DESCENT

Also by Tim Johnston

Never So Green
Irish Girl

DESCENT

a novel

TIM JOHNSTON

ALGONQUIN BOOKS
OF CHAPEL HILL
2015

Published by
ALGONQUIN BOOKS OF CHAPEL HILL
Post Office Box 2225
Chapel Hill, North Carolina 27515-2225

a division of
WORKMAN PUBLISHING
225 Varick Street
New York, New York 10014

A portion of this novel appears, in slightly different form, as the short story
"Up There" in the author's story collection *Irish Girl,* 2009, University of North Texas
Press. Another portion first appeared, in slightly different form, on NarrativeMagazine.com
as the short story "Two Years," and was then anthologized in *Best of the West 2011:
New Stories from the Wide Side of the Missouri,* 2011, University of Texas Press.

This is a work of fiction. While, as in all fiction, the literary perceptions
and insights are based on experience, all names, characters, places, and incidents
either are products of the author's imagination or are used fictitiously.

LIBRARY OF CONGRESS CATALOGING-IN-PUBLICATION DATA
Johnston, Tim, [date]
Decent : a novel / by Tim Johnston.
     p. cm.
"Published simultaneously in Canada by Thomas Allen & Son Limited"—
Verso title page.
ISBN 978-1-61620-304-7
1. Missing persons—Fiction. 2. Abduction—Fiction. 3. Families—Fiction.
4. Loss (Psychology)—Fiction. 5. Rocky Mountains Region—Fiction.
6. Psychological fiction. 7. Domestic fiction. I. Title.
PS3610.O395D47 2015
813'.6—dc23   2014024023

10 9 8 7 6 5 4 3 2 1
First Edition

I dedicate this book to your daughters, and to mine.

What we chang'd
Was innocence for innocence; we knew not
The doctrine of ill-doing, nor dream'd
That any did.

—WILLIAM SHAKESPEARE

May she be granted beauty and yet not
Beauty to make a stranger's eye distraught.

—W. B. YEATS

THE LIFE BEFORE

Her name was Caitlin, she was eighteen, and her own heart would sometimes wake her—flying away in that dream-race where finish lines grew farther away not nearer, where knees turned to taffy, or feet to stones. Lurching awake under the sheets, her chest squeezed in phantom arms, she'd lie there gasping, her eyes open to the dark. She'd lift her hands and press the watchface into bloom, blue as an eye in which blinked all the true data of her body, dreaming or awake: *heart rate 86 bpm, body temp 37.8°C, pace (0), alt. 9,015 feet.*

Alt. 9,015 feet?

She looked about the room, at the few dark furnishings shaped by a thin light in the seams of the drapes. To her left in the other bed lay her mother, a wing of blonde hair dark on the white pillow. In the adjoining room on the other side of the wall slept her father and brother. Two rooms, four beds, no discussion: she would not share a room with her fifteen-year-old brother, nor he with her.

The watchface burned again with its cool light and began to beep and she pinched it into silence. She checked her heart: still fast, but it wasn't the dream anymore, it was the air at 9,015 feet.

The Rocky Mountains!

When she'd seen them for the first time, from the car, her heart had begun to pump and the muscles of her legs had tightened and twitched. In a few weeks she would begin college on a track scholarship, and although she had not lost a race her senior year (COURTLAND UNDEFEATED! ran the headline), she knew that the girls at college would be faster and stronger, more experienced and more determined, than the girls she was used to running against, and she'd picked the mountains for no other reason.

In the bathroom she washed her face and brushed her teeth and banded her ponytail tight to her head and then stood staring into the mirror. It wasn't vanity. She was looking to see what was in this girl's eyes, as she would any girl, so she would know how to defeat her.

She stepped back into the room and for a moment she thought her mother was awake, watching her from the bed, but it was only the eyelids, pale and round in that dim light—a blind, unnerving effect, like the gazes of statues— and Caitlin opened the connecting door and stepped from one room into another exactly like it and shook the boy awake.

THE SUN WAS STILL climbing the far side of the mountains, and the town waited in a cold lake of shadow. The black bears that came down at night to raid the garbage bins and lope along the sidewalks had all gone back up. The streets were empty. No one to see the two of them passing under the traffic light, no one but them to hear the slow blink blink of its middle eye.

Caitlin was not yet running but high-stepping in a brisk pantomime of it, like a drum majorette for a parade consisting of the boy alone, wobbling along behind her on the rented bike. The boy wanted to go back for sweatshirts, but it was July, she reminded him, it would warm up.

His name was Sean but she called him Dudley, a long-ago insult which had lost its meaning. They'd come into town the day before, up from the plains on the interstate, up through Denver and then into the mountains on a swinging cliff of road that swung their hearts out into the open sky, into dizzy plungings of bottomless green, the pines so thick and small on the far slopes. Up and up they'd climbed, up to the Great Divide and then down again—*down* to nine thousand feet, where the resort village appeared suddenly in the high geography like a mirage. The wintry architecture of ski shops and coffeehouses at midsummer. Chairlifts hanging empty over the grassy runs. Impossible colors at this height and air like they had never breathed before.

Now, in the blue morning, they drew this air into their lungs and coughed up white clouds. The smell of pine was like Christmas. "Here we go," Caitlin said, and she turned onto a road called Ermine and began to run in earnest, and the boy followed.

Not bad, he thought at first—wide, smooth blacktop with plenty of sky overhead. But then the road grew steep, the trees loomed denser and nearer, and the bike began to jerk in mechanical palsy as he cursed through the gears. He stood on the pedals and rode openmouthed, sucking at the air. Where his stomach overspilled his shorts the sweat ran hot and slick. Ahead on the black road the pale shape of her grew small and dim like some leggy and teasing sprite. *"Slow down!"* he called, at great cost of breath, and then fell to watching his own quivering thighs. It was snowshoes all over again: Caitlin stomping out ahead of him on the lake and he slogging behind, the old wooden snowshoes colliding, tripping him—the lifeless heap of himself in the snow (the whole dark lake underneath, the thin floor of ice), red-cheeked Caitlin appearing suddenly and reaching down. *C'mon, Dudley, stop screwing around . . .*

When he looked ahead again she'd stopped, and he rode up to her, and planted his feet. "Jesus Christ, Caitlin . . ." Trying not to sound like a desperate, gasping fatty. His heart whopping.

"Shh," she said. Her chest was heaving too but she was smiling. Her burning lungs, her banging heart, were ecstasies to her. Back home, across a wall of her room, track ribbons lay feathered like the wing of a brilliant bird. "Do you see it?" she said.

"What?"

"Up there."

"What?"

"Just off the road. He's right there."

Then he saw it: a small red dog with a thick tail. But not a dog. Something wild, with black little eyes and huge, listening ears.

"What is it?" he said.

"I think it's a fox."

"What's in its mouth?"

"I don't know."

"It's a pup," he said. "It must be her pup."

"No, there's blood."

"So she killed it. They do that sometimes."

They watched, the fox watching them, until at last it about-faced, the small body yet in its jaws, and went trotting up the road and was gone.

The boy swung the backpack around and rooted inside for the spouted bottles. Caitlin had stopped not because of the fox but because she'd come to an intersection and was unsure of the way. She remembered the young man at the bike shop with the oil-stained fingers (with the tattoo spider climbing his throat, with the very green eyes) saying there'd be signs, but there weren't any, not here.

They squeezed cold water into their mouths and Sean removed his helmet and they unfolded the map between them.

"That way," she said, and he looked up the narrow gravel road she indicated and shook his head. "That's not right." They promised to keep to the paved roads, the county roads, he said, and she looked at him: his red, serious face and the high, greasy bird crest of hair his helmet had styled. Hard to remember sometimes he was fifteen and not twelve, not ten, not seven.

She checked her heart and it was fast just standing still. Their altitude was 9,456 feet.

"Dudley," she said, jamming her bottle back into the pack. "Did you rent a *mountain* bike so you could go tooling around on county roads?"

THE SUN HAD SPILLED into the valley, and a yellow blade of it opened a seam in the drapes and fell across the bed and across the eyes of the man who lay there sleeping. After a moment, the man turned away from the light and blinked the alarm clock into focus: 7:15.

A motel room. Colorado. To his right sat the other bed, empty and unmade.

In the bathroom, on the counter, the boy's toothbrush lay in its puddle. The man, whose name was Grant Courtland, splashed and dried his face and returned to the room and parted the drapes. The sky was a pale early blue, a few thin clouds skimming the peaks. A beauty hard to believe in. A postcard. Some far-off bird rode the thermals, hovering there for the longest time before suddenly diving, bullet-shaped, into the trees. He watched to see if it would return to the sky but it didn't.

He wasn't sure where his kids were, geographically. It might be that near mountain there, those trees, which looked so close. The night before, they'd all bent over the maps, but Grant had not looked closely; it was their adventure to plan and carry out. In a few weeks Caitlin would begin college back in Wisconsin, on scholarship for track-and-field, and the mountains had been her idea, her choice, a graduation gift.

College. Already.

He stared into the distance until he thought he saw something—a wink of chrome, a flash of white running shoes. But there was nothing, of course, only the green and more green of the pines.

He picked up his cell phone and pressed a series of keys but then hesitated, his thumb hovering over the send button. The dream he'd been having came back to him—partially: a woman's cool, exploring hand, that was all, but Lord.

He set down the phone and stared at it. After a minute he pulled on a pair of jeans, a T-shirt, and stepped barefoot into the adjoining room.

THE PATH GREW NARROWER, less a gravel road now than a kind of gully snaking up the mountain, and finally there was no gravel and no path but only this bald jawbone of rounded stones, like the dry bed of a seasonal stream shaped, year after year, by water's only thought, which was to go down, always down, and never up.

"*This isn't right,*" Sean yelled up the gully.

Ahead of him she kept going, leaping stone to stone like a goat.

He struggled on, wheezing, his body quaking and his jaw jibbering on its hinges until at last he said, "Fuck this," and let the bike jolt to a stop, then let it fall to the stones as he staggered away.

"*Caitlin!*" he yelled.

He felt enormous and weightless, both. His legs took an unexpected step. Some flying thing struck his helmet, shrilled in the vents and sped away. "Bitch," he said.

He picked up the bike and began fighting it over the stones, but in another moment he was attacked again—something under the pack now, buzzing against his back, and he dropped the bike and began to twist from the straps before he understood it was a phone, and by the time he had the pack off and the phone in his hand the buzzing had stopped. He watched the little window for the new message alert, but there was none. He checked his own phone, then dropped both phones back into the pack.

Then he picked hers out again. Stood a minute with the ruby heft of it in his hand, looked up the gully again—and then sat on a stone and punched up her text messages and read them. The most interesting thing was the names: *Colby. Allison. Natalie. Amber.* Lean, athletic girls who arrived in baggy shorts and tight, chesty tops to drink his Diet Cokes and stomp barefooted up and down the stairs. Girls who left impressions in the furniture and their scents in cushions and creases. Girls of constant texting and laughing and talking—always talking. The time he crouched outside the basement window and heard Allison Chow tell the other girls about her boyfriend's big thing almost choking her. The time he walked in on Colby Wilson in the bathroom, bare-thighed on the toilet. Track shorts pushed to the knees.

Nice knock, tubs.

HE WAS CLOSER TO the top of the gully than he knew and when he reached it he found a road, another steep blacktop like the one they'd first been on. Or the same one. He found a sign that said CO RD. 153 and he found the sun on his hot neck and he found the silent pines and that was all. Up-road the blacktop made a right hook out of sight, and downroad it dropped away like a cliff. All of him, his every cell, wanted to go that way—*down:* the speed and the breeze and the long free ride on the back of gravity. But she wouldn't do that, she wouldn't go down, God damn her, and he turned the bike and stood on the pedals and began once more to climb.

He'd not gone far when something burst from the trees, so near and terrible he howled and leapt from the bike. It only lasted a moment before he heard that donkey-laugh of hers, and the blood came rushing to his face.

"God damn you," he said.

"Oh God, Dudley, you should've seen your face!"

He lifted the bike from the blacktop.

"I never knew you could move so fast!" she said.

"I never knew you could be such a cunt," he said.

She stopped laughing. And into that new silence dropped a man's voice— from nowhere. From everywhere. In a moment it broke decidedly over the rise below them and with it came two figures, helmeted and hunched over their bikes, a man and a woman. The man stopped talking when he saw them, and he and the woman came on in winded silence, their faces uplifted and bright. The woman was younger than the man, she might've been Caitlin's age, and she gave Sean a smile. One of the man's lower legs was not a real leg but a black post locked into a special pedal, so that it was hard to say where the bike ended and the man began. He said Howdy and Sean said Howdy back. When they'd rounded the bend and were gone again, Caitlin said:

"What did you call me?"

Her face was burning. So was his.

"Christ, Caitlin. I was *looking* for you. We were *supposed* to keep an eye on each other."

She regarded him darkly. Then she looked away and shook her head. She adjusted the band at the root of her ponytail and came forward and he flinched, and she told him she did have her eye on him, she knew exactly where he was the whole time. What kind of person did he think she was?

BOTH BEDS IN THE adjoining room were empty and unmade, their layers cast off like torments. The room, which had been so cold when the girls went to bed, was now hot and reeking faintly of perfume and sweat. Grant went to see that the heating unit was off and then crossed to the small staging area outside the bathroom where the two suitcases lay open on the racks, their insides distinguished at a glance by the colors and cuts of under-things, bras and panties.

The bathroom door was ajar, steam playing in the gap. The rasp of a toothbrush. He pushed at the door and there she stood in the steam, wrapped in a white towel, going patiently at her teeth. She might have been twenty again, in that towel. College days. Her little apartment on Fairchild over the bakery ovens. Winter mornings in bed with the smell of her, the smell of baking bread. She'd had a twin sister named Faith who drowned when they were sixteen and this somehow fascinated him. He was reading books then, literature, poetry. Then came pregnancy, bills, a baby. He went to work for a builder and she stayed in school, sometimes taking the baby with her to class when Mrs. Turgeon was sick. The baby eighteen, now. A young woman. Going to college herself. Fast as the wind and his father's heart pounding each time she ran, *My God look at her, my God don't let her fall.*

"Fan dudn't wuk," Angela said around the toothbrush, and he came to stand behind her, his face appearing above hers in the portal she'd wiped in the glass. Her hair wet and heavy and drawn by comb into many neat, fragrant rows.

"Did they call you yet?" he said, and she bent to spit, bumping her bottom into him. She rinsed and brushed, bent over. "Not yet," she said. "But it's early." She stood again and found his eyes in the mirror. "Another hour, I'd say. Easy."

"You missed some." He touched the corner of his mouth and she put a matching finger to hers. "You need to rinse better," he said.

She smiled and bent again to the running water, bumping him again, and he gathered the damp strands of hair into a single rope and held it while she rinsed. She turned off the water and flattened her hands to either side of the sink. He lifted the white towel into the scoop of her back and gazed down on her, on buttocks so white and smooth.

"Grant," she said.

His hands upon her were like things forged in some furnace, pulled huge and dark to rest here, to cool and heal on these pale surfaces.

"Yes," he said.

"Let's go lie down. I want to see your face."

SHE'D FOUND SOMETHING WHILE she waited for him, and now Caitlin walked back into the pines and Sean followed on the footpath, and soon they were surrounded by the white trunks of aspens. A subforest within the forest. The footpath wound through the aspens and delivered them all at once into a small glade, a sylvan grotto within which there stood, waiting for them, the Virgin Mary. Life-sized, bone smooth, purely white. Around her had been built a carapace of stones and mortar, the rounded stones like those Sean had cursed in the gully. Two fingers of her right hand, raised in a saint's greeting, were snapped off at the second knuckle, giving her less an air of beneficence than of disbelief, as if she'd been sculpted in the instant before blood and panic.

"Did you see that?" Sean said, pointing to the hand.

"I know, right? Like Dad's."

"What's it doing up here?"

"I'm guessing it has something to do with those," and she pointed to a cluster of stone tablets rising from the ground like teeth, thin and chalky and pitched every which way.

Next to the Virgin was a stone bench, and they sat down to drink water and eat waxy energy bars in the shade.

"Who do you think they were?" he said, and she shrugged and said, "Settlers."

"Donner party," he said.

"Wrong mountains. Look, there's a plaque." She pushed scrub growth aside at the base of the Virgin to expose a bronze plate and its verdigrised inscription:

> *Right Reverend Tobias J. Fife,*
> *Bishop of Denver, Mercifully Grants,*
> *In the Lord, Forty Days of Grace*
> *For Visiting the Shrine of the Woods*
> *And Praying before It,*
> *1938.*

"The right reverend," said Caitlin. "I like that."

"What's forty days of grace?"

"I think it means you don't have to pray again for forty days. Like a vacation."

"Maybe it means you're safe for forty days. Like nothing shitty can happen to you."

"Maybe. Hand me my phone."

He groped into the pack and handed her the red phone. She checked for messages, then aimed it and took a picture of the shrine.

A breeze came to stir the aspen leaves. The boy chewed on the energy bar and made a gagging sound and Caitlin told him not to eat it on her account.

She raised an eyebrow at him. "Go ahead. I don't care."

He hesitated. Then he tossed the energy bar into the pack and fished into the cargo pocket of his shorts and fetched up the big Snickers and began to peel back the wrapper.

"Want some?" he said, and she took the candybar and opened her mouth as if to jam the whole thing in but then only clipped a little off with her front teeth. He ate the remainder in three great bites, mouth open, chewing and gasping. He took a long drink of water and caught his breath. He drummed his fingers on the backpack and stared at the Virgin's fingers. Their mother believed in God but their father said they had to make up their own minds.

"Caitlin," he said.

"What."

"Do you think Dad's screwing around?"

She leaned away from him, twisted at the waist, and beheld him from this new vantage.

"What?" she said.

"Don't you think he's been kind of weird lately?"

"Dudley, he's *always* weird. How do you go from that to *screwing around*?"

Sean looked off into the woods. "I saw something. A while ago," he said. It was at their father's office, the steel building behind the house out of which he ran his contractor's business. Sean had been there earning his allowance—cleaning, sweeping, putting away tools. But one of the chests had been locked and he'd gone back to get the key and the office door was open and . . .

"And what?" said Caitlin.

"And he was sitting there. And there was a girl."

"A girl?"

"A woman. Sitting on his desk. And she was wearing a skirt."

Caitlin waited. "And what else?"

"Nothing else."

"That's all she was wearing?"

"No—that's all I saw."

"Jesus Christ, Sean." She crossed an ankle over her knee and snatched at shoelaces and swept the shoe from her foot and shook it as if it were full of beetles, and then she fit her hand into the humid cavity and felt around. She pulled the shoe back on and retied the laces. "Then what happened?"

"Nothing. The girl—the woman—got off the desk and shook my hand and went away. He told me she was a client."

"So what gave you this *screwing around* idea?"

"I don't know. Shit." He rezipped the pack with a violent yank and sat staring at it. "Forget it, all right? Let's just get outta here."

Caitlin stood and looked down on him. "Don't bite your fingernail. It's gross." She brushed at her bottom and walked toward the graves.

Sean looked at the Virgin, and then got up and followed.

She stood at the edge of the little graveyard with her arms crossed, an elbow cupped in each palm. Her body was cooling. She needed to get running again. The boy stood next to her.

"It wasn't anything," he said. "Forget it."

She rubbed her arms. She remembered a line from a poem she'd read the night before, *I cease, I turn pale.*

Then she told him about the time their father had stopped living with them—three, maybe four months in all, though it had seemed much longer. Sean had been very young and wouldn't remember. Their mother said it was nothing to worry about but Caitlin had heard the way she spoke to him on the phone, and she remembered her mother's face—this new face she'd never seen before. She remembered the words her mother said into the phone too but she didn't repeat them now.

She was silent, and Sean stared at the old tombstones. At the base of one, in the grass, lay a small black bowl, or saucer. After a moment it became what it was: a plastic coffee lid with a sippy hole. A piece of trash, the only piece, come to rest here, at this stone, way up here, and nowhere else.

"When he finally came back home," Caitlin said, "his fingers were missing. I always thought that's why he came back—because wherever he'd been was a place where you lost your fingers." She shivered, remembering. She hadn't cared about the fingers, all she needed was his arms, the sandpaper of his jaw, the thrill that rolled through her each time he said *Caitydid, my Caitydid.*

"He used to tell me—" Sean gave a strange snort of laughter. "He used to say they fell off from smoking."

"Did you believe him?"

He didn't answer. In an instant everything was changed, each one of them.

"What do you think will happen this time?" he said, and Caitlin released a breath that seemed to stir the spangle leaves of the aspens into their dull chiming, a sound like rain.

"Nothing," she said. "Let's go," she said.

THE DRAPES WERE DRAWN and sunlight leached from them along the wall and upward in a bright coronation. Naked under the bedsheet, Grant stared at this. He'd dozed a few minutes and then popped awake with his heart kicking. What bed was this? Whose arm across his stomach?

Now there was a gasp, a spasm, and Angela said, *"No,"* and he said, "It's all right," and touched her shoulder. Long ago, she'd described a dream she'd had longer ago still, in which a voice told her she needed to be with her sister. *Which one?* she'd asked the voice, *which sister?* but there was no answer.

"—What?" She lifted her head, her brown eyes.

"You said no."

She drew the hair from her face, unsticking it from her lips. "I did?"

"Yes."

She shifted, resettled her head on his chest. She breathed. Somewhere a door slammed and a joyful stampede shuddered the hallway, many small bare feet racing for the pool. The high summer voices.

"It's going to be weird, isn't it," she said. She was looking beyond him to the other bed. The scrambled heap of bedding, the illusory suggestion of a body within it. She spread her hand on his chest.

"What is?"

"You know what."

Grant regarded the empty bed. "It went fast," he said.

"That's what everyone tells you: You won't believe how fast it goes. In a few years, Seanie too." She sighed.

She tapped a finger twice on his chest, like a soft knock. She did it again.

"Don't even think it, Angela."

"We're not too old. I'm not."

"I am," he said, and she said, "No, it keeps you young."

In the room next door a woman began a violent hacking. A TV came to life, an anchorman's voice, some urgent new development in the world.

"They saved some money on these walls," Grant said.

"Was I loud, earlier?"

"I don't give a damn."

He swung out his legs and sat with a scrap of bedsheet over his lap. His right leg took up a restless dandling.

"There's nothing to do, Grant," she said to his back. "You are far away in a magical land where nobody works."

He was silent. Then he said: "What?"

She reached for the water bottle on the nightstand and he handed it to her. "They'll be back soon, though," she said. "And we wouldn't want them to catch us in bed"—handing back the water bottle—"would we."

He took a drink, his heart skipping. On the nightstand was a book— small, hardbound, tented on its pages. He lifted it, trapping his thumb in the crease, and read the cover.

"Are you reading this?"

"It's Caitlin's."

"Where'd she get it?"

"Someone gave it to her."

"Who?"

"I don't know."

"It's D. H. Lawrence. Did you know that?"

"Yes. So?"

"So I didn't know she read this kind of stuff." He opened the book and silently read the lines to the left of his thumb:

> *When the wind blows her veil*
> *And uncovers her laughter*
> *I cease, I turn pale,*

And with a deep shift in his chest he remembered when she was small. Small and warm under his arm, clean girl-smell of her filling his heart as he read, *Oh, I'm lookin' for my missin' piece, I'm lookin' for my missin' piece, hi-dee-ho, here I go, lookin' for my missin' piece.* The total absorption of a child, no matter how many times. Her little hand on his forearm, rising to hang hair behind an ear, to scratch her nose—the abandoned, the bereft place on his arm until the hand returned.

He replaced the book carefully, facedown, on the nightstand.

"What kind of stuff?" Angela said.

"Poetry," he said.

He turned to look at his wife. "Is something funny about that?"

Angela shrugged. She shook her head. They'd lain in the lamplight and Caitlin had read one of the poems in nearly a whisper, a poem full of kisses and touches. Angela wanted to stroke her hair, crawl into bed with her like a sister. She almost could have. The way it often went with mothers and daughters—the screaming, door-slamming days of adolescence, the terrible old warfare of the home—was not how it had gone with Caitlin. The girl had run her way through all of that. They knew how lucky they were.

"Should we call them?" Angela said.

"In a minute."

"We'd better call them," she said.

"I'm going to open up these drapes."

"I know," she said. "I'm ready."

SHE LAY THERE A while longer getting used to the light, watching the shape of him, a naked dark sculpture of himself before the sun and the world. There was something about being in a strange place that made everything, even the most familiar things, strange. At last she went to him and put her arms around his hips and pressed herself to him. To skin that no longer smelled of smoke, or alcohol, but only of him.

"Someone will see," she said, but there was no one to see them, just the sky and the mountains, heaped and stacked in diminishing brilliances of green. The great distant peaks higher than anything ought to be that still stood on the earth.

"It's incredible, isn't it," she said. "You can imagine how it was, two hundred years ago. No roads, no rest stops. Just this vast, wild . . . unknown. Like another planet. No wonder men wanted it so badly."

"Men," he said absently, "not women?" He had her phone in his hand, scrolling through the menu.

"Oh yes, your eighteen hundreds woman couldn't wait to load her nine kids into a wooden wagon and haul them across the Rocky Mountains." She released him and gave him a spank on her way to the bathroom. "Press fifteen. Or eighteen," she said, and he turned and said, "Still doing that?"

"I'll stop when she's twenty. That will just make me feel old."

He hesitated before entering the code, glancing around the floor, *Put some goddam shorts on at least before you talk to her,* he thought, and an image of his daughter flashed in his mind, pale and long-legged on the black cinder—that stride of hers, so light, an illusion of weightlessness, of never quite landing, but with something terrible in it too when she came up on a girl from behind—and in the next moment another phone began vibrating on a hard top somewhere and Angela said from the bathroom, "That's them," and then hurried into the other room. Grant followed but she'd already picked it up. He stood at the threshold watching. The missing tips of his fingers began to jump with heartbeat.

She was frowning at the number. The phone buzzed again in her grip.

"Angela," he said.

She raised the phone and said, "Hello?" Staring blankly at him. "Hello? . . . Yes, this is his phone—who is this, please?"

She lowered the phone slowly, watching it, and Grant could see it happening. Every second of it. The unbelievable, the irreversible moment.

"She hung up," she said. Looking at him. Her eyes already changed.

He reached toward her. "Let me see the—" But she stepped away, turned from him, and began punching at the keypad. He pursued her in a thick warp of movement. He had won her back, little by little. Like bringing someone back from the dead. Years of truthfulness, years of love, all undone by a simple switch, an unthinking exchange of phones. He could not even see the woman's face, her body. She seemed a creation they'd pieced together out of nothing, out of old materials, right here in these rooms.

He looked at his wife, standing with her back to him. Somehow they would need to get through this hour, this day, this vacation. The long drive home.

"Angela—"

"Don't," she said. "Just—" She was trembling. "Answer it, will you?"

The phone in his hand was ringing. For how long? He read the screen with illogical dread.

"It's Sean," he said, and his wife said nothing.

THEY'D LEFT THE ASPENS and stepped into a high, intense sunlight, their shadows thrown back on the blacktop. The morning had burned away. The air was sere and smelled of weeping sap and of the brown, desiccated needles. They'd unfolded the map and tried to get their bearings. In a moment, and for the first time that day, they heard an engine, and then a gaining thumpbeat of music, and above them at the curve there banked into

view a truck, or a jeep, or something in between, some mountain breed they
didn't know, and it was coming and Caitlin said, "Get over here," and Sean
crabwalked himself and the bike into the scrub growth and wildflowers while
the strange vehicle, all sunlight and bass, veered wide of them. In the window
was a face, a man's jaw, yellow lenses fixing on them for a long moment before
the jeep-thing passed on and, reaching the crest of the road, dropped away
body and engine and music and all.

They'd set off again then, and when they came around the bend there was
another road, unpaved, intersecting the blacktop at an oblique angle like an
X, and without hesitating and without consulting him, Caitlin simply took
it. And although the road was unmarked, and although it appeared as though
it would take them higher up rather than down, he said nothing. Later, he
would think about that. He would remember the shrine of the woods. The
graves. He would see the Virgin's face and her mutilated blessing and he would
remember thinking they should pray before her just the same, like the right
reverend said, just in case. Forty days was forty days. But Caitlin had already
been on the path, moving toward the road. She was wearing a white sleeveless
top, white shorts with the word BADGERS bannered in cherry red across her
bottom, pink and white Adidas, and for a moment, in that place, she had
looked not like herself but like some blanched and passing spirit. A cold wan-
derer around whom the air chilled and the birds shuddered and the leaves of
the aspens yellowed and fell.

HE RAISED THE PHONE and said, "Hello, Sean," and a man's voice
said, "Is this Mr. Courtland?" and Grant's head jerked as if struck.

"Yes. Who is this?"

At these words, the change in his body, Angela came around to see his
face. He met her eyes and looked away, out the window. The man on the
phone identified himself in some detail, but all Grant heard was the word
sheriff.

"What's happened?" he asked. "Where's Sean?" There was a pain in his forearm and he looked to see the white claw fastened there. He pried at it gently.

"He's here at the medical center in Granby, Mr. Courtland," said the sheriff. "He's a tad banged up, but the doctor says he'll be fine. I found his wallet and this phone in his—"

"What do you mean a tad—" He glanced at Angela and stopped himself. "What do you mean by that?"

"I mean it looks like he got himself in some kind of accident up there on the mountain, Mr. Courtland. I ain't had a chance to talk to him yet, they doped him up pretty good for the . . . Well, you can talk to the doctor in a second here. But first—"

"But he's all right," Grant said.

"Oh, his leg's banged up pretty good. But he was wearing that helmet. He'll be all right. He had some good luck up there."

"What do you mean?"

"I mean he could of laid there a lot longer, but it happened some folks come by on their bikes."

Grant's heart was hammering in his skull. He couldn't think—his son lying there, up there, on the mountain, hurt—

"Mr. Courtland," said the sheriff. "Where are you all at?"

There was something in the man's tone. Grant shook his head. "What do you mean?"

"Well, sir. We found your boy way up there on the mountain, on a rental bike. So I'm just wondering, sir, where *you're* at."

"Caitlin," Angela said suddenly, and Grant's heart leapt and he said, "Yes. Let me speak to my daughter. Let me speak to Caitlin."

"Your daughter . . . ?" said the other man, then was silent. In the silence was the sound of his breathing. The sound of him making an adjustment to his sheriff's belt. The sound of a woman's voice paging unintelligibly down the empty hospital corridor.

When he spoke again he sounded like some other man altogether.

"Mr. Courtland," he said, and Grant stepped toward the window as though he would walk through it. He'd taken the representations of the mountains on the resort maps, with their colorful tracery of runs and trails and lifts, as the mountains themselves—less mountains than playgrounds fashioned into the shapes of mountains by men and money. Now he saw the things themselves, so green and massive, humped one upon the other like a heaving sea. Angela stopped him physically, her thumbs in his biceps. She raised on her toes that she might hear every word. "Mr. Courtland," said the sheriff. "Your son came in alone."

Angela shook her head.

"No," she said, and turned away and went to the suitcases and began to dress.

When they were young, when they were naked and young in that apartment of hers above the bakery where the smell of her, and the smell of the bread, had been a glory to him, Grant had tracked her heartbeat by the little cross she wore—by the slightest, most delicate movements of the cross down in that tender pit of throat. *Touched it with his finger and asked without thinking, Wasn't it ironic, though?*

Wasn't what?

That God took your twin sister, whose name was Faith?

She turned away. She would not speak to him. Her body like stone. I'm sorry, he said. Please, Angela . . . please. He didn't yet know of the other heart, the tiniest heart, beating with hers.

Now in the little motel room, his wife's phone to his ear, he begged: *Please God, please God,* and the sheriff was asking him again where he was at, telling him to stay put. The boy was safe, he was sleeping. He was coming to get them, the sheriff—no more than fifteen minutes. He would take them up there himself, up the mountain. He would take them wherever they needed to go. But they wouldn't be here when the sheriff arrived, Grant knew. They would be on the mountain, on their way up. The boy was safe. The boy was sleeping. Grant would be at the wheel and Angela would be at the maps, the way it was in the life before, the way it would be in the life to come.

THE LIFE TO COME

Part I

1

He was up at first light. Earliest, frailest light of another day. Sitting on the edge of the bed hands to knees in bleak stillness, staring out the window as his life came back to him piece by piece. Finally, as always, there was only one piece, the missing piece, his little girl.

He crossed the narrow hall and looked into the other bedroom to see if his son had come home, but the bed sat neat and empty as before. The wood floor barren as before. In the bathroom the left-behind toothbrush stood bristles up in its enameled tin cup. He passed it under the faucet to wash off the dust, returned it to the cup, then made a bowl of his hands and lowered his face to the icy water.

On the porch he lit a cigarette and stood smoking. It was just September, the chill of autumn in the gray morning, but the sun would come up over the pines and burn that off. The old black Labrador crept out from her place under the porch, stretched, and sat at the foot of the stairs and waited. The ranch house had once been the only house on the property and was now a kind of guest house, or had become that when Grant moved in. *You need a break from these mountains,* the sheriff had said, *and that old man of mine could use some help.* The old man, Emmet, meeting them triple-legged in the drive: cowboy boot, cane, and cast. Toes like a little yellow family all bedded together in the plaster. *Come down off a shedroof the fast way but I ain't looking for no goddam babysitter,* he'd said, his first words.

A full year ago, that meeting.

Grant backed the truck up to the machine shed and spent some time in there preparing the chainsaw, longer than he needed to, taking his time amid the shed's oily plentitude of parts and tools and machinery. Breathing that air. Then he loaded the chainsaw and a bale of barbed wire and the wire-stretcher into the back of the truck and when he opened the truck door the Labrador came up and looked at him but he told her No, you stay here.

He drove the truck bouncing and squeaking to the far corner of the front pasture, near the county road where the big oak grew. A limb had come down in a storm a few days before, snapping the top line of wire, and it hung there still, its withered leaves chattering like the sound of winter. The rest of the tree was yet thick with summer's leaves and the morning air was green with the smell of grass and alfalfa. The haze had burned off. The sky was intensely blue and empty. No cloud, no hawk, no helicopter. As he stood looking things over, the two mares came to snuffle at his hands, dewing up his palms with their velvet snouts. He pulled on his gloves and primed the saw and jerked the cord and the horses went cantering big-eyed across the pasture, ears pricked back at him.

He lopped off the smaller branches at a point just beyond the fence, then tumbled the remaining log onto the ground and sectioned it into cordwood lengths. He made a pyramid of the logs in the back of the truck and set to work mending the wire. Now and then a car or truck rolled by on the county road, and he would raise a hand to the ones he knew and only stare at the ones he didn't, at the strange faces that turned to stare at him, this solitary working man in a pasture, this human face among the trees and the grasses and the mountains and the sky. There was such randomness in the world, the passing faces told him, such strange and meaningless intersections—this man could be him, or this man. He looked for some ordinary man in a certain kind of car, any kind of car or truck that said mountain, that said unmarked roads and mud, deeply rutted paths, and he would follow. It was madness, but it was all madness; if a man should randomly pick his daughter, then why shouldn't that same man randomly cross his path? Wasn't this the way of the world? Wasn't this the way of the god of that world? He'd trail the man out of town, up into the mountains, his heart racing, his heart growing hot, until the truck he followed, the jeep, would turn at last into a driveway, an ordinary mountain house, smoke spilling from the chimney . . . a child's dropped bicycle under the pines, a big dog bounding out and leaping at the man who looked back, who caught Grant's eye and nodded and waved and turned to his house as the door opened, and there was a woman in jeans, in a loose white sweater, leaning for a kiss.

The time he followed one man to the end of a high road that turned out to be no road at all but the man's driveway and no easy way to turn around, and the man was a ranger and knew him. Angela and Sean were back in Wisconsin by then and Grant was alone in the motel, alone in the resort town at nine thousand feet. A year by the calendar since she'd vanished, one hour by the heart. *You need a break from these mountains,* said the sheriff.

Now Grant shook his head like a man coming out of a dream and turned back to his hands, the clip they were fastening to a steel T-post, the pliers twisting and tightening.

Other times he would pause altogether to stare into the hills beyond the ranch, up into the climbing green mountains. The sunlit creases in the pines where some living thing might travel, bear or moose or hiker or daughter. One speck of difference in the far green sameness and he would stare so hard his vision would slur and his heart would surge and he would have to force himself to look away—*Daddy,* she'd said—and he would take his skull in his hands and clench his teeth until he felt the roots giving way and the world would pitch and he would groan like some aggrieved beast and believe he would retch up his guts, organs and entrails and heart and all, all of it wet and gray and steaming at his feet and go ahead, he would say into this blackness, go ahead god damn you.

A moment later, when a cigarette had been placed in his lips, a flame made to light its tip, the smoke drawn into his lungs and held there, and held there, and released at last into the sky, Grant would be calm again, and he would get back to work.

2

They carried the walkie-talkies and they carried their phones and they remembered a show they'd once watched about a girl locked in an underground bunker texting her mother (remembered their own daughter sitting between them, a thin and budding girl of twelve in summer pajamas, bare knees drawn to her chest, smelling of her bath, riveted), and they played and replayed the one message from Caitlin, the last one, her voice breaking on the single word. The sound of an engine in the background and the sound of wind and then a sound like the phone dropping and then the silence.

Daddy, she'd said—but they had not heard her. Had not heard the call. They'd been in bed. They'd been fucking.

In those first days, those early disbelieving days in the mountains, they did not hold each other and they did not weep in bed at night. They spoke of what had been done that day and what must be done the next and who was going to do it—who would sit with Sean at the hospital and who would take sandwiches to the volunteers and who would get more posters printed and who would contact the school back home and who would meet with the sheriff or the FBI men or the reporters again and who would go to the Laundromat, a grotesque feverdream of the domestic, and when they had talked themselves to exhaustion, when sleep was coming at last, Angela would pull them back to pray. She would pray aloud and she wanted Grant to pray aloud too, and he would, in those early days, though it made him nearly sick, the sound of his own voice, the sound of those words in the cheap little room.

Days into weeks. Grant wheeled Sean out of the hospital and the three of them took two rooms on the ground floor of the motel and those rooms were now

home and headquarters—papers and supplies and lists and maps on every sur-
face. In town, when a poster came down, Angela somehow knew, and the poster
was restored. Weeks into months. In early November Sean turned sixteen; they
remembered two days later and went out for pizza. Angela's calls began to be
returned less promptly and sometimes not at all, and when she called the sher-
iff she was no longer put right through but had to speak to a deputy first, and
often the sheriff was not in, nor was he up in the mountains searching some un-
searched quadrant of forest. Such helicopters that sounded overhead—the sound
of urgency itself in those throbbing blades, of all-out human and mechanical
response, massively adept—beat across the sky toward some other purpose.

It may not be just a case of a needle in a haystack, the sheriff told Grant. It
may not even be the right haystack.

How do you mean?

I mean a smart man don't steal a pony from his neighbor. Pardon the analogy.

You mean he might not be local. This man.

I mean a man might drive quite a ways looking for just the right pony.

They'd come to the Rockies thinking it was a place like any other they might
have chosen: chronicled, mapped, finite. A fully known American somewhere.
Now Grant understood that, like the desert, like the ocean, the mountains were
a vast and pitiless nowhere. Who would bring his family—his children—to
such a place?

He returned to the motel and checked with Sean in front of the TV, and then
stepped into the other room and shut the door and went to her where she sat at
the desk staring at the laptop.

Angie. He needs to go home.

What do you mean?

He needs better care for his leg. He needs to be back in school. Back with his
friends.

She turned to look up at him. What are you saying?

I'm saying it's no good for him, keeping him here.

Are you sure you're talking about him?

Grant didn't answer.

We can't go back now, Grant. You see what's happening here. You see what's going on.

One of us can go back with him. For a little while.

You mean I can go back. You mean me.

I can keep things going here. I can keep Sheriff Joe going.

And who will keep you going?

He stared at her, and she turned away, and she began to shake.

Angie. He put his hands on her shoulders. He raised her to her feet and pressed her to his chest. He held her as her legs gave out, then moved her to the bed and eased her down and held her. After a while she stopped shaking and he swept the hair from her eyes and kissed the tears up from her cheeks and he kissed her lips and she kissed him back and then she kissed him truly and something broke in his chest and, kissing her, he put his hand between her legs, and at first she let him, but then suddenly her thighs tightened and—No, stop it!—she shoved at him and fled into the bathroom and slammed the door and he could hear her in there moaning into a towel.

Dad . . . ?

He got up and opened the connecting door, banging it into the footrest of the wheelchair. I'm sorry, did I hurt you?

Is Mom all right?

Yes.

What happened?

Nothing, Sean. We had an argument.

What about?

Grant shut the door and went around the wheelchair and sat on the bed. Nothing. Just an argument.

She woke up that night clutching at him. It's all right, he said, it's all right.

No, she said, her eyes bright in the dark. I was driving a dark road. Just me, and she came out of the trees, into my lights. She was naked and covered in dirt. Like she'd been buried alive. But she got out. Oh God. She got out and she was trying to come home.

He held his wife until she slept again, then he lay with his eyes on the ceiling thinking about that girl in the bunker, the one who texted her mother. Her abductor thought she was just playing games on his phone. He'd kept several girls down there, eventually burying them all nearby. One girl, he said, he kept for two years; they were like husband and wife, he said. People wanted to know why. Mothers in ruin begged it of him. The man shook his head. He looked to the courtroom ceiling as a man would to God. It won't help you, he told them. I'm sorry, but it won't.

He looked like any other man, this man: glasses, blue eyes, halfway bald. In prison now, this man, way back in there, where none of the fathers could touch him.

3

In the hours before dawn, in the storm's first cool blows, thin curtains fill and lift in the dark. They belly out over the bed, rippling, luffing—and abruptly empty again, and for a moment everything is still. The world paused. There's a terrific light, the room conjures for a white instant, and almost at once comes the shuddering boom, and before it has entirely died away the door opens and a small figure stands in its frame, back-lit by the hallway nightlight. Fine muss of dark hair, pink-hearted pj's. Angela lifting the bedding and the child slipping into that sleeve and shaping her little backside to her as a hand within a hand.

I'm scared.

It's all right. It's just a storm.

The small shivering shoulders. The quick-beating heart.

Where's Daddy?

I don't know but we're all right. We're safe. Okay?

Okay.

A kiss to her silken skull and Angela holding her as she quiets, watching the doorframe for the boy to come too, but he doesn't, and here's the rain pattering heavy on the roof, on the firm green leaves outside the window, and she is drifting down, smelling the rain, feeling the small girl in her arms, the deep drumtap of the girl's heart, and her only prayer in that hour of love is Dear God, may the morning never come.

But it does, of course it does . . . and all Angela held in her arms was a pillow, and the door was shut, and the room was not her room, and the bed was not her bed.

Before her, on the bedside table: A plastic bottle of water. A small book of poetry with a blue first-place ribbon for bookmark—*I cease, I turn pale.* A digital alarm clock preparing to sound. An amber vial of pills. She stared at the pills. At the clock. She listened to the house that was not her house, its total stillness. Get up, she thought. Get up now or else lie here and cease.

Cease then.

You can't, Angela.

Why not?

The girl's heartbeat still played in her arms. In her chest. She remembered the hour, the minute, she was born: precious small head, the known, perfect-formed weight of it. All her fears of motherhood—of unreadiness, of *unfitness*—vanishing at the sight of that plum-colored face mewling in outrage. *My child, my life.*

She pushed aside the covers and sat up. Got to her feet. Crossed the creaking floor and opened the heavy drapes on a gray dawn. No movement in the leaves of the elm tree. The street and the sidewalk dry. The most ordinary of days. Of worlds.

When she came downstairs in her outfit and makeup, the children were at the table. She touched the boy's head and then the girl's on her way to the coffee, one, two. They watched her as if she were someone who'd just walked in off the street.

At the stove in the climbing steam he turned and said, "Well, you look nice."

"Thank you."

"Will you eat some eggs?"

"No, thank you."

"Are you sure?"

"Yes. Thanks."

"These are my special cheesy eggs with dicey ham."

The smell is enough, please spare me the description.

"No, thanks, really," she said.

"All right. How about you two monkeys? Who wants more?"

Angela sat at the table to drink coffee and chew at a cold triangle of toast. He served himself and returned the pan to the stove and sat to her left. "Are you excited?" he said.

After a moment she looked up. "–I'm sorry?"

"I said are you excited. About today. About teaching."

She thought how to answer, thinking for so long that he stopped chewing. He swallowed, then picked up and sipped his coffee.

On the wall at the foot of the stairs a vintage sunburst clock ticked prodigiously. As if sound was its only mode of timekeeping.

The children began to talk to him. He listened and smiled and talked back and she remembered the little girl—*her* little girl—coming into her bed. The firm small body pushed against her. That heat, that smell like no other.

"I'd better be going," she said. "I've got a long walk."

He reached and touched her then, two fingertips, lightly to the bone of her wrist, and picked up his cell phone and showed it to her. Some sort of colorful image like a bright whorl of bruise.

"That's something," she said.

"That's rain. You should let me drive you, Angela."

She looked at him. His kind face. The clear blue eyes with their overcasts of worry. She knew how she must look to him. To all of them. It's going to be all right, she wanted to say, we're going to survive this, but at that moment behind her a step creaked, and then another, and there was the scuffing whisper of slippers over linoleum, and fingers swept the back of her head, and she watched as her younger sister made her way around the table in her robin's-egg robe, swooping down to kiss the boy on the head, the girl on the cheek, and lastly the man, fully on the lips.

"Good morning," Grace said to her husband, to her children, and to Angela. "Good morning, my loves."

4

The moment she walked into the classroom she knew she'd made a mistake, but some of them had already seen her and it was too late. Rebecca Woods whose mother, Anne, liked a good martini in the afternoon; Ariel Suskind with her tremendous brown eyes and a father who taught graduates at the university and who had left Ariel's mother for one of them. Angela had a brief smile for these daughters of friends and once friends, and they had the same for her before the girls were moved to urgent doodling, to matters of the cell phone. She saw the flushing young cheek. The spill of fine hair which must be rehung behind the ear. Girls of high bloom and maturity enough to know wreckage when it stood before them but not to bear it, and in that instant she abandoned every plan she'd made and asked them to open their books please and just read, and this they did without a whisper or passed note or pen poke among them. Instead there was the mute fervency of secreted devices, messages firing lap to lap like cells along a nerve chain, and she sat out the hour staring into the paperback and letting them take her in as the news reached them one by one: *She lost her daughter in the Rocky Mountains, then she lost her mind; she was in the "hospital" for three months & now she's our sub? Is that even like, legal?* Yes, children, here is your lesson, here is all I can teach you, until the bell sounded at last and she stood and pretended to search the contents of her tote bag while they shouldered their packs and trooped wordlessly out and—

"Good-bye, Mrs. Courtland."

"Oh, good-bye, Ariel. Please tell your mother hello."

"I will." The girl slowing, not quite stopping, books held to her chest, the great brown eyes. She had an older sister with the same eyes who had run track with Caitlin but who'd broken her neck diving into a pool and lived now in her wheelchair, and Angela digging intently at the tote bag, muttering, a glance and a smile—"Bye now"—and the girl Ariel nodding and turning and going on, and Angela's heart racing high in her chest as she shut the door and shook out a palmful of pills and then spilled them back into the vial, all but two, and clapped them into her mouth and swallowed them dry. When she opened the door again some minutes later the hall stood empty left and right. She stepped out and walked it with the rap of her heels bouncing off the tin lockers like the footfall of some following soul. Like the twin sister who still spoke to her, whom she saw in the mirror. Two old dears alone in that church-quiet corridor, they might have been, childless where a thousand living children ran.

How do you go on?

You just do, honey.

The clack-clack of heels. The gray rectangles of doorlight ahead.

Why?

Because He asks you to. And for your family.

She pushed through the doors and there was the smell of rain and she sat on the wooden bench and slipped off one heel and pulled the white sock onto her foot, the white sneaker after, and then she did the same for the other foot and tied the laces. She lifted her face to the sky and shut her eyes against the first cold drops. *Your family.* She tried to think. She tried to remember what that meant. How you were supposed to feel. Above her, the flag lapped silkily upon itself, susurrant as some creek or stream making its way across the sky. The drops fell harder. Colder. She pulled the black umbrella from her tote bag and thumbed the button and the device shot forward and flapped into tautness over its bat-wing joints. She felt the pills under her heart like a hundred small hands holding it aloft.

At home—at Grace's—her little sister, who did not work on Mondays, was putting the kitchen back in order. She was getting dressed, she was brewing fresh coffee and reading the paper, she was listening to that clock. She was waiting for Angela to walk in the door and tell her how it went. She was waiting to talk. Grace had no memories of another sister, of Faith. To her there was Angela, and there was this girl who looked exactly like Angela in the old albums—identical pretty young girls smiling, dazzling the camera, no way to tell which was the girl who would live and which the one who would not.

Angie.

Yes.

We can't just sit here.

I know.

She sat a moment longer beneath the umbrella, inside the dark bell of it, listening to the drops drumming. Then she stood and walked away from the school, and away from Grace's.

5

Two days of heavy snow before the pass opened again and they could go. Unbelievably bright and crystalline Saturday morning, the little resort town gilded end to end in a deep wonderland sugar. Skiers racking their skis on a shuttle bus outside the motel and clomping aboard in splendid plastic boots. A foursome of boys jostling up the walk waving snowboards—Hold the bus!—eighteen, nineteen, careless as lords.

It was the day before Thanksgiving. They had lived in the motel for four months. Family of four when they checked in, family of three checking out.

Everybody in? Grant said unthinkingly.

They were the only car going upward against a long, down-snaking procession of inbound traffic, as if they alone defied the laws of the divide, of physics. The whitened pine forests rolling by like a child's dream of winter (if anything moved, if anything stirred in all that whiteness the eye would see it at once, seize on it—but nothing did), and they wound their way up one side of the divide and down the other without a word among them, slipping at last into a vein of freeway that carried them through the city toward the plains to the east, the great peaks rising behind them, more massive somehow with distance, undiminishing, the car doing seventy but dragging, straining, the sensation of a climbing ride that would reach its vertical limit, falter, and plummet backward. As it must. As it should.

They drove on, away from her, mile by mile.

In the back the boy had his homework, the things the school had sent, arranged on his lap, his naked leg pillowed along the length of the seat, the entire length of it, no other way for him to be in the car, so where would she have sat?

East of the city nothing but the road ahead and the wintered plains and the blue sky. They drove over a ruddy stain where an animal had been struck, and Angela reset her sunglasses. Deeper into the plains dark rags of meat and hide littered the road. Black hooves in the ditch like strange blossoms. They came upon a fully intact animal in the median, a newly antlered buck on folded legs, no blood but no life either in the eye that watched them pass. Oh God, said Angela, and Grant said, Don't look.

How can I not look?

Watch the horizon. Close your eyes.

That doesn't help.

What do you want me to do?

There was the rattle of pills and her head kicked back once and then again as she drank from her water bottle. If she looked over her shoulder all she would see of the boy was his leg. The lurid seams. The gleaming steel brace clinging to his knee and holding the pieces together under the skin. A thing from the future that from time to random time probed with its needle legs raw, deep beds of nerves. Since they'd gotten into the car she hadn't looked back, not once. As if her head no longer moved that way.

Grant tabulated through the stations and switched off the radio. How you doing back there? In one of his pockets were Sean's pills.

Fine.

The leg okay?

The boy looked at his leg. The steel arachnid.

Are there any rest stops in this state?

When they stopped, Angela's head, lolled against the window, did not stir. Grant pulled the collapsed wheelchair from the rear of the wagon and after a few minutes the boy was in it and they were pushing into a bitter wind, his bare leg pink and white in the cold.

No warmer inside the men's room but at least windless, the wind whistling around the glass blocks where the caulking had pulled away. A large man in a checkerboard winter vest glanced at them and turned back to his loud pissing. Sean wheeled himself to the handicap stall and Grant said, Will you be all right? and Sean didn't answer, his heart rising furiously. At school was a bath-room with a blue wheelchair sign on the door and the door would swing open when you came near it with a certain kind of card, and the only people who had the card were the janitors and a boy in his class with MS and an older girl, a friend of Caitlin's who'd broken her neck diving into a swimming pool. And now Sean would have the card too and he would go into the cripple's bathroom and sit like a girl when he pissed.

Some minutes later he wheeled out of the men's room and steered toward the glass doors of the lobby and stopped. Out in the car, his mother's head rested as before. Sunglasses like black outsized eyes, blind and unblinking. To the west was nothing, the mountains gone, absolutely, as if into a sea. They were the survivors; all they had now was each other. Like in a book, or a movie.

Want something from these machines?

He wheeled around.

They've got Snickers bars. Coke, his father said.

Sean stared at the machines. I'm not supposed to eat that crap.

You can eat whatever you want.

Why?

Because you can, that's all.

Because I'm in this thing?

Because you're sixteen, Sean.

They were silent. Wind pushed at the glass doors, rattling them like a man locked out.

What is it? his father said.

Nothing.

What, Sean?

Is she going to be all right?

His father stared at him, his eyes glassing over, and Sean said, I mean Mom, and his father looked out at the car.

She's going to need time. And help. She's going to need your help.

And yours too.

Yes.

But you're going back. To keep looking.

Yes.

I'm going with you.

You need to get back to school, Sean. And you need to heal that leg.

They were not on the highway long before his knee took up an intense pulsing—rhythmic flashes of pain he thought he ought to be able to see like light in the eyelets of flesh where the spiderlegs sunk in. A quasar of bone and nerves throbbing under the zippered skin. He stared at his knee and he remembered the ground up there. The brown bed of needles, the weeds and the dust. Lying there looking up into the trees with the feeling of piss in his crotch. Hot piss in his crotch and a leg all wrong and his heart pounding and still seeing the man's face behind the wheel, no surprise no fear no nothing, just the yellow lenses, and he'd closed his eyes when the man came up—Don't touch him, she said—and he'd kept them closed like he was sleeping as they put the man's blanket that smelled of wool and gasoline over him and he kept them closed as she knelt and talked to him one last time, and he kept them closed and he kept them closed with the piss going cold in his crotch.

How's the leg? his father said. As if the pain were visible after all, burning like headlights in his mirror.

Fine, he answered.

6

Angela walked.

She walked and her mouth was dry and there was the supermarket sign across the street like a bloodstain in the gray, side-blown rain. The trees were lashing themselves. The umbrella filled with wind and lifted, brute and purposeful. When the little walking figure lit up she stepped into the crosswalk and a man said *Shit* and she stopped just short of the collision—bike and bicyclist skidding by quarter-wise to the road, tires locked, rainwater fanning, a wet grimace of face under the helmet and then the wheels unlocking and the bike righting and the man glancing over his shoulder not to see if she was all right but to tender his disbelief, his fury, before facing forward again and pedaling on through the rain.

She crossed the road, crossed the parking lot, and the glass door swung open and she stepped into the supermarket's vast fluorescence, thinking of the winter day she'd first seen him on that bike, that three-speed from another century, himself an unlikely figure in army surplus trench coat and canvas haversack, like some courier of the tundra. *Grant Courtland,* someone told her. Pulling up next to her another day at a crosswalk and turning to her and waiting for her to look. Waiting. And when she looked at last she saw first the redness of his face, the bright blooms of cold on his cheeks, blooms of some essential enthusiasm, and next the eyes, stung-wet and very blue, and lastly the lips as he smiled and said, *You look nice today.* And rode on.

In her apartment over the Polish bakery he would read to her, fragments of which she could still recite: *Homeless near a thousand homes I stood,* and *O! speak again, bright angel-a,* and *I'll example you with thievery.* Years later he couldn't believe she remembered the lines when he himself did not.

Such days, such nights. Such heat in the dead of winter! How could it ever end?

The sun's a thief. . . . The sea's a thief.

Can you recite too what the father said that day? said Faith.

Yes: *God does not ask His children to bear that which they cannot.*

Right.

But neither does He permit them to not bear it. Therefore He asks His children to bear the unbearable.

He knows you have strength you don't know you have.

"Excuse me." A woman was reaching past her for a bottle of water. Angela said, "I'm sorry," and moved aside.

Angela stared at the bottles. So many choices. She selected one and studied its list of ingredients: water. A little boy of perhaps five was standing beside her. She looked down at him and he looked up. Brimming blue eyes and teartracks on his cheeks.

"Where's your mother?"

He shook his head.

Angela looked around.

"All right. Don't worry. Come on." She turned and walked and the boy followed. After a moment he took hold of her skirt. As they passed the long produce bin the indoor thunder sounded and a fine mist fell from unseen jets, dewing up the bright tomatoes, the perfect heads of lettuce. *The thunder is to warn you,* Sean said, ten years old, *so you don't get sprayed.* Caitlin said, *Oh, really?* and stepped forward with her summer arms.

"Bradley!" came the cry. A quick breathy commotion bearing down from behind. "Where are you going?" Wild, puffy eyes and all the goods her arms could carry as she groped for the boy's hand. "Where are you going with my son?"

"Nowhere," Angela said. "We were going up front to—"

"You just walk off with someone's child in a grocery store?"

Angela looked at the woman. Then she looked at the boy, his face buried now in the woman's thighs.

"He looked like a very nice boy," Angela said, and the woman's mouth convulsed mutely. She dropped a bag of cornchips and let it lie there so that she might palm the boy's head and lead him away.

Angela paid for her water and walked outside. Still raining, though the wind had moved on. The little trees of the parking lot seemed to be collecting themselves, checking for damage. Under a concrete shelter sat a number of iron tables with a number of people using them: supermarket employees on smoke break, businesswomen stabbing at salads. Was it lunchtime already? One old man writing in his notebook. She stood across from the old man and asked if she could sit down and he looked up over thick plastic frames, one eye pinched nearly shut and the other a clouded blue marble. He said, "By all means," and she sat down and opened her bottle and drank from it, watching the rain.

She looked at the old man again. Bent over his notebook with what looked like no pencil at all in the twisted and swollen fingers. Heavy brown overcoat and a tweed cap finger-darkened at the brim by a lifetime of donnings and doffings. A wooden cane was hooked on the table edge, thinner at its topmost curve as if by heavy sanding. She looked at his hands again and saw the tiny pen.

"What kind of pen is that?"

He held it up. It resembled an elongated black suppository.

"That's a space pen," he told her.

"A space pen."

"It's the pen they use in outer space."

The pen itself pointed to where that was.

"It's antigravitational, is why," he said.

"What does that mean? It defies gravity?"

"It doesn't, the ink does. You can write upside down. You can write on the moon."

He gave her a last good look at the pen and resumed his writing.

Angela drank from her bottle. The rain fell steadily on the parked cars. Women in sneakers made a run for it, water spinning from the cart wheels.

"Do you mind if I ask what you're writing with such a pen?"

The old man hesitated. He didn't look up.

"I'm writing notes. For my grandson."

"Where does he live?"

"He doesn't. He's dead."

"Oh. I'm sorry . . ."

"He died serving this country."

"I'm sorry."

"Well," said the old man.

Angela was silent. Then she said again that she was sorry, and the old man scratched at the tip of his nose. He stirred a finger in the white hair of his ear. "I figure I'll go on writing him like before. He's got a wife and a little boy and I figure that's why I'm still here, so I can tell him how they're doing. I know how crazy that sounds."

Angela shook her head. "No," she said.

He wrote for a while and then he put down the pen and took his writing hand in the other and rubbed at the knuckles. He looked over his shoulder at the rain as though it had been hounding him all his life. He said: "An old aunt of mine told me one time, Simon, if you knew what growin' old was you wouldn't be in no rush to get there. I didn't know what to make of that at the time."

She waited. "And now?"

"How's that?"

"What about now?"

"Now?" He looked at her, somehow keenly for all his eye trouble. "Now I wonder why a man lives so long he doesn't even know the world he's in anymore."

"Granddad?"

A woman came up behind him, a little boy in tow. Same woman, same little boy. The woman didn't seem to believe what she was seeing.

Angela smiled at the old man. "Thank you for letting me sit with you."

The old man touched the tweed cap and got slowly to his feet. The little boy handed him his cane. "The pleasure was mine, young lady."

7

At midmorning Grant helped the old Labrador into the cab, then drove the three miles through the foothills to the cafe for his coffee and eggs and the Denver paper. Other such Saturdays, when he would return to the truck an hour, sometimes two hours later, the dog would be asleep on the bench seat, having been asleep the entire time, but on this morning, when he returned after only thirty minutes, the dog lifted her head and watched him glassily, as if puzzled in her dog brain to see him back so soon. He got in and said nothing, and did not scratch her ears, nor turn on the radio, and as he drove back through the hills she cast baleful looks at him until at last without looking he said, "She wasn't there. So what?"

By the time he pulled into the long gravel drive he'd not been gone an hour, but it was the hour in which the black car returned.

Billy.

He brought the truck to a stop and sat staring at the car across the front pasture. Bright, glossy black and parked at a careless angle next to the old man's blue Ford at the side of the house. The two bay mares grazed the fence line near the county road, as far from the house and the black car as they could be. The dog sat watching him, quietly panting.

"Not a thing to do about it," he said finally, and drove on toward the house. He parked beside the El Camino and stepped out of the truck and the dog spilled out behind him and limped around the corner of the house and disappeared.

He lit a cigarette.

Heat rose from the black hood. In the cab a litter of coffee cups and burger bags and crushed Marlboro packs. In the bed nothing but a flat tire and a tire iron, flung there, from the look of them, in a moment of disgust.

Grant walked around the side of the house and onto the dirt cul-de-sac with its grassy island and the blue spruce at its center, and as he came around the spruce he saw the aluminum ladder leaning against the eaves of the old ranch house, the old man up on the pitched tin roof in a blaze of reflected sunlight, on his knees, clinging one-handed to the brick chimney.

"Shit," Grant said. He stepped on his cigarette and went to the foot of the ladder. "I see you couldn't wait for me."

Emmet shifted for a look down, his lenses flaring. "—How's that?"

"I said I see you couldn't wait for me."

The old man turned back to his work. "Did wait, by God. Waited all morning while this roof got preheated."

"I'm coming up now."

"Bring some Crisco with you."

"Some what?"

"Crisco. You can't fry your ass without Crisco." He frowned under the brim of his straw cowboy hat. You could make him smile with a joke, but when he made one himself he frowned. Beneath his coveralls he wore only a sleeveless undershirt, baring the white knobs of his shoulders to the sun. His red windbreaker lay on the ground below like a fallen helper.

Grant climbed the ladder and stood watching the old man scour the base of the chimney with a wire brush. "You might've got your boy to spot you on the ladder at least," he said, and Emmet glanced across the sky to the other house, then resumed his work.

"He come in a little after you left and went straight to his room. Walked right by me like a ghost." The back of the old man's neck was a dark leather chamois, red in its seams. Thick smile of scar running under the jaw where part of the throat had been removed, the scar a bright crimson in the sun. Grant thought to say something more about Emmet's son but then remembered his own son, gone one morning without good-bye, without even a

note. Half a year ago now. More. Taking Grant's blue Chevy for good mea-
sure. Could've called the cops. Still could.

"You think that's clean enough for fresh jack?" Emmet leaned away from
the chimney and Grant looked for the place to grab him if he slipped.

"I think that'll do." A five-gallon bucket hung from the top of the ladder
and inside was a bristle brush, a small spade trowel, and two fresh tubes of
roofing cement. When Emmet was finished with the bristle brush, he took
the caulking gun from Grant and began to squeeze the black cement into
the deep crack where the flashing had split and pulled away from the brick.

"She's thirsty up here," said Emmet.

"Is she?"

"Like a tick on a tumbleweed." He emptied both tubes and took the little
spade trowel and began to work the cement like black icing. After a while he
wiped his brow with his forearm and said: "How's that look to you, contractor man?"

"Like I did it myself. Better."

"Like hell. You'd of tore out half this roof and put new flashing on."

"This will do for now."

"That's all I'm asking. The next man after me can do it his way."

Back on the ground Grant stowed the ladder and they went up on the
porch for the shade and looked out at the sky as if to watch for the storm that
would now come along and test their work. But the sky was clear and the old
man's joints told him there'd be no rain today nor any day soon. The dog lay
under the porch in the dark with her chin on her paws, listening.

"Come up to the house for lunch," Emmet said. "I got coldcuts, and we
could fry us some bacon, and not that goddam fake bacon neither."

Emmet's house sat stark and handsome in the sun. From the outside it appeared to be a large two-story log cabin cut from the very pines that marched
down the hills to surround the ranch's meadows and pastures, when in fact it
had arrived in sections on the back of an eighteen-wheeler ten years before,
and the men who brought it had put it together in two days and the walls
inside were as smooth and white as any art gallery's. Emmet had done it for

Alice, his wife, but she got to enjoy the house for less than a year before she died, all of a sudden in the night, from a clot in her brain. Guess what you can count on, said the old man: nothing.

Grant put his weight on a sprung board in the porch floor and said he had half of a leftover steak he'd better eat. "Split it with you, if you like."

"Don't feel like steak today. Don't feel like coldcuts neither but I gotta eat something so I can take my goddam pill. Which reminds me." He peered at his wrist and began to rub at a smear of black. "I put a few of my prescriptions in there, in your cupboard. Behind your Cheerios. They're ones I don't take too often but they cost a damn fortune. If you wanna put them someplace else that's fine by me, I'll just ask you when I need them."

"All right."

The old man took one step down and stopped and looked off. He stroked craftily at his throat and said: "You see that waitress this morning at the cafe?"

"Which waitress?" Grant said.

"Which waitress, he says." He took the remaining two steps to the dirt and bent for his red jacket and spanked the dirt from it and fed his arms into the sleeves. He sunk a hand in one pocket and said, "The hell? Oh, that," and he stepped back to the stairs and reached a fist up to Grant. "You might as well take these too. For the time being." Grant put out his hand and Emmet spilled the shotgun shells into his palm like candies. The old man zipped his jacket up to his jaw and tugged his hatbrim down and began to make his way across the clearing, hunch-shouldered and small-looking, as if the storm had come after all.

8

The bus rolled to its hissing stop and the door swept open and Angela climbed up into a smell she loved. You couldn't define it but it was a smell all buses had and it was the smell of childhood. The school bus, yes, but her father had been a driver for the city and he would tip his cap when they came aboard, *Good afternoon, ladies,* and they would drop their quarters coolly—*Good afternoon*—and go down the swaying aisle in their summer shifts, their sunglasses, bikini strings playing at their napes, and they would sit where they could watch him, the way he turned the great wheel like a ship captain, swinging their hearts through space when he took the corners, the cordial way he had with every kind of person who stepped on board—and then coming to their stop and tipping his cap again, and these two girls, these identical sun-browned girls kissing him on the cheek, one, two, and skipping down the steps into the sunlight and not turning but feeling the following eyes, the men especially, as the bus rolled on.

Summers of secrecy and love and something else. Of hearts aching for something they could feel just beyond them, around the next wide-swinging turn surely, or the next.

An old woman sat directly behind the driver with a kind of mesh duffel in her lap and after a while a tiny head poked out of the duffel with enormous bat's ears and round, wet eyes to look about, licking its muzzle with the smallest tongue. At the very back of the bus were three slumping teens, two boys and one girl, skinny black jeans everywhere, oblivious to all but their phones.

Angela watched her town go by. The shopping center. The university. The church where she was married. The soccer field that had been a drive-in theater in its last days when they were sixteen and dating, do you remember that?

Those Meyers twins everybody thought we must *go out with?*

Identically ridiculous.

Identically boring.

Identically bonered.

Oh my God!

The bus stopped and the old woman with the tiny dog stood and went carefully down the steps. Angela watched her open up a yellow umbrella on the sidewalk, taking care to keep the dog dry. No one else got on. The door swung shut again and the driver signaled and suddenly Angela was on her feet. "Wait! Wait, please," she called to him, "we need to get off."

The teenagers, the driver—everyone—watching her make her way, just her, down the aisle.

THE OLD WOMAN TOOK the path that led to the old section of the cemetery, her umbrella climbing a far hill like a cartoon sun amid the dripping trees, the wet ancient stones, and Angela took the path to the newer section, with its smaller trees and its modern stone benches. She'd not been here for so long, but somehow she was calm; the markers and the grass plots and what lay beneath them did not frighten her. Perhaps it was the rain, the absence of sunshine, of birds singing. Perhaps it was the pills.

Her father was here, awaiting her mother, who lived on, half oblivious, in the nursing home. Faith was here too. And next to Faith's plot was an island of empty grass, the turf undisturbed, unstoned. Back then there'd been plenty of empty plots, but Angela had known. She'd known. Her parents could not imagine the girls separated; they could not imagine Angela a grown woman with a husband, children of her own. You could not imagine burying your children—putting their bodies into the earth while you went on living, growing older—until you had buried one. This was what the second plot had told her.

Do you remember how freaked out you were? Like you were expected to go too?

It wasn't that. I thought I should go. It wasn't fair for you to go alone.

Fair to whom?

She swept the water from the bench as best she could and sat down and at once felt the dampness in her skirt, the deep chill of the stone. She breathed in the sodden air and blew a faint mist. The rain beat dully at her umbrella. The blood was moving thickly in her veins, dividing, seeking its separate ways.

The bench was cold and hard and the air was cold and there was the smell of leaves and earth and rain, and the umbrella spread over her like a dark canopy, and she sat very still in that sheltering space until the bench became the same stone bench where Caitlin had sat—looking at these gravestones, this pale and cold Virgin with her missing fingers like Grant's and the brass plaque at her feet, *Right Reverend . . . Mercifully Grants, in the Lord, Forty Days of Grace.*

Did she pray before the shrine, her daughter? She would ask Sean—did Caitlin pray? Did you?

What would it mean if they didn't? What would it mean if they did?

There was a sound, a small rustling, and she saw at her feet a black beetle scrabbling over the yellow aspen leaves. It carried another beetle in its jaws, this second beetle smaller, weightless, inert with death, or perhaps the paralyzing bite.

Pray with me now, Angela.

Somehow she was alone in the woods. Grant, the sheriff, the rangers, the dog handlers, the volunteers—all had fanned out and moved on. Nobody noticed she was not with them. She picked up the walkie-talkie and looked at it: something was wrong with it, the battery was dead.

Pray now? she said. Before this shrine?

Yes.

Is this Lourdes? Cures and miracles? Our Lady of the Missing Fingers.

Please, Angela.

The bland white face like a china doll in the dusk. The clipped, bloodless fingers. Stump-Fingered Lady of Our Missing, keeping watch over the old stones. Crooked old markers of once living Americans, frontiersmen and their kin, drawn west by such scenes and dreams as their minds could conceive. There was that documentary they'd watched about the Donner party: women, children, whole families, freezing and starving in the mountains, eating each other. Some party, said Sean, twelve years old. Caitlin said she would have done what they did: she would've eaten to stay alive. Grant—Grant was not there.

The sun was down. The air gone autumn cold, October cold. Her breaths pluming and dispersing like a series of ghosts.

Do you remember when he came back that time, that summer, with his hand in bandages?

Yes, of course.

How he got down on his knees at my feet? How he begged for my forgiveness? The promises he made?

Yes.

No more drinking, no more women. He wasn't asking for forty days, he was asking for a life. A whole new life. And I gave it to him. I forgave, and I took him back, and I believed God would grace us the more for our fight, for our resilience. And now here we are. And you ask me to pray before this rock?

You did before. After that day on the lake. You didn't stop praying then.

You didn't leave me. You never left me!

Neither has she, Angie. Neither has Caitlin. You'll see. But you have to fight. For her, and for God, but most of all for yourself.

What if I can't? What if I'm broken, like these fingers?

Oh, honey, *said Faith, and said no more, for there were lights in the woods— swinging, wayward lights, like headlights knocked loose. Voices out there, calling.*

Angie! Angela!

Her heart leaping wildly—Caitlin! What is it, she cried, what is it?

They were upon her, they came crashing over the fallen leaves in the dark, putting their hands on her. Grant's face, inscrutable behind the beam of light— Angie, Christ . . . we thought we'd lost you.

9

On certain hot days after the work was done Emmet would step onto his porch across the way with a beer and sit in one of the wooden rockers and stare out at the land. In time Grant would come over and they'd sit and talk about what the weather was bringing and what must be mowed or painted or planted or mended the next day, watching the dusk slide down. Emmet would tell Grant to smoke and Grant would say he'd get around to it but then wouldn't because of the old man's throat, and in silence they'd watch the stars swim up over the hills. The bats and swallows in their soundless, extravagant dances.

At this day's end in early September Grant filled his mug and stepped outside and went down the steps, the dog rising stiffly from her place under the porch to follow. The black El Camino sat as before, as it had sat all day.

"I see you had the same idea," Emmet said, raising his coffee.

"Seemed like a night for something warm."

"Fall's coming. Set down, partner."

Grant lowered into the other rocker that had been meant for Alice Kinney and for the remaining days of the old couple's lives. The dog sniffed up a spot farther back on the porch, turned twice, and dropped with a huff to the boards.

Emmet had napped and shaved and there was pink in his face above the red windbreaker and he'd dragged a comb dipped in scented oil through his white hair.

"That patch looks good from here," said Grant.

"How's that?"

"I say that chimney patch looks good from here."

In the west a large bird sat atop the ridge on the point of a lodgepole pine that had long ago shed its branches and pointed like a needle at the sky. This same bird found this same perch at the same hour every day, as if to maximize its own effect before the sunset, resting in silhouette until prey or some other bird impulse set it moving again. By its regularity it had become an unspoken fact of the ranch, like the hills themselves—although once, early on, Grant had commented on the bird, and the old man had grown silent and still. Then he told Grant that his wife liked to say that if she must come back to this earth and not to heaven she hoped God would let her come back as such a bird—hawk or eagle or falcon. And if she did come back as one of these, said Emmet, she hoped she would have no memory of ever having lived as a human woman. She wanted to look down from the air and know the things a bird should know and nothing of what men thought or did, but just to watch them as a bird would, from up high, no more curious and no less wary than any other creature.

They'd sat watching the bird.

Do you believe it? Grant had said.

Believe what?

That a person can come back.

Emmet had set his boot down from his knee. Sipped his beer. Raised the opposite boot to the opposite knee. At last he said he didn't know if he believed such a thing in any religious kind of way, if that's what Grant was getting at, but he said his wife had been the one true thing of his life and when he looked out on this land and saw that bird setting atop it that way, well. He blew as if expelling smoke from his lungs. *I believe a man is likely to surprise himself with what he believes. Don't you?*

Now the bird pushed off and beat its wings twice and rode them south along the piney ridge, and the men were quiet and the dog slept, and into the heart of that calm there came a sudden piercing sound—a high, sharp whistling that sliced through the screens and made Emmet duck in his rocker as if struck to the back of the head. They both turned and found the whistler standing in the door, in the screen, lips pursed, looking from man to man. After a moment he turned the latch and brought the shrill notes out onto the porch.

"Quit now, by God," Emmet said.

The whistling ceased midnote and Billy stared at him. "You don't like that tune?"

"That wasn't no tune I know."

"That was Hank Williams, Pops. Here, listen." He stepped between the rockers and turned to face the men. A tall, lean young man in a black leather coat and crisp white shirt. Dark hair stashed behind his ears and a small tuft of beard clinging to the underside of his lower lip. The coat was of a sporty cut and creaked when he moved.

"No, now, stop," Emmet said. "You are painin my ears."

Billy stopped, one hand paused in the air, a longneck beer bottle swinging in a noose of finger and thumb. He turned to Grant: "All of a sudden he hears like a bat."

He sat on the railing and crossed an ankle over his knee in a mirror image of his father and began to jitter a black cowboy boot as if it were something they should all watch. His eyes appeared very blue in the twilight. He set his beer on the rail and got out his cigarettes and shook one up to his lips and began to put the box away but then gestured it at Grant.

"No, thanks."

"You quit?"

"No, just holding off a bit."

"Ah," said Billy. He dropped his boot down from his knee and straightened out his leg so as to snake two fingers into his jeans and said around the cigarette: "So how's tricks, Grant? I was wondering if you were still around."

"Still around, Billy. How's tricks with you?"

"Holding down the old fort over there, are you?"

"Just till the landlord kicks me out."

"Ha," said Billy. He uncapped a silver Zippo and spun the flintwheel and lit his cigarette and shut the cap again smartly. He blew smoke in the direction of the old ranch house and said, "I hope you like it cold. A man will piss icicles of a winter morning over there. And then what happens the second he moves out? They build themselves this overheated Ramada Inn over here." He recrossed his leg and jiggled the boot in the air. The lighter moved restlessly in his fingers, silver, then blue-violet, silver again.

"Don't you believe it, Grant. He's had that whole house all to himself whenever he wants. Him and his friends."

"Used to," said Billy.

Grant sipped his coffee.

"What is the matter with you, son?" Emmet said.

"You're welcome to it, Billy," Grant said. "I can make other arrangements."

"What? Hell, I don't want in there. I don't want nothin to do with that place."

Emmet shook his head and looked away. Billy drew on his cigarette and blew the smoke thinly.

"Those are good-looking boots, Billy," Grant said.

Billy held his foot still. He aimed the pointed toe at the porch ceiling.

"I took them off a man down in Denver thought he could play nine-ball. A fool and his boots are soon—hey," he said, looking beyond Grant, "there you are, girl. Come on over here."

The dog lay in the shadows watching him. She looked at Grant.

"Don't look at him, come here." Billy pinched the cigarette in his lips and spanked his thighs and the dog rose slowly and went to him, her head low. "You don't remember how to come when you're called?" He took her head in his hands and shook her.

"Let up on her," Emmet said.

"Aw, she loves it. Don't you, Lo, don't you, huh? We used to wrastle like goddam alligators."

"She's too old for that now."

Billy stood and removed the cigarette from his lips. "Damn it, Pops. Don't you think I know my own damn dog?"

Emmet stared at him, then looked away.

Billy picked up his beer and tipped it back, the sharp knob of his throat working until the bottle was emptied.

"All right then," he said. "Can you loan me a few bucks, Pops?"

"What for?"

"What for. So I don't starve. All I got is eight bucks and a check I can't cash till Monday."

"Why didn't you cash it before you come up here?"

"Because I didn't, that's why. Now can you loan a man a couple of bucks or can't you?"

Emmet pulled his billfold from his hip pocket and adjusted his glasses to peer inside. "All I got is a twenty."

"That'll do." Billy stashed the note in his shirt pocket and looked at the dog again where she'd resettled herself on the floor next to Grant. When he stared at her the dog pinned her ears.

He began tugging at the patch of hair under his lip.

"Well, Grant," he said. "It's good to see you again, if you don't mind me saying so."

"Why would I mind?"

"Why would you mind?"

"Yes."

"Why would you—?" He looked from Grant to Emmet, and back. "Because seeing you here means that that brother of mine still hasn't found that daughter of yours, that's why."

Grant looked at the young man. Held his blue eyes. The first he'd known of Billy Kinney was in the mountains, in those early days when they lived in the motel—the sheriff stopping by one day to say he'd be gone for the day, driving down to Albuquerque. Angela staring at the sheriff with eyes that held only one concern, one question, always: *What did he know?* It's nothing, said the sheriff, I gotta go get my little brother out of jail, be back as quick as I can. It had stunned them—the first time since they'd known him that the sheriff had not seemed to be entirely theirs, devoted exclusively to their needs. They could not object, they could not blame the sheriff, but neither could they bear it, this abandonment, because within it was the message that, in time, the investigation, the manpower, the reporters, the world, would all move on.

"God damn it, Billy," Emmet said, leaning forward in his rocker, clutching the armrest with one hand. "What in the hell is the matter with you?"

"What? Nothing's the matter with me. What's the matter with you? I'm just trying to be friendly here."

"Why don't you go be friendly somewheres else?"

"Jesus Christ, I didn't mean nothin. He knows that. Don't you, Grant."

Grant sipped his coffee. "We'll see you later, Billy."

Billy looked from one to the other and shook his head. He flicked his cigarette into the dirt and went nimbly down the steps. A moment later the El Camino roared and a red stain of taillights spread over the dirt at the corner of the house. The tailgate came briefly into view and then lunged forward, throwing up red fans of dirt. They heard the car progressing down the drive, heard it idling at the county road, revving throatily, but there was no squealing of tires, and after a few seconds the sound of it faded away altogether.

Across the way, over the doors of the machine shed, the automated farm light had come on, lighting up a scrim of grit in the air they could taste.

"I gotta say I'm sorry for that, Grant."

"No you don't, Em. I got a boy too. He's just young."

"He ain't that young. And I'm too old. I was already old when we had him. I wonder if that's why." Emmet stared into his coffee. Grant stared out at the night. A bat dove blackly into the light to snatch a moth and wheeled away again. Soundless as a thought.

"I'll say one more thing," said the old man. "Though I know a man ain't supposed to say such things aloud. But if it come down to just one of these boys coming home, yours or mine? I'd of voted for yours."

10

The truck, a long-bed blue Chevy, moved down the interstate under a low moon and the fading vault of stars. No crew cab, three years old, in good shape. No bumper stickers or decals. No gun rack. It held cruise control steady at 77 mph, two miles over, all its bulbs alight and nothing out of the ordinary but the out-of-state plate. The driver was heading north and if there was another passenger or any kind of luggage or possessions in the cab with him, these were stowed out of sight. Ten miles from the upcoming town on a steep grade, the Chevy swung into the left lane to pass a flatbed hauling a tremendous black stone, a monument of some kind, and then it swung back into the right lane again, and the silver SUV that had been following did the same and bloomed with flashing lights, red and blue, red and blue, strobing soundlessly in the dark predawn.

The officer sat back there running the plates. In the truck, the boy squinted at the headlights in the rearview and pushed the mirror out of true.

Out over the desert the moon had struck a black edge of sky, the flat of a mesa, and sat flat-sided itself in a field of stars. Tossed, unknown stars; a strange heaven. With his head half out the window he looked and looked, disbelieving, almost dizzy, until at last there was Pegasus, and from there the others: Cepheus, Cassiopeia, and Andromeda, the king's daughter, chained to her rock. Naked, forsaken, watching the sea. He was not a great student but he had learned the stars. The idea that they'd been there, in their places, long before their names, long before the first eyes saw them.

The officer, walking up, put his light on the boy's face, and then into the passenger's seat, lighting up a red roll of sleeping bag and a green duffel, the duffel incompletely zipped on a gray nest of tubesocks. Below the duffel on the floorboards sat a canvas carpenter's bag with leather grips and a brass buckle fastened across the mouth. It looked full and heavy.

The officer lowered his light and stood in the frame of the window, half lit like a moon in the beams of the cruiser. Under the hatbrim he was black-eyed and smooth-faced and he wore a black shiv of mustache. His jacket bore the insignia of the sheriff's department but he was too young to be sheriff. He asked for the boy's license and registration. He put his light on one document and then the other and then flicked it to the boy's face again, throwing white pain into his eyes.

"This your license, sir?" In his voice was that lilt of another land, another people, older than anything.

"Yes."

"This says you're seventeen."

The boy waited.

"That correct?"

"Yes."

"How long you been sucking on those cancer sticks?"

The boy glanced at the cigarette between his knuckles. "Sorry?"

"You the oldest seventeen I ever saw."

The boy waited. "How come you pulled me over?"

"Failure to signal when you passed that flatbed. Who is Grant Courtland?"

"My father."

"This his truck?"

"Yes."

"He know you got it, way out here?"

"What do you mean?"

"What do you mean what do I mean? Does your Wisconsin daddy know you are driving his truck in New Mexico."

"He knows I've got it."

"But he don't know where you're at?"

"No."

The deputy watched him. "What did you do back there?"

"Back where?"

"Wisconsin."

"Nothing," said the boy.

"You did something."

"No, sir."

"Yes you did. You left."

The boy kept looking at the deputy. No sound but the cruiser's idling engine. After a minute the deputy leaned a little closer and lifted his face in a peculiar way. As if to take the boy's scent.

"Where you coming from, bro?"

"What do you mean?"

"That's twice you asked me that. I mean where you been *at,* before you come through here?"

"I was in California for a while."

"California."

"Yes."

"What for?"

"Sorry?"

"What were you in California for."

"To see the ocean."

The deputy stared at him. "These are some poor answers, bro."

The boy waited.

"You steal this truck from your daddy?"

"Was it reported stolen?"

"I asked you a question."

"No, sir. I borrowed it."

"You borrowed it."

"Yes, sir."

The deputy squared himself and glanced up the highway to where the truck's shadow on the road reached long and thin for the dark beyond. His torchbeam slashed mildly up and down as if he were testing the flashlight's weight in his hand. He told the boy to step out of the borrowed truck and go stand behind it in the lights of the cruiser.

Dawn was coming, a creeping shade of violet in the east. The boy smoked his cigarette and dropped the butt and mashed it under his boot toe. The air smelled dryly of sage and juniper and rocks and dirt but it was a cold smell, and even without the cigarette his breath smoked white. September, he thought, early September. The seasons might be changing but they were not his seasons and he didn't know the signs. He shuddered and tried to shake the pain out from under his kneecap. He'd slept a while at the rest stop, the sleeping bag as pillow, but then the cold and pain had got to work on him and he'd driven on.

The deputy's black eyes appeared in the rear window of the cab, above the passenger's seat, and were gone again. Between the highway and a far mesa ranged a field of pale grass with the dark heads of chaparral rising out of it like the humps of sea monsters. Standing there not thirty yards away was an antelope, or pronghorn. Sharp corkscrew antlers, one obsidian eye fixed on the boy. The boy stared back, his own eyes aching, and he thought of the Chinese man leaning down, widely unlidding one eye between finger and thumb and sinking his needle light into the helpless ball, smell of rubber fingers, *Hello, Sean, I'm Dr. Lee. White lights beyond the Chinese man's needle light flooding in and then the sudden bomb of leg pain that sent all lights streaking like comets across his vision—and within the streaking lights was the car or the jeep-thing that had come out of the trees and locked its tires in the dirt, the yellow lenses of the man behind the wheel and the look on his face which was no look at all just his yellow eyes as the jeep-thing slid. And then the boy must have slept again because he woke himself talking. Answering questions when he became aware that he was answering questions. No feeling at all in his leg, as if they'd cut it off. His mother and father off to one side and another man looking down on him, big man in a sheriff's jacket. Holding a sheriff's hat in his hand, big serious face trying to look friendly.*

Good, Sean. You're doing just fine. Now, I need you to do something for me. It's real important. I need you not to tell anybody else who ain't a lawman what

you just told me. Do you understand? Anybody else asks, you just tell them you
don't remember a thing. Nothin about no sunglasses, nothin about no blanket,
none of that. Do you understand?

Everybody staring. Mother father Chinese man sheriff.

Can you do that for me, son?

"Step on back here," said the deputy.

The boy came up and glanced in the window. Socks and T-shirts strewn over the unrolled sleeping bag and down on the floorboards, the canvas bag on its side with the gear tumbled out. The glove box gaping, all its junk stuffed back in as if to gag it. *Don't say it, Dudley. Don't say a word.*

The deputy said, "What's wrong with your leg?"

"Is that it, then?"

"You borrow those tools from your daddy too, in that grip?"

"Some. Some are mine."

"You sure?"

"Yes, sir."

"My daddy come in the house one day to take a shit and when he comes back out to the garage his table saw is gone. Somebody borrowed it."

"That wasn't me."

The deputy turned his face and spat.

"Tell you what, bro. You don't look to me like nothin but dumb white trouble, and I don't want none of that anywhere near my town or on this highway even. You copy?"

The boy gazed over the truck into the east where the dawn was coming. The stars and their kings and their creatures all swept away in the tide of light.

Little brother, the man with the yellow eyes called him.

"Yes, sir," he said, "I do copy. But I need gas. I was planning on stopping for gas."

The deputy raised his beam like a great sword. "There's a Shell station fifteen miles up the road, exit 151," he said. "They got all kinds of gas there."

11

February. *The days dull and leaden and cold. Sitting at the dining room table head bowed to his homework when she came down the stairs and hushed by in slippers and housecoat stirring the air with her sleep-smell on her way to the kitchen. Watching her pour water from the filtered pitcher and stand at the sink holding the glass to her chest, staring out.*

An hour after school, an hour before dark.

Do you want to go somewhere? he said. Pen stilled and denting his finger in a dull bite.

She turned as if surprised. Her hair a lifeless drapery. Eyes backed into shadow.

We could go to the store, he said.

No, sweetie. Parts of a smile came to her face and she turned back to the window. Do you need money? she said, lifting the water, sipping.

He shook his head. She held the glass to her chest.

It's still there, she said, more to herself than to him.

The twenty-seventh of February, this was. Two days after her nineteenth birthday. The two of them had been back in the house for three months. His father was in Colorado, in the same motel room where he and the boy had lived.

The boy got into his jacket and his crutches and went out the back door and over the icy pavers to the metal building and unlocked the door and stood a minute at the threshold staring at his father's desk, his breath mushrooming into the trapped cold. The woman in her skirt. Her bare legs. Getting up to smile, shake his hand. A client, his father said.

When he emerged from the metal building he seemed to move along on strange implements: elaborate clattering fusions of crutch and shovel and yard rake. In this way he came around to the front of the house and to the curb and he swung down into the street under the black arms of the sycamore where he and Caitlin used to climb and he looked back. The window was empty.

It was a red squirrel, spread-eagled as if to embrace the road, the world, preserved by cold, skull crushed. The county said they'd come but they didn't.

He stood in his crutches looking at it. Why didn't you stay in your nest, stupid?

He set the rake tines over the body and the square-point shovel behind the plush, riffling tail—but some clinginess would not let him rake the body into the shovel and instead he had to work the blade spatula-wise under the tail and under the little hind feet and along under the belly and finally the head, prizing that up with a small ripping sound. He took the rake and crutches in one hand and bent on his good leg and lifted the weighted shovel and held it level while he got the black bag open, and then he spooned the shovel carefully in and tilted until the stiff body dove splashing down into darkness. He bread-spun the bag and put a knot in it and got on his crutches again and looked back and the window was empty.

What could he tell her that would help her?

What did he know?

He knew everything up until the moment he was hit, was in the air, was watching himself in the air, as if he would not participate in such a thing, was struck again, and there was nothing to know but the brilliant new pain of brokenness.

As for the rest.

It rolled on despite him, without him. Things he shouldn't know, couldn't know, but that were no less true for that. As if something more than his knee had been changed in that slamming instant. As in the comic books he once loved: the ordinary made fantastic by fluke cataclysm, by the weird laws of accident.

It felt like shame. Like crouching outside the basement window listening. You couldn't say what you knew without saying how you knew it: I crouched. I listened.

And who would believe him, anyway? Not even himself. Least of all himself.

What happened up there, Sean?

Only what I've told you. Only what I've told you.

12

She took the turn and he didn't call out to stop her and she ran on down the un-paved road, forty, sixty yards before looking back, and then running backward a few strides and then stopping and running in place, hands on hips—and she'd taken two steps back toward the road when he came laboring out of the shadows, heaped over the handlebars, and he didn't call out and she turned and ran on and did not look back again.

The light grew thinner here. The forest lusher and wilder the higher they climbed. As if they were entering a peculiar kind of wildness that thrived on al-titude and lack of oxygen. It must have occurred to her to wonder what purpose such a road served and where it might lead. The instant before she stepped on it a lizard the size of a man's finger twitched from the red silt and slashed away into weeds.

Afterward, she would believe she'd known it was coming. She would believe she'd seen and not seen something back in the trees. Heard the low breath of it, or smelled it, or merely sensed it back in there, just out of view. Or maybe it was only that it seemed, later, like the sort of thing that would have to happen on such a road, in such woods. In any case it came, monstering through the trees at an incredible speed, crushing deadfall, the whip and scream of branches dragged on sheet metal and then the suddenly unobstructed roar that made her wrap her head in her arms, the sound of tires locking and skidding and the thing slam-ming into what sounded like the sad tin post of a stop sign and then the meaty whump and the woof of air which was in fact the boy's airborne body coming to a stop against the trunk of a tree.

A haze like atomized blood rolled uphill and beyond it sat the car—or truck or jeep-thing—come to rest perfectly broadside to the road like a barricade. Completely still and soundless.

Sean was not in the pink haze of dust. Was not on the road anywhere. She saw the bike, the incongruent orange of it far back in the green and she knew the boy was there too because of course he would be where the bike was. But then something moved in the foreground and it was an arm, lifting as if in lazy hello from the scrub growth at the base of the tree, and she went to him with a barb of irritation in her heart—you are ruining my run—and then she said, Oh, shit, and dropped to her knees beside him, the pink haze all around her like the tinted air of dream. When she saw his leg her heart slid coldly. The purple balloon of knee and the lower leg folded at some exceptional angle.

Shit, she said, shit.

But no blood that she could see, no flowing blood anywhere for her to stanch with her hands or tie off with her top. He began to lift his arm again and she said Don't. Don't move. Lie still. Did you hear what I said? There was a stink in the weeds, as of some animal marking territory. Then she looked at him again and the stain she thought was sweat in his shorts had spread and was spreading and she placed her hand on his shoulder and said, Oh, Dudley.

Don't, he said, and she withdrew her hand.

Sean? Can you hear me?

His eyes were hard shut. A claw mark on his face had begun to weep scarlet beads. The helmet strap was sunk in the fold of his chin. The helmet was on his head. It seemed to nod.

Don't do that, she said. Don't move your head. Don't move anything, okay? She laid her hand on his shoulder again and with her other hand she unzipped and rooted inside the pack until she felt her phone. The feel of this small familiar thing, undamaged, poured relief into her heart. Just relax, she told him. You're gonna be fine, and she thumbed the keypad and she watched the little window for the signal.

It won't work, said a voice behind her, and she gave a small hop and a cry, there on her knees, like a crow.

He stood just behind her. Having arrived without sound. Inhumanly large, in that first view. Rubbing his neck one-handed like a man who'd been working long hours and had taken a break to come check on them, this girl and this boy by the side of the road. The movement of his hand on his neck made a fleshy, intimate sound, and part of her mind dwelt on that. On the fact that she could hear it so clearly.

There's no reception up here, he said. There never is. He raised his other hand and showed her a small black phone, as if this were proof.

She peered at her phone. She redialed and watched the screen and watched the man at the same time.

I came out on the road and there he was, he said. Right in front of me like a deer. I didn't believe it. A kid on a bike, up here. Son of a gun. What are the odds?

He took a step and dropped to his haunches all in one motion, and this new position—or the sudden, easy way he achieved it—changed him from an upright giant to a man with a much lower center of gravity, one for whom squatting was perhaps the more natural position, like an ape. He sat studying the boy through yellow lenses.

How you doing, little brother? he said, and she nearly said, Don't talk to him. He smelled of pinesap and gasoline and sweat, and his existence took some-thing away from her. After a moment of only feeling this, she knew what it was: it was her sense of herself as the eldest. The strongest. The one in charge.

And yet . . . he might be an expert on injury, on proper mountain procedure. It was his outfit: the pressed and tucked-in khaki shirt, the glossy black belt, the new-looking blue jeans and good hiking boots and the clean tan baseball cap. She looked more closely at the belt for gadgets and pouches, at the shirt and cap for insignia. She looked beyond him at the car or jeep-thing blocking the road but nowhere found any sign to tell her not to watch him, not to be ready.

You got knocked pretty good, didn't you, little brother?

The boy didn't move. His eyes were shut. The inflamed red of the scrape on his cheek had spread to his entire face and neck. It was the color he turned when he was very angry or embarrassed.

I think he's out, said the man.

Sean, said Caitlin. Sean, open your eyes.

The man said, Let him sleep. His body needs it.

She gave the boy's shoulder the smallest shake. Sean, open your eyes.

I wouldn't do that, said the man.

He's my brother, she said flatly, without looking at the man.

All the same, he said. He squat-walked one step forward and from there reached and pressed two fingers into the flesh of the boy's throat.

His heart's going like crazy, he said. After his hand was back out of view it occurred to her that he wore a gold ring. He's just traumatized, said the married man. Help me get him into the truck.

No, she blurted, don't touch him.

Okay, he said, okay.

His neck could be injured. She turned to him. Do you have a blanket or something?

A blanket?

Something we can cover him with? In case of shock?

Shock? It seemed a new word to him. He didn't move. Then he said: I'll go look.

When he was gone she tightened her grip on the boy's shoulder and pressed her free thumb to the keypad again. Come on, God damn you. She shook the thing. She held it at arm's length in every direction. She raised it high over her head.

Go, said the boy.

What? Sean, what did you say?

A door slammed and the man's boots came gritting back toward her. How had she not heard that, his boots in the dirt, earlier? He carried a thick square of cloth, military in color, and when he snapped it from its folds it released a rich kind of animal smell. He floated it down and got into his monkey-squat again to help her tuck it around the boy.

Wait. She peeled back the blanket and reached into the pack again and found the boy's phone and brought it out and pressed it into his palm. The fingers closed slowly around it like a dying spider. Sean? she said. Nothing. His eyelids were shut but not at rest, the delicate skin busy with minute twitchings. As if he were a small boy again and she were watching him, waiting for him to talk in his sleep (so she could tell them at breakfast, them trying not to laugh and the boy burning red).

The man stood behind her, a little to the left, and after a moment Caitlin pushed up from the dirt and began to brush fine pebbles and grit from her knees. She continued brushing after there was nothing but the red impressions in her skin.

Okay, said the man. We best get going.

She turned to him. She was a tall girl, five eight, most of it legs, and in his boots he stood no taller.

I'll drive you on down to where your phone works, he said. Drive you to your folks, if you want. Or the sheriff. Whatever you want.

And what? she said. Leave him?

He'll be all right here. Nothing will touch him. The man hung his hands on his belt by the thumbs and gave her a kind of smile. Don't be afraid, he said, and until that moment she hadn't been.

I'm not afraid, she said. It just doesn't make sense. You can drive down until you get reception. Call 911, tell them where we are.

He stood looking at her with the yellow lenses. Maybe you misunderstood me, he said. I'm offering to take you down where you can make a phone call. Heck, I'll drop you in front of the sheriff's office if that's what you want. But if you send me down there alone, well. That's likely to be the end of it, far as I'm concerned.

Her face, she believed, was a perfect blank. She stopped herself from lifting her phone again. When she spoke, her words sounded to her like stones dropped into sand.

What's that supposed to mean?

It's supposed to mean that I hit this kid with my vehicle and I may not feel like getting sued by his daddy.

She crossed her arms and uncrossed them.

You'd really be in trouble then. If you left, she said.

No, he said. I'd just be more careful.

I've seen you. I've seen your car.

Miss, do you have any idea where you are?

She stared into the yellow lenses. What kind of a woman was waiting for this man? Slept in his bed?

Fine, go. Go down the mountain and go to hell you white piece of shit, we don't need you.

Please, she said aloud. Please.

The man sighed. Look, he said. Here's the situation. Stay here with little brother and roll the dice on me making a phone call, and maybe he goes into shock and dies in front of your eyes, okay? Or, after I'm gone, try and run down to where you can make a call yourself. You could ride that bike, but I doubt it, from the looks of it. Or come with me and be down within range in ten minutes. I'll let you out the second you have a signal, that's what you want, and the sheriff or daddy can grab you on the way up. Now that's the deal on the table, miss, you can take it or leave it but you need to decide quicklike. He began patting his pockets—jeans, khaki shirt—looking for cigarettes or keys or some other misplaced thing. Have yourself a minute to think while I get this vehicle straightened out.

He walked away and she looked up the road and then down the road. Treetops swooning in a high wind. Sunlight spilling bough to bough to reach a random spot on the forest floor. Or not random at all, she thought, but the same boughs, the same spots of floor, day after day, the sun on its fixed course and every bough fixed in its place and nothing random about it but the eyes seeing it from this particular vantage at this particular hour of the day. She saw the face of the Virgin, and the memory of that place—the white aspens, the hard chill of the bench, the smell of chocolate and the sound of his desperate chewing—took hold of her like a memory of girlhood and left her heartsick.

She knelt and touched his shoulder again.

Sean, I have to go. I have to go down where I can get a signal, and then I'll be right back, with Mom and Dad. With an ambulance. Then we'll all go back down together. Okay? All you have to do is lie here and I'll be right back, I promise.

She began to rise, and stopped. He'd said something.

What? she said. Sean?

Don't, he said.

Don't what?

Don't go.

You want me to stay?

No.

What do you want me to do?

His slack, red face. Nothing in his eyelids but the tremblings of dream.

He said something else, hoarsely, weakly, and she leaned closer. What? she said, nearly as weakly, and held her breath, watching his lips.

13

The old Chevy that his son had left him still had good kick in the mountains, but Grant was content not to pass the logging trucks and other rigs laboring up the steep switchbacks. He lit a cigarette and watched the range rear up around him, the patterned thick walls of pine and more pine and now and then a copse of yellowing aspen like a blight on the green. At the top of the pass was a paved lot, a scenic overlook, a refuge from the harrowing turns—irresistible to a family from the plains who had never seen such country before.

Why do they call it the Continental Divide if it's not the exact middle of the continent? his son wanted to know. Standing with their backs to the view while a stranger aimed the camera, found the button. *Because,* said his daughter, *this is where the water changes direction. On the eastern side the streams and rivers all flow to the Atlantic. On the western side everything flows to the Pacific.*

Looking out, each of them, as if they might see these streams and rivers running obligingly toward their endings.

Grant drove to the far end of town, to the Black Bear, and parked, and made his way to the counter. *I am starving,* said Sean. *How shocking,* said Caitlin. A few faces looked up—looked again, then bent to their sandwiches, their soups. Waylon Reese appeared from the kitchen, raising his hand in an automatic wave, but then came forward with his hand held out. He asked Grant how he was and Grant said he couldn't complain, and Grant asked after Waylon's family and Waylon looked away at something and said they were fine, they were all just fine.

He'd been one of the good ones, Waylon Reese. Free sandwiches and coffee for the sheriff's people, the government men, the volunteers. He'd hauled his whole family up into the mountains, Julie and the two boys, to help look. He'd kept the poster up at the Black Bear long after others in town had taken it down.

A good man who now flipped to a fresh page on his little pad and, staring at it, said, "What can I get you, Grant?"

A CAR HONKED AND he looked up. The light was green.

He accelerated around the corner and drove down the old street, past the school playground, the town hall, until he reached the sheriff's building. Inside was the woody, dusty, faintly sour smell of a church. The groaning floorboards, the rack of shotguns aligned ceilingward like organ pipes. He looked over the head of the young deputy to the bulletin board and felt his heart fall out of him—his daughter's face, there amid the postings. Her good teeth, her sun-squinted eyes. Black hair whipping away as if she were in full sprint. It was the picture taken at the top of the divide by a stranger. Grant and Angela and Sean, mountains and sky, all cropped out. He had looked on it a thousand times and it never failed to kill him.

The young deputy sent him on back, and at Grant's rap on the doorjamb Joe Kinney swiveled and brought his chair level with a sharp mechanical outcry. "Well now," Kinney said. He got to his feet and Grant came forward to shake his hand. The sheriff's hair was getting whiter and thinner, coming into the blown, snowy style of his father. But unlike Emmet, the sheriff was yet a big man, with a high, hard gut he wore as if according to some official stipulation.

Grant told the sheriff he'd got a hankering for the Black Bear, and Kinney, hitching his thumbs in his belt, affirmed that it was worth the drive.

In the outer room the young deputy opened a drawer, shut it, and muttered something.

"Do you mind if I close this door one minute, Joe?" Grant said, and the sheriff said, "No, sir. Shut it and sit down. You want Donny to get you a coffee?"

"No, thanks. I'll only take a minute here."

"Take as long as you like."

On the desk between them a walkie-talkie faintly hissed. Grant knew the exact heft of it, its leathery, electronic smell. Off to the right, staged with a father's pride, stood the picture of Kinney's daughter on her horse at the rodeo, cowboy hat sailing behind her.

Kinney offered him a cigarette and he took it and leaned to meet the lighter. The sheriff lit himself and said, "Everything all right down there at Dad's?"

"Well," Grant said, and the other man said, "Shit, don't tell me he fell off another roof—"

"No, nothing like that."

"Man his age, climbing on roofs."

"Nothing like that," Grant said. He gazed critically at the tip of his cigarette. "I just wondered if you knew Billy's come home again."

The sheriff leaned back and drew on his cigarette. "Last I heard he was in Nevada."

Grant sat forward to tip his ash into the glass ashtray. "No, he's back. I thought you might like to know about it, if you didn't already."

"I appreciate that, Grant. But I guess if anything was wrong I'd of heard from Dad."

Grant nodded. "It's not my place, Joe. But your dad and Billy. Well, your dad's getting on."

The sheriff smiled crookedly. "I know he is, Grant. But if you're sitting here telling me he can't handle that piss-ant little brother of mine, well, I'd say you ought to know better by now."

"I'm not trying to tell you anything, Joe. I probably shouldn't have said anything at all. I just thought you might like to know he's come home again, that's all."

The walkie-talkie crackled, throwing a quick, reflexive flurry into Grant's heart. Kinney scooped it up and frowned at it and set it down again.

Grant said, "Well," and he stabbed out his cigarette and began to rise. But the sheriff motioned with his hand and said, "Now, hold on a minute, Grant. I got something to tell you too."

"All right."

"It's about Angela."

"What about her?"

"She's been calling again. Day, night, it doesn't matter. 'What are you doing, Sheriff? What's your plan? What are you people doing up there to find my girl?' She's been working that phone and ... I don't know how else to put it, Grant, but she don't sound like she's got both feet altogether on solid ground. I'm sorry for what she's had to go through—what you've both had to go through—you know that. But ..." He lifted a hand and dropped it again.

Grant studied his own hands. The truncated two fingers. He'd heard this tone from the man before—that first time, that first morning, when the sheriff wanted to know what a fifteen-year-old boy was doing way up on that mountain by himself.

Kinney tapped his cigarette, staring fixedly at the ashtray. He had something more to say but he wasn't going to say it, not today. Behind him was the large green map of the front range; in a few square yards of paper and ink it contained all the millions of true, godless places a person might be. How long was long enough when it wasn't your child?

And when it was?

"I'm sorry to hear this, Joe," Grant said. "I'll talk to her."

Kinney shook his head and stubbed out his cigarette. "I just thought you might like to know, that's all." He came around the desk and opened the door and followed Grant into the outer room. At the front door Grant turned and the two men shook hands again.

"I want to thank you for keeping that up," Grant said.

The sheriff didn't turn to look at the bulletin board. He looked down and scuffed the old floorboards with the sole of his boot and he studied the scuffmark a long time.

"I don't believe it's in the papers here yet, I haven't looked. But I heard from a lawman yesterday about this gal in Texas got kidnapped when she was twelve. Dragged into a car right in front of her house. Fifteen years ago and they just now found her. Living in a garage all this time behind the man's house not ten miles from her home. Neighbors never knew a thing. Say they never saw her. Never saw the little girl she had by the man, neither."

The sheriff looked up. "Twenty-seven years old now, this girl. A little daughter same age she was when she got taken and who don't know a thing about this world but that garage." He drew a breath through his nostrils and shook his head.

Grant held his eyes.

"I didn't know if I should tell you about it or not," Kinney said. "I guess I decided I should."

Grant nodded. "Thanks, Joe."

"Oh, hell." The sheriff drew himself up. "You'd of read about it anyways."

14

She walked in the rain's aftermath along wet sidewalks and under dripping trees with the clouds coming apart in the sky like rotted fabric. The old brick library was gone and the new one with its soaring glass facade like a church stood in its place. There was a history. During construction, people had called it the Lindsay Suskind Library because it was Lindsay Suskind who'd gone rolling backward down the wheelchair ramp of the old building, and it was Lindsay's mother, Jeanne, newly certified in the law, who threatened action.

Wide, smooth sidewalks now coming and going, glass doors parting at ground level, book aisles like boulevards. Walking into the building was like walking into a botanical atrium, plant life and the sound of water chuckling somewhere, bright shafts of daylight. But the smell of the new library was like the smell of the old library: paper, bindings, the faint whiff of mold. Like the smell of buses, it was a smell of childhood. Of young girls out on their own on a summer day. Long empty days of sunburn and ice cream and the pursuing eyes of boys. Of men.

Angela stood staring at the new releases. Picking one up. Putting it back. Choosing another.

On a stool behind the counter sat a plump older woman who'd been at the old library and who had a way of smiling that made you believe she remembered you, though it had been years. Angela handed her the book and looked beyond her. A seated young man with a silver hoop earring, gazing into a computer screen. That was all.

"Does Lindsay Suskind still work here?" she asked the woman.

The woman scanned the book and smiled. "Oh, yes. She's taking her lunch break."

Angela glanced about.

"She'll be back in fifteen minutes, if you care to wait."

Angela took the book and her card. "Thank you, it's not important."

She walked into the cafe annex and ordered a small black coffee and sat at one of the smaller tables and opened up the book.

The girl was parked at one of the larger tables, reading. Dipping her fork from time to time into a Tupperware. In a final act of amends or whatever you wanted to call it, the new library had installed Lindsay herself at the checkout desk, where she excelled. After a year, Angela heard, she earned her library science degree through the evening and weekend program at the university where her father taught and slept with graduate students, and the library had promoted her accordingly. Mike and Jeanne, separately, were prone to boasting about her in a way they hadn't when the girl ran track.

Angela remembered the day—her own daughter walking in, hair still dripping from the Owensby pool, so brown and lean in her bikini, so beautiful it startled her. As if some undressed woman had come striding through her front door. *You walked home like that? she was about to say when Caitlin ran damp and sobbing into her arms.*

What is it, sweetheart, what happened? Her mind leaping to the worst—rape, pregnancy, HIV. It was like falling into blackness. The end of everything. A daughter was your life; it was as simple as that. Her body was the only body, her heart the only heart. The most absolute, the most terrible love.

The July sun was burning in the kitchen window. The air was roaring. The girl couldn't, or wouldn't, speak; her body was convulsing (the feel of that body pressed to hers, the wet and sun-hot skin, the softness and the firmness, the smell of the pool, of coconut, of the sun itself in her skin, in her dripping hair!).

It's all right, just tell me, just tell me, sweetheart . . . She'd heard the sirens, she would remember later.

Lindsay, Caitlin said at last. Oh, Mom, it was awful . . . and Angela holding her the tighter and her heart crying, Thank God thank God thank God, and only later thinking of her own sister, Faith, diving off the dock.

Then the day, the bright December day perhaps a week after returning from Colorado when she answered the door and a dark-haired girl was on the stoop in a wheelchair and for just a moment, just an instant, she'd thought, *Caitlin.*

Angela closed the book and walked over, and the girl looked up. Smiling in recognition, and then true recognition taking hold and the smile falling.

"Mrs. Courtland," she said. "Gosh. Hello."

"I'm sorry to bother you, Lindsay. I know you're having lunch. I just wanted to say hi."

The girl closed her book and set down her fork. "No, gosh." She put a hand on Angela's wrist. "Would you like to sit down?"

"No, you're eating—"

"Please, sit down."

Angela pulled out the chair and sat and the girl studied her, searching her face with large brown eyes. For a moment Angela was lost in them. Why had she come? What did she think she would say to this girl, this young woman whom she'd once picked up and dropped off, fed, watched over like one of her own?

"Mrs. Courtland, is there . . . I mean has something . . . ?"

"Oh," Angela said. "No. No, I'm sorry, I should have said so right away."

"It's just, I haven't seen you here. I mean I've never seen you here before. I thought maybe . . ."

Angela shook her head.

"I'm so sorry," said the girl.

A man came to the counter and ordered something in a low voice, as though he didn't want anyone to know, and the barista girl set to making it.

"I saw Ariel this morning," Angela said.

"You did?"

"Yes. I was substituting."

"You were?"

The girl didn't want to look or sound surprised, Angela knew, but she couldn't help it, she had no guile. Her heart had been through too much.

"I'm sorry," Lindsay said, "I thought you were . . ."

"I was. But that was months ago."

Lindsay nodded. "Did she behave herself—Ariel?"

"Yes."

Angela stared at her hands where they lay upon the book. They looked like someone else's. Her heart was aching.

"She's gotten to be a pain at home," said the girl.

"I'm sorry, Lindsay."

Lindsay shrugged. "She's what they call a teenager, I believe."

"Not for that." She held the girl's eyes. "I'm sorry for the way I was that day you came to the house."

Lindsay shook her head. "Don't, Mrs. Courtland—I shouldn't have come like that, out of the blue. It must have been a shock."

"It was. But everything was. Everything. I didn't know what to say to you."

"It's all right."

"No, it's not. I never came to see you at the hospital either. After your accident. I'm sorry for that too. That was hideous of me."

"It was hard for people . . ."

"You were friends with my daughter. I was friends with your mother. I should've come."

Lindsay looked down, and for a moment Angela saw her in flight, one long leg thrown out before her and the other folded under like a wing as she took the hurdle. Effortless, magnificent.

"Caitlin came," Lindsay said. "Every day after school. Or after practice. I'll never forget that, Mrs. Courtland."

Angela smiled. Lindsay smiled. Without thinking, Angela reached and thumbed the tears from the girl's face, one side, then the other.

"I'm sorry I ambushed you like this. I'm sorry to upset you. I just wanted to talk to you."

"I'm not upset. I'm glad to see you."

Angela stood to go.

"Mrs. Courtland?" said Lindsay.

"Yes?"

"I know about what happened."

Angela stood looking at her.

"Between my mom and your—with Mr. Courtland. Years ago. I know about it. I know that's why you and my mom stopped being friends. I know that's why you didn't come to the hospital."

Angela stared at her. Then she remembered—but it was like something she'd lost, or buried. She had no idea what it once felt like to know that her husband had slept with—was sleeping with—Jeanne Suskind. She thought of her own mother in the nursing home, who sometimes called her Faith, who asked, *Where's Angela?* Did the mind break down or did it simply correct? Vectoring away from pain? They'd never told her mother about Caitlin and they never would. The old woman would die without ever having lost her granddaughter.

"That was so long ago, sweetheart," Angela said at last. "None of that matters anymore."

"I know. But Caitlin and I talked about it sometimes. I think it made us closer. Almost like sisters. Weird as that sounds."

Angela nodded. She smiled. "I'm glad I got to see you, Lindsay. Will you please tell your mother I said hello?"

"I will. And please—" The girl's eyes filled again. "Please come back."

Lindsay watched her walk away. From where she sat she saw Angela pass through the library's automated glass doors and stop to open the small brushed-nickel door of the deposit chute, lift her book, and drop it in. She seemed to listen for the dull bang, then she let go the little door and walked on.

15

A whistle shrilled and three girls burst bare-legged down the black lanes, pony-tails whipping, but then pulled up laughing and loped onto the field where other girls lay strewn and twisting on the grass. Cross-country girls, not sprinters, they'd mostly been freshmen when Caitlin was a senior, yet they all knew her and they all knew him, and when one girl contorting in the grass looked up the hill and saw him, and tapped the hip of the girl nearest to her, he turned and limped away.

Deep painful blue of sky, the first stains of autumn in the elms and oaks.

The buses were long gone and there was nothing to see or hear at the front of the building but the snap hooks lashing at the high barren flagpole with that silvery hollow sound, and when he reached the street he turned south toward the railroad tracks. VFW stood for Veterans of Foreign Wars and the old vets would hail him and arm him with a pool stick and tell him stories of shitstorms in the jungle where men, boys really, not much older than he, best buddies, brothers, were there one second and gone the next. Headless. Cut in two. They wouldn't let him smoke or drink. They called him the Young American. They swore they would find the piece of shit who did that to his leg and make the cocksucker beg them to put a bullet in his cocksucking eye. The old vets knew nothing about Caitlin—there one second and gone the next.

Before he reached the tracks a truck pulled alongside him in the street, and the passenger's window descended and behind the wheel was his father. The boy stopped, and the blue Chevy stopped too.

I was up at the school, his father said. Up and down those halls. Where were you?

*Just walking. The boy felt dizzy. The sun appeared to yo-yo in the sky. What
are you doing here?*

Came to talk to you.

The boy waited.

*It's not about Caitlin, he said. Hop in, he said, and the boy breathed. He
slipped the backpack from his shoulder and hauled himself up into the cab.*

Where were you going?

Nowhere. Just walking.

Just walking, his father said. That knee must be feeling pretty good.

*The boy shrugged. Though the windows were down, the cab held a humid
personal odor like a bed just vacated. It was the smell of a man's long drive alone.
His uncounted cigarettes and coffees. His souring skin and all his human ema-
nations, including his thoughts, all the miles and miles of them collected within
the cab like a dew that would lift from the glass on the tip of a finger.*

*The Chevy joggled over the tracks and Grant turned left and drove past the
old VFW lounge with its antiaircraft gun aimed at the sky. The faded flag lifting feebly from the pole and falling again.*

You've got your aunt Grace pretty concerned with all this just walking.

Is that why you're here?

No, I was coming anyway.

Why?

To talk to you, like I said.

You could've called.

*That only works when the other party answers his phone. Did you lose your
phone again?*

The battery died. So you drove all the way here to talk?

Do I need a better reason?

*They drove south, out of town, on Old Airport Road. Grant had just come
from seeing Angela, from sitting across from her at Grace's kitchen table, a mug
captured in her thin hands, her eyes dark and strange. As if watching a scene
that had nothing to do with that kitchen, with him. There was one morning she
couldn't forget, she said.*

A twin-engine Piper raced the Chevy on a parallel course and rose from the runway and immediately banked and headed for them as if in attack. It droned overhead, darkened them in a blink of shadow and went wobbling off into the west. When Sean was small they would come here to watch the small planes take off and land, and Grant had told him the story of Sean's great-grandfather who had been a navigator on raids over Germany and whose plane had been shot down. How one of the crewmen came home two years later to tell that he'd seen the boy's great-grandfather parachute out just ahead of him but had lost him in the night sky, and when the crewman was captured he expected to see the navigator in the camp, and when the war was over he expected to see him at the army hospital, and then he expected to see him back in the States, but he never did. No one ever did.

The story had put into the boy's mind the story of a man who dropped into a forest far from the war and the cities, a black forgotten forest where a man could walk for years and never come across another man nor the end of the forest. Back home his young wife and his son wept over his gravestone but the man was alive in the forest and he lived there for so long that he forgot that there were such things as wars and cities and families. He simply became, like the deer, the owl, the fox, a thing of the woods. And like them he one day died, not from war, or the violence of another man, but because he'd grown old and could no longer hunt and could no longer protect himself from the other things in the forest.

I think you should come back with me to Colorado, Grant said.

Why?

You don't seem very happy here.

Am I supposed to be happy?

Grant looked at him.

The boy took hold of the brace he wore over his jeans, the steel bars to either side of his knee, and gave an abrupt, adjusting jerk. What about Mom?

What about her?

She needs me here, remember?

Grant nodded, absently. I think it would mean more to her right now if you came back with me, he said. To help look.

For a time the boy said nothing. Then he said: She bought me something, out of the blue. Guess what.

What.

A model airplane.

Grant studied his son's face—grown thin in the last year, like the rest of him. The soft blond mustache he ought to just shave. His son had lost interest in model planes years ago, he knew, though dusty fighters still patrolled the skies of his room.

Sean, he said. Did Mom ever tell you about her sister, Faith? Her twin?

The one who drowned.

Yes.

No. Caitlin did.

What did she tell you?

That mom had a twin sister named Faith who drowned when they were young.

Grant nodded. *They were sixteen, he said. Your age. Their folks, your grandparents, would rent a house on the lake for two weeks every summer—swimming, suntanning on the dock. One day they left the girls alone to go into town. They left little Grace with them. Grace was walking by then and she walked right off the end of the dock. Do you mind if I smoke?*

No.

He lit the cigarette and went on, describing the day as Angela had described it to him one night just before their own daughter was born (long wretched night of no sleep, of fears bursting all at once from his wife's breast): the two teenage girls on the porch painting their toenails, talking to a boy on the house phone, accustomed to their mother watching the baby. The moment when something splashed and they looked at one another—each seeing in the other, in her twin, her own face of immediate comprehension. Immediate fear. Two girls running as one to the end of the dock and diving in. Angela could see little Grace down among the rocks like a sunken doll. The water wasn't deep and she quickly had her in her hands and she came up kicking, reaching for the dock, calling out, *I got her, I got her.* But Faith hadn't come up. Was still down there looking, she *thought. She got Grace onto the dock and turned her on her stomach to push the water out and then turned her over again and as she blew into the tiny mouth, filling the tiny lungs, she was thinking about both sisters: the one she was trying to save with her breath and the one who wasn't there, who wasn't coming up. She had this feeling that, as a twin, her twin self ought to be able to dive in after Faith, her actual twin. She thought she ought to be able to be on that dock and in the water again, both places, at the same time.*

The ember of the cigarette flared, and he let the smoke out slowly.

Finally Grace coughed and began to breathe, he went on. And as the life came back into her baby sister, your mom told me she felt another life going out. Going out of herself. She dove back in the water and searched, and she came up to make sure Grace was still on the dock, still crying, and dove under again. It took too long. She could feel that other part of herself slipping away. Just slipping away.

Grant stared into the distance as if into those waters. Faith had misjudged her dive, he said. She hit a rock on the bottom and her lungs filled with water and she drifted under the dock, into the shadows.

He took a last drag on the cigarette and crushed it out.

The boy had found photo albums in his aunt Grace's garage, the plastic pages separating with a loud kiss of time on the twin girls as babies, as blonde birthday girls, as teenagers who with their pure, rudimentary features looked more like daughters of the grown woman he knew than his sister did. After sixteen, it was one blonde girl alone, and to study pictures of his aging mother was to wonder if, in some other, ongoing world, some divergent world, that identical sister once so happy and pretty remained happy and pretty, or must she grow as well into the same tired, beclouded woman who went on in this one?

He didn't know what to say. He understood that his mother grieved not only for a daughter but for the lost half of herself.

But it didn't change anything.

School just started, he pointed out, and Grant said they would get him into school up there or down in Denver; they'd have to look into it.

You've got your license now, don't you?

Yes.

And you can drive all right? He glanced at his son's knee.

Yes.

He handed him a key and took three twenties from his wallet and handed these over too. He told him to go over to the house after dinner and get the old green Chevy and gas it up and drive it back to Aunt Grace's. Pack up his things. Be ready to go at 7 a.m. sharp.

Your mother knows the plan, he said.

16

It was a modest but handsome house, gable-roofed, with large ground-floor windows that caught both the morning and evening light. There was a time, pulling up to it, when her heart would fly out of her, like seeing the ocean, like seeing the mountains. Here was the shape of her life, of all she loved. A solid house. Nothing in disrepair. The house of a carpenter. Grant had done the bedroom over the garage himself when Angela was pregnant with Sean, and when it was finished, Robert and Caroline across the street, who'd watched the whole process, said they couldn't believe it hadn't been there all along.

It was late and the sun was dropping through the washed and dripping trees. Above her reached the long arm of the sycamore where her children once swung. She became aware of a dog barking but only when it ceased. Lights coming on in the houses. Yellow-warm lights in houses where once they'd gone for dinners, drinks, to see new babies. Birthday parties in the backyards. She was almost surprised to see no lights in her own windows. No boy doing homework at the dining room table. No woman at the kitchen sink.

A minivan rounded the corner with its lights burning and Angela went up the walk fishing in her tote bag for keys. Finding them and getting the right one in the lock and opening the door as the car prowled by and stepping in and shutting the door as if casually behind her.

In that first moment, that silence, she heard the clicking of little toenails as Pepé came skating around the corner. But Pepé was years ago, his crooked little body buried out back under the elm in a pine box that Grant and Sean had built. Such a profound absence for such a small creature. Days of grief and Sean lobbying for replacement.

We'll see.

When? When will we see?

After Colorado.

She stood looking up the stairs into the shadows. The absolute stillness of the house. Silence like a pulsing deafness. Smell of some depleted candle perhaps but otherwise nothing, not even the smell of dust.

She poked at the thermostat and listened for the furnace to kick in, and then she went into the kitchen and turned on the light and ran water in the sink—something to do with the traps, you had to keep water in them. In the basement she filled an old plastic pitcher at the utility sink and poured water down the washing machine drain and into the floor drain. Finally there was nothing to do but go up to the second floor. Three sinks up there. Two showers. Two tubs. Two toilets.

We need to talk about the house, Angela.

All right, let's talk about it.

Neither of us has worked in over a year.

That was the point of the second mortgage, I thought.

It was. But we're burning through it. All these flights back and forth. The bills. The hospital bills.

Grant.

It's just a house, Angie. It doesn't mean anything.

Just a house?

You know what I mean.

Is that what we tell her? Sweetheart, it was just a house? It didn't mean anything?

She stood before Sean's door at the end of the hall. Her impulse was to knock, and she shook her head at that and opened the door on a fantastic scene: military airplanes swarming in outer space. The sun's last rays flaring along wings and stabilizers against a backdrop of stars.

He strode before the wall-sized map like a little explorer, *Here's Polaris, Mom, the North Star. Here's Andromeda.*

Just above her in diving attack was a fighter plane with its wicked shark's smile. It banked and shuddered at her touch.

She shut the door and took a few steps and stood before her daughter's door. Her hand on the knob.

You don't have to, Faith said.

I know.

She turned the knob and stepped inside.

Posters. Pictures from magazines in the way of young girls since there were magazines. Wild-haired crooners at the microphone, one shirtless guitar player, but mostly athletes, caught in one marvelous instant or another, the unbelievable physiques.

The white girlhood vanity stood as Caitlin had left it. Scattering of makeup. Books, CDs. Small gifts from friends: a rubber heart with legs and arms, standing on clownish shoes and waving hello. An open jewelry box holding mostly hair bands. Pictures of family, pictures of friends. Lindsay Suskind and three other girls in the air, in casual stances, as if levitating. Angela saw her movement in the mirror but did not look, her gaze landing instead on the silver brush, a thing she'd always loved. The rich weight of it, the raised cameo of a young woman on the back, head slightly bowed as if to receive some blessing. Burnished by generations of young girls' touching. *Our family hair-loom,* Caitlin called it when she was little. It rested on its back. After a long moment Angela reached and touched. Fine lacings of hair deep in the bristles. Hairs still eighteen and silky. Hairs that would never age.

Here were her trophies in a fine dust. Here the layers of ribbons, so many of them blue. The handsome small Christ on his cross. The neatly made bed. The pillows. A stuffed ape with gleaming eyes, a lapsed, shabby bear of countless washings and dryings, propped like a couple, just as she'd left them.

Dusk had come into the room. She was so tired.

She slipped the tote bag from her shoulder and set it on the bed and reached into it for her phone, the bottle of water from the market, the amber vial, placing each of these with care on the white lamp table by the bed. Then she moved the ape and the bear and lay down with her hands over her stomach, over her womb. The room slipped into darkness. Heat breathed in the vent. The dog began yapping in the backyard, mad little Pepé, tormented by the neighbor's fat gray tom. In the metal building a blade hummed to life and went singing into a length of hardwood—oak, maple perhaps—Grant calling to Sean to feed it smoothly, *smoothly,* and any moment now the front door would swing open and her gym bag would drop from the height of her hip to the floor with a joyous whop and she would be so hungry, she would be *famished, my God, Mom . . . when do we eat?*

17

In the bleary daybreak the boy passed a gas station just beyond the off ramp and drove into the little town the deputy had told him to stay out of. He took Main Street at the posted speed, parked among the spaces, and fed two of his dimes, and a third, into the meter.

The cafe door opened with a disturbance of small bells and he stood a moment in the warm, ancient reek: ages of coffee, ages of bacon. The quiet tink tink of knives on chinaware. A girl said, "Anywhere's fine," and he went to the row of stools at the counter. She came around and poured him a coffee and handed him a menu. She had the black hair and round face of a native people, although native to what he didn't know. He ordered an English muffin.

"That's all you want?"

"With butter and jam, please."

She looked at him more closely. He seemed all bone and muscle under his denim jacket, and with that limp she'd first thought rodeo, but the boots were wrong and he wore no hat. He looked as though he'd slept on a rock. She imagined touching his yellow hair, dirty as it looked.

She played the thickness of her ponytail through her fist and held his eyes. "Douglas back there pours a humongous flapjack, and it only costs a dollar more than an English muffin."

The boy glanced at some men behind him, their jaws working at their meals.

"No, thanks," he said, and with a sigh, with an air of having done all she could do, the waitress left him. A minute later a toaster popped and she placed the muffin before him and stepped away to the cash register.

"How was breakfast, Gabe?"

"I reckon I'll live." The man winked a leathery lid at the boy and slipped a twenty from his wallet. The drawer rang open with a rich slosh of coins.

MORE DINERS CAME IN and the waitress carried loaded plates along her forearms. On one trip a plate appeared before the boy, the great flapjack steaming. When she returned to the counter it hadn't moved. She inched a small china bowl toward him.

"Real maple syrup," she said.

The boy popped the last of the muffin into his mouth. "Thank you. But I won't eat it."

She made a birdlike motion with her head. "Why not?" Behind her in the pass-through a man appeared. Large man stooping to look. Toothpick in his lips. One dark eye looking at the boy and the other wandering off into the world.

"I ate that muffin and that'll do me," the boy said.

She looked at the man in the pass-through until, muttering to himself, he went away, and then she turned back to the boy and collected the plate and turned again to upend the flapjack into a bin, and with each turn of her head her ponytail swung like a girl on the move, like a girl in a race, that thick and fitful, that alive.

He left the diner and walked along the sidewalk until he came to a Laundromat. He cupped his hands to the glass and then stepped inside. He thought he was alone but he wasn't—a dwarfish round woman turned and blinked small black eyes at him and then turned back to monitor the portal of a dryer, her head cocked as if listening for some false note in the thumping heartbeat of it. The air was humid and sharp with the ammonia stink of piss. He went to the back by the soap-dispensing machine and stacked his quarters on top of the pay phone and pulled the slip of paper from his wallet and stood looking at it. He'd stopped calling her cell phone months ago because of the way she answered, and because of the way she sounded when it was not the call she wanted.

He got a cigarette to his lips and dropped two quarters in the slot and dialed the number and a voice told him to deposit more money and he did so and then lit his cigarette and waited.

"You can't smoke in here."

It was the woman, the dwarf monitress, torn from her vigil.

He nodded and showed her the receiver at his ear.

"This here's a nonsmoking facility," she said. "Says so right there."

The ringing in his ear ended and he turned from the little woman as a voice said thinly, electronically, over the miles, "Hello? *Hello . . . ?*"

"Hello, Aunt Grace?" he said. "It's Sean."

"Sean?" she said. "I can barely hear you. Where are you? Are you still in California?"

"I'm in New Mexico now."

"New Mexico! What's—Jordan, please stop poking him with that, now he asked you to stop, so stop." There was a pause, a clatter of silverware, a young girl's despairing voice. Covering the mouthpiece with her hand or her breast, his aunt said, "Right, young lady, just keep that up till I get angry, okay?"

The boy drew on his cigarette and sudden pain lanced into his knee, deep between the bones. White hot and twisting. He shifted his weight to that leg to force the blade back out.

His aunt said into the phone, "Ugh. I'm sorry. Are you there, hello—?"

"I'm here."

"New Mexico!" she said again. "What's in New Mexico?"

"I've got some work," he said.

"You should come home, Sean. You can do that kind of work here, can't you?"

He knew that if there were news from Colorado his aunt would have said so.

"Is Mom around?" he said, and for a long moment it seemed the connection had failed. At last his aunt said: "Sean, haven't you talked to your dad?"

He said nothing. Then he said, "Why?" and his aunt said, "Seanie, your mom's back in the hospital."

He saw a dim phantom of himself in the face of the soap-dispensing machine.

"When?"

"Two weeks ago. She took too many pills."

"She tried to kill herself."

"No, she didn't, Seanie, it was an accident. She was just taking too many of those damn pills."

"Do the doctors think it was an accident?"

"The doctors are . . . cautious. They want to watch her for a while, that's all."

Behind him a harsh alarm sounded and the little woman opened the dryer and began hauling laundry hand over hand into a wire basket on wheels. Next to the soap-dispensing machine was a corkboard thick with fliers and ads: trucks and farm equipment for sale, offers of trash hauling and baby-sitting. Reflexively he looked for his sister's face among them.

"Sean—?" said his aunt, and he drew soundlessly on his cigarette. Tapped ash to the dirty floor.

"Is she okay?"

"Yes. I mean, what's okay?"

They were silent.

"She's safe," said his aunt finally. "She's resting."

They hung up and he spread the remaining quarters in his palm, tallied them, and dropped two more into the phone. He punched in a number from the corkboard and watched the little round woman backing herself through the glass door, her body rocking with the weight of two swollen garbage bags at the ends of her arms. "You ain't got the right to smoke in here," she said, pinning him with her black eyes. "You ain't got the right to give other people your cancer."

18

Grant left the sheriff and drove back over the divide and down again to meet the climbing dusk. He exited the freeway while still high above the city and took the county road back into the foothills, to the old mining town that lived on though the copper was long gone.

Inside the Whistlestop on his way to the back a man reached out to grab him. "Where's the fire, mister?" It was Dale Struthers, the old veterinarian who owned the ranch down the road from Emmet's. He and the wife, Evelyn, smiling up warmly. They told Grant to join them and he glanced at his watch and said he couldn't, he only had time for one cold one and then he had to go see what kind of trouble Emmet had got up to.

"We were going to stop by on the way here, see if we could feed that old bird," Struthers said. "But then we saw Billy's car there and, well . . ."

"We didn't want to intrude," Evelyn said.

"He been back long?" said Struthers.

"A few days," Grant said, and the old man said, "That right?" and put his silverware in order as if for surgery. His wife patted Grant's arm to free him.

He continued back to the bar and sat down, nodding to Jack Portman and to the man Jack was serving whom he did not know. He got out his cigarettes and then remembered and put them away again. Jack drew him a pint of beer and poured a shooter. Grant tossed back the shooter, chased it, nodded for another. He sat watching the bar and the restaurant beyond in the backbar mirror. He used the mirror to study the man a few stools down. The man's face was ordinary and revealed nothing of his character.

Maria Valente came into view in the glass, stopping before a booth of high school kids to take their order. For a moment, before she returned to the kitchen, Maria seemed to look in Grant's direction, but her face was obscured by a large silver cataract in the old glass.

He thought about ordering another shot and another beer. He rubbed his thumb over the blunt ends of his two fingers and looked in the glass again for the man with the ordinary face. The man was gone. Grant ordered another shot and another beer.

"Is this seat taken?"

Maria was there, at his left, her dark eyes finding his in the mirror. She got onto the stool and set the plate of food between them. "I got the big steak and extra fries," she said. "Here's some silverware."

"No, that's your dinner."

"Are you kidding? Look at the size of this thing. It should've come with a deed." In her voice, the way she formed her words, were long-ago scenes of a little girl in Italy. Grant knew he tended to watch her mouth.

"Are you off?" he said, and she shook her head.

"Debbie-Lynn called in sick. Otherwise known as a hot date. How about you?"

"How about me?"

"Big plans tonight?"

"Sure." Grant took up a French fry. "Me and Emmet are throwing a party out to the ranch. Gonna be a hootenanny. You should come by."

"Really. A welcome-home party for Billy?"

He looked at her and she said, "He was in earlier. With that Gatskill girl who likes to French-kiss in public." She watched him in the mirror, then picked up her knife and began sawing into the meat. After a few minutes he joined her.

They had just finished the steak when Maria's daughter appeared at her side, planting her elbows on the bar and levering herself forward for a look at the bloody plate. "That is revolting. Did you even cook it?"

"Carmen, *tesoro*—you remember Mr. Courtland?"

"Yes. Good evening, Mr. Courtland."

"Good evening, Carmen."

The girl had her mother's dark eyes and dark curly hair but her skin was darker than Maria's. That was all Grant knew about the father.

"Anyway," the girl said, snapping down a credit card. "Here's this."

"Did you have them check the transmission fluid?"

"I checked it myself. It's fine."

"Who showed you how to do that?"

"This hitchhiker dude I picked up."

"Oh, that's funny. Isn't she funny, Mr. Courtland?"

There was a sound, a playful chirrup, and the girl glanced at her phone. She kissed her mother on the cheek and dismounted from the bar. "Gotta go, Jenna's waiting."

"You two be good," Maria said.

"You too."

"And not one second past midnight, I mean it."

The girl strode back through the restaurant and the high school kids watched her go. One of the boys bugged out his eyes and Grant's heart filled with violence. He saw himself crossing over and lifting the boy out of the booth by his throat.

"So she got the car," he said.

Maria looked to the ceiling in wonder. "When she drove it off the lot, just her, sitting behind that wheel, I thought, This can't be happening, look at her, look how young!"

She turned to him and touched his forearm. "Oh God, I'm sorry—"

Grant shook his head. *Hush.* He patted her small hand.

When she got off work at ten o'clock she found him where she'd left him, hunched over his drinks. There was a kind of scene outside in the yellow lamplight when he would not surrender his keys, but finally he dropped them into his pocket and got into her Subaru. Maria was not expecting anything. There had been plenty of time for something to happen and it hadn't, and she was fine with that.

Grant sat with his hands capping his knees, his eyes fixed on the road unspooling in the lights. Maria punched on the radio, listened a moment to some country song, and punched it off.

"She's a beautiful girl," he said.

"Who is?"

"Your girl. Carmen."

"Thank you."

"And smart. Smart. I bet she's ready to drive that car right off to college."

Maria looked over at him. He pawed at the chest pocket of his jacket and then stopped and put his hand back on his knee. "You can smoke if you want to," she said. "Seriously. I think I've even got one of those lighter things . . ."

"Right here," he said, thumbing in the knob. He got a cigarette to his lips and gapped the window. The lighter popped and he guided the coil with care. He blew the smoke through the opening, and then held the ember as near to the wind as he could without destroying it. The wedding band on his finger glowed a dull green-gold in the light from the dash.

"Well," Maria said. "What about Sean?"

"What about him?"

"Is he getting ready for college?"

"I don't know."

"You don't know?"

"No, ma'am."

"Doesn't that—" she said. "Don't you want to?"

He nosed the cigarette slowly to the wind, absorbed, until the embers flared and flew off like bright little hatchlings.

She said: "I'm sorry, I'm overstepping."

"No, you're not."

"I'm taking advantage of the circumstances."

"Which circumstances?"

She glanced at him, then looked back to the road. Slowing for a blind curve, her beams swept a stand of aspens—white skins flashing for a lurid instant and dodging back into darkness.

After a silence Grant said, "Ask me something I can answer," and she nodded and said, "All right. All right, I've always been curious: what happened to those fingers?"

"Which fingers?"

She gave him a look, and he opened his hand before the windshield.

"Was it a work accident?" she said. "Like a saw or something?"

"No. Well, there was a saw, but it wasn't a work accident. It was a drinking accident."

"Oh."

"I used to be a drinker."

"Oh."

"The turnoff's coming up."

"I know. But thanks."

When they reached the ranch he had her circle around the big spruce and park in front of the old ranch house. He struggled with the seat belt until she leaned over to get it. The black spill of her hair, the up-close smell of it.

"Maybe I should come in and make you some coffee," she said. "Do you have coffee in there?"

The Labrador met them on the porch and Maria put her knuckles to the dog's nose and tousled the soft ears. Grant held open the door and flicked on the light and saw at once the drab utility, the male disregard. Whiff of laundry he'd let pile up because he didn't like the sound of the machines, that humming and thumping, that false lulling.

"Make yourself at home," he said.

"Where are you going?"

"Over to check with Emmet. Come on, you," he said to the dog.

From the window over the sink she watched man and dog cross the clearing in the blue light. Grant walked upright and steady in a way that made her heart shift. She had tried to imagine it—what happened to him happening to her, her daughter—but she could not, not even for a second. Bad things happened to good people. God had his plan, always. But how did that help this man? His family? That girl? She began looking for the coffee.

Grant stopped short of Emmet's porch and stood before the living room window. Through the glass he could hear the argument between two TV crime solvers. Electric auroras of blue and green played over the walls and over the old man's white-socked feet on the footrest. The remote stood upright in his spotty hand but his eyes were shut and his stubbled jaw had fallen. Grant thought of his children, his own children—of carrying them to their beds when they were small. The limp human weight of them, the young scent of their skins, the murmurs as he lay them down. Angela waiting downstairs with a glass of wine, bare feet up under her on the sofa. He stood outside the old man's window remembering that this had happened, that it was true.

19

The edge was not keen but the cottonwood logs were dry and they split well, the halves leaping away as the blade sunk into the face of the block, which was the trunk of the cottonwood itself. The boy split each log in half and then split the halves in half, family of four, over and over, pausing only to carry the pieces to the corner of the house and add them to the stack, turning each piece for fit. The house was stucco of some defeated color, with vigas stumps jutting from the face. About it lay a graveyard of trucks and farm equipment and other wreckages, all of it wallowing in tall yellow grass. In the shade of the narrow portico at the front of the house sat a muscular brindle dog, tracking the boy's movements. It seemed to be waiting for an excuse to attack him.

Around noon, with the sun roaring down, he walked to the hand pump near the smaller house, the casita, and struggled with it until at last the water retched up and ran in a cold stream that tasted of stones and iron. He bowed his head under the stream, and then lifted his T-shirt to towel his face. When he dropped it again a girl was sitting in a chair in the shade with the dog. A thin-armed girl in a black bikini top and enormous round sunglasses, her insteps gripping the wooden railing.

The boy lit a cigarette and stood smoking it in the shade of the casita.

Later the man came out with two bottles of beer and a ham sandwich on a plastic plate. He was a large red-faced man in a black T-shirt tight across his gut, his feet stuffed into a kind of sandal. He had a bad back and moved like a man in ankle chains. His name was Tom Carl but the boy didn't know if Carl was his last name or the second part of his first.

He took the sandwich and one of the beers and said, "I don't think I can do much with these right now. But thank you."

Tom Carl looked at the stack of cordwood near the house. "I can see you know how to work. You don't have to try to impress me."

The boy looked around for a place to set the sandwich and the beer other than the face of the trunk.

"We came out here to work too," Tom Carl said, surveying the ruined machinery of his kingdom. "Spend more time together, fix the place up. A family project. Angela lasted five months and high-tailed it back to Phoenix, and now my daughter is counting the days. One day, that dog will go too."

"Angela," said the boy.

"Angela. My wife," said Tom Carl.

"That's my mother's name."

The older man looked at him, and then took a long swallow on his beer.

The boy stood holding the sandwich and the beer.

"Give 'em here," said Tom Carl, and when his hands were full again he turned and took two steps toward the house and pulled up short. "How long you been sitting there?" he said.

The girl's painted toenails made a ruby necklace in the sun. She did not look up from the magazine in her lap. She turned a page. "Since the dawn of time," she said.

THE BOY WAS AT the corner of the house stacking cordwood when the girl rose from the chair and reached in a stretch for the portico ceiling, showing her dimpled stomach, ladder of ribs, and he thought of Caitlin and her friends in their track shorts and their tight tops—barefoot empresses of summer days, conspiring in voices that made no effort not to be overheard by the male in the house, the plain, meaningless lump of boy who burned at their periphery.

That boy older now than those girls were then. Older than this one before him.

"Come on," said the girl, and she made a kind of dash past the dog. She bent and slapped her thigh. "Come on," she urged. She waved a hollow length of bone. "You want this? You want this?" The dog rose to all fours and sluggishly followed. The girl waggled the bone before the dog and said, "Go get it!" and flung the bone into the high blazing grass. The dog took a step toward the thrown bone, swung its head to watch the boy returning to the tree trunk, and then slunk back to the shade and to its dirty square of carpet. The girl stood with her back to him, drenched in the reddening light, young and hip-cocked, preposterous, beautiful.

"CAN I BUM a smoke?" she said.

She stood to his left, hand to her forehead, shielding the big sunglasses from the sun. White well of armpit giving off faint scent.

"Sorry?"

"A cigarette?"

He saw himself reflected in the dark glasses. He looked at her bare feet, the dusty ruby toenails. He pulled the flattened pack from his pocket and held it to her. She pinched up a cigarette and tucked it under an edge of her bikini top and then offered these same fingers.

"Victoria," she said.

He wiped his hand on his thigh and took hers, small and warm, and he said his name.

"What's the matter with your leg, Sean?"

"It was in an accident."

"A car accident?"

"Yes."

"Are there scars?"

"You better step back," he said.

She stood by as he swung the ax down on another log, retrieved one of the halves and set it up. Swung again. He thought about every movement, every pause.

"So, Sean," she said. "Can I ask you something?"

"Yes."

"What are you doing here?"

"Here?"

"Out here." She glanced about the arid world.

"Making gas money."

"To get to someplace else."

"Yes."

"Someplace in particular?"

"No."

"So, pretty much you just drive around in that truck."

"Pretty much."

She nodded. She watched him. He passed a forearm over his brow. Far above in the sky a threesome of large birds turned a slow wheel. He stood another log on the block.

"What about company?" she said.

"What about it?"

"Don't you get lonely?"

He brought the ax down on the log and the two halves leapt. He picked up one of the halves and stood looking at it as if the new yellow face of it would tell him something. Then he placed it on the block and split it in two.

"Well," said the girl. "Everybody needs some company sometime." And without waiting for his reply she turned and walked back to the house, and knowing she knew he watched, he watched just the same.

Why not her? he thought. Why not this girl instead of Caitlin? The idea of such carelessness, such arbitrary selections in the world, made him almost sick.

By sundown there were only a few logs left and he quartered these and stacked the cordwood. On the horizon a yellow moon rose from the mesas. Tom Carl returned carrying two sweating bottles of beer.

"You hungry now?"

"No, but thirsty."

They stood in the song of insects. Tom Carl looked at the Chevy and said the boy was a long way from Wisconsin, and the boy said he didn't live there anymore, and Tom Carl asked where did he live and the boy looked at the

moon and said the last place he lived under a regular roof was up in Colorado
with his father.

"How long ago was that?"

"February," he said.

"And you've just been driving around since then? Job to job?"

"Yes."

Tom Carl sipped his beer.

"Is there more of you up there in Colorado, with your father?"

The boy looked at him.

"More of your people. Your family."

The boy shifted his weight to his bad leg and Tom Carl said, "It's none of
my business. I'm just curious if your dad's alone up there or not."

"There's an old man on the ranch where he's living."

Tom Carl raised his drinking arm and slapped at it with his free hand,
killing a mosquito.

"How come you left? If you don't mind me asking."

The boy was silent a long time. A hard, bitter morning, he remembered,
Perseus, the slayer of Cetus, setting in the west, and the old green truck
wouldn't start, so he took the good truck, the blue Chevy. He'd been living
with his father in the ranch house for five months and he hadn't thought,
until he was miles away, how it would be when his father woke to find another child gone.

"It just seemed like it was time to go," he said at last, and took a drink.

Tom Carl put a hand to his back and grimaced. "I thought maybe you had
some kind of trouble."

"Trouble?"

"Trouble."

The boy met the older man's eyes. Then he looked into the dusk and said,
"No, sir. No trouble. I'm just trying to make gas money."

Tom Carl showed him the casita and the daybed there and the shower-
head over the stone floor. On his way out he stopped and asked the boy if he
had a cell phone.

He did but the battery was shot.

His host stood gazing about the little room. "If you need to call someone," he said, "come on over to the house. I got a cordless you can take outside and that's about as good as it's gonna get, privacy-wise."

He thanked him and Tom Carl tipped his bottle good night and closed the door.

The boy removed his boots and socks and lay back on the narrow bed, his knee pulsing with the old damage and his shoulder answering where the muscle and bone went on chopping, and he lay in this dialogue of pain thinking about his father up in Colorado, his mother in Wisconsin, in the hospital, and Caitlin wherever she was—and he didn't think he would sleep but he did, and in his sleep he climbed a path in the woods, in the dark, making his way by the progress of the animal he followed, a dog or wolf of such whiteness it raised shadows from the things it passed, the trees and stones. He kept pace with the white dog until the path grew steep and he began to fall behind, and soon he was in total darkness. Clawed at by the limbs of trees, falling to all fours, he scrabbled on until he came to her suddenly on the path. Pale and naked and curled upon herself, and though she was very young he knew it was her. He said her name but she only lay there holding her knees, and when he looked up again he saw the white dog watching him. He moved to pick her up and the dog advanced, and he let go and backed away. The dog came on and he backed away until he could no longer see her, until she'd slipped wholly back into the dark. Then the dog walked to her and by its light he saw her again, saw that she was sitting up, and that she was grown. Covering her breasts with one arm and gesturing to him with the other, beckoning him back, *Come back . . .*

20

There was one morning she could never forget, Angela said. Bright, battering morning when she'd awoken in her own bed after so long away, her own room— the first morning back from Colorado and it had not been a dream, she hadn't thought so even for an instant—and the moment she was awake she knew Grant was gone. Knew he'd not even come up to bed but had slept a few hours on the living room floor and left in the dark or at first light, so as to spare her this departure, this separation—let her wake to it in her own time and on her own terms. It was like before, when he'd left them, her, for some other woman, some other bed, she said. Only now she was not sorry; every moment he was here with her was a moment he was not in Colorado, searching, and those were hard, hateful moments.

Grant picked up his coffee and sipped. He sat across from her at the kitchen table in the middle of the afternoon, the middle of September. Sean was in school; Grace's kids were in school, Grace and Ted at their jobs. The house was like a house where everyone has been murdered: breakfast dishes in the sink, a boy's plastic truck on the counter, the terrible wall clock ticking and ticking. Grant had come back at Grace's request, to see Angela, to see his son, whose leg was now healed, or as healed as it would ever be. She wouldn't say it outright but Grant knew that what his sister-in-law wanted was for him to see how things had become in her small and crowded house.

Caitlin had been gone for a year and two months.

That morning, that first morning back, Angela had come down the stairs in her robe. Sean was on the sofa under the bedding, books and homework and other things from his room spread out over the coffee table. The wheelchair within reach. He looked asleep, and Angela passed quietly into the kitchen and found Grant's note by the coffeepot—I didn't want to wake you, etcetera. She was standing at the kitchen window staring out when Sean rolled in. She looked at him and smiled. How are you feeling?

Did Dad leave?

He didn't want to wake you. He said he'd call from the road.

Sean looked around the kitchen as if it he'd never seen it before. He was getting used to seeing everything from a lower vantage. As if he'd grown small again. Angela turned and looked out the window at the stark cold day. No cars, no one on the sidewalks, everyone shut up inside recovering from their Thanksgivings. They themselves had gone to a restaurant where they'd picked in silence at hot turkey sandwiches. The restaurant so quiet they clearly heard the young waiter in the kitchen ask, Christ, who died?

Mom? said Sean.

Hmm? She turned back to him. Yes?

He elevated his leg just a little and lowered it again. Nothing, he said. I think I'll have some cereal.

Oh, I'm sorry, I should have asked. Do you want some eggs?

No.

Do you want an English muffin?

No, just some cereal.

Okay. Stepping to the cupboards, pulling down the boxes. We're going to have to put stuff down where you can reach it, aren't we. She set a place for him and moved the chairs away and she arranged all the cereal boxes and the milk and she watched him get himself parked before the bowl.

Aren't you going to eat? he said.

Not right now. I'm going to go up and shower. Will you be all right?

I think I can take it from here.

She touched his shoulder and walked back through the living room and she understood, she told Grant, how everything had shifted in the house, like pieces in a puzzle: the boy's room empty and the living room now a bedroom, her own bed half empty, another bedroom empty beyond all comprehension or belief. She climbed the stairs. Then, at the top, she heard Sean say something, but she didn't stop, and she didn't look back.

Grant waited. Angela lifted her mug and sipped and returned it soundlessly to the table.

That's it? he said.

That's it. Yes.

Grant looked toward the stairs.

Christ, that clock, he said. He turned to look out the window. Finally he turned back. Angie, you were in shock.

She thought about that. Do people remember being in shock? I remember the moment vividly. He called out to me and I pretended not to hear him.

Grant stared into his coffee. He shook his head. You can't blame yourself, Angie. I know that's your instinct as a parent, as a mother, but you can't.

He heard the hollowness of these words in the ticking stillness of the borrowed kitchen.

She waited for him to look up. It's worse than that, she said.

What is it? God? You blame God?

I wish I did.

He moved as if to reach for her hands and her hands withdrew to the edge of the table.

He watched her, studying her, and she saw the instant when he understood, and she knew that he had thought it himself, that it wasn't just her.

But, Angie, my God, he said quietly. He was just a boy. And he was hurt. What could he have done?

I don't know, I don't know. Her eyes were dry. Dark. Grant didn't know them. But he just lay there, she said. He just lay there while she got into that man's car and I can't help it, Grant, when I look at him all I can think is, why didn't you do something? Why didn't you stop her?

21

The boy awoke with a start, disoriented, lying in a narrow bed in a small room. It was the sound of animals that woke him, a high ungodly yipping nearby, and the distant baying of hounds. His heart pumping and his T-shirt soaked, staring in utter confusion at these ceiling poles, these blank walls.

He smelled the smoke and then he saw the ember arcing and lastly he saw the girl, sitting not far from the bed on the only other piece of furniture in the room, which was a rickety wooden chair. She sat with one bare knee drawn up to her chest, one thin arm roped around the knee.

"Christ," he said, getting onto his elbows. "What is that?"

"What's what."

"That sound."

"Coyotes. Fucking coyotes. Or, perhaps, coyotes fucking."

He looked away from her, listening to them. She was watching him.

"What time is it?" he said.

"Three a.m. I couldn't sleep with all of this." She drew on the cigarette and exhaled. The chair creaked. "Do you want me to go?"

He stared at her, the milky shapes of her arms, her legs. She seemed to be wearing almost nothing.

He shook his head to clear it but it would not clear.

"Is that a no?" she said.

After a moment, he said, "—What?"

The girl watched him. If he moved just a little, toward the wall, she would take the space next to him, the way his little dog used to. The warm little body against his stomach.

She peered at him in the poor light. "Are you all right? You don't look so hot."

The animal sounds abruptly stopped, and the girl cocked her head, listening. Then she lowered her leg and leaned toward him. "Who's Caitlin?"

"What?"

"You said Caitlin in your sleep. Is that your girlfriend?"

Before he could answer, the door swung open and they turned to see it fill with the shape of Tom Carl.

The ember flew like a firefly to the stone floor.

"Hello, Thomas," said the girl.

Tom Carl stood there. The brindle dog panting just beyond his legs. With surprising grace he stepped forward and took the girl by the arm and hoisted her to her feet and pushed her toward the door.

"Having a conver*sation* here, Thomas!"

"Conversation over. Go into the house. Now."

She stood at the threshold rubbing her arm. They glared at each other, their kinship undoubtable, until at last she sighed and turned and strode away, her white legs scissoring at the dark. Tom Carl turned to the boy.

"Did you touch her?" His tone was not accusatory, nor hostile; no question in it as to what the boy had wanted to do—and no judgment about that either. There was only the wish to know if he had done it.

"No, sir."

Tom Carl shook his head. He ran a hand through his hair. "I gave you work. I gave you a bed to sleep in. She's fifteen, did you know that?"

The boy sat up and reached for his socks. His boots. "Nothing happened."

Tom Carl watched him work his feet into the socks. He sniffed the air, looked about him, and stepped forward and brought his sandal down on the cigarette. He left without another word, and the dog, putting a last look on the boy, swung its square head and followed.

Outside, the moon was high and a weird spectrum of light lay over everything—the trucks and the ruins of trucks, the looming mesas and the juniper and piñon that grew from their walls. All of it saturate, phantasmal.

The boy drew on his cigarette and looked to the north, to the place in the sky where he thought the mountains of Colorado must be, the white backbone of the Rockies, and there was nothing there, only the black, star-blown heavens on and on. A falling star put a scratch across Cancer and was consumed again, and with that signal the coyotes resumed their crying, their yelping and keening, very close.

He walked around the casita, but when he reached the opposite side he was sure the animals must be on the side he'd just left. He went back around and experienced the same certainty. There were things in the world that would not be explained. Entities were birthed from moonlight or from their own uncanny wills to be, to howl and to run and to mate and to hunt. Andromeda on her rock watches the sea for the thing it hides, the black scales and the black mindless eyes, the hungry smile. Not far away, in mountains to the north, in the highest ranges, she knew these beings well. She fought and wounded and escaped them but more came on to snatch at her and carry her back, and *Don't go,* she was about to say in the dream, *Don't leave me,* and she fought and she ran, and the moon looked down from its bed of stars and did nothing.

22

Don't do it, don't you do it, don't you get into that car, but she did, and he told her to buckle up and she did that too and they picked up speed, rocking along over the dirt road, his hand on the upright stick shift as upon some elegant cane, until he would suddenly throw it with slamming violence, as if this were the only way it would work.

They abandoned the dirt road in a hard right on the blacktop and she twisted around but there was nothing to fix in her mind but the red cloud of dust and the featureless world of trees and You just left him there, with nothing but the animals. Busted up and all alone and just a boy and you left him there.

She tried to read the odometer but couldn't—and then remembered her watch.

What's that? said the man. What are you doing there?

Setting the mileage, she said. She saw her heart rate and took a slow, deep breath.

You don't need to do that, the man said. You just tell them take Fox Tail Road offa County Road 153. Sheriff'll know exactly where to go.

She checked her phone.

Down the blacktop they went, banking left, right, the rubber sending out faint cries, the wind lashing the unravelings of her ponytail across her face. The pines stood back and blurred like bicycle spokes.

If he slows down you could jump, you could jump out and go into the woods and go back up to him. Or down.

She wanted the ground, the forces of the earth against her, each tree as she passed it singular and essential, like girls on the track. She would know what to do. Primally agile in flight, the pattern of the woods opening up to her, she would see path upon path and all of them going down.

Down to where? It might take hours. You could get lost, and what would happen to him then?

So, the man called, as if over a greater noise. What were you all doing up there, anyway?

She might have asked him the same thing. She checked the phone.

I say what were you all doing up there, anyway?

Running.

Running?

Yes.

Running from what?

She was watching the phone. What?

I said running from what?

From nothing. Just running. For training.

Oh. He braked into a sharp turn, downshifted, hit the gas again. Training for what?

For running, she said.

That's good, he said. That's funny. You got a good head on your shoulders, don't you.

Will you just please shut the fuck up? said the good head but not aloud.

The road intersected another unpaved, unmarked road and he took it, plunging them down through the trees until they landed abruptly on another blacktop, or the same blacktop, and he took that road and she lost all hope of being the one to lead the way back. But the sheriff would know. The sheriff would know. How could you just leave him?

What's your name, anyway? the man yelled.

What's yours? she said automatically. Like a child.

He grinned and said something but she didn't hear it, she'd turned back to her phone. It had changed—the tiny array of icons had changed. She thumbed the keypad, and waited, and her heart leapt as the radiant pulses of dialing graphed across the screen.

So what's yours? said the man.

She pressed the phone to her ear.

It was late morning. They'd be up by now and showered. Sitting in the cafe next to the motel drinking coffee and reading the local paper and trying not to look too often out the window—trying not to even though they'd chosen the table, without discussing it, for the view that would include, any second now, the paired familiar shapes of daughter and son, exactly as their minds saw them, demanded them, moving carelessly up the strange street. Maybe, waking up in the strange rooms, even in separate strange rooms, but waking up without kids in the strange rooms in the strange mountain light and the air that made the heart work, maybe they'd felt closer to each other. Maybe they'd laughed. Touched. Maybe their hearts were beating with a new old love over their coffees when the phone rang.

She was smiling, she was crying, already hearing his voice: Hello? Caitlin? Where are you, sweetheart? And then she did hear his voice, deep and steady and familiar in her ear, and though it was only his voice mail she began to sob.

Daddy, she said, before the first blow landed.

23

At the end of sleep there was music, low and thumpy and harassing him back into the world. Grant lay on the sofa with his knees drawn up, her lap replaced by a coarse little cushion she'd somehow slipped under his head. He sat up, boots to the floor, and passed his hand roughly over his face. The music was outside, the deep bass pulsing over earth and floorboards. He looked around the darkened room. What had he done? He'd kissed her, there on the dusty sofa. He'd put his hand on her breast and she'd put her hand over his. But when he began on the buttons she stopped him. Rubbed his shortened fingers in hers like coins. She didn't want to be a drinking accident, she said. He'd put his head on her lap then and she'd traced slow circles on his temples with her fingers. She'd turned off the light when she left.

But no, here she was—the shape of her, at the kitchen window, framed in the blue light beyond.

"You'd better come look," she said.

He got to his feet and went to her and they both looked out.

Six of them over there on Emmet's porch. Three boys, two girls, and Emmet. All but Emmet holding beers. Two of the boys and one of the girls sat on the steps while above them in the rockers like lord and lady sat Billy and the Gatskill girl, the rockers close so she could keep her fingers in Billy's hair. The El Camino was parked before them in the dirt, the beat pumping from the open windows like blood.

"There's your hootenanny," Maria said.

Emmet stood in the light from the screen door, one hand yet on the latch, his white hair wild on his head. He had taken the time to pull coveralls over his pajamas and to put on his old brogans though not to lace them. With his free hand he gestured toward the El Camino and spoke to Billy, and Billy said something in reply over his shoulder, and the others ducked their heads in laughter.

Grant raised his watch to his face. "Almost midnight," he said. "Your daughter will be home soon."

Maria stared at him in the dark. "This is a good time for me to go, you're thinking?"

"No, probably not. But—"

Something was happening over there; Emmet was crossing the porch. He took two steps down between young hips before Billy stood from the rocker and seized him by the upper arm. Emmet looked in amazement at the hand on his arm and then into his son's face. His glasses flashed blue in the farm light.

Maria took Grant's wrist and said his name.

"Hold on," he said. "Hold on."

"He's going to hurt him."

"Hold on."

Billy said something to Emmet and Emmet said something back and then Billy was hauling him back up the steps by the arm. Emmet dug at his son's fingers and planted his feet but with a modest tug Billy yanked him off balance and got him clomping pitifully toward the screen door. Billy opened the door and guided the old man through and shut it again. They stood staring at each other through the screen. Then Emmet turned away and his shadow on the porch floor grew small, and then it was gone. Billy took his seat again to cheers and raised bottles.

"I'll be right back," Grant said.

"Grant, we should call someone."

"Who?"

"Sheriff Joe."

"He's way up there in the mountains."

"Then Sheriff Dave down here."

Grant opened a drawer and began rooting through batteries and old tin flashlights.

"What are you looking for?"

"Nothing." He stood and slipped the cartridges into his pocket.

"Grant, you know what he did to that Haley boy."

"I heard about it." He went out the door and down the steps, and the old dog came out from under the porch and limped along behind him.

"Evening, neighbor," Billy said, hailing him from the rocker. "Everyone, this here is Grant, the old man's hired gun, as it were. Grant, this here is everyone."

The young people raised their beers and bid him good evening.

"And you brought my dog too, I see. Where's he been hiding you girl, huh? Get on up here. Get up here girl. Come on now." Billy leaned forward in the rocker and the black leather jacket, hangered on the high chairback behind him, stirred like wings.

The dog lowered to her belly and flattened her ears.

"God damn it," said Billy, slapping his thigh.

"Let her be, Billy."

"Don't tell me what to do, Grant."

"She's just a scared old dog."

"She's my scared old dog. Now get up here girl goddammit before I come down there and get you."

Grant turned to look at the dog. She looked up and he made a shooing motion and she rose to all fours and slipped away into the dark.

"There goes your dog, Billy," said one of the boys on the step. A lank and pimpled boy with a cigarette in his grin.

Billy stared at him until the boy's grin collapsed and he looked away.

"I think maybe you better call it a night, Billy," Grant said. "I don't think your dad can sleep with all this. And fact is neither can I."

"Really," said Billy. "I didn't think you had sleeping in mind, Grant."

"That's that waitress's car," said the pimpled boy. "The one what's got that nigger daughter."

Grant stepped up closer to the boy. He was truly a boy, younger than Billy by perhaps ten years. They were all younger, including the Gatskill girl. "You need to watch your mouth, son."

"Is that right, Dad?"

"That's right."

"Shit, Vernon, that is right," said Billy. "You talk like your dad fucked his sister and out you popped whistling Dixie." There was laughter, and Vernon bared his bad teeth and said, "Hilarious, Billy."

"I'm going inside for a minute," Grant said. "I'd appreciate it if you all went on home like I asked."

"I am home, Grant," Billy said. "And there's your irony: this wouldn't even be happening if my old house over there weren't otherwise occupied."

Grant glanced back at the ranch house. The kitchen window a dark and featureless square in its face.

"There's nothing to do about that tonight," he said.

"No," said Billy. "I agree with you there."

Grant went up the steps and on inside and climbed the stairs. Emmet was in his bedroom, sitting on the edge of the bed. He appeared to be giving great thought to his boots, down there on his feet. Grant sat beside him, raising a faint cry from the coils.

"I'm sorry if they woke you, Grant."

"Oh, I was up."

"They got no respect. Not one speck of it."

"Em. Maybe we should make a phone call."

Emmet looked up, his eyes behind the lenses bleary in their folds. "Who the hell to?"

"Maybe Joe needs to know about this."

"I ain't doing that, Grant. I ain't calling one brother on the other. I told you that before." He shook his head. "These kids will get tired in a bit and go home."

"It doesn't look that way to me, Em. Looks to me like they're gonna make a show of it, especially now that I've come over."

Emmet ran a hand over his face. "Who is that boy? I don't even know who that boy is."

They sat there, the beat from the El Camino like a heartbeat in the bed. Old sunken bed of marriage where the old man went on sleeping year after year on the side nearest the door.

"Where do you keep that shotgun, Em?"

"That what?"

"Just for show."

Emmet looked at him. Then he flung a hand toward the closet.

Grant found the softcase and set it on the bed and unzipped it, releasing a smell of walnut and steel and gun oil. It was an old Remington 20-gauge side by side.

"You know how to handle that?"

"I used to have one not too different. It was my dad's. Angela wouldn't have it in the house once the kids got older." He unbreeched the barrels and sighted the bores and snapped the barrels back. "You took good care of this," he said, but the old man didn't seem to hear him.

GRANT WENT DOWN THE porch steps and reached into the El Camino and turned the key, killing the engine and the music. The chromium tailpipe shuddered out a final blue cloud and was still.

"Fuck me," the pimpled boy said, "the hired gun's got a gun."

"What are you up to, Grant?" said Billy.

"I asked you to call it a night and now I'm not asking."

"Did that old man put you up to this?"

"No, he was against it."

"Well, what do you intend to do, shoot us?"

"No. I'm going to shoot the tire on one of these cars. After that, if you're still here, I'm going to shoot another one. If I have to buy new tires tomorrow I will, but tonight the party's over."

"How we gonna leave if you shoot our tires?"

"Shut up, Vernon. Grant, I don't believe you've got any ammo in that old gal."

"You're right about that." He thumbed the lever and broke the shotgun, chambered two red shells and snapped the gun shut again.

"All right," said Billy. "There's phase one. But I guess we're going to have to see phase two before these negotiations go any further."

"Jesus, Billy," said the girl on the steps. "Let's just go somewheres else before this old man does something crazy."

"Sit down and shut up, Christine."

"These aren't negotiations, Billy," Grant said. "This is what's going to happen next if you go on sitting there." His voice was even, his chest calm. He thought about that as Billy lifted his cigarette to his lips and crossed a black boot over his knee. Billy tugged the hair under his lower lip, that shapeless brown tuft. Then he nodded, and Grant stepped around the El Camino and raised the gun on the front tire of a battered GMC pickup and with the stub of his forefinger squeezed the forward trigger. The gun kicked and a flap of rubber flew from the tire in a gaseous cloud and the truck buckled like a stricken horse and swallows burst from the spruce and wheeled amid the stars while the boom echoed away in the hills. The night air bittered at once with the smell of cordite and the rubber tang of old tire air.

"You shot my tire," said Vernon, rising. "You fucking whackjob."

Grant took a step and raised the gun on the toylike tire of a small red Honda.

"Billy!" cried the girl on the steps, and Billy laughed and said, "All right, all right." He put his cigarette in his lips and gave a few claps. He stood from the rocker and offered a hand to the Gatskill girl. "Time to go, those who can."

"What about my goddam truck, God damn it?"

"You heard the man, Vernon. Said he'd get you a new tire tomorrow, and you've already seen he's a man of his word so quit your crying and get in the car."

As the young people loaded into the El Camino and the Honda, Grant looked at the stars. The patternless bright birdshot of ancient, monstrous bodies. Forces unthinkable. Passing him, Billy stopped and looked beyond him, peering into the dark foothills. He squinted as if he saw something out there and spoke: "What the hell—?"

Grant didn't turn to look, and Billy dropped his cigarette and ground it into the dirt with the toe of his boot.

"Thought I saw somebody," Billy said. He looked up into Grant's eyes. "But there ain't nobody out there. Is there, Grant?" He winked, and tossing the leather jacket ahead of him onto the Gatskill girl's lap he swung down into the El Camino.

Taillights withdrew into the night. Grant stood with the Remington on his shoulder, the weight of the barrels, the shapely walnut grip, the warm triggers, the slam of the stock yet playing in his bones—all a strange pleasure to him.

Emmet stood at the screen door, one hand on the handle as if he were making up his mind whether to step out into the dark or latch the door against it. Grant held the old man's eyes a moment, then he turned and began to walk back to the ranch house. A black shape separated from the shadow of the spruce and slid along the ground toward him and became the old dog at his heels, half crippled in her hips, panting softly, halting suddenly when Grant halted: there was movement at the ranch house, someone passing through the dark square of the kitchen window. A woman. She came back and remained there in the frame of the window, doing something with her hands, preparing something, as if she belonged there.

Grant stood beside the spruce with the gun in his hands, the dog quietly panting. He looked to the north and made out the shape of the mountains by their erasure of the stars along the base of the sky. In his dreams she was running—always running. Her heart strong and her feet sure, never stumbling, never tiring, mile upon mile, coming down like water. He looked to the north and he began to speak, as he did every night. He began to speak and the old dog stopped panting and grew alert, cocking her ears to the dark.

24

She was running well, her stride long and light, her feet rolling loose through their landings, her lungs working hard but not too hard and her heart like a liquid clock in her chest. And while part of her mind roamed through her body this way—observing, evaluating, adjusting—the greater and forward part processed the messages of the run as she received them through her narrowed senses: the sound of soles on packed cinder and the sound of many lungs; the smell of dew in the April grass and the good petroleum stink of the sun-heated track; the blurred cheering faces of a Saturday morning beyond the blade of vision that was the length of lane before her, the next few meters of track, her own shadow there, black and soundless and one step ahead, always one step ahead, goading her on until it was just the two of them, far ahead of the others who had nothing left to run for now but just to finish—second, third, what did it matter?

And she was gaining; she was hard on this shadow's heels as they banked into the final turn, ready to open her stride and take the race away, just take it, without mercy or apology, like taking a boyfriend—Whoosh, mine now, not yours! She ran without fear or effort, a strong, leggy girl of eighteen, an undefeated girl, with nothing before her but more races and more life and the never-ending love of her family, and hers for them, a family who waited beyond the finish line to collect her once again, to claim her in pride and love and take her off for breakfast. She ran and it was like a dream of running under the spring sun, and the day was so beautiful and her heart was so full that she hardly noticed the shadow when it returned, darkening the cinder ahead as if she'd rounded another bend, though she hadn't. Her heart pounding, legs pounding, giving everything, everything, and it wasn't enough, the shadow held its lead, it stretched, and she watched in dismay as it—parted. Severed itself foot by foot from her own feet and fled down the track untethered, uncatchable, gone.

And from that, to a scene that should be the dream but isn't—this dark, rough space of raw plank walls and low plank ceiling, dark floor of thick timber where small life comes and goes through the gaps. A room of such squareness and sameness it might roll like a toy block and do just as well, wall as ceiling, ceiling as floor, and she blinks heavily, the light and colors of the race leaving her, sunlight leaving her, wind and speed leaving her, the heat and smell and heartbeats of the other girls—all gone, and the only arms that wait to claim her are the arms that took her, without apology or mercy, just took her, from the mountain.

Part II

25

A few miles outside of a small town on the eastern half of Nebraska, some two hundred miles yet from the river border, the boy switched on his hazards and pulled over on the pitched shoulder, stepped out, and went around to the passenger's side and found the rear tire nearly flat. He had gassed up in the small town and now he looked back that way.

"Forgot to check your tires, Dudley."

He pulled his jacket from the cab and put it on and got a cigarette lit and stood looking out over the land. In the wires of the near fencing, tumbleweeds trembled like living things, and beyond the fence the land combed away in a vast litter of bleached and severed cornstalks. Late February, he thought. Maybe March. To the west a darker scrim of gray sky swept the ground, rain or snow, coming along, its smell already there, and looking out over the whole shelterless world he wondered what you would do or where you would go if you were out there on foot with nothing but the clothes you wore, alone in that emptiness when the storm came. It was what he always wondered, plains or mountains or desert.

He was now eighteen. She would be twenty-one.

He dropped his cigarette and stepped on it and considered the truck, its stance on the pitched shoulder, and seeing no way to improve it he set the parking brake and freed the jack and the tire iron from their clamps behind the seat and got to work. He set the tire iron on a lug and bore down on it, and bore down on it harder, but to no effect. Some weeks back at a small station near the Mexican border he'd had the tires rotated by a man who had reset the lugs with his pneumatic driver and charged him ten dollars.

He reseated the iron and taking hold of the Chevy's bed rail he stepped onto the thin bar and eased down his weight, until the iron twisted off and rang on the shoulder. He crouched and found three edges of the lug smoothed over with small thin forelocks of steel.

Nice, Dudley. What's your next trick?

As my father liked to say, his father would say, enacting some sly mechanical solution, *even a monkey knows the value of a stick.*

The first drops of rain began drumming the bed of the truck. A single drop burst coldly on the back of his neck, and then the rest of it came hissing over the road behind him and he braced as if for a blow and it was on him, drilling his head and shaping out the truck in a violent riddling and blackening the road as it went.

He leaned into the cab and unlatched the buckle on the kitbag and as he did so he looked through the fogged rear window and saw a figure coming toward him in the rain, alone and as gray as the rain itself. He swiped the glass with his hand and watched the figure come on, his progress casual, thumbs hooked under the straps of his backpack, stains of rain-soak along the shoulders of his jacket.

"What in the hell," the boy said.

He came away from the cab with the big twenty-ounce Estwing, and he got down on his knees again and seated the iron on a lug and held it there with his left hand and cocked the hammer back and brought it down squarely on the bar but with no result other than a wild, electric jolt in the bones of his left hand. He raised the hammer and brought it down again, and another time, and once more before he looked up into the pelting rain and into the face of the young man who had come up behind him on the shoulder and stopped there, rain dripping from the bill of his cap, regarding the boy through round unreflecting lenses. To the boy in that instant the young man seemed older than he by several good years; but to the young man the same was true of the boy before him on the shoulder with the big one-piece hammer.

Without unhooking his thumb from the backpack strap the young man opened his hand and said Hola, and the boy nodded and said Hola back.

"Somebody was serious when they set those nuts," said the young man.

"And all Chevy gave me was this little toy wrench."

The young man sniffed and looked down the road ahead as if he would walk on. Then he made a survey of the tire iron and the tire and said: "Looks to me like a question of leverage."

"You don't happen to have a two-foot length of pipe in that pack, do you?"

"You tried stepping on it?"

"It slipped off and tore up the nut."

The young man nodded. "Well." He studied the tire. "I've got an idea, if you're about done with that club."

The boy seated the iron once more as instructed and held it with both hands while the young man came around next to him and got a grip on the truck and stepped up on the bar with one wet sneaker, then the other, and stood a moment getting his balance, and then began lightly springing so that the boy could feel the bar flexing in his hands, could sense in it a quality of steel that would only give so much before it sheared, and he was ready to tell the young man to stop when the bar shuddered in his hands and the nut gave an eerie cry and the young man rode the bar like a mechanized lift down to the blacktop and stepped off.

"There's one," he said.

"There's one," said the boy.

The rain continued but with a lesser violence and the little iron held, and soon the boy was setting the lugs on the spare while the young man stood turning the flat tire, blackening his wet hands until he stopped and said, "There she is," and the boy looked. A nickel-colored nailhead flush to the tread.

"I worked some construction down in Texas," he said. "But that was weeks ago."

"They do that sometimes. They plug the hole for a while and then they don't. My uncle Mickey's a contractor and I've seen him about fire a man for letting a nail lie in the dirt." He lightly fingered the nailhead. "This one's got a flat side on it. Like a nail-gun nail."

The boy considered that, then stood up, his knee cracking and popping, and he restowed the tire iron and the jack behind the seat while the young man hefted the tire into the bed of the truck and swiped his hands one against the other. "I'll be seeing you," the young man said, and when the boy turned he was already walking down the highway.

He called to him and the young man turned around and stopped.

"I'm going that way if you want a ride."

"Thanks, I don't mind walking."

"Well," he said. "I'd like to return the favor."

"That's not why I did it."

The boy squinted into the sky as if to locate the sun in all that sodden gray. "I've seen better walking weather," he said.

"Me too. But I'm already soaked and I don't want to foul up that truck."

"It's just a truck, and I'm soaked too."

He rebuckled the kitbag and piled his duffel and his sleeping bag between the seats and the young man swung his large pack into the truck bed and swung himself into the cab. The boy put the truck in gear and pulled back onto the highway, unsheltering a perfect dry rectangle of shoulder as the Chevy drove away into the haze.

THE YOUNG MAN REMOVED his wet cap and set it like a bowl in his lap and said his name was Reed Lester, and the boy gave his full name in return and they said nothing more for a while but only listened to the clicking wipers and the wet sizzle of the tires. The air in the cab was dense with the smell of unwashed bodies and damp, unclean clothing.

"How long you been walking?" the boy said.

"I left Lincoln two days ago."

"And you walked all that way?"

"Mostly."

"Where you headed?"

"Noplace special. How about you?"

"Same place."

Reed Lester looked about the cab. "This is a nice truck, isn't it."

"It's all right."

"It looks about brand new."

"It was brand new, four years ago."

The young man laughed and the boy looked over, surprised. As much by the sound of laughter in the truck as the idea that he had caused it.

"Mind if I smoke?" he said, and Reed Lester said, "Hell no, it's your truck."

"You want one?"

"No, thanks."

He pushed in the lighter and returned his hand to the wheel.

"That uncle of yours ever see a nail-gun nail in a tire?" he said.

Reed Lester watched the road. "Those nails don't usually lie around in singles."

The lighter popped and the boy touched the coil to the cigarette and pulled the smoke into his lungs and cracked the window and exhaled into the cold draft.

Reed Lester adjusted his glasses. "You think somebody put it there for you?"

The boy watched the road. "Down in Texas I met a man at a gas station and he hired me on the spot. Said he was way behind on this house outside Austin. The next day I jumped in with these Mexican boys been there for months and I don't think they knew what to make of me. White boy out of nowhere in his nice blue Chevy."

Reed Lester shook his head. "They don't know what to make of you and it's your own damn country."

The boy smoked.

"Then what happened?"

"Nothing. I worked for two weeks and moved on."

"With a nail-gun nail in your tire."

The boy said nothing. Watching the road. Then he said: "Those Mexican boys worked harder than anyone I ever saw. They were making good money and I never saw them eat anything but beans and tortillas. They were sending every dime back down to their families."

"Well," said his passenger. "There you have it."

"Have what."

"The whole problem with those people. Crying about discrimination and deportation and all the while they're throwing U.S. currency over the border and it's never coming back, not ever. Uncle Mickey won't hire them anymore, not even when they've got papers. Says there's plenty of Americans around who can swing a hammer."

The boy stared ahead with nothing to say. He put some air on the fogged windshield.

"Some people want to call that racism," Reed Lester volunteered. "But if Americans don't get the jobs, then they don't get the capital to build houses, and if they don't build houses, then Uncle Mickey can't give jobs to ten other guys. It's not racism, it's Economics 101."

The boy drew on his cigarette. He tapped the ash in the draft. "I never said it was racism."

"I know you didn't, boss," said Reed Lester. He picked up his wet cap and sat weighing it in his hand.

"Hell," he said. "My girlfriend back at school was Cuban. Pure Cuban. All her family crossing over on a boat hardly more than a raft. Daddy and grand-daddy and all her aunts and uncles. Her mother eighteen and pregnant with her. They hit a storm in sight of Miami. They could see the lights one second and then they couldn't. When the Coast Guard got there it was just girls in the water—her mother and her mother's sisters. All the men, Mia's daddy, her granddad, all her uncles, all drowned." He scratched at his jaw. "They didn't send them back because what would become of four teenage girls in Cuba with no family and one of them already pregnant?"

"Why did all the men drown?"

The young man looked up, as if roused from a daydream. "What?"

"Why'd the men all drown."

"Because there was only enough life jackets for the girls."

The rain was turning sleety, dashing like insects on the glass and collecting in slushy berms at the outer reaches of the wipers. Along the road the mile markers flared green in the truck's daylights. Ten miles on, sixty miles outside of Omaha, something appeared in the road ahead and the boy lifted his foot from the gas and began tapping the brake.

"What is that?" said Reed Lester. "Is that a coyote?"

"No, it's too big."

The wipers flicked and they watched the animal grow larger in the gloom. It was a dog. A German shepherd on its side, half on the road and half off. It lay with its long spine to them and one dark ear aimed at the sky, the tail limp and rain-flattened on the shoulder. The boy pulled over and brought the Chevy to a stop a few yards short of the dog and killed the engine and the lights.

"What are you going to do?" said Reed Lester.

"Go look, I guess."

"At what? That dog is dead."

The boy reached and unbuckled the kitbag at his passenger's feet and brought out his gloves and then switched on his flashers and pulled the key from the ignition and stepped out into the driving sleet.

Reed Lester stepped from the truck with his cap on and stood with his hands deep in the pockets of his jacket. The boy tugged on his gloves and walked over to the dog and Reed Lester followed.

The dog did not appear to have been there long. Its thick coat was not saturated but stirred yet in the wind at the haunches and at the hackles. Over the road lay a sleety film and a fine white pebbling unbroken but for the black stripes where tires had passed. In both directions the tracks ran straight as far as the eye could see. There was no sign that any car had swerved or braked or pulled over on the shoulder.

The boy came up slowly, watching the dog's ribs, the black pointed ear. Nothing moving but the sleet and the windblown fur. He came closer, bent at the waist, and came closer yet and suddenly the dog lifted its head in a lunging motion and the boy dodged back, and Reed Lester's feet went out from under him and he sat down on the shoulder saying "Holy shit," then scrambled up and moved off.

The dog returned its head to the pavement and the boy stood there, stunned and chilled. The shepherd had tried to bite him but it had no lower jaw. There was the muzzle, the upper canines, and that was all. The tongue and lower jaw had been shorn off and flung away somewhere. Or else they rested in the bumper of a car on its way to Iowa.

He removed his gloves and came forward again and knelt to his good knee, and this time when the dog's head snapped up he set his bare hands on its body, one at the ribs and the other at the neck, and he worked his fingers into the fur and he told the dog Shh and met its wide desperate eye. The head went down again and he listened to the high whimpering in its bloodied nostrils and he said Shh and moved his hand to the dog's skull and rubbed the great ears. Everywhere he looked he saw damage. Bleeding rents in the fur, disfigured bones under the hide. The dog had known that sudden astounding flight, that long ride in the air and the return to earth with its snapping sound of breakage. The only unbroken part seemed to be the neck, and pressing his fingers into the fur there he felt the collar. He dug deeper and raised a length of blackened leather. He rotated the collar until the tags came jingling into view.

"King," he said. "It's all right, King. It's all right, boy." There was a phone number. He undid the buckle and slipped the collar from the shepherd's neck and folded it into his jacket pocket and got slowly to his feet while the animal watched him with its skyward eye. It lifted its head again, not aggressively but as if to rise, and he showed his palm and said "Stay," and Reed Lester watched him turn and walk back to the truck and lay his forearms on the rail of the truckbed.

He went to stand beside him.

"What're you going to do, boss?"

"I don't know."

"There's nothing you can do for that animal."

Grains of ice ticked in the bed of the truck. A dark station wagon hissed by on the highway, the face of a young girl in the window.

"There's one thing," said the boy. He went to the cab and reached into the kitbag and pulled out the Estwing and turned back to the shoulder, back to the dog, and Reed Lester watched him and he saw the dog's ear prick to the sound of the boy's step, and as the boy came nearer he saw the dog's tail strain to lift, and he watched the boy lower himself to his knee again and set his bare hand on the dog's neck and speak to the dog, telling it something he couldn't hear. He saw the boy move his hand to the dog's ears, rubbing, and then to its brow, and with his hand over the dog's eyes he saw him cock the hammer high and bring it down once, very hard, very close to his hand.

They lifted the dog and carried it into the ditch and set it down again. The boy looked up and down the highway. Then he returned to the truck and reached behind the seat for the red mechanic's rag his father kept there, and he carried the rag back through the ditch and tied it to the uppermost fence wire. He stood looking down on the dog as the sleet fell and he looked at the sky and he shuddered. He went once more to the truck and reached again behind the seat and returned to the ditch and unfolded the blue tarpaulin and spread it over the dog and tucked its edges under him. The tarp had been his shelter, his plastic roof on nights under the stars when the dew came down. He stood back and the sleet pocked loudly at the plastic, as if angered by it. He returned his hammer to the kitbag and the two of them got back in the truck and he turned off the flashers and started up the Chevy. The wipers leapt back to their noisy work. He checked his mirror and pulled back onto the highway and in silence he lit a cigarette and in silence they drove on.

26

There is a beam of light, shaped by an eye-sized hole in the battened window over the cot, a light with no purpose other than to push a burning coin of itself over the seams of the floorboards—irregular demarcations of an illogical timepiece. The beam is pink in the dawn and turns yellow-white on its sweep as the sun moves westward over the earth—as the earth spins eastward away from the sun—progressing from one corner of the room where a locked chest sits, to the opposite corner, the beam going ruddy, and then pink again, and then dying altogether at the lion's foot of the stove, as if dispirited, as if defeated daily by the black iron thing.

Some days the beam never arrives at all and it's as if the sun, and time with it, has stopped. Other days the beam flickers and withers midfloor, signaling the arrival of a storm front. And when it dies all at once, as if by a switch, she pins herself against the wall side of her cot and waits for the beam to come back and for the peeping eye that stopped it to move on again.

Currently the beam is midfloor. She could reach out and place her hand in it and feel it pool in her palm, a warm autumnal yellow, a weightless continuum to the outside world, free to come and go.

She doesn't move, not in the least. Her heart down-beating from a race it believed it was in, a dream-race against nothing but her own shadow.

You should get up. You should get up. You should not lie here like this.

The coin of light rests in the center of her vision, severed in two by a crack in the timber. The longer she fails to get up the more it's as if her real self has continued on in the dream, leaving behind this heavy, dark-minded thing, this shell. Why get up? Why move? Hopelessness falls like the shadow of a great bird; black thoughts rise like water. Then, suddenly, without deciding to do so, she sits. Is sitting up. A pair of hands in her lap. Hers. She can make the fingers move like so. My fingers. My legs. Mine.

27

They rode the storm eastward and by the time they reached the outskirts of Omaha it was dark and the ice had grown thick at the edges of the windshield where the wipers and heat fought it back, and when the Chevy's tires strayed from the tracks in the whitened road, rails of slush crushed beneath them with a wet, explosive sound.

They came into more lanes and more traffic. A semi plowed by casting a filthy wave over the windshield, and through the wash of it they saw a pair of taillights ahead but in a strange place and at a strange tilt. A little farther on they saw the tire tracks cross suddenly before them, twining in helices before trailing away into the median, and then they saw the black SUV down there and the blue glow of the phone inside and the man's lips moving calmly as if he were only continuing the conversation he'd been having before he spun off the highway.

"All that rig and there you sit in the median," said Reed Lester.

"We could be next," said the boy.

"I doubt that."

"Four-wheel drive isn't any good on ice and I haven't got any weight in the back."

"You want me to get on back there, boss?"

The boy looked over. "Would you mind?"

"Hell, no. Just pull over a second."

"I thought you might just go on out your window."

"I could. But if I fall, then where will you be?"

The boy watched the road. The red starbursts of taillights. The bleary lit signs of gas stations and motels drifting by.

"Maybe we ought to just pull over someplace and see what happens with this," said his passenger.

"You said you were just going to the other side of town."

"I am but it's a big damn town and this traffic's gonna get a whole lot worse, and I'm in no hurry. Are you?"

The boy stared out at the storm. "You know any place to go?"

They left the highway and drove along a business strip of car lots and liquor stores and many dark, derelict buildings. In the midst of it sat a small restaurant of boxcar shape with neon beer signs burning in its windows and a radiant sign in the shape of a palm tree declaring its name which was the Paradise Lounge.

"You like burgers?" Reed Lester asked.

"Sometimes."

"This will be one of those times."

Lester directed him to park in back and he did so, bringing the Chevy to rest in the cratered gravel lot among another dozen cars and trucks. They transferred the wet backpack from the truckbed to the cab and the boy locked the truck and followed Lester toward a red metallic door.

Inside was a noisome crowd which somehow gave the impression of having arrived out of the inclement night hours before, and all together. Faces turned to take stock of them and turned away again with no show of impression good or bad. The air smelled of seared beef and perfume and alcohol. Islandy music piping down from the ceiling and everywhere on the walls large, richly colored images of white sands and turquoise waters and brown-backed girls.

They found two stools at the bar and sat in the electric glow of tiki torches and ordered two beers from the bartender, a large yellow-haired man in a Hawaiian shirt who, in a practiced glance, saw two men weary from the road and the weather, and turned to draw their beers. Placing the pints before them he said, "You gents going to eat here or wait for a table?"

Lester looked to the boy and the boy shrugged and Lester said they'd eat there if the bartender didn't mind.

"I don't mind if you don't mind."

"Why would we mind?"

"I know I'm pretty, but most dudes come in here would rather be served by Barb or Patti."

They rotated on their stools and took in the waitresses, one blonde, one redheaded, both in Hawaiian shirts and both older than either of them by ten years or more.

"We'll keep an eye out for a table," said Lester, and the man made an approving face and took a pencil from behind his ear. "So," he said. "What do you want on those burgers?"

THEY DRANK THEIR BEERS and watched without comment the college wrestling match under way on a TV above the bar, two muscular near-naked men twining like pythons, until the channel switched unaccountably to a basketball game. In the backbar mirror the boy saw himself and Lester sitting side by side and it seemed an odd, implausible thing to see. When the bartender brought their burgers, fat and tottering on nests of fries, they both set into them gratefully, though the boy was not hungry.

The bartender indicated their glasses but only Reed Lester was ready for another.

"I don't much follow college sports," he said to the boy around a mouthful of beef. "You?"

"Not much."

"What do they call them in Wisconsin, is it Buckeyes?"

"Badgers," he said. The word flaring red on the white field of memory—her running shorts on the mountain, in the woods.

"Know what they call them here?"

He didn't, and Reed Lester leaned and said cagily: "Cornhuskers. You believe that? Who can say that word without thinking cornholers?"

They finished the burgers and worked the fries. The bartender came to check on their glasses and rapped a knuckle on the bar. "Nothing personal against you gents, but there's a booth opening up over there if you want it."

They looked and Lester said, "What do you say?"

The boy glanced out the near window. The sleet was still coming down hard. Endless needles shooting through the red haze of the neon beer sign.

"I don't mind sitting a while, but I won't drink any more."

"You sit and I'll drink."

They carried their glasses to the booth and the redhead, Patti, took their order and went away.

"How old you think she is?" said Lester.

"I don't know. Thirty."

"I think more like thirty-five. Still, she might be about as good as it's gonna get in the old Paradise tonight." As he said it the front door swung open and two young women blew in hunched and clutching each other and gathering control of their skating bootheels and laughing. "Holy fuck my hair," one said, and they laughed again and cast their made-up eyes around the room.

Reed Lester raised an eyebrow at the boy.

The girls spied the two empty stools at the bar and hurried over and seated themselves with considerable tugging on short skirts and shifting of bottoms and tossing of hair.

"Bombed," the boy said.

"They might not mind being bombed in a booth," said Lester. He looked at the girls and his grin died away. "Shit."

Two men had come across the floor to bookend the girls. Or not men but large boys in red and white football jerseys, baseball caps set backward on their skulls. Each bent toward the near girl, stiff-arming the bar in reverse images of capture. The name on the bigger boy's jersey was Valentine. At a table across the room two other boys also sat watching, and after a minute the girls turned to look at the table, and then leaned and consulted into each other's hair, and then they laughed and rose together from their stools and with more skirt tugging preceded the boys across the room. The smaller of the jerseyed boys snatched two chairs from an adjacent table without asking and all sat down and introductions began.

"Cornholers," Reed Lester said.

The waitress returned to set their drinks before them and moved on again. The boy didn't want to be there, but he wanted to be sober and so he drank his Coke while Lester drank his Jack and Coke.

"I used to watch such geniuses as these watching Mia at the bars," said Lester.

The boy looked at him.

"My girlfriend—the Cuban? I'd see them huddling up and calling the play. Sure enough, some cornholing genius would come on over and start talking her up, like I wasn't even there. She'd look at me like she didn't know what the hell was going on, like what was she supposed to do, she'd just been sitting there. And she *had* just been sitting there, is the thing, boss. That's all she ever did and still they came." He swallowed half his drink and sat pondering the remains. "Well," he said. "That's all she did whenever I was around. But I wasn't always around. And then, after a while, neither was she."

"Where was she?"

"Where was she? Where was she, you ask? I asked myself the same thing. I began to get a little dark in my mind, boss, I confess it. I went by her building. I went over there just to see if I could catch her coming or going. I wanted to see her face, I wanted her to look me in the eye, that was all." A cheerless smile crept into his lips. "Well," he said. "You can guess where this is going. I'm standing there across the street one night and this black Caddy pulls up and sits there idling for five minutes, twenty minutes, I don't know, until finally the dome light comes on and out she pops, smiling back at the man in the car, wiggling her fingers at him. Mia. My Mia. Jesus."

He hunched over his drink, raised it to his lips and drank and then returned it to its wet ring on the table.

The boy wanted a cigarette. He looked in vain for a clock.

Lester watched him from under his eyebrows. "The thing is, I knew that car, boss. And I knew the old bald head that lit up when the dome light came on. It was the writer. The famous writer the college had rented for the year."

The boy waited for the name of the writer, but Lester only lifted his glass again and swallowed and winced.

"About two nights after that first night, I see that black Caddy parked outside a certain bar, this certain local craphole where the old professors go to run their hands up the skirts of their students in the back booths. So in I walk and there they are. Having the conversation of their lives. Just about knocking their goddam heads over the table and him with his old claw on her wrist and the next thing I know I'm walking on back there. I'm walking back there and they both look up and at the sight of me Mia's smile falls away, just falls away."

He stared into some remote place, some sector of vision beyond the boy's right shoulder, turning his glass slowly in his hands.

"I stand at the booth and the great writer looks at me. With his bald head and his goatee. He looks at Mia, and he looks at me again and he says: 'The jealous boyfriend, I presume?' And I look at him and I say, 'It's an honor to meet you, sir, I'm a great admirer of your work,' and he nods and says, 'That's very kind,' and I say, 'How do you like fucking my girlfriend?'"

Lester lifted his drink, sipped at it, set it down.

"Mia says something but I don't hear it. It's just me and the writer now, and we're just staring at each other. 'Young man,' he says finally, very quiet. Very serene. And I remember every word, boss. 'Young man,' he says, 'I can only assume by such a comment that you have made the assumption, based perhaps on my age, perhaps on my demeanor, perhaps on God knows what, that I will not stand up from this booth and knock you on your insolent ass. That is a poor assumption. On the other hand, it is absolutely true that I would prefer to stay seated as I am. Why don't you sit down and allow me to buy you a drink?' To which I replied: 'I read one of your books once, you old cocksucker, and I would sooner have another one force-fed up my ass than have to read it.'

"Well," said Lester. "The great writer turned to Mia and excused himself, as if he was going to the head, and he got out of the booth and turned and took this funny, old-school jab at my gut, but he caught me on the wrist and I heard some of his bones go and before he got his hand up I came around with the left and sat him back down in the booth with the blood pouring from his nose, just gushing from it, all over his nice shirt and his sport coat and all over Mia's hands when she came around and tried to sop it up with cocktail napkins. Jesus, she looked like a nurse trying to stop a gut wound with those little goddam napkins."

He lifted his glass for the watery dregs.

The boy looked away, his eyes drawn to the electric tiki torches at the bar. An erratic simulated guttering that, when watched, was not erratic at all but cyclical and predictable.

"So then what," he said, turning back.

"Then what what."

"What happened?"

Lester regarded him dully. "I'm sitting here with you, aren't I?" He tipped his empty glass and crushed some ice in his backteeth. "I got hauled up before the dean, and do you know what he says? Says I can get the hell offa his campus by five p.m. or go directly to jail, my choice. I told him I didn't take the first swing and he says that's not what the great writer says, and I said that that bar was full of witnesses and he says that's not what a single one of them says. I said there's one who didn't say that and the dean says which one is that and I say Mia, the girl who was sitting there through the whole thing. And he shook his head at me, the dean, and said, son, there was no girl sitting there."

The boy got up to have a smoke. He walked past the bathrooms and he saw the pay phone he hadn't seen coming in, and he thought about the time of night and he thought about the last time he'd called—a few days after she'd gotten out of the hospital, and although she was upbeat, although she said she was happy to hear his voice, all he could hear in hers was that place: the hall walkers, the mutterers, the TV gazers, the weeping, the forgotten, the broken.

He stepped through the metal door and into the cold and sleeting night.

A man stood smoking under the yellow light, his back to the wall, one leg cocked and the heel of his cowboy boot set to the bricks. The sleet blew over the scant eve and fell at an angle to a place just a few inches in front of the toe of his other boot. He touched the bill of his cap and said, "It ain't much but it's dry."

The boy put up his collar and got a cigarette in his lips and the man produced a lighter and lit him.

"Pretty night," said the man. His face was deeply lined, the stubble on his jaw half gone to silver, his eyes in shadow under the cap bill. "You all got far to go?"

"Not too far."

"That's good. I believe this will turn to snow, and snow on top of ice, that's about as fun as it gets."

The boy nodded. He smoked. "You going far?"

"Not as far as I come. But it's those last miles, ain't it? Especially when you got something worth getting to." He turned and caught the boy's eye and the boy half smiled and looked away.

The man gestured at the trucks in the lot. "I'm guessing that one there. That Chevy."

"Sorry?" said the boy.

"I'm saying that's your Chevy there, the blue one."

The boy stared blankly at the truck. He could see the man watching him in the corner of his eye. "What makes you say that?"

"Well. From the look on your face when you stepped out here I took you for a man who has not had the pleasure of this particular smoker's lounge before. And I see them Wisconsin plates. And I see what looks like a fair amount of gear in the cab there, like a man on the road."

The boy drew on his cigarette. "Which one's yours?" He was scanning the lot for an off-duty cruiser, or a detective's car.

"Black Ford over there with the topper," said the man.

The boy looked. In the rear window of the topper was an American flag decal and on the bumper below was a sticker with the words SMITH & WESSON and nothing more.

"I guess you could sleep in there if you wanted to," said the boy.

"You could, it weren't packed so tight a mouse can't lick his nuts."

They smoked and looked out on the foreshortened night. The patter of the sleet on the roofs and hoods of the trucks. The boy's head felt clearer for the cold air.

"Coming here I found a dog by the side of the road," he said. "A German shepherd. Had a collar and tags." He shifted his weight and didn't look at the man.

"Dead?"

"No."

"Somebody hit him?"

"Yes."

"What'd you do?"

"There wasn't anything to do."

"So what'd you do?"

"I finished him. Then I set him under a tarp by the fence. There's a phone number on the tags."

The man looked at the boy and looked out at the storm. "My daddy shot a dog once. Old Jim-Jim." He smoked and shook his head. "I can still hear that rifleshot like it was yesterday."

Out on the frontage road a police cruiser crept slowly by, the dash-lit face of the officer turning to take them in, filing their images away.

"Whoever hit that shepherd didn't even slow down," said the boy.

"Does that surprise you?"

The boy studied his cigarette. "Maybe they didn't know they hit it."

The man looked at him. "You always think so well of people?"

"No, not always."

The man took a last pull and held the butt before him as if it were some strange new thing. "Used to be a man could chase a good meal with a good smoke and never get up from his table. You remember that?" He tossed the butt into a pothole brimming with slush and pushed off from the brick and touched the bill of his cap. "You take it easy now."

"You too."

"Stay out of trouble."

28

There's the jeep-thing, of course—somewhere. Stowed in a cave of scrub woods with more scrub piled on top to cover it. She knows when he's used it by the smell of gas on him and the smell of the places he's been, a hamburger joint, a barbershop, a bar. The smells inside these walls are finite and the ones he brings back from the outer world must be sniffed and identified, like guests confronted by the family dog. She sniffs for the smell of the motel where she stayed with her family. The restaurant where they ate, the Black Something. She sniffs for the smell of her mother's perfume.

Once a month he fetches groceries and she knows it's once a month by the dates on the magazines he brings, National Geographic, Field & Stream, *and this is how she knows roughly how long she's been here too. No newspapers. Nothing to tell of herself or of the search, nothing to tell of her brother—how long he lay there and who found him and how they got him down the mountain and how his leg is and You never should've left him, never should've done that, lying there so scared and his leg all wrong, and the man said he saw on the news when he went down that the boy was fine so stop asking him—and sometimes he brings a bright new shirt from the boys' department because he won't shop in ladies', nor buy tampons or liners, such things were already here, stacked and stacked on a shelf above the toilet. The sight of them telling her everything that first day, everything.*

People see him when he goes in the jeep-thing, when he goes down to wherever he goes. They must. He moves among them like anyone would. Completes trans-actions. Trades pleasantries. He wore a ring that first day but not since and there is no woman down there, she knows this as any woman would. Does anyone give him a thought? Think him strange?

The yellow coin of light has slipped over the ninth gap in the floorboards and she pushes herself up from the cot and shuffles into the bathroom following the blue beam of the hiker's headlamp that precedes her like eyesight itself.

Bathroom. Please. It is like some prairie outhouse with a dry, house-style porcelain bowl. She pulls the thin door and fits the little hook into the eyelet, takes down a box from the shelf and drops one tampon unwrapped into the water bucket where it swells and floats like a small drowned thing. Four more in this box. Twenty more in each of the four remaining boxes. Was this her schedule, her tenure here? Behind the toilet, low in one corner in the dark old wood, is a patch of a lighter shade. Once, she got down on hands and knees and looked closely. Felt with fingertips. Faint small scarrings in the wood. Hatch marks. Months and months of calendaring, incompletely sanded away. It sickened her and taught her: Don't count. Don't mark. Don't believe in a foreseeable end with its nothing to do but wait, and wait.

She sits and pees with a hollow pattering sound into the dry bowl, lifts the tampon from the bucket by the tail and drops it into the bowl and with a tilt of the water bucket sloshes everything down to wherever it goes when it goes down, obeying laws of gravity and geography. The Great Divide deciding even this.

In the dull small mirror screwed to the wall is a pale miner, halogen moon in the center of her forehead. The pajamas lie on the floor and she stands as if risen out of them, all her flesh crawling in the cold. She soaks the washcloth in the remaining bucket water, soaps it and washes herself while the girl in her head takes up her story again midsentence . . . but there was one thing I had to tell myself every morning when I woke up in that place . . . the voice not hers but the voice of an older, tougher girl, speaking as though to a gymnasium of girls, all their faces composed while their bodies imagine and their hearts beat with strange excitement, and she is one of them, knee to knee with her friends. Listen, is the girl's message, this could happen to you.

She takes up the sour gray towel and dries herself quickly and begins to dress.

What did I have to tell myself?

There is only you. There is only you.

In the outer room she throws her arms one way and then the other, limbering her spine. Rolls her head on her neck and bends at the hips to grab her toes. So bent she clasps her arms around her knees and hugs herself into a compact human fold, breathes in, her upside-down heart thudding evenly, breathes out. She touches the thick band at her ankle, the hard iron within the leather liner, no more strange to her now than her own foot. She releases her legs and gathers up the chain in her fists and stands, leaning until all her weight is opposed to the remaining length of chain, and she begins to walk, clockwise, like a mule turning a mill wheel.

The steel plate, about the size of an index card, makes its minute adjustments under the four bolt heads, revealing hairlines of raw wood as she half circles the compass and then returns. The movement of the steel plate is good, but her focus is the ringbolt itself, the small half hoop of steel welded to the plate, its gritty underbelly of red-brown where she has nurtured corrosion on a diet of water, sweat, orange juice, urine, and Coke. (Rust particles are harder than steel, sweetie, her father told her once, by way of comfort when a swing chain dropped her on her fanny; abrasive wear is inevitable.) With her every straining pass the connecting link traverses the arc of the ringbolt, and back again, transmitting a grinding kinking code up through the links to her hands. The turnings have become grainier, noisier, and she stops every six passes just to listen—for whistling. For footfalls.

The coin of light is on the last floorboard before the lion's foot and she releases the chain for the day. Kneels down facing east and tests the ringbolt with the tender backs of her fingers. Hot. She wets a fingertip and blots up tiny particles like spilled salt. Presses fingertip to lips and tongues up the taste, the peculiar rusty tang she loves now, so like the taste of blood. Good work. And off in the woods she hears the whistling and she stands and brushes off her knees. Good girl. And the whistling is coming and she goes to the cot and lies back and picks up the magazine and opens it and stares at the picture of an Egyptian mummy. The magazine is trembling, her fingers trembling from her labor, the jumpy kinking and twanging of the chain still alive in her hands like crazy heartbeats. Good work. Good girl.

29

Reed Lester sat toying his glass around on its base, wheeling the naked cubes around and around. He had a new red hue to his face like the faces of the people who sat near the windows where the red beer lights burned. The waitress brought him a fresh drink and asked the boy if he was ready for another and he told her he'd take a glass of water and she went to see about the group of young people in the corner who had taken to ordering shots—downing them in some kind of game, slamming the glasses hard on the table and cheering. People at the tables next to them had paid their tabs and left. One of the boys in jerseys had his arm around one of the girls. Another boy leaned to say something into the ear of the other girl and she shoved at him and said, "Get your dog breath offa me. Jesus!"

Outside the window the sleet was turning to snow.

"Know what I'm thinking, boss?"

"No."

"I'm thinking you should come with me to Uncle Mickey's. He'll hire us both like that." His finger snap was soundless. He leaned back in his seat and regarded the boy with whiskey eyes. His eyelids slid down and were a long time opening again, and then only in reaction to the commotion from the table of young people. A chair scuffed the floor and a clump of keys were dropped and retrieved. "Ah, sit down, Courtney," said one of the boys, "c'mon."

"Abby," said the standing girl, "I'm serious." The girl Abby said something and the standing girl said, "I'm serious, I'll take the car. You'll be stuck here."

Reed Lester watched them without expression.

"She won't be stuck," said one of the boys.

"Abby," the girl said. "Abby."

The girl Courtney crossed the floor alone, fierce and unstable on her bootheels, and pushed out through the front door. In a moment a pair of headlights flared, thickening the snowfall, and swung around and were replaced by the red eyes of her taillights and these went bobbling over the pitted lot and arced onto the frontage road and vanished.

"Stupid," said Lester. "Stupid, stupid."

"I think it's time to hit the road," said the boy, and Lester gave an extravagant wave.

"Let's do it. But gimme one minute here. My head is rollin like a BB in a teacup. I need water. One glass and I'll be shipshape." His head went back again and his eyes closed. The boy looked for the waitress. She was behind the bar staring into a computer screen. He sat looking at Lester for a while, then got up and walked down the hall to the men's room.

"Leave him, Dudley," he said to the cracked plaster over the urinal. To the large curving phallus carefully penned there. "Bring his goddam bag in and go."

Outside in the hall a group was passing. Someone of size thudded into the bathroom door. A man whooped and the restaurant's back door groaned open and after the group had passed through it groaned shut again and he could hear them faintly in the parking lot laughing. An engine revved to life, car doors slammed, and the sound of the engine faded away.

He washed his hands and crushed a paper towel and stepped into the hallway and went to the metal door and stepped outside again and looked for the man who'd given him a light before, but the man wasn't there, no one was. He lit his cigarette and leaned against the wall. The sleet had gone completely to snow and there was a good white inch on the ground, on the Chevy, on the black Ford with the topper, on everything but the rectangles in the gravel where cars and trucks had recently sat, and these were quickly filling in. His eye fell on the freshest of the rectangles and stayed there. Then he looked to the side of the building where he himself had driven around to park. He looked back to the rectangle. The tire tracks leading away from it did not run that way but banked in the opposite direction, disappearing into a narrow gap between the Paradise Lounge and the cinder-block building next door. The boy leaned on the bricks and smoked and watched. In a moment, at the corner where the tire tracks disappeared, came a cloud of white breath. Only one.

He looked at the blue Chevy under its coat of snow and he thought of his kitbag inside the cab and he thought of the Estwing inside the kitbag and he remembered the weight of it and the sound of it landing and he drew hard on his cigarette. He looked at the corner again, then stepped on his cigarette and went back inside.

He took a few steps toward the dining room, then turned around and went back into the men's room and stepped into the stall where the stool was. Next to it in the stinking corner stood a cheap plumber's helper. Crusted black rubber and a grimy wooden handle.

The value of a stick, he thought.

He trapped the rubber cup against the floor with his boot and unscrewed the stick and took it into the light and looked at it. Beyond the stick he saw the stick again and himself holding it in the square of glass over the basin, his face sallow and shadowed by the ceiling fixture, darkness in the wells under his brow.

What are you up to, Dudley?

30

She knows the world of the sleeping bag. The satiny inside that goes from cold to warm, the head hole string-drawn down to the size of a child's fist, the humid, breathing lung of it, of one's own self. Such pleasures long gone.

Kiddo, comes his voice, down through the hole. Comes again: Kiddo, and she stirs so he won't put his hand on the bag—on her shoulder, her hip. She follows her own fingers, arms, head out into the cold morning, blinking. Bacon spitting in a skillet. The air smoky and pungent. His back is to her. He came in late, she remembers, and went straight to his cot, trying not to wake her.

She down-zips to the smaller opening at her feet where the chain feeds in, swings her legs over the edge of the cot and plants her bare feet into the slippers. She wears flannel pajamas but in the morning a girl needs to get out of bed without being watched, and he keeps his eyes down as he kneels at her feet and unlocks the cuff.

Do you know what today is? Handing her the plastic plate. A child's juice box for her other hand. He has stopped offering coffee, knows she doesn't like it. She sits on the cot and he pulls up his camping chair. Fresh cordwood is stacked near the stove in a tidy pyramid. The ax and the saw are outside somewhere. The pistol is on his hip.

She picks up the plastic fork and looks at the yellow clot of eggs, Eat it, Courtland, and forks up a bite and says, Monday.

No—

Thursday. Sunday.

No, not the day of the week, kiddo. Bigger than that. Think bigger.

She chews the egg and with her fingers breaks off a chip of bacon and slips it into her mouth and chews on that and shrugs.

What is the biggest day of the year? he says. The day everybody looks forward to most?

She looks at him. Then she turns and looks at the little fir tree at the foot of his cot. The necklaces of red berries and popcorn she'd sat there stringing while Johnny Mathis sang from the small speaker. Stabbing her fingers with the needle to keep her mind there, with her, in this place and not back in some candle-scented memory of home.

A large red box sits under the skirt of the tree. Oh, she says.

Oh ho ho, he says.

After they eat he gets Johnny Mathis going again and sits in his chair with his coffee, watching the snowfall in the small square of window. He tells her he likes it like this, Christmas morning: simple, quiet. When he was a kid you couldn't get his old man out of bed before noon and still he'd be drunk. Look at all these goddam presents, he'd say. Jesus H. Christmas. Why didn't somebody tell me we were rich?

He swings his chair and opens the iron gate and jabs his stick into the fire, setting off a brittle collapse. The stove is serious business. Deadly serious. If she doesn't do it right while he's away, if she gets careless . . . can she imagine a more terrible way to die than fire?

Um . . . to die by fire while chained like a dog?

He tosses in a length of wood and maneuvers it with the stick. One Christmas, he says, all I wanted was a Swiss Army knife. The big one with a hundred uses. A real survival knife. Didn't ask for anything else. Dad worked for the forest service and he wasn't home much but when he was he made sure his boys weren't becoming a couple of pansies in his absence. If we cried when he whipped us he'd keep going till we stopped. I wanted the knife because I thought it was the last thing a pansy would want.

He stares into the fire. The new log hissing and whistling.

Did you get it? she says.

He looks up. What?

The knife.

No. He told me: I know you wanted that knife, boy, but what kind of father would I be giving a knife to a boy still wets the bed, what kind of message would that be? He had me confused with Bobby, of course, my little brother, but you couldn't tell him that. Nor remind him that it was him, not Bobby, passing out and pissing himself on our couch.

His hand moves to his hip, where he hangs the big hunting knife, but finds nothing and moves back. He shuts the gate and swings back to her. The knife, in its sheath, waits in the locked footlocker by his cot. Or under his pillow.

He sips his coffee. She looks at the length of chain where it lies on the floor. She is free of it and yet her hands ache for it.

Two years later, he says, just a few months after Bobby hung himself with a power cord, he—Dad—was up in Oregon when a load of logs rolled off a rig and crushed him where he stood. He raises his coffee but doesn't drink. Thirty-man crew coming and going all day and it's my old man walking by when those logs decide to go. Some might see the hand of God in that.

She waits. Then says, Do you?

Do I? He laughs. When you have seen your little brother swinging from a rusty pipe in the basement you pretty much know all you need to know about God.

A tear runs down her cheek, surprising her. It's the day. Her family. His voice. It's Johnny Mathis singing to these walls, these cots, which in a glance betray every raw, unbelievable thing they've witnessed.

She wipes away the tear and he says, Hey, I'm sorry. What am I thinking? Who needs to hear that crap? It's Christmas! The coffee cup rises and his head hinges back for the last of it—single hard convulsion of the throat knuckle under the skin—and when he looks at her again his eyes are bright with atonement.

I've got something to cheer you up.

He fetches the red box and places it on her lap, surprisingly light for its size, and her heart dives at the thought of the dress inside, before she remembers he wouldn't do that, that he's too careful.

I didn't get you anything, she says.

He waves this off.

I couldn't get away, she says.

He gestures impatiently at the gift.

She peels back the wings of paper and takes in the image on the box. For just a moment something opens in her chest, like excitement, like happiness, before she understands the cruelty of it.

She lifts the lid and crushes back tissue paper and her heart sets up a thick beating.

Is this some kind of joke?

Expensive joke, he says, taking one of the snowshoes from the tissue. I thought you might like to get out for a while. Have you ever used them before?

31

He stepped out through the metal door again, out into the cold and snow, and he moved unhurriedly along the wall, toward the corner where he'd seen the white plume of breath, where he now saw another. He began to mutter, and he made his footfall heavy and he fumbled with his fly as he gained the corner, and when he saw the white jersey there in the shadows he took a clumsy step away and said, "Oh, sorry."

"Take off, jack," said the boy in the jersey.

"Apologies, boss," said the boy. "Just came to empty the tank."

"Empty it someplace else, jack. Piss yourself and fuck off." It was the big one, Valentine. His jersey brilliant white in the unlit alley. Number 10 in deep red on a white field.

He looked beyond Valentine into the alley and the larger boy stepped forward to block his view.

"What part of fuck off don't you understand?" His breath sour and alcoholic in his face. The boy back-stepped the way he'd come and stopped, looking at Valentine. Valentine took another step and the boy back-stepped again. In this manner they both came around the corner, and when Valentine was all the way around it the boy moved no farther. He let the wooden handle drop from the sleeve of his jacket, catching it at its threaded end, the threads like a grip. In the snowlight he saw flecks of black in Valentine's glassy blue eyes and he brought the stick up in a whistling arc that caught the larger boy across his ear. Valentine clapped a hand to his head and slipped to his knees and then forward onto his free hand, his face contorted in a soundless wail.

The boy stepped around him into the alley, moving toward the other jersey he could see there in the deeper dark, white like a signal, like a flag. On the jersey was the name Whitford and this boy Whitford stood at the rear of the truck in a sure stance, his jeans and underwear spanning from knee to knee and his white buttocks clenched and working. The other two boys from the table leaned over the truckbed rail, their hands down in the dark of the bed like ranch hands at some act of animal husbandry. When they looked up, the boy saw in their eyes that he was not himself—was not the boy he knew himself to be but some dark contour of man, shaped out of the light and snow behind him, ageless and faceless and moving certainly toward them.

One of the boys said, "Shit," and the thrusting Whitford looked up, looked over his shoulder, and without pausing in his work said, "Who the fuck are you?" He didn't see but heard the stick as it came whistling out of the dark and struck him just below the jersey, laterally across the buttocks, as if to recleave them yet again crosswise. He howled and spun away from another strike and received it instead to the face. He raised his hands and went staggering until the shackles of his jeans tripped him and sent him flat-handed to the snow. "Motherfucker," he said, crawling away. "Motherfucker."

The boy raised the stick again and the two boys leaning into the truckbed let go their holds and fled down the alley and the facedown girl began to slip from the tailgate, and he placed a hand in the small of her back to stop her. Her hair lay over her face like black webbing and there was the smell of vomit and he could see where it had melted the snow and pooled in the bed of the truck.

He dropped the stick and set his hands in her armpits and considered how best to proceed, and as he was doing this he heard the heavy steps and he braced for the blow, and it landed with such force it slammed him down over the girl's body. An arm collared his neck and lifted him and he let go the girl to grope at the arm and the girl began to slide again, slipping limp and heavy over the tailgate. She spilled over and her chin struck the tailgate's lip and her head rocked back and she toppled doll-like down, her head landing last and bouncing once dully on the snowed-over ground.

The boy was lifted from his feet and he could feel the skin of Valentine's face against his own, the jaw working as he told him quietly, "I got you, jack, I got you." The boy bucked and horse-kicked and punched blindly at

Valentine's head but the arm only grew harder and tighter until he could no longer breathe but could feel the other boy's breath in his ear saying, "Quit that now, it ain't helping you any."

"Turn him this way, Clayton."

The boy was swung and before him stood Whitford, head down, patiently attending to his fly, his beltbuckle. When he was finished he reset his backward cap and regarded the boy. He touched his fingers to his own cheekbone, gently probing, and inspected his fingertips. He looked to the fallen girl, and back to the boy.

"Give him some air, Clayton. He looks about to pass out and he don't wanna do that."

Whitford walked over to the girl and began searching the ground. He kicked at the black twist of her underwear and said, "That ain't it. Ah, there you are." He bent and pulled the length of stick out from under her leg. He looked it over as if it were some rare specimen of weaponry.

"Is this what I think it is? Damn." He put the stick to the girl's hip and flipped up her skirt. He looked at the boy again, hung there like a pelt in Valentine's arms.

"You could've had your turn when we were done, bud. You had no call to get violent. Set him to the tailgate there, Clayton."

The boy fought but Valentine was too big and too strong and when the boy was pinned against the tailgate Whitford reached around the boy's waist and began to undo his belt. The boy grabbed at Whitford's wrists and the stick whipped across his fingers and Valentine squeezed until the boy raised his hands again and held on to the thick noose of arm.

"Don't fight," said Whitford. "And don't worry, I ain't no fag. All I'm gonna do is this. Are you listening? You got enough air? All right. All I'm gonna do is, I'm gonna take your little friend here and I'm gonna put him up your asshole, far as he'll go, all right? How's that sound, bud?"

The boy bucked and Valentine brought his weight forward and folded the boy over the tailgate until his face was nearly in the girl's vomit and he twisted as his jeans and shorts were jerked down to midthigh and the air was cold and the snow was like cold insects alighting on his flesh. There was a long sickly moment of nothing before the stick made its whistling sound and struck him hard. He flinched but made no sound.

"There," said Whitford. "Now we both know what that feels like. This next part, well. You'll just have to let me know. Hold him good, Clayton."

The boy clenched himself as if he could make that part of himself shut and vanish altogether by the sheer will to do so. Something touched him on the hip and he flinched and it was the other boy's fingers there. "Easy now." Fingers settling gently one at a time and lastly the thumb, finding a purchase that would give him leverage. From the parking lot there came the sound of an engine's turning—coldly laboring at first but then firing in a deep exuberant roar, sustained and incensed by a series of stompings to the gas pedal, and the fingers on the boy's flesh were stilled and the arms that held him were like the fixed arms of a statue. The engine revvings brought to his mind the black Ford and the man who drove it. SMITH & WESSON. *Stay out of trouble.* Yellow light spilled into the alley and searched along the cinder-block wall but in the next moment was eclipsed by the building as the driver made his turn, and then driver and car and light and sound all faded away into the night.

Fingers reset themselves on the boy's hip, and Whitford told him quietly that it would all be over before he knew it, and in the long ludicrous moment to follow there came another sound, unexpected, one that halted everything under way in the alley, all movement, all breathing, even their hearts. Only the snow went on as before, mutely falling. It was the crisp steely sound they all understood to be the chambering of a round in a gun.

"Drop the stick, number twelve," the man with the gun said.

The stick hit the ground in a soft clatter.

"Step away, over there. And you, number ten. Big man. Let him go and step over there with your faggot buddy."

Released by Valentine, the boy drank the cold air into his torn throat and pushed up from the tailgate.

He pulled up his jeans and redid the fly and buckled the belt and turned around.

"Didn't I tell you, boss? Cornholers."

32

He has gear for her—snow boots and jacket and gloves and sunglasses, all rising from the footlocker and all in the style of a young and self-conscious boy. Things her brother would like. Yet she knows as she slips into the jacket, into the boots, that they have never been worn by a boy but by a girl more like herself, some predecessor whose traces she can't see or smell but that are here just the same, like a left-behind shadow. The shadow in these clothes, in the fit of the boots and the jacket and the hat and the gloves is profound, and comforting, and sickening.

When he opens the door and stands aside she thinks she's prepared but she isn't. The whole white world crashing into her eyes, the cold, incredible brightness of it. She puts on the sunglasses and sees this world as the girl before her saw it: the mountain pines rising in their entirety toward the white sky, boughs heavy with snow. The piney air so intensely white and clean and cold it's as if she's never breathed before, never smelled before. She is so dazzled she almost doesn't look back, but then she does. It isn't a cabin but a shack. Hardly that. A low wooden storehouse half buried in the snow. Smoke like white birds fleeing the pipe. A stripe of red catches her eye and it takes her a moment to understand what it is, which is the painted runner of a sled. Long wooden child's sled parked along the wall. It's how he moves logs from the woods, provisions from the jeep-thing. Other loads.

It's going to feel strange when we get in the deep snow, he's saying, down in his monkey-squat at her feet, setting her bindings. It's like learning to walk all over again, he says. But there's no way to learn but to do it. Just remember to keep your legs apart, and try not to drag the tails, you might snag on something under the—

She sets off ahead of him across the small clearing, downslope, and when she falls, the arm she puts out to stop herself sinks and sinks, as if into fog. She comes to rest in her own impression, her face turned from the snow. She half rolls and tries to push herself up with the other arm and finds the same deep nothing below her. She understands she needs to get the snowshoes under her again before she can stand, but the gymnastics of that—the rolling, the grunting, the immodest exertions on her back—is a performance he won't see, not out here.

He walks to her on the snow and helps her up. You stepped on one shoe with the other. Legs apart, remember?

She brushes snow from her legs, her hips, and sets off again, and makes it to the trees.

Better, he says, better. But let's go this way. And he turns from the downward slope and leads her up instead. Up the mountain and into a woods of spruce and fir and utter stillness. Her breathing is coarse and her quad muscles throb and he stops to check with her and she goes stomping by.

Don't push yourself, he says. You can get sick at this altitude, and she says, I'm fine, and stomps on.

They make slow headway against the slope and against the gravity of her body that wants only to go down. She searches for a change in the trees, for the suggestion under the snow of an order imposed by the path of a creek bed, or a road. She looks up compulsively for cables, listens for the sound of anything at all: traffic, chainsaw, helicopter. She remembers the blue road markers from that day in July and looks down expecting to see them like tiny heads trying to keep themselves above the snow.

How you doing? he says behind her, and she flinches at the sound of him. She takes two more steps and falls.

You're getting tired, he says, appearing above her. Blocking the falling snow, her view of the trees. When you get tired you get lazy, and you can't be lazy in snowshoes.

Where are we? she says.

What do you mean?

I mean where are we? Are we far from where you—from where my brother and I were? She hasn't mentioned the boy since the beginning, since those first days.

He looks down on her. Nothing at all in his eyes behind the yellow lenses.

Why?

Why what?

Why do you ask.

Because I want to know.

Why?

Because I do. Wouldn't you?

No. What difference would it make?

It might make you feel less lost.

Or more. Where you are is where you are, not where you're not.

She stares at him. But I don't know where I am.

Yes you do. You're with me, right here.

He watches her, then looks away. You want to go back? Is that it? You want to spend Christmas day indoors? Aren't we having a good time out here? Isn't it beautiful?

The pitch grows steeper and the woods grow thicker, obliging them to weave around the trees in a series of switchbacks that make the climb easier but longer. And where the slope turns gentler, fewer trees confront the way, as if that were the design, until at last they reach a wide expanse of snow where the trees grow sparsely and are no taller than herself. Unless these are the tips of the trees and she is crossing a deep lake of snow.

Ahead, the trees vanish altogether, and then so does the mountain—abruptly, entirely, like the edge of the world. Nothing beyond but the gray sky and the snow swarming out of it as though here is the place where snow begins, where it's made. She goes on toward the edge but he calls out Stop, and she stops and looks back.

He stands between a pair of small fir trees; they give him the illusion of great stature. We don't want to go beyond this point here, he says.

Why not?

I'll show you. Come back here.

She returns, and he draws off his glove in his teeth and reaches under his jacket and there's the sound of a metallic snap and he's holding the pistol.

It is the black, hard center of the white world. The only thing to look at or care about. Dizzily she sees her body here, left behind in the lake of snow to freeze and thaw with the seasons. Or maybe never to thaw but to lie in its last, fallen state for centuries, the story of her death preserved with her body, and she will ask him to please please not take the gear off, at least, the boots and the jacket and the gloves, to please at least do that much.

He raises the pistol and fires into the gray void. The sound is unexpectedly small, like a summer firecracker, yet it carries unexpectedly, caroming and returning to them from invisible reaches. In the instant after, she thinks there must be something out there he can see but she can't, and she peers with aching eyes for the man, mountain climber, lawman, to come stumbling from the fog, hands to his guts, face twisted in pain and amazement.

Instead there's a second, greater crack, like the gunshot amplified, and in the foreground a ragged blue seam appears in the snow like a vein shot full of dye. The vein widens, turns a deep glacial blue and then fills with white as the entire length of ridge shrugs and slips away down into the gray, pulling her eyes and her heart and the pit of her stomach down after it, down into the sky. The ridge falls and crashes and pounds against the side of the mountain. It takes a long time and sounds all the while as if it's no farther away than when it began. Then it stops, or seems to stop, and there's nothing more to hear but the distant replay of thunder in the far, unseeable gorges.

They stand in the aftersilence. He ejects the shell from the cylinder and it falls hissing into the snow. He fetches up another bullet and slips it into the cylinder and snaps the gun back together again and returns it to the holster under his jacket and there's the sound of the metal button snap and he puts his glove back on.

One bullet at a time. She never knew it but she understands it at once: if she ever got her hands on the gun she could only shoot him once, and he likes his chances of that shot missing or merely wounding him in some nonlethal way.

It's safe now, he says, and they advance together, the space between them widening as they near the edge, like an understanding. She looks out into the tumbling snow and feels the pull of the gorge, the unknowable drop, the thinness of the space between doing and not doing—between a step of the mind and a step of the body, the unreal moment when it's done and there's no undoing it and there's only your rolling heart and the roar of the blurring world.

Careful, he says, and reaches for her, and she steps alertly back. The wind can carry you off like a leaf, he says.

They stand staring into space.

On a clear day you see as the hawk sees, he says. You see as God sees.

He looks at her. To observe the effect of such words.

She swipes at her dripping nose.

Ready to go? she says, and he steps toward her, and she steps away, back from the edge.

What are you doing? he says.

Nothing. I'm afraid of the edge.

Don't be afraid, he says. As he'd said that other day, long ago.

She takes another step and stops and he comes up to her, aligning his snow-shoes carefully with hers. He takes her upper arms in his hands: I don't want you to be afraid, Caitlin.

I'm not. Not now.

Good.

He stands staring at her. He shakes his head.

What, she says.

Nothing. He squeezes her arms. You're just so beautiful, out here in the light. In the world. Did you know that?

She takes his wrists in her hands, smiles, and he comes a little closer, his fingers clenching and relaxing. Clenching, relaxing. He comes only so close and will come no farther.

After a moment, looking into the yellow lenses, she comes the rest of the way to his lips.

33

Freed from Valentine's embrace, the boy put his hand to his throat and looked at the gun at the end of Reed Lester's straight and level arm. The slender chasing of light along the chromium barrel.

"I wasn't really gonna do it," the boy named Whitford said.

"Shut up," said Lester.

"I just wanted him to think I was."

"Say one more thing, cornholer. I dare you." He looked back to the boy. "What the hell are you doing?"

He was down on his knee working his arms under the girl's shoulders and under her knees. He hefted her to himself and his leg trembled as he stood but it held. The girl's head lolled and her upturned chin began to bleed and he shifted her so her face rested against his chest. "She's hurt," he said hoarsely.

"I think we'd be smart just to vacate, boss, and most ricky-tick."

"We're taking her."

Lester opened his mouth again but what came out in an unmatched voice were the words *Oh my God* and he and the two boys at gunpoint turned to see what the boy had already seen, which was the redheaded waitress standing at the mouth of the alley in the light. "What are you doing with that girl?"

"Hospital," said the boy.

"What did you do to her?" said the waitress.

"He didn't do a damn thing," said Lester. "Go back inside." The boy limped forward with the girl. He reached the waitress and said again, "Hospital."

She opened her mouth and shook her head.

"Where's the goddam hospital?"

She turned around. She ran a hand through her hair and got her bearings. She pointed south with her cigarette. "Down the strip, about four miles. You'll pass under the highway and you'll see the sign. Sisters of Mercy. But let me call an ambulance, okay? Just bring her inside."

He limped away from her into the parking lot and after a moment the waitress turned and ran back toward the door.

WHEN REED LESTER REACHED the Chevy his pack was on the ground in the snow and the boy was folding the girl's legs into the cab from the passenger's side. Lester picked up his pack and tossed it in the truckbed with the boy's gear and went around to the driver's side and helped him arrange her in the middle of the cab. "I'll drive, boss."

The boy settled the girl's head back on the seatback and gave a tug to her short skirt and shut the door and walked around to the driver's side and stood staring at Lester.

"You're right, you drive," said Lester, and he hustled around and reopened the passenger's door and pushed in next to the girl and slammed the door. The boy started up the Chevy and hit the wipers and they creaked but didn't budge.

"Got a scraper, boss?"

The boy put a hand to his throat. "Under your seat."

Lester found the scraper and jumped out and left his door open while he went to work on the windshield. The red door of the Paradise Lounge opened and the waitress and the big blond bartender stood watching them. The bartender began to cross the lot and Lester faced him and said, "It's all good, boss," and the bartender abruptly stopped as if reaching the end of a tether.

"The police are coming," he said. "I think you boys had best leave that girl here."

"So do I," said Lester. "But it ain't my show." He reached into his jacket pocket and the bartender took a step back. Lester underhanded the wad of keys through the air and the bartender caught them in his fist and looked at them.

"What're these?"

"Keys."

"No shit."

"They go to that truck parked in the alley."

He climbed back into the Chevy and the boy put the truck in gear and drove out of the lot. He turned onto the frontage road and got the Chevy up to speed in the snow.

Reed Lester looked at the boy, then at the girl. Her split bleeding chin and the wet dark ribbon tracing her bared neck, the small pool of blood in the pit of her throat and the dark ribbon running on, down over breastbone, down under a bridge of sweater and into shadow. As the cab warmed there was the smell of her perfume. Of alcohol and bile.

"I won't ever tell," he said.

"Tell what?" said the boy.

"About back there."

The boy watched the road. He reached for his cigarettes but the fire in his throat stopped him.

"Where's that gun?" he said.

"Put away. Why?"

He looked over and Lester looked up from what he'd been staring at, which was the girl's bare upper thighs, the hiked hem of skirt. They held each other's gaze. The wipers made their noise. The boy turned back to the road.

"Loaded?" he said.

"What?"

"The gun."

"Not much good otherwise, boss."

"You had it all along."

"You never know what you might run into on the road."

"Like a dog."

"Sorry?"

The boy stared ahead. "You just stood there and watched me. With that hammer."

Lester watched the boy's profile for a long moment.

"Well, what if I'd whipped out a gun right there, boss? What would you have thought?"

The boy stared ahead into the diving flakes.

"Damn," said Lester. "You'd think you'd be happy I pulled that gun when I did."

The sound of sirens reached them from some uncertain direction. Lester looked around window to window until the sirens began to fade. His eyes fell again to the girl's thighs. Pale flesh rolling slightly with the drift of the truck. The high black hemline of skirt.

"What are you doing?" said the boy.

"Nothing."

"Don't even think it."

"I wasn't thinking a damn thing, boss. Jesus. You think I'd do something like that?"

The boy got a cigarette in his lips and lit it and held the smoke in his mouth, fighting the instinct to inhale.

"On the other hand," said Lester. "A person might wonder what you were doing back there in the first place, boss. What'd you go looking for that got you into that fix?"

Before the boy could respond there was a sudden blooming of red and blue, and the sirens wailed up again and the cruisers multiplied all around them and the boy pulled carefully to the shoulder under the highway overpass.

The cab was shot through with the white light of the cruisers' spots, and in that brilliance the cab's dome light when it came on made no impression at all, and so the boy didn't know that a door had opened until he turned to tell Reed Lester not to say or do a goddam thing, and found him gone. The door still swaying on its hinges, men shouting out there in the lights. Engines raced and tires spun and some of the colored lights went strobing away down the road.

All around him, officers crouched behind their doors with guns drawn and they were shouting at him. He looked again at his open passenger's door and saw the ice scraper where Lester had left it on the floorboard and, beside it, something else, half stowed under the seat and pulsing blue and red with the cruiser lights. He stared at it for a long moment. Then he looked straight ahead and raised his hands and spread his fingers, as if to designate the number 10. Up ahead, beyond the cruisers and their lights, less than a hundred yards from where he sat, there hung in the snowfall a lambent blue sign with the silvered words SISTERS OF MERCY.

34

Hold up, he says, and she stops and waits for him to come up beside her, no sound in the world but the soft whupping of his snowshoes.

He thumbs the pack from his shoulders and brings out two plastic bottles of water and they uncap them and drink, the water gurgling its way around clots of ice in the necks. She caps the bottle and unzips her jacket and fits the bottle into the pocket near her breast, and then rezips the jacket.

He watches her do this. And watches her after it's done.

It's too cold to drink, she explains.

He lifts his bottle again and then returns it to the pack, and she says: What else you got in there?

Granola bars. A couple of Snickers. Are you hungry?

I'll take a Snickers, I guess. What else?

Nothing else. Nothing else to eat.

Tissue?

What?

Did you bring tissue?

Like Kleenex?

Like anything. She stares at him, into the yellow lenses, until he understands.

I have a small pack of Kleenex, that's all.

Can I borrow it?

Of course. He digs into one jacket pocket and then another until he finds the small package.

She slips it into her jacket pocket with the Snickers, then she turns and begins to walk back the way they came, in her own tracks, downslope.

Where you going? he says after a moment.

She doesn't look back. She points ahead to a squat, solitary spruce, wide and thick and hung with snow as if snow is its blossom and its only purpose. She missteps, totters on the snowshoes, rights herself.

Careful, he says, and she gives him the thumbs-up over her shoulder.

From the far side of the spruce she looks back through the snowy boughs, and the cold runs into her heart to see him standing dark against the snow just as she left him, far closer than she thought he would be. As if the distance she crossed to the spruce was an imaginary distance. Or as if he has moved as she moved but without sound and without tracks or effort.

She falters and then finds her voice: I can see you watching me.

I can't see a thing, he says, and she knows it's true.

She bends to tighten the bindings over her boots. I can see you watching, she says again. He doesn't move. Standing there. I can't go with you staring, she says, and at last, with an air of parental exasperation, he turns his back to her.

She takes a side step in the snow, downslope. She thinks she's made no sound but can't be sure because of the bloodbeat in her ears. She stands a moment in the stopped time and stopped breath and stopped heart of the starting blocks—
Breathe, Courtland—and then she takes another step, and another, keeping the tree between herself and the Monkey, and when she is twenty paces from the spruce she turns and she begins to descend the mountain in great, soundless, weightless strides.

35

All that followed that long night and into the morning was a perverse waking dream that would not end but only taunted him with the taste of ending, with scraps of near sleep wrenched from him at the last second and replaced by more noise and more walking and another bare room or the same bare room with the same man or men across a steel table or different men but always the same questions and the same hard light and the only break in it all, the one brief escape, was a real dream that rose up during a lapse in procedure, some miscue among his keepers that left him alone long enough to sleep, and in his sleep he climbed a path in the woods in the dark, making his way by the progress of the animal he followed, a dog or wolf of such whiteness it raised shadows from the things it passed, the trees and stones. Then the woods cracked with thunder and he jolted awake to the iron bars and the concrete and to the backlit man telling him to get up, and he was led in handcuffs once more down the corridor into the bare room.

The man at the table did not look up but sat studying the pages of a file that lay open before him while the man who brought the boy removed his cuffs and wordlessly left, pulling the steel door shut behind him.

The man at the table wore no jacket, only a white long-sleeved shirt buttoned at the wrists and at the collar, his tie well-knotted and pristine. The leather straps of his gun holster had a defining effect on the shirt, suggesting the good health and fitness of the torso beneath it. He had a full head of short black hair razor-line-parted on one side, and his jaw was blued with stubble. He wore a gold wedding band.

This man at last looked at the boy. Searching his eyes as if he might see there what none of the men before him had thought even to look for. Whatever he saw he dropped his gaze and let it rest on the boy's denim jacket, buttoned nearly to the throat. They had taken his white T-shirt with its catalog of bloodstains.

He looked again into the boy's eyes and said: "Sean, my name is Detective Luske. I'm with the Omaha PD Sexual Assault Unit. Would you like some water?"

"All right."

The detective filled a paper cup from a dispenser in the corner and set it in front of the boy and sat down again.

"Sean. As you know, since you say you saw it in progress, that girl you had with you in that truck last night was raped. By at least one assailant. Maybe as many as three. Now, she was inebriated and she was passed out for much of it, but I've talked to her and she believes she can identify those boys who were sitting with her inside the Paradise Lounge, if not necessarily those who raped her. Do you understand?"

"Yes."

"Do you?"

"Yes."

"What I want to do, Sean, is I want to bring another officer in here and take a sample from you. Would you agree to letting me do that?"

"What kind of sample?"

"A DNA sample. From the inside of your cheek. Your mouth. It takes about two seconds. Would you agree to letting me do that?"

"I won't try to stop it."

"That's not good enough. I can't take the sample without your consent unless I get a warrant. But it will look better for you if you give your consent."

"You mean verbally?"

"Yes."

"All right, I give my consent."

Luske sat back and the door opened and a tall thin woman stepped in. She wore a white medical smock and white latex examination gloves. A silver badge swung from her neck on a lanyard. She asked the boy to open his mouth and she scraped at the inside of his cheek with a plastic wand and he smelled her latex gloves and remembered the doctor at the hospital, the Chinese man with his needle light, and the woman placed the wand carefully inside a plastic tube and capped the tube and went away again.

"How long will it take?" said the boy.

"How long will what take?"

"The test."

"That has no bearing on this investigation, Sean. The test is for the State, for its case, should it decide to bring one."

The boy sat, hands on the table.

The detective picked up his pencil and began drumming the eraser on the table. The boy watched him.

"I don't suppose I can smoke," he said, and Luske shook his head and said, "There's no smoking in this building," and he reached into the pocket of his suit jacket draped over the chairback. He held the boy's pack across the table and the boy pulled a cigarette free and the detective lit it with the boy's lighter. He watched the boy draw in the smoke and blow it toward the ceiling.

"Sean," said Luske. "Tell me why you went into that alley."

"I had a feeling," the boy said, once again.

"A sexual feeling?"

"No, just a feeling. I heard some people leaving when I was in the bathroom but when I went outside for a smoke I saw by the tracks that they'd pulled into that alley. And I thought something was wrong about that and I had an idea what it was."

"Why didn't you go back inside and call the police? Or tell one of the staff at the restaurant?"

"It was just a feeling. I wasn't positive until I got back there."

"All right. So you went back inside the Paradise Lounge and you got this—what was it, the handle of a plunger? You didn't go to your truck and get your hammer?"

"No, he'd have seen me."

"Who?"

"The one at the corner keeping watch. The big one with Valentine on his shirt."

"All right. So you walk to the corner and you and this boy have words and then you strike him with the handle from the plunger."

"After I saw what was going on in the alley, yes." He recounted again his hitting the second boy and trying to keep the girl from sliding off the tailgate and being put in a choke hold by the first boy and being struck with the stick by the second boy.

"Where did he hit you?"

"In the alley."

"Where on your person."

"Same as I did him. Across the ass."

"Across the bare buttocks."

"Yes."

"Why were your buttocks bare?"

The boy regarded the ash on his cigarette. He readied to tap it into his palm but the detective told him to tap it on the floor and he did.

"Why were your buttocks bare, Sean?"

"Because he'd pulled down my jeans. The smaller guy. While the big one held me."

"Then what happened, after he struck you."

"Nothing. That's when Reed Lester showed up."

"Nothing more happened to you sexually?"

"No."

"All right." The detective scratched the side of his nose. "What made Reed Lester go back there?"

"I don't know. You'd have to ask him."

"Do you have an opinion?"

"I think he got to thinking I'd taken off without him."

"With his backpack in the truck?"

The boy shrugged.

"Where did you first meet him, Reed Lester?"

"On the side of the road. He was walking and he helped me change a flat so I gave him a lift."

"You never met him before that?"

"No."

"You didn't spend any time with him in Lincoln?"

"No."

"You didn't know he was wanted on sexual assault charges in Lincoln?"

"How would I?"

"He might've told you. Two guys in a bar, drinking and jawing . . ."

The boy shook his head. "He said something about a fight in a bar with a writer over a Cuban girl."

"A fight in a bar with a writer over a Cuban girl?" The detective stared at him. "This was a forty-five-year-old woman he attacked, in a parking lot. One of his professors. There wasn't any Cuban girl."

The boy drew on his cigarette and blew the smoke and waited.

"You didn't know he had a gun either, I suppose," said Luske.

"Not till he pulled it in that alley."

"So you two didn't get to talking, inside the Paradise Lounge, and decide to go on back there together with that gun and that stick and maybe finish what those boys started?"

"No. It happened like I told you."

The detective watched him, then he read the paper in front of him and underscored something with his pencil.

"All right. So now you've got those two boys at gunpoint and the girl is lying there unconscious. Why didn't you call the police at that point?"

"I don't know. I thought they'd take too long. She was bleeding and I wanted to get her to the hospital."

"Reed Lester and his gun didn't factor into your decision?"

"No. I didn't care about him or his gun."

"How do you think the gun ended up with you, in the truck, and not with him?"

"He left it there when he ran off."

"Some friend, huh."

"He wasn't a friend. I just met him that day."

"Tell me about the hammer."

"It's an Estwing, twenty ounces. It belongs to my father."

"How did it get blood on it."

"I had to kill a dog by the side of the road."

"You had to kill a dog by the side of the road."

"Yes, sir."

"Why?"

"Because it was hurt and there wasn't any help for it. Somebody had run over it."

"So you hit it with the hammer and killed it."

"Yes, sir."

"And Reed Lester was there at the time?"

"Yes, sir."

"Why didn't he use the gun? Or let you use it?"

"That's what I asked him later."

"What did he say?"

"He said something about not wanting to scare me off."

The detective stood and refilled the boy's cup of water and filled a cup for himself.

"Sean. What were that girl's panties doing in your jacket pocket?"

"I guess I put them there."

"Why did you do that?"

"I don't know. I don't remember doing it. I must've seen them lying in the snow and thought they were hers and she would probably want them back. I don't know."

"I've been doing this work for ten years, Sean, and I can't even tell you how many times I've found the panties, or the underpants, of the victim either on the perpetrator or in his home. He doesn't seem able to help himself. He's gotta have that trophy. That memento."

The boy drew on his cigarette and exhaled and waited.

The detective watched him.

"So you get a flat tire. You pick up a fugitive from the law. You have to kill a dog with a hammer. And you get pulled over with a raped girl and a gun in a truck that isn't registered to you. That's what I'd call a bad day, Sean."

The boy nodded. "I've had worse."

"I know you have. I know about your sister. I know how you got that limp."

"You know about her, huh?"

"I know what happened to the two of you up there in the mountains, yes."

"Then you know more than me. You know more than the entire state of Colorado and the FBI."

They stared at each other. The detective tapped the eraser of his pencil on the top sheet of the file and the sound seemed to remind him that it was there. He looked down and turned the page over and turned it back. At length he said: "Here's what we do know, Sean, all right? Here's what our investigation knows as fact. It knows that on the night of the assault you were pulled over in a truck that was not registered in your name. It knows an eyewitness can place you at the scene of the assault. It knows that you were pulled over with the victim in the cab of the truck, constituting possible kidnapping. It knows there was a gun in the cab of the truck, constituting possible kidnapping at gunpoint. It knows that in the bed of the truck was a backpack belonging to a man wanted on sexual assault charges in another county. It knows there was a hammer in a tool bag with blood on it. It knows that the victim was bleeding and that you had fresh blood on your T-shirt. It knows that the girl was wearing no underpants and that there was a pair of girl's underpants in your jacket pocket. Lastly it knows that there is no one, including the girl herself, to corroborate your statement that you did not rape her but instead tried to help her."

Luske folded his hands again over the file. The boy met and held his gaze.
"Sean."

"Yes."

"You're eighteen, correct?"

"Yes."

"And you do understand your rights?"

"I think so."

"You understand that the State will appoint a lawyer to you if you ask for one."

"Yes."

"Why haven't you asked for one?"

"Because I haven't done anything wrong."

The detective's face darkened. "The State will decide that, not you. Do you understand? The State will not give one cartwheeling fuck about you. When it decides to prosecute you, all the innocence in the world won't help you. At that point you are a piece of dumb meat in the jurisprudence system and the jurisprudence system, Sean, will take away your life."

The boy smoked and the detective watched him.

"What about your folks?" Luske said.

"What about them."

"Don't you want to talk to them?"

"No."

"Why not?"

"Does it matter?"

"Not to me," said the detective.

He was returned to the cell. He sat on the hard bunk and stared into space while a man in the adjacent cell who had not been there before snored and muttered. He lay down on the bunk, staring at the pocked and gray concrete ceiling and as he stared he saw in the edges of his vision other men moving restlessly about the cell, and he could smell them and he could hear them, yet when he moved his head to look there was nothing but the concrete and the bars and the buzzing yellow light throwing more bars across the floor.

36

The snow swarms about her, thick and white as in a snow globe, a white dust that dazzles the eye and promises a painless fall but that holds for the girl trying to keep on top of it nothing but the terror of the fall and the suffocating struggle of climbing out of it, of getting upright again while the Monkey comes on, sure-footed, step by step.

Childhood days of snow angels and snowmen were wasted. Days on the lake with Dudley were squandered opportunities—the two of them out on the frozen lake in very old snowshoes, clumsy wooden things with cane-bottom decking and tired leather bindings.

But these! These are like a sprinter's trackshoes; they move as she moves, their tails snapping up smartly with her heels. They do not wobble or stray and they are narrow enough that she doesn't have to hold her legs apart uncomfortably yet broad enough that they keep a good float on the snow, as the Monkey promised they would.

She's been watching him, listening to his breathing, and she knows that with a good lead she can outrun him. Outlast him. Not running, exactly, but moving fast enough in her careful striding to keep her lead and even to improve it. This snow is his snow too and he will not want to make a mistake either, will not want to risk a fall, the time and energy to climb out of it, but will count on her panic, on her inexperience and the weakness of her body, all her time of doing nothing in the shack, to bring her down. He was counting on it when he decided to buy the snowshoes and take her out. When he allowed her to go behind the spruce without him.

And now he would find out if he counted correctly.

HER BREATHS BURST WHITE before her and when she passes through them she hears No fall, no fall, and each successful footfall is rejoiced and praised, and the landing leg dares the trailing leg to do it even more cleanly, even more impressively, and she does not look back but only listens, the way she listens on the cinder track, and for a long time there's nothing but the no fall, no fall of her breaths and the quieter cadence of the snowshoes meeting the powder, and she knows that even if he sees her up ahead in the distance, a glimpse of her in her snowy globe, he will be too far away and there are too many trees between them.

For what?

For the pistol.

Sweat has come to her chest, her back, wetting her shirt under the jacket. When the temperature drops and she stops to rest as she knows she must, she'll be cold. There are stick matches in her pocket, with the headlamp—but no, what you need is darkness, and distance, and stamina, and no fall, no fall, no fall . . .

She attempts to unzip her jacket on the fly, trying to collect the metal pull in her gloved fingers, glancing down to locate it, and in that distracted instant the snowshoes collide with a sharp clack, her right foot fails to come forward, and she pitches downhill in the onset of a head dive. Yet even as her hands reach out for the snow, her legs react to keep her from it, pushing against the forward crampons so that she leaps altogether from the snow and draws the snowshoes forward in a kind of leapfrog, separating the frames in time to land downslope again with a deep whump. But in landing she pitches too far back and is falling again, backward now, all her weight on the tails of the shoes, arms pinwheeling, momentarily skiing down the slope before the tails begin to sink, and she slows, and her body swings forward and she takes a stumbling step, thighs howling, and is stable once more on the shoes and You did not fall, you did not fall.

She stands on the snow, sucking the cold into her lungs, her heart pounding. Reflexively she raises her wrist but the training watch is gone. It lies at the bottom of some gorge along with her phone.

She unzips her jacket and sweeps the cap from her head. Behind her, upslope, nothing but trees, falling snow, her tracks. Enormous repeating tracks unbroken, unmissable. Foxes, and maybe other hunted things, know somehow to backtrack.

But she does not understand how the instinct to backtrack can override the instinct to go forward, always forward, to keep as much distance as possible between you and the thing that wants you.

Water. You need to drink, Courtland. She takes a fast swallow and returns the bottle. Glances upslope once more and then lifts the left snowshoe against the dumb reluctance of her muscles, against a punishing gravity, and then the right, and she is moving again, going down again.

37

He awoke to a man's loud hacking and sat up in the buzzing yellow light. He put his fingers to an itch on his chest and was confused by the buttons on his T-shirt until he looked down and saw the denim jacket.

He stood before the bowl, then bent over the basin and splashed the cold water on his face and ran it through his hair and scooped it into his mouth and scooped more of it despite its taste of old pennies. When he stood again the man in the adjacent cell was watching him. The man lay on his bunk propped against the concrete wall, his white-stockinged feet crossed at the ankles and his arms crossed over his stomach. He was a skinny dark-skinned man with a skullcap of wiry silver hair. He stared at the boy and said with a graveled throat: "Is there something I can help you with?"

"What?"

"What?" said the man.

The boy held his gaze, the glassy, red-stained eyes.

"I said," said the man, "is there something I can help you with."

"I don't think so."

"Then why are you eyeballing me?"

"I wasn't."

"Hell you wasn't, motherfucker."

The boy went to stand by the bars of the door, as if doing so would compel the door to open and release him. You saw it in the movies and on TV but none of that gave you any idea of what it was like to be caged, to be kept against your will and against reason and against the truth for even one hour of your life.

The man in the other cell got to his feet and stepped to the bars separating the two cells and stood watching the boy, his wrists draped over the crossbar, his hands hung into the boy's space.

"Hey," he said.

The boy turned and the man showed his teeth, large and white, as if smiling. "I was just messin with you."

"Ah," said the boy.

"Just taking your temperature, my man."

The boy nodded and looked away.

"Hey," said the man.

The boy looked back at him.

"Name's Jonas." He held his hand out for shaking. Held it there.

The boy stepped over and took it. Cold and thin and raspy as the hand of an old woman. He said his name and stepped away again.

"What they got you in here for, Sean?"

"Nothing."

"Nothing?" The man watched him. Then he said: "What do they *think* you did, Sean?" and the boy said without turning, "They think I raped a girl."

The man gave a low, portentous whistle. "White?" he said.

The boy looked over.

"White pussy or dark?" The man laughed and said, "What am I saying? Pussy ain't got but one color, ain't that right, Sean?" He laughed until he dislodged something from his throat and turned and spat in the direction of the stool in his cell.

"Hey, Sean. Sean," he said. "I can see you ain't no rapist, my man, shit. I'm just messin with you."

The boy stared out into the corridor.

"You talk to your lawyer man, Sean? Or lady? Half the time it's a lady nowadays."

"No."

"What's this? You ain't talked to no lawyer?"

"No."

"Why not?"

"Nothing to talk about."

"What do you mean?"

"I mean there's nothing to talk about."

"'Cause you didn't do nothin."

The boy was silent.

The man peered at the boy's profile and said, "How old are you, Sean?"

"Eighteen."

"No you ain't."

The boy said nothing. The lights buzzed.

"Eighteen. God damn, I got a daughter oldern you." He hung his head. Then he raised it and said: "Boy, do you even know what kind of trouble you're in?"

"I got an idea."

"It must be a pretty poor idea or else you wouldn't be here chatting with me, you'd be talking to your motherfucking lawyer."

He turned away as if he'd finished with the boy. He walked to his bunk and stood staring down at it. Then he came back to the bars, his hands back into the boy's cell.

"Where your folks at?" he said. "They know you're in here? They know the shit you're in?"

"No."

"You ain't called them?"

"No."

"Why not?"

"It's not their problem."

"Not their problem."

"No, sir."

"You they son?"

"What?"

"Are you their son?"

"Yes."

"Blood son? Born to them some eighteen years ago? Born to them and to no others?"

"Yes."

"Then motherfucker you are nothing *but* their problem. And you are always gonna be and I'll tell you something else, Sean. The judge and the jury might set you loose in the world again but set you loose to what? Loose to what? You understand what I'm saying?"

The boy turned and looked into the man's bloodshot eyes.

"Boy, look at you. You a young man, but you already on a road that don't go but one way." His hands rolled in space and he drew the air into his flared nostrils in the manner of a man gathering in the aroma of some exquisite dish.

"Mm-hmm," he said, "I can *smell* it. I can smell it on you like shit on a dog's ass."

Luske was waiting in the same room, at his chair, hands on the file. He now wore his jacket and he had shaved and the room smelled of shaving cream and coffee. When the boy was seated and they were alone, Luske pushed one of the two large coffees across the table, the smell of it rich and darkly delicious. A smell of the normal, the free world. Luske rooted in his jacket pocket and reached across and unfisted onto the table a pile of packets and cream containers.

"I didn't know how you take it so I grabbed everything."

"I usually take it with a cigarette."

"I told you there's no smoking in this building," he said, then slid the boy's cigarettes and lighter across the table.

The boy thanked him and got one lit.

Luske watched him.

"Do you know what day this is, Sean?"

The boy thought and said, "Sunday?"

"No. This is your lucky day."

"It is?"

"You better believe it. We picked up the owner of that Ford truck, this boy named Valentine, and he fell to pieces like a china doll. I never saw a boy that size cry so hard. Did he cry like that when you hit him with that stick?"

"No, sir. He didn't say a word."

"Well, he's got plenty to say now."

"I don't suppose he said I wasn't any part of what they did to that girl."

"No, he didn't. He rubbed his big red ear and said you just wanted to get you some of that free pussy." The detective lifted his coffee and sipped it and set it down again.

"He's lying," said the boy, and Luske said, "Maybe. But who's to say?"

"I am."

Luske seemed to be waiting for him to say more. When he didn't, the detective said: "He did give us names, however. And this morning I gave the girl a photo array to look at and she picked them out, all four of them. And she'll testify."

The boy drew on his cigarette and exhaled the smoke.

"I guess my picture was in there too."

Luske nodded. "She didn't look twice at it."

"And I guess that doesn't count for much since she was passed out."

"No. But other things do."

"What other things?"

"The waitress's account. The fact that you were pulled over within sight of the hospital. That dead dog we found where you said it was. Although there was no blue tarp."

"The wind might've got it."

"Or somebody took it."

The boy tipped his ash and watched the flakes fall to the floor. "What about the gun?"

"Sold by a dealer outside Lincoln. Purchased by Reed Lester five days before you picked him up."

"And what about him?"

"Lester? Still at large."

The boy observed the tip of his cigarette. As if reading some message in the thin scroll of smoke.

"So now what?" he said.

"So now I'm compelled to release you, Sean. Your father's waiting at the front desk."

Some heavy thing like an ax swung in his chest. He stared at the detective.

"We called him about the truck, Sean."

"How much does he know?"

"I don't know. I just know he's here."

The boy said nothing. He stared at his cup of coffee.

"I'm compelled to let you go, Sean, but I'm not happy about it."

"You're not?"

"No."

"Why not?"

"Because I got a feeling about you, despite what it looks like you did for that girl. Maybe because of it. Maybe because of the way you did it. The fact that you didn't call the police and you didn't look for any help whatsoever but you just walked back there and whipped those two boys with the handle of a shit plunger. The fact that you had Reed Lester in your truck for whatever reason. There's something in the eyes of people who are capable of certain things, and I see it in yours."

The boy did not look away.

"I'd never do what they did," he said.

"I didn't say you would. But there's plenty more a man can do that will end just as bad. He might not go looking for it, and he won't think he wants it, but he won't do enough to avoid it either and it will find him. It will find him, Sean, sooner or later."

38

Some unknown hours later, unknown distance, she becomes aware of a change in her stride, in the nature of the effort it takes to keep moving forward, and in the sound of that effort.

She stops and looks around at the valley she's come into. A mountainous small amphitheater. The angle of the trees confirming what her body has been telling her, that she is no longer going down but is crossing snow that has massed evenly on level ground. Without the feeling of down in her legs, a stone of fear rolls from its place behind her heart. All she knows, all she counts on, is down. Without down, and without a thing in the sky to go by, with no horizon to lock onto, she might walk and walk until she arrived suddenly in the cold night at her own tracks.

To either side of the valley the banks of the mountainsides rise into the gray. Whatever lies ahead at the far end of the valley lies behind the veil of falling snow and the dusk, and there's no way to know but to go there. It seems very far away and I wanted to stop, says the girl in her head, the girl in the gymnasium, I wanted to dig into the snow like an animal, bury myself, listen to him pass over me in the dark. Sleep. Wait for the spring. But I didn't. I knew if I stopped, I died. I asked my legs to keep moving and somehow they did.

She goes down the center of the valley in the failing light and there is more valley here, though narrower, the wings of mountain drawing steadily closer, moving toward a fusion she can't see. She notices the shifting, scuttling snakes of powder at her feet and then notices the tailwind that drives them. It whips up and gains strength the nearer she comes to what she expects to be the convergence of the two mountainsides—the hard inevitable slamming that will crush out any passable trail and leave nothing but a steep rocky crotch, a dead end. It will almost be a relief.

The wind plays a cold note in the boughs of the trees, in the needles; the sound of absolute aloneness. She moves forward and the mountains move together and she is under the trees again, their laden arms dragging against her, the snow spinning up from the ground and littering the back side of her lenses with a distorting rash of crystals. She removes the glasses and stows them and works her way through the dark underworlds of the boughs, the wind rocking her on the snowshoes one way, and then the other, and finally forward, only forward, like the current of a river. It pushes her onward through a pair of low boughs crossed like swords, and stepping through these with her arms raised to protect her face she almost does not see, and nearly goes over, the edge of a sudden drop in the mountain.

Down.

She stands looking down the straight and treeless chute of what she knows is the bed of a stream, a dry wash like the one they went up that day in July. Not the same one; she knows she's a long way from that place. But this one brings her closer to that one. Or closer to some conjoining artery by which she can spill once more into life, into family. The wind howls in the gap behind her, the hysterical snow rushes past, and within that funneled gale she hears the droning of a motor. A large and laboring motor such as a semi in low gear, dragging its load up the mountain. A man sitting warm in the cab, country music in the speakers, his solitary headlights boring into the storm. The image is so stark in her mind that she can imagine nothing at the bottom of the dry wash but the paved and plowed road itself.

It's steeper than she expects and her instinct is to lean back, but when she does so the tails of the snowshoes slip and ski. She shifts her weight to the forward crampons but feels she will pitch headlong over the snowshoes. Finally she turns herself crosswise to the slope and continues her descent in a series of deliberated steps, like a newly walking child on a staircase.

It takes her five minutes, it takes her five hours. All she knows when she reaches the bottom of the dry wash is that she's reached the bottom and there is no road.

Here the stream when it runs spills into a broad wallow in the mountain where it either pools or else drains away in multiple smaller streams, none large enough to carve a recognizable path through the trees. No road. No truck. No wind here. No sound again but her own ragged wheezing, in which she hears some desperate note and says, Stop that, God damn you.

And there comes an answer—a whooping cry from the woods. From far up-slope. The far-traveling call of some great bird, announcing its greatness to the mountain, and it splits her open, this sound, and takes her heart in its claw.

She turns to look back up the dry wash and there's nothing but the white rising chute and the dark conical shapes that are its borders. Then, arriving out of the heights, there appears a dark falling thing on the snow. Black as night and gliding down. An immense bat of the woods. A black angel on skis.

She takes two wild steps away and on the third the snowshoe doesn't rise and she falls heavy and facedown into the snow. She kicks but the snowshoe won't move, it's snagged on something, gut-hooked like a fish. She tries to get her other foot up and around but can't drag it through the weight of the snow, the weight of herself. Worse than that: she sends the signals to the leg and nothing happens, no response from the muscles. She begins to dog-paddle in the snow, trying to get herself turned over. Though she can't see it she knows there's a tree nearby—the sensation of needles raking her face as she fell, the piney smell of them is still with her. If she can get a hand on a lower branch she can pull herself out.

She shoves at the empty snow, and twists, and manages to turn herself enough to see, over the edge of the depression, the last of his descent. Arms out and legs spread in flying rapture, riding the tails of his snowshoes. When he hits the level snow at the bottom, his crampons bite and he pitches forward, aloft, and lands in a sure-footed concussion of powder two feet from where she lies. In the darkness above her his teeth are brilliant.

He squats down and puts a hand on her snowshoe and all her flesh trembles. She stares up into the steeples of the trees, the falling snow, with weird absorption. The flakes in their slow, distinct tumblings—the brightness and clarity of each one of them. They fall without care or intent, will go on falling no matter what. Her mind knows this, and disbelieves it, and is sick with it.

You're snagged on something under the snow, he says, breathing hard. Didn't I warn you? He wrestles the snowshoe free and gives her foot a kind of rough toss. He looks down on her. This curious thing in the snow.

You know what? I don't believe you never snowshoed before. Nobody moves that good their first time. Damn. I about gave up. I puked up eggs and bacon three hours ago.

Christmas Day, she remembers then. In two months she would be twenty.

He shrugs off his pack and brings out his water bottle. Look at this—frozen solid! Doesn't take long. He scoops a gloveful of snow and pushes it into his mouth. Works it around. Swallows. He glances about the dark woods.

You've really done it now, haven't you? We're way the heck out here now. No tent. Too far and too dark and too cold to walk back tonight. There isn't anything we can do but get under the snow and try to keep each other from freezing to death.

He stares at her and she looks beyond him. The black-and-white patterns of the trees. The careless ghostly flakes. You got any ideas how we do that? he says, and she shakes her head.

I do. Now give me your hand and let's get you on your feet. I want to see what all you got in your pockets.

No, she says.

What's that?

No.

Don't tell me no, kiddo. He grabs her by the jacket and lifts her into a twisted, half-sitting position and holds her there—and then lets go, and she falls onto her side again. He stands and reaches down and takes her jacket in both fists and hauls the dead weight of her up and onto her back, where she sinks once more into the snow. He stands over her, bright clouds like fury erupting from his lungs.

I could use a little cooperation here, he says, and a small voice in the dark says: Please. I just want to go home.

What did you say?

Please, says the voice.

He looks into the black sky and fills his lungs and wails. There's no other word for it. The sound tears away into the night and stops the small hearts of whatever small things hear it.

He walks straddle-legged over her and drops to his knees, his weight landing squarely on her hips and sinking her more deeply into the snow. He takes glovetips in his teeth and pulls one glove off and tugs off the other and seizes the zipper-pull at her throat and jerks it down, opening her chest to the cold.

Kiddo, he says. Don't you understand you are home?

His hands are up inside her jacket. They find the water bottle and slip it into his own jacket, then they pull up her flannel shirt and push the dingy sports bra roughly from her breasts. Steam lifts palely from her pale skin, rising and moving off like some banished layer of herself. He is talking but she isn't hearing him, she is deep in the snow and within the snow is the gymnasium, and Allison Chow is on her left and Colby Wilson is on her right, and they are sitting in the wooden bleachers listening to the girl who's come to speak to them, to tell them this story, and their eyes are wide as they listen, and their hearts are beating. But although they know that what the girl is saying is something that could happen to them, it hasn't, not yet. It has happened to her, to this girl standing before them. To her, not them. And for that they love her, as fiercely as they love each other.

Part III

39

When Sean appeared suddenly from the back of the station, emerging without escort through a steel door, his hair in oily disarray and a blond whiskering on his jaw—an older boy by far looking out from his blue eyes—Grant stood and rubbed his own jaw in an effort to keep the surging of his heart from reaching his own face. He put his hands in his pockets to keep them from reaching out and taking the boy into his arms.

Sean came to him, and they stood looking at each other.

"You didn't have to come."

"Do you think I could not have come?"

Sean sat on the hard bench and reached into the plastic bag he was carrying. After a moment Grant sat down too and watched his son feed the laces back into his boots, his belt back into the loops of his jeans.

They were driven to the impound lot in the backseat of a cruiser, retracing the route the boy had taken to the station the night before, down the same frontage road where the Paradise Lounge still sat, squat and ugly and meaningless in the gray cold morning. Though the snow had stopped only hours before, already a layer of grit seemed to have settled over everything. The officer dropped them at the lot another mile down the road and wished them a good one and then drove off with his radio squawking.

They reclaimed the key and crossed the lot toward the blue Chevy Grant had not set eyes on, like the boy, in more than a year.

"I changed the oil every three thousand," the boy said. "Rotated the tires."

Grant stripped a garish orange decal from the windshield and then reached into the truckbed and put his hand on the damaged tire. Finding the silver head of the nail with his thumb, he stood a moment touching it, as if he might divine from it all that had happened because of it.

Behind him, the boy looked at the flat and wanted only to sleep and to sleep.

They drove to a motel near the highway and Grant checked them into a single room with two large beds. He thought Sean would want to shower, he suggested as much, but instead the boy sat on the nearest bed, pulled off his boots, fell into the pillows, and was asleep. Grant drew the curtains and peeled the duvet from the other bed and settled it over his son, then sat down on the mattress across from the boy. He sat in the dimmed room studying the shape of the boy under the blanket. Eighteen now, he was. The age she had been.

After a while he wrote a note and placed it close to Sean, then retrieved it and went out the door to stand on the narrow concrete balcony. He seemed very far away from the mountains and the ranch and the people he had come to know: Emmet and his sons, Maria and her daughter. Farther yet from Wisconsin and Angela and the house where they'd raised their children; his onetime life.

He inhaled the cold air with its highway tang of diesel, and lit a cigarette. He looked west into the wind until his vision blurred, and then he turned to the east, to the city's low industrial horizon under the low pewter sky. Semi after semi droning down the highway toward the sky.

WHEN HE RETURNED, THE sun was low in the west behind the clouds and the room was nearly dark. The duvet had been thrown aside, and at the sight of the empty bed his heart dropped for a disbelieving instant before he saw that the bathroom door was shut, before he saw the seam of light at the floor and heard the exhaust fan groaning away on the other side.

He set down the grocery bag and opened the curtains and stood looking out at the highway in the gray dusk until the bathroom door opened and his son switched off the fan and stepped out. He wore a blue T-shirt and the same weary pair of jeans. The room filled with the scents of soap and shaving cream.

"I didn't think you'd wake up till tomorrow," Grant said.

The boy looked at him but saw only his dark shape before the window. He picked up his duffel and set it on the bed. "I don't like motel rooms," he said, fitting his things back into the duffel.

"I gather that from the inside of that truck. Have you been sleeping in there this whole time?"

"No. I slept out sometimes. Sometimes people put me up."

"If you'd asked, I would've sent you money. Or a credit card."

The boy zipped up his duffel, then stood and raked his damp bangs back with his fingers.

"I bought some orange juice," Grant said. "Cokes. A couple of sandwiches."

The boy got into his jacket. "Can we just go?"

The Chevy was still warm and Grant fit the key in the ignition but did not turn it, and they both got a cigarette lit and sat with the windows half down, saying nothing, until the boy said without looking: "You want me to drive?"

"No, I'll drive."

The boy flicked his ash. "You were gone a while."

Grant looked over but the boy would not meet his glance.

"I was looking for a place to get that tire fixed," he said. "But it's Sunday. Everything's closed." He took hold of the key, then let it go again.

"Sean."

"What."

"Talk to me. We have to talk."

"What about?"

"Sean."

The boy inhaled, blew sharply at the window. "What am I supposed to say?"

"I don't know."

"I don't either."

They both looked to the west, where the dropping sun flared suddenly between the clouds and the horizon like the eye of a great bird cracking open, round and blazing.

"I only tried to help her."

"I know you did, Sean."

"How?"

"How what?"

"How do you know?"

"Because I know you. Because you're my son."

"Those aren't the same thing."

"They are to me."

The boy sat without moving. Grant crushed his cigarette in the ashtray. After a while Sean did the same.

"So now what?" he said.

"What do you mean?"

"Are you going back to the airport, or what?"

"I don't know. Where are you going?"

He didn't answer.

"Where were you going?" Grant said. "Were you going home?"

"What home?"

"Wisconsin."

The boy was silent.

Grant said: "She's home from the hospital, did you know that? She's back at Grace's."

"I know. I talked to her."

"When?"

"Just after she got out."

"It wasn't prison, Sean. She was there voluntarily."

"I know."

"She's doing much better. She's talking about teaching again."

The boy nodded. "That's good."

Grant drew his fingertips along the dash, looked at them, rubbed the red dust with his thumb. "Do you want to go there now? We could put you on a plane. Or—" He didn't finish.

"Or what?"

"Or we could drive there together. If you wanted to."

The boy glanced at him, and turned back to the sun. A tepid orange disk sitting exactly on the edge of the world as if it could go no further. It didn't seem possible that the whole western half of the country lay before it and not beyond it. The mountains, the deserts. The wide plate of the sea, all waiting for their own sundowns.

Without turning he said, "We can't do that."

"Can't do what?"

"We can't leave her there."

Grant said nothing. In his chest were two hearts, two thudding fists. One of these hearts beat with the memories of his daughter, and the other beat with the sight of his son before him. Each the more furiously in the presence of the other.

He put the Chevy in gear and pulled out of the lot. He found the on ramp and accelerated up it and merged into the westbound traffic, into the lanes of cars and trucks and semis all racing toward the horizon as if they meant to catch it, as if they might go flying over it as if over a rise in the road, thereby forcing the sun back up into the sky, again and again, keeping it indefinitely aloft, the day indefinitely alive.

40

They drove the long midwestern state again, end to end, exactly as they'd driven it that July long ago when there had been four of them and everything, even Nebraska, had been worth looking at, and then had driven it again when Grant and the boy returned in the two trucks. Now it was just the two of them once more, in the single truck, and they drove at night and there was nothing to see but the same length of highway, the same median, and the same bleak radius of snow-blown nothing that came along with them and around them like a moving island they could not escape. Just outside of North Platte Grant stopped for gas and to use the restroom, and when he came back out Sean was still asleep, slumped against the door, against the roll of sleeping bag.

Later the boy sat up and squinted into the oncoming lights and asked where they were, and Grant said they were just inside Colorado, and did he want to stop for dinner? Sean said Okay and they took the next exit, but when the waitress came to the counter in the overlit diner he set aside the menu and ordered only coffee.

"That's all?" said the waitress.

"Yes, please."

"How about a little plate of hot beef sandwich? Folks drive from all over for the hot beef sandwich. I've got this old couple drives all the way from Sterling for it. Though I guess I would too if I lived in Sterling. And was old," she slyly added.

Grant told her that they themselves had driven from Omaha and the waitress cried, *"Omaha!"* as if announcing some appalling discovery on the floor. "What on earth were you doing in *Omaha?"*

The boy looked to the window, which held only the reflection of the diner: himself and his father sitting there.

Grant handed the waitress the menu and said they'd just been passing through on their way to the hot beef sandwich.

When she was gone he said, "I thought you were hungry."

"I never said I was hungry."

"I asked if you wanted to eat and you said yes."

"You asked if I wanted to stop for dinner. I figured you were hungry so I said okay."

"When was the last time you ate?"

"I don't know. Why?"

"What do you mean why?"

"What's the difference?"

He stared at his son, his thin face, and for a moment he could have been just some young man in the diner, just off the road like himself.

The waitress returned and filled their coffee mugs and went away again.

"When I was fat everybody tried to starve me. Now they want to shove food in me I don't even want."

"You were never fat," Grant said, and the boy looked at him. "You just had some vertical compensating to do."

They got back on the highway and the boy drove while Grant slept. The night was clear and there was little traffic and he tracked a three-quarter moon as it overtook him on the left, cold and steady. In time this same moon pulled from the black foreground a luminous row of teeth, and he watched in bleary confusion before he understood what he was seeing, which was the first snowy reef of peaks, yet hours away, baring itself to the plains.

Grant raised his head to see the mountains rising in the night, and they both found their cigarettes and sat waiting for the knob in the dash to pop. They gapped their windows and smoked while the cold night spooled in and whistled around them like a mad spirit. The boy thought of the jail cell, the hard cold stink of that place, and he saw the man from the adjacent cell like a projection on the windshield: his bloodshot eyes, his disembodied hands hung in space. *I can see you ain't no rapist, my man.*

He blew smoke and tapped his ash in the gap.

"Do you think we'll ever feel normal again?" he said.

"I don't know. What's normal?"

"I don't know," said the boy, watching the road, the mountains. "Not this."

A few miles on, Grant put out his cigarette and powered up his window and the boy did the same and the whistling stopped and the cab grew warm again. Don't forget about the airport, Grant said, and the boy said he didn't forget, and two miles later they took the exit for it, and they found the green Chevy in the sea of cars, and after that they drove the two trucks in tandem toward the lighted city.

41

The boy kicked off his boots and fell back onto the little bed and watched as a multitude of near-invisible bodies rose into the space above him. Dense nebulae coalescing into shapely whorls like the formation of stardust into stars and planets and moons. Himself rising bodilessly and traveling through systems of light and color and mass that he alone had ever seen and that were his alone to name. But in the next moment, or what seemed like the next moment, there was a sound, and the alien worlds dispersed as if in fright and he opened his eyes and listened, and after another moment it came again, a kind of cry. A single windy note, short and uncertain. It came at slow intervals and he thought it must be his father in the bedroom across the hall fashioning some new kind of snore in his nose. But then he realized it wasn't coming from across the hall but from his own room, and he sat up and listened, and then he leaned and looked under the bed, finding only dust and the old floorboards. The sound, louder and nearer, came again while he was bent over looking. After a minute he pulled on his boots and trod quietly down the hall and out onto the porch into the cold dawn.

He stood on the porch listening, his breath smoking. Then he went down the steps and got down on his good knee to look under the porch. Nothing there but packed dirt and a kind of smooth wallow, roughly lined by the remains of a once-red blanket. He dropped to all fours in the snow and crawled just under the porch to peer into the recesses of the crawl space, and when he was under there, waiting for his eyes to adjust, boots clopped overhead on the floorboards, the storm door hinges croaked, and boots came clopping down the steps.

"Did we bust a pipe?" His father stood stooped in the light behind him, hands on knees, face upended.

"No. The dog's under here."

"She's under there?"

"I'm looking at her."

"What's she doing?"

"Looking at me."

"Why doesn't she come out?"

"I don't know." He called the old Labrador by name and told her to come on out of there. She made her whimpering sound and the boy said, "I think she's hurt."

Grant came up beside him on hands and knees. "Maybe it's her hips." He gestured and called to the dog and she scrabbled forward a few inches on her forepaws and stopped and whimpered. Grant watched her. He surveyed the crawl space and the dirt and said with his eyes on the dog, "Think you can crawl back there?"

They got the dog out from under the house and arranged her gently in the cab of the blue Chevy, and doing so the boy remembered the girl bleeding in the truck, and in his exhaustion he thought that that must have been something he dreamed.

They climbed in on either side of the dog and Grant drove to the county road and turned west, away from town, and a mile later he parked in front of a white two-story farmhouse, pink in the dawn, and after a moment a stately white-haired woman appeared on the screened porch and called down, "Is that you, Grant Courtland?" and Grant called back, "I'm afraid so, Evelyn."

"I see you got your truck back."

"Yes, ma'am."

"Who's that with you?"

"He came with the truck."

"Don't say? How are you, Sean?"

"I'm fine, Mrs. Struthers. How are you?"

Her head tilted back and she peered down at him from the height of the porch, the height of herself. "Mrs. Struthers is what my students call me. Were you ever my student?"

"No, ma'am."

"I thought not. In that case call me Evelyn." She held the door wider and gestured them up. "Come on, come up out of the cold and let me get some coffee in you."

When the old man came down, Grant said, "I'm sorry about this, Dale, I know you're retired but I didn't know where else to go."

"Oh, stuff," said Evelyn, sweeping in behind her husband and going to the coffee pot. "Neighbors are neighbors."

Struthers regarded the back of her head, then turned to Grant and the boy and jerked his thumb at her, as if to say there was nothing more to say nor better way to say it. She turned and fitted a mug of coffee into his waiting hand and so armed he said: "All right then. Let's see what you got."

Grant pulled the truck around and parked before a small red outbuilding, and he and the boy carried the dog inside and settled her onto the stainless-steel table. The boy cupped his hands and blew into them and the old vet said, "I'm sorry about the cold. I don't hardly heat anything but the house anymore, and hardly that, cost of gas."

Cold as it was the air smelled richly of kennel and ammonia and pine.

The old man set down his coffee and reached into the pocket of his white coat and put something under the dog's nose and in one chomping instant the offering was gone. He placed his hands on her, playing them slowly through her fur, watching her eyes, frowning, pausing, moving on again and waiting for his hands and the dog's eyes to tell him something. He slipped one hand underneath her and she gave a yip and swung as if to bite his wrist but only licked at it furiously. He reached into his pocket again and again she took the treat and licked her chops and watched his hand.

"Way under the house, you say."

"About as far as you could get," Grant said. "Had to send skinny under there to pull her out."

The three of them looked at the dog. The dog watched the vet.

He sipped from his coffee and set it down again. "She's got at least two cracked ribs under there. One is just about broke but not quite. I'd guess a horse kick right off. But of all the horse-kicked dogs I ever saw I never saw one got itself kicked from underneath like this. I don't know what kind of horse could pull that off, do you?"

Grant held the old man's eyes. Then both turned again to the dog, as if she might put an end to speculation with her testimony. Grant stood in silence and the boy watched him and watching him understood that something had been discussed between the two men that though he'd been right here, was not available to him—as if he'd dozed on his feet, or blacked out.

"Can you do anything?" Grant said.

"How do you mean?"

"For the ribs."

"There's not a whole lot I can do for cracked ribs but wrap them up. And she's old."

"Right," said Grant. "Meaning?"

"Meaning she'll be a long time healing, if at all. And she'll be in pain."

Grant nodded. "Is there something for that? For the pain?"

"Sure, sure," said the vet. "But."

Grant and the boy and the dog waited. Struthers took his clean-shaven jaw in his hand and worked it over. "I'm not sure she ought to be going back there, Grant, is the thing," he said.

"No," Grant said.

"I mean it ain't my business . . ."

"No, I think you're right."

"And I can't keep her here."

"I wouldn't ask you to, Dale."

"I'm just not set up for it anymore. And Evie can't have an animal in the house for her allergies, never could, all these years. The Lord said no children and then he said no pets either, all you get woman is this old man comes in end of the day smelling of horse and dog and everything else."

"Seems to me she's had plenty of kids, Dale," said Grant. "Hundreds of them."

Struthers didn't seem to hear this, but then he looked up from under his silver eyebrows and said, "Thirteen hundred and twelve."

Grant watched him.

"She's got ever last grade book going back to her very first class, year we were married. Takes them out time to time. Goes through them one by one, like picture albums."

"Now what," said the boy.

"Now we go see a friend."

They were in the truck again, driving back toward town. The dog in her trussings nested between them, blinking drowsily as the painkiller found its way into her blood. The sun climbing the pines, washing the snowy boughs in a restless glitter. They came around a turn and Grant brought the Chevy to a stop behind a school bus. Flushed little faces in the rear window, too listless at that hour even to stick out their tongues.

The boy got a cigarette to his lips and depressed the lighter knob.

"Give me one of those," Grant said. "I'm out."

The lighter popped and they took turns with it.

"Are you gonna tell me what's going on?" said the boy.

"What do you mean?"

"You know what I mean."

Grant shook his head. "Can't tell you what I don't know."

"Well, what do you think then?"

"What do I think?" Grant flicked his ash. A young girl and a younger boy came out of a small clapboard house and made their way to the bus. The bus door folded open and the little boy stood stomping some last-second imperative into the snow until the girl nudged him and he hauled himself aboard and she climbed up after him. The door rattled shut and the stop sign clapped to and the bus rumbled on, towing the Chevy behind at a distance.

Grant said: "I'm wondering if Billy didn't do that to her."

"Billy."

"Emmet's son. That's his car at the house. The El Camino."

The boy looked at the dog. He watched the rear of the bus.

"Why would he do that?"

Grant drew on his cigarette. "I'm not saying he did."

They were silent. The little faces at the back of the bus watched them. The boy took a last drag on his cigarette and crushed it in the tray.

"Yes you are."

They followed the bus through town and for another mile beyond that before Grant turned into the woods down a narrow drive where the snow lay brilliant and trackless between the pines, a small one-story house at the end of the drive, cornflower blue with darker blue shutters and a bloodred door. Grant made a space for the Chevy on what might have been the lawn so as not to block either of the Subaru wagons parked before the house, and when he opened his door the dog forgot about her injury and tried to stand and he placed his hand on her skull and said, "You stay here. Both of you."

He shut the door and the dog began to wheeze in distress for what she couldn't see, and the boy spoke to her. "He's walking up to the house. He's knocking on the door. Someone's at the window. The door opens. It's a woman. Dark curly hair. It's the woman from the diner, that waitress, I forget her name. She looks out and waves . . . I wave back. He steps inside and the door closes. Maria is her name. Maria Valente."

The red door opened again and Grant returned to the Chevy and got the dog halfway into his arms and the boy came around to collect the remaining half, and when they were free of the truck Grant said to put her down but hold her up, and the dog looked around in confusion until he told her to do her business, at which signal and without the appearance of another thought she lowered her haunches and released a long hissing stream into the snow.

They carried her into the house and placed her on the bed of blankets Maria had prepared on the tiled entrance, and Maria squatted to stroke her head. Then she stood again and all three looked down at the dog. They were still standing there when the girl arrived from somewhere in the house, sock-footed and carrying a large backpack in one hand and a cell phone in the other. With the barest of glances at the two men she dropped the pack and sat on her heels before the bandaged dog and began to pet her.

"What happened to her?"

The dog sniffed at the girl's bare knee. Licked it.

"We're not sure," Grant said. "She might've got herself kicked."

"By what?" She looked up—she looked from Grant to the boy, and back. She seemed about to say something else but didn't say it. She turned to the dog again, stroking her ears.

"Poor Lola," said the girl, "poor Lo."

The boy looked at his father, then at the girl again. "You know this dog?"

She glanced up, her brow furrowed, as though there must be something wrong with him. "Of course I know her."

"She goes over there some Saturdays," Maria explained. "To help with those horses."

They were all silent but the girl, who went on soothing the dog with her hands and her voice.

Grant said he'd come by later with food for the dog and to take her out, and Maria handed him the key and he slipped it into his pocket. He said he'd find someone who could take the dog in for a longer time but she told him not to worry about that, that they would see how this went, and the girl said with finality, "We'll take care of her."

Maria went to the kitchen to find a water bowl, and the girl stood and with a tug at her skirt turned and put her dark eyes on the boy. "I'm Carmen."

"I know." He said his name and the girl said, "I know. I just didn't think you knew mine."

"You were in my history class," he said.

"Briefly," she said. "A brief history."

At their feet the dog showed her old fangs in a great yawn.

The girl checked her phone, then turned and opened a closet door and withdrew a red woolen jacket and got into it. She dipped her white-socked feet into suede boots of a plush, primitive style, and bent once more to rub the dog's ears. She hoisted the pack from the floor and called, "I'm outta here, Mom," and Maria called back, "Okay, *tesoro*. Be careful on the snow, I love you."

"Love you too."

She gave Grant and the boy her smile, and then she stepped around the dog and opened the red door and for a bright instant as the morning sun found her she blazed in a red pirouette and was gone.

WHEN HE AWOKE AGAIN the room was sun-swamped and hot and he lay staring at the large yellow blister directly overhead. Empty smooth eggshell of plaster shaped by a leakage long since moved on to some other course or else hunted down and stopped at its source. He listened for the sound again, the dog or the ghost of the dog restored to her foxhole beneath the floorboards. But when the sound came again it came distinctly through the pine door. Through the two pine doors shut to each other across the narrow hall.

He got up and opened one door, waited, and carefully opened the other.

This room on the western side would not see daylight until the afternoon and his father lay on the bed in the chill gloom, facing him. The blanket drawn over his ribs but his shoulder and arm exposed, bare and white, the arm hooked over a pillow as a child holds a stuffed animal. As a man holds a wife. When he spoke he seemed to be speaking to the boy, his voice as plain and clear as if he were asking the time. But his eyes, or the eye that was visible, was shut. The face slack.

"What?" said the boy.

"Where is she," said the sleeping man.

"Where's who?" He took a step forward and the cold floor cracked and he stood still.

"Where is she," said his father, and he looked more closely. The curvature of eyelid trembling and rolling with the restless ball it held.

He drew the blanket up over the bare shoulder.

"She's fine," he said. "She's safe."

He got into his jeans and T-shirt and stepped onto the porch barefooted and stood where there was no snow and lit the cigarette and sucked in the smoke and leaned against the post and blew the smoke out. Almost at once, across the way, an answering white cloud sallied from the porch of the house. He brought his cigarette to his lips and squinted. The old man would sit there in his rocker in the mornings with his hands clamped around a smoking mug. But the old man did not have brown hair hooked behind his ears and he did not leave the house T-shirted and barefooted even on the warmest of days and he did not smoke.

The two smokers regarded each other across the way. They took another drag each, exhaled, and as the smoke tattered away in the cold the young man on the far porch raised his cigarette in a mannered way—princely, pontifical—and lowered it again.

The boy raised his in answer.

42

Spring comes, even there. Or perhaps false spring.

Snowmelt dripping from the shedroof and ringing faintly on the floors of tiny wells in the snow, frail airholes to the earth. Note upon hollow note. The shingled roof, bared to the sun, flexes and cracks like something coming awake. When she puts her nose to the peephole in the wood over the window, she can smell the heated sap of the pines beyond the glass and she aches with the feeling of spring after the long Wisconsin winter. The cinder track rising through the snow like a hot, primordial ring. She listens for the sound of water running, of snowmelt finding its way in thin cascadings, meeting, gaining mass and speed, churning for the far valleys, for the great rivers to the sea. But which sea?

He is staying away longer. Days, sometimes. The food runs out. The wood runs out. She hoards her water. In the dull little mirror is the shape of her skull. No one is there.

SHE KEEPS AT HER *work, her diminished body pitched against the length of chain, milling halfway around and then back again, listening to what the links are telling her. On the surface of the steel plate, spanning the two thick welds of the ringbolt, lays a tiny field of dull glitter, winking and changing visibly every few passes with the addition of some new and sizable granule of steel or rust. The largest of them fall at the moment when the mated crooks of the bottom link and the ringbolt grind and fight and give way in a sudden twangy jump that makes her heart jump too with the momentary loss of resistance and the feeling, as on that long ago swing set, that the link has broken and she is about to go sailing, free, into space. Again and again, that deception.*

After one such twang so profound she must take a hop for balance, she stands in dismay when she finds the chain still taut, still unbroken at the ringbolt. Something breaks within her then and she begins to haul wildly at the chain, and it's her own noise, she understands later, the torrent of curses upon the tormented chain, that causes her to miss the sound of footsteps outside in the crusted snow.

The first she hears of him is his voice.

Hello? he calls, freezing her.

She drops the chain. Her heart slamming.

It comes again: Hello? Someone in there?

It's not him. It's some other man. Close, and not close. Well back from the door. Keeping his distance, according to some law of mountain etiquette. Or fear at what he heard, her wild thrashing.

Her throat constricts, her jaw opens, and a voice she does not know calls out, Hello? Is someone out there?

Hello, the man calls. I saw the smoke. I thought it might be a fire.

She takes a step toward the door and her right leg halts painfully in midstride and she looks back in confusion at the length of chain on the floor. The leather-wrapped cuff at her ankle, the big padlock with the word Master *at its base. Her own naked foot, filthy and alien.*

She turns back to the door. Are you the police?

He doesn't answer. Then: Who are you? And she knows he is just a man. Not the police. No gun. No dogs. No walkie-talkie. No helicopter on its way. No father no mother no brother.

Who are you? he says again. Are you all right?

She puts a hand to her throat and feels the words in her fingers as they come up, as she says her own name for the first time in so long. Her family is looking for her, she says. The police are looking for her. A man has been keeping her here, please help.

The snow crunches and the man is approaching.

All right, he says, all right. Take it easy. Did you say Caitlin? Close now. On the other side of the door. She hears the padlock shift. Hears him tug on it. Caitlin? he says.

Yes?

Where is he?

I don't know. He left me.

How long ago?

She shakes her head. Two days? She swallows down her climbing heart. Please help me. She can hear him breathing hard in the thin air. There's an ax somewhere, she says. Do you see it?

He takes a step back from the door. No.

It's out there, she says. She can see it so clearly. I hear him chopping all the time. The man takes a few steps away, then comes back.

Is there another way in? A window? he says, and she says, On the other side, but it's locked too, and his footsteps move away from the door and grow faint as he makes his way around the shack.

She drags the chain across the floor and steps onto the cot and puts her eye to the small burning hole in the window board, stopping the coin of light.

Incredibly, he is already there—exactly there. Dark shape of him in the white nimbus of vision. Dead-centered like a figure posed in a lens not yet focused. There he stands before her, and yet the sound of his footsteps reach her through the wall to her left. He is standing still and he is walking around the shack, both. She blinks in the tearful light and the figure in the peephole clarifies, taking its true form, and a blade comes into her chest to halve her heart like an apple.

The footsteps progress around the corner and grow louder, nearer, and then they halt, short of the window, short of what she can see of the world, and she hears the man say Jesus. He makes a sound like a kind of laugh. Where'd you come from, buddy?

Same place as you, I reckon. The Monkey smiles and his face begins to turn toward the window and she drops like loose bones to the cot.

I saw the smoke, the Monkey says. Thought there was a fire.

So did I, says the man. But there's somebody in there. He takes two steps and stops. There's a girl inside.

Slumped against the wall, knees hauled to her chest, she hears them as though they stand in a tunnel, voices tubing along the stone walls toward the opening.

I know, I heard, the Monkey says. Heard her say a man's been keeping her up here.

These words roll and die in the tunnel.

You wouldn't be that man, would you? says the Monkey.

Hell no, says the man. And nothing else.

They are silent, the world silent, until a crack detonates in the roof timbers, relaying in the wall where her shoulder touches it and jolting down through her.

Pretty funny the two of us arriving at the same time, says the Monkey, and the man says, I saw the smoke.

You said that. The Monkey sniffs. You don't look like a ranger.

I'm not.

You're not?

No.

What are you then?

What am I? Hell, I'm just a hiker.

A hiker. The Monkey shifts somehow in his jacket. You're a ways off the trail, aren't you?

Like I said, I saw the smoke.

The Monkey shifts again. You saw that?

I smelled it first.

Ah.

They are silent. Water drips from the roof and rings in its wells.

What about you? the hiker says.

What about me?

What brings you up here?

I'm a volunteer ranger.

A volunteer ranger. What's that mean?

It means I've got a cabin down the mountain I don't want burning up.

The hiker says nothing. Then he says, Hadn't we better see about getting her out of there? She might be hurt. Are you hurt in there? he calls.

Run, damn you, she whispers. Get away. Get down the mountain.

She sounded fit enough a second ago, says the hiker. There's a padlock on the door, but she said there's an ax out here somewhere.

I heard that. Is that it over there?

Where?

Behind you. Under that tree. Where that wood is.

The hiker changes his footing in the snow, is still, and then moves quickly in the direction he came. Okay, he calls. It's an ax. I found the ax, he calls to her. There's another man out here. He's a volunteer ranger. We're gonna come around and knock the padlock off the door, Caitlin.

He is walking again and she tracks his footfalls, and the Monkey's, as they circle the shack, and soon the hiker arrives once more at the front door.

Don't, she breathes. Don't, don't . . .

Don't do it like that, says the Monkey. Use the poll.

The what?

The blunt end.

Why?

Cause you'll ruin the edge.

Who gives a damn if I ruin the edge?

There is silence. Then the hiker says Wait and through the door comes a sound she knows, a sharp festive pop, like a single firecracker. Hardly loud enough to startle a bird yet sudden and sharp enough to cleave open a mountain and send it shearing down itself. Immediately the door shudders in its jamb, as if he has decided to throw his weight at it, but feebly, and then in defeat has slid slowly down to the snow.

I do, says the Monkey.

She hears him click open the pistol. Eject the casing. Snap the pistol shut again. Something scuffs at the outside of the door, down low, near the floor. Like an old dog scratching to be let in. There is a second pop and the scuffing stops.

SHE IS ON THE cot as before, unmoved, legs drawn up in the same tight ball of herself, when she hears him returning. His footsteps, the sled runners, moving more easily through the snow. She remembers the high snowy ledge, *the tumbling emptiness beyond, but he has not been gone long enough for that, has stashed the body someplace nearby. As he unlocks the padlock the timbers crack overhead and her legs spasm, kicking as they do in dreams of running, and her mind plays her a scene in which the last thing she sees and feels in life is the cold, blued face of the only other human being in all this time who knew where she was, who heard her voice. A stranger with whom she will now lie through however many years, centuries, nothing to do but hold each other until they're found, rags of cloth and mummy's flesh inseparable, histories inseparable, locked in each other's bones. More in love by the look of them than any man and wife of the living world.*

43

They rose together for coffee and cold cereal and they worked through the mornings at chores, together and separate, and then they sat with Emmet for lunch, the boy quietly chewing and Emmet telling his stories as before and never asking the boy where he'd gone or what he'd done in all that time away, and Emmet's son Billy passing through these scenes like a character in a play, commenting in merry disdain and moving on, never stopping, always on his way to more promising scenes, more promising company.

At the waitress's house they watched from the door stoop as the dog stepped gingerly through the snow, finding the places that suited her, the two of them standing in a draft of warmth and scent from inside the little house until the door was shut again and locked. Later they rang the bell over the cafe door and Maria smiled to see them.

Saturday found Sean up with the dawn to shower and shave, to brew the coffee and carry a cup of it out onto the porch. Cold silence and no movement in the treetops along the ridgelines and not a trace of cloud in the sky. Second week of March and no change anywhere, no sign of winter's end. Across the way sat the El Camino, black and gleaming.

The mares nickered and blew at his approach and he stepped to the stall with an apple rolling in his palm.

He was leading the mare named Belle from her stall when the old man arrived at the bay door with his cup of coffee, dragging the red cap from his head as if entering a church.

"You thinking about riding?" he said, and the boy said that he was. He hitched the mare to the post and went back for the other while Emmet scooped oats into the galvanized pails fixed to either side of the post. When both mares were hitched and feeding, the boy returned to the stalls and began raking the soiled straw into a heap.

Emmet stood patting the near mare's neck. With his eyes on the horse, he said: "You look a might fussed up for such work."

The boy took up the pitchfork and said, "No more fussed than usual."

Emmet patted the mare's neck. "You might have yourself some company, you're not careful."

"I might?"

"Might." He sipped his coffee. "Since you been gone there's a gal been coming over Saturdays and helping with the horses."

"That's what I hear."

"She don't come every Saturday, of course. Sometimes she gets busy with other stuff. Fact is, I'm surprised she comes a'tall, lately." He coughed and turned his face and spat, and toed a little mound of dirt over the spot. "She keeps on coming when she feels like coming, though. Calls me up when she don't."

The boy pitched the last of the straw into the wheelbarrow and rolled it out into the sunlight and came back in and took up the curry brush and began brushing the mare named Nellie.

"She ain't called today," Emmet said. "The gal. Why I said that about you maybe having some company."

The boy said he'd figured as much.

"Did you figure you might save that curry work till after, when they'll need it?"

The boy said he had nothing better to do and went on brushing.

Emmet stood watching him. Then he said, "That leg pain you much?"

"What leg?"

"What leg he says." He sipped at his coffee. He scratched at the scar on his throat. "I ever tell you about my old granddad who had that same hitch in his step?"

"No, sir. How'd he get it?"

"Asked him that very thing, one time. Asked him, 'Granddad, how came you to have that hitch in your step?' and he looked down on me with a look to make the clocks run backwards and said, 'Boy, I'm gonna tell you this just this one time 'cause I know you don't know no better, but you'd best learn that a whelp never asks a growed man any such questions.' Then he told me how he'd had three brothers, each one hardly older than the next and him the youngest. Well, the Great War come along and off went the eldest named John Junior, eighteen years of age and not over there two weeks before he got blowed in half. A month later the second brother named James snuck off in the night and never made it to the continent but got torpedoed by a U-boat in the North Sea. Two weeks went by before the third brother named Thomas slipped over there and was never seen nor heard from again."

Emmet paused for a sip of his coffee.

"'Well,' said Granddad," said Emmet. "'There I am in the bed one cold night, fifteen and the bed all to myself for the first time in my life, and I'd just got to sleep when I woke up screamin. Felt like my foot had been dipped in molten steel, and me lying there a twistin and a cryin, and when I could finally see through the pain what do you think I saw? I saw my daddy standin over me holding the handhatchet my mother used to chop the kindling with. I looked to see did he chop my foot off, but he hadn't, he'd just given it a whack with the blunt end, breaking every little bone they was. So I asked him, What'd you do that for, Daddy? And do you know what he said? Said, 'Cause your momma tolt me to.'"

Emmet lifted his coffee halfway to his lips and stopped. The boy had stopped brushing, the brush held still on the mare's shoulder.

"You think I'm making this up?"

The boy resumed brushing. "You might be telling stories."

"True stories. Years later, at Granddad's funeral, I kissed my granny's cheek and said, 'Granny, he sure will be happy to see his brothers again, won't he?' And she blinked at me and said, 'Brothers? What are you talkin about?' And I said, 'His three brothers what all died in the war, which is how he come to have that hitch in his step on account of his momma telling his daddy to bust his foot with the handhatchet.' Well. Granny stared at me and then started laughing. *Laughing,* at her husband's funeral. 'Boy,' she said, 'your granddad never had no brothers a'tall. He come by that limp thirteen years old when he kicked a mule and broke his foot.'"

Emmet lifted his coffee and sipped noisily, and when he lowered the mug he was frowning happily.

The boy brushed along the mare's back in slow, mechanical strokes. "That reminds me of this dog I found one time by the side of the road," he said.

"Dead dog?" guessed the old man gamely.

"No, still alive. Big German shepherd. Whoever hit him had driven off. His lower jaw was missing."

Emmet said nothing. He watched the boy.

"Lifted his head and looked right at me, this dog. He couldn't bite if he wanted to, but I don't think he wanted to. Somebody had run him over and left him there like that, but he let a stranger walk right up and touch him."

"He knew you didn't mean him no harm."

"I killed him with a hammer."

Emmet looked at the boy. The boy went on brushing.

"You did him a mercy, that's all. You did what any decent man would do."

The boy went on brushing.

Emmet combed his fingers into the mare's dark mane. He was quiet. Then he said: "I bought these two animals for two reasons. One was so Alice and me could ride them, time to time, and the other was to give my boy Billy something to do with himself. But after Belle here threw him and busted his arm he wouldn't have a thing to do with either one of them. They was already tame as lambs when I bought them and when I asked him what he did to make her throw him he looked at me and said, 'Nothing. She's just a crazy mean bitch of a animal.'"

The old man coughed and sipped from his coffee.

"Alice and me. We didn't do nothing different for that boy we didn't do for his brother before him. We did a good deal more for him, truth be told. But it was just one heartbreak after another, year after year. That poor gal.

You think the heart gets harder but for a mother it never does. It just breaks and breaks and breaks once more."

The boy glanced at Emmet and went on brushing. "Not for a father?"

"For a father too. But a father don't know it so well. A father keeps busy in his body. A father don't stop. Then one day his wife of forty-five years is gone and then he knows. Then he knows. He gets up one day and he's got too much love. Just too much love. What's he supposed to do with it? Where's it supposed to go?"

The boy held the brush on the mare's croup. The old man stared into his coffee mug, then glanced up, abruptly, as if surprised to find he was not alone with the horses. "You was gone a long time," he said plainly. And the boy resumed brushing.

"I shouldn't have done it how I did it," he said. "I know that much."

"Something tells you it's time to go and you go. In that respect a young man ain't so different from a old one."

The boy brushed down the mare's hindquarters and moved to the other mare, Emmet beside him. The mares puffing and smacking at the empty pails.

"Well," said Emmet. "I won't chew your ear no more."

"You weren't."

"Well," he said. He moved as if to go but then stopped, and the boy turned to see the blue-green Subaru wagon come around the corner of the house, swing around the big spruce and stop short of the bay door. They watched the girl step from the car and come across the snow in her cowboy boots and her cowboy hat. She raised up to peck Emmet on the jaw and the mares turned their heads from the pails and flared their nostrils at the changed air and snorted.

Under the wicker weave of her hatbrim her dark eyes shone.

"They think I have carrots," Carmen said, and Emmet said, "They know you do," and she said, "I know. But that's for later." She stepped between the mares and raised a hand to each and they pushed their muzzles into her bare palms and snuffled and blew, and for a moment with the two horse heads balanced in the cups of her hands she seemed to be weighing them one against the other, like some figure of equine justice come to decide their case.

44

From where he stood at the western-facing window, Grant saw the horses splash abreast into the winter wheat, blackbirds flushing before them, parallel seams chasing behind. The girl sat her horse erect and easy, her ponytail in a matching swing with the mare's, while his son clung to his horse with his knees, his arms and shoulders all out of compliance with the gait. He watched to see if they would turn to look back but neither did, and he watched them come out of the pasture and he watched their shapes grow fitful and watery in some distorting effect of distance and light before they vanished altogether into the tree line, boy and girl lost to sight, and he turned from the window and looked about in confusion at the empty and foreign room.

When they gained the tree line she took the lead and they rode single file up the trail, the boy's mount passively following hers so that he had little to do but watch the rainfall of broken light through which she and her horse passed. The air full of the smell of pine pitch and no sounds but horse sounds: the creaking saddles, the stepping hooves, the champing and blowing.

He held the reins loosely and followed as he had followed another girl long ago, up and up, and for an unfocusing moment he saw her again, moving up the blacktop pale and lean and light, the pink alternating flash of sneaker tread—until the trail crested onto level ground and he rocked back in the saddle and they stopped.

Before them lay a broad glade of aspens, white and spare; the pinewood rising beyond, and in the far distance above the highest pines stood the snowy crags of the Rockies, fantastic in scale and burning in the light of their own immensity. He sat the horse, his gloved hands on the saddle horn. The cowboy at rest, he thought. The Marlboro man himself. He was reaching for his cigarettes when the other horse stepped on, and his horse did the same; side by side into the glade, punching their hooves into the plate of snow where smaller, lighter creatures had recently tread.

The horses diverged as the trees demanded, and they'd not gone far into the glade when, angling back toward Carmen, the boy's mare abruptly balked, tossing her head and whinnying. He gave her rein to step around the trouble and looked down on it as they passed—the welter of bloody paw prints and the torn bag of hide and bone which no longer resembled any animal he knew.

He saw the cabin through the last of the aspens: a solid and unnatural dark geometry ahead, unexpected and improbable. For a troubling instant he thought he knew it—all of it, all that they would find inside. But this was not that place, this was not that place, he understood that as they crossed the small clearing where the trees had long ago been axed to build the cabin itself and where nothing had grown up in their place.

The horses halted perhaps twenty yards from the cabin.

"Is it Emmet's?" he said.

"No. This isn't his land."

The cabin's doorjamb looked built for a smaller race of human. There was no longer a door in the jamb and nothing but darkness visible within. The roof was a caved rib cage of lodgepoles, clinging at their high point to the stone chimney.

"The horses don't like to get too close," Carmen said.

"Why not?"

"I don't know."

They sat the horses, watching the cabin.

"What's inside?"

"I don't know. I've never looked."

THEY LEFT THE HORSES and walked to the cabin. The boy's knee had gone rigid in the stirrup and each step was like a sprung trap seizing on the bones. Carmen saw his face set blankly against it, and walked on. She passed under the lintel and the boy, stooping, followed. A window had been cut into the far wall and as they stepped into the room an animal went scrabbling out, long-bodied and black.

They stood looking around, like potential renters. There was just the one room, and they found in it no identifiable trace of former occupancy, not even the expected litter of beer cans left by passing hunters or teens hunting for privacy. On the stone floor of the firebox, nothing but soot and the same gray coat of grit that lay over the dirt floor, the floor itself hard as stone and bowled smoothly toward its center as though by some tireless human milling. They each moved unknowingly to this depression and stood back to back, their breaths coming thick and white.

"Someone once lived here," she said.

"Maybe," he said. "Might've just been for hunting."

She shivered and crossed her arms. "I think somebody lived here." She looked around and sniffed the air. Then she turned toward the boy, and in the bleak light he looked less like the boy she remembered from school and more like some older, rougher brother, and her heart dipped strangely, and she turned away and stepped back outside.

He did not follow but stood there alone, trying to imagine a man building the cabin. Swinging the ax to clear the land tree by tree. Peeling and mortising the logs and mating them at the corners and carving out the openings. Long nights rocking in his chair before the flames, smoking his pipe while the wind howled. Did he dream of company? Did he dream of women?

Outside, Carmen had found a stump and cleared away its mushroom cap of snow and sat with her legs straight before her. He stepped from the cabin and she swept the snow from a second stump and he sat down. The mares raised their heads to look at them.

"I never touched a horse until these ones here," he said.

"You could've picked worse ones," she said. "Emmet told me one time that when he bought these mares the man wanted to sell him just one of them and one other horse. He said it wasn't good to have two sisters together. Said they never learned any sense of independence or were hard to train or something. But Emmet saw how these two moved, how they stayed close to each other, and he said that was all he needed to see. He said that if one just stuck with the other, then he wouldn't ever have to worry about the other running off wild with his wife on its back when they went out riding."

She stopped and found the boy looking at her.

"What?"

"Nothing," he said. He got out his cigarettes and lit one.

She watched him and he said, holding up the cigarette, "Does it bother you?"

She shook her head. "I don't like it but I like the smell of it." Her nostrils widened very slightly and she turned to watch the horses. "My father was a smoker, maybe that's why. I haven't seen him since I was seven," she said.

"Where is he?"

"I don't know."

"You don't care to see him again?"

"Why would I want to see a man who doesn't want to see me?"

He tipped the ash from his cigarette. He said that he hadn't seen his mother in over a year and he knew exactly where she was.

"Why haven't you?"

He shrugged. He uncrossed his ankles and crossed them the other way and the movement set off the pain in his knee again—wires of outrage from the deep nerveball where bone met bone.

After a while Carmen stood and went to the mares. "Know what I saw, one time?"

"What."

"I saw that dog, Lola, walk under these horses and just stand there, for the shade."

She turned and stared at him, waiting for him to understand what she was saying. Which was that she knew it wasn't one of the mares that had cracked the old dog's ribs.

THEY RODE BACK NOT as they'd come but along what remained of a backwoods road in a deep seam of pines where the boughs forced the mares to walk with their hindquarters bumping, the stirrups clacking together, his left and her right. The sun was well into the west and they rode slowly where there were no tracks other than those of mule deer and the snowed-in hoof-tracks of the horses themselves from the last time she'd ridden here. They rode and she talked about the colleges she'd applied to, speaking soberly of their virtues and shortcomings, of what she reasonably expected to hear from them, but also of what she hoped to hear. They'd ridden perhaps a mile along the path when the mare the boy rode snorted and began to step more briskly. He attempted to rein her back but she only slung her head petulantly and trekked on. The other mare sped up and when the animals were abreast again the boy said, "She's just plain ignoring me."

"Smell of the barn."

"What?"

"She's drunk on the smell of the barn. Don't take it personally."

"Don't take it personally she says," he said to the horse. "After all the apples you've eaten right out of this hand."

"If you turned her around she'd behave herself again. Of course you'd have to get her turned around."

"I might do that."

"Show her who's boss?"

"That's right."

"Let's see it, cowboy."

The boy glanced about him. "This is no place to turn a horse around."

"You ever been to the rodeo?"

"No. Why?"

"A horse can wrap around a barrel like a snake."

"Some other horse. Not this horse."

"It's a poor carpenter blames his tools."

He looked at her. "Where'd you hear that?"

"I heard a man say it once."

"What man?"

"What man?" She pushed out her lower lip. "A man going by the name of Grant Courtland."

"That's what I thought."

"You know him?"

"I've heard of him. And guess what?"

"What?"

"He doesn't know shit about horses."

She tossed back her head and laughed.

They were coming to a bend in the road and well before they reached it both mares trimmed their ears and began snorting, swinging their heads into each other's neck and careening bodily together, pinning the riders' legs between them. Carmen worked her reins and said Whoa, whoa and the boy merely held on. Then they heard what the horses had already heard—the high, thin warbling of electric guitar, the deep air-throb of bass. The sound grew, and the animals pressed on, at war with themselves and with their riders until at last they all came around the bend and saw the car, and the mares drew up snorting.

He'd pulled onto the old road from the county blacktop, and he'd pulled in just far enough to make going around him difficult. Nor could they detour through the woods for the density of the trees. He'd left the car running and the window down, and leaning against the forward black fender in his black leather jacket he appeared a dark extension of the car itself, just as inanimate but for the motion of his thumb over the keypad of his phone.

Carmen looked at the boy, and then she sat forward in her saddle and said, "Hey," and then louder, *"Hey,"* until without taking his eyes from the phone Billy raised his free hand in a silent appeal for patience. At last he lowered the phone and pocketed it and faced them benignly, ready now to learn what he might do for them.

Beneath the scales and bassbeats of the music was the low throb of the idling engine.

"We can't get by," said Carmen.

Billy cupped a hand to his ear and she repeated herself and he raised one finger and reached into the window and the music stopped, the engine stopped, and all was silent again but for the snorting of the horses and the restless stepping of their hooves.

"Afternoon," Billy said. He smiled at them and the smile was friendly. "You two look like a postcard sitting on those horses."

"We can't get by," said Carmen.

He glanced behind him and turned back to her and said, "Sure you can. There's just room on this side here."

"The horses won't go around the car."

"What do you mean they won't go around the car?"

"I mean they won't go around the car."

"They're horses, darlin. They do what you tell them to do." He smiled at her and he looked at the boy who had so far said nothing. "It sure is nice to see everybody getting along so well, I have to say. Everybody so friendly. Know what I heard the other day?"

They said nothing. The horses tossed their heads.

"Heard that old man of mine humming a tune." He shook his head. "Can you beat that?"

Carmen smiled thinly. She looked at the boy. Turned to Billy again.

"Are you going to back up and let us go by?" she said.

Billy held her eyes. Smiling still, but the smile nowhere now but in his lips. "Where you all been to, anyway?" He squinted at them. "You been up to that cabin, haven't you. Old man Santiago's cabin?" Mirth and lewdness playing in his face. "I knew this old boy one time went to the doc with a load of number five birdshot in his ass cheeks. Doc takes one look at the boy's jeans all blood-soaked but not a hole in them and says, Damn, I thought old man Santiago passed on years ago."

To the boy he said: "The way you sit that horse, I'd say maybe that old cuss has done kicked off after all."

The boy said nothing.

Carmen said, "Are you going to move that car or not?"

Billy studied her. He tested the little patch of hair under his lip with the tip of his tongue and smiled again. "Why you gotta take that tone with me? Isn't that my horse you're sitting on?"

"It's Emmet's horse."

"Wrong. That's my horse between your legs, darlin." He stepped toward them and the mares shied and stamped and he stopped. "Not that I'm proud of owning such a pair of contrarian nags."

Carmen reined the horse and said, "Okay, this has been fun. Really. But I'm turning around and going back."

"Going back?" said Billy. "With him?"

She was trying to back-step the horse so she could get it turned around but the horse only squatted and tossed its head and would not back-step.

Billy shook his head. "Pitiful."

At last she curbed the horse violently and it reared and slammed against its sister and came down on its forehooves facing the way they'd come and she reined it to a standstill and looked at the boy and said, "Are you coming? She'll turn around now."

The boy sat watching Billy.

"Sean," she said.

He slipped his off-boot from the stirrup and swung his leg over and stood down into the snow and looped the reins over the mare's neck and held her by the cheek strap as she shook her head. When she was calm, he walked away from her toward Billy.

Billy waited with his arms loose at his sides, smiling placidly until the boy stopped and stood facing him.

"Well?" said Billy.

"Are you going to move that car?"

"Sure I am."

The boy waited.

"You mean now? This second? No, I don't believe I can do that."

The boy walked on toward the car.

"Where you going?" said Billy, following.

The boy stepped to the driver's side and reached for the handle.

"I wouldn't do that."

He lifted the handle and opened the door, and Billy stepped up and kicked the door with the heel of his boot, wrenching the door from the boy's grip and slamming it shut again. The sound echoed down the canyon of pines, and both horses reared and Carmen held on and said Easy, easy. She watched and the mares watched wild-eyed as Billy took the boy by his jacket and spun him around and pinned him against the fender and brought his face close to the boy's and said, "Like father like son. What is it with you people? Don't you know any better than to touch another man's vehicle?"

The boy had not resisted being spun around and pinned to the car. Now with Billy's face in his face and the feel of his spittle landing on his skin, he reached up and filled his hands with the leather lapels and shoved off against the car and spun around and pinned Billy, in turn, to the car.

"Stop it," called Carmen. "Sean, stop it."

"Best listen to her," Billy said. "How you gonna tap that little brown ass if you can't even walk?"

The boy let go of one lapel and swung but Billy turned his head and the blow only grazed his chin, and before the boy could swing again Billy pulled him close and fitted his head alongside the boy's head jaw to jaw as if he wished to say something into his ear, and the boy tried to separate but Billy held him and said into his ear: "Too bad you weren't so tough when you lost your sister." And he drew back and head-butted the boy's nose. There was a brittle sound and the boy felt the blood flow hot over his lips and Billy slipped away and stepped around him and punched him once, deeply, in the back, and of some command not his own the boy dropped to his knees in the snow.

Carmen tried to turn the horse again but it would not turn, and at last she dug in her heels and the horse burst forward at a gallop and she looked back once to see that the other mare followed, and then she released the horse to its own desperate heart and it fled up the narrow way, the huge body rocking under her and her hat whipped from her head in the wind and lost behind her.

Watching her go, Billy did not see the boy get to his feet, or the swing that caught him in the temple and sent him stilt-legged toward the trees. He planted one hand in the snow, saving himself in this tripod fashion from a knockdown, and when the boy stepped forward to kick, Billy caught his swinging boot and held on to it and the boy went down and Billy let go and stepped away with a hand to his head. The boy scrabbled to his feet and turned to him again, came forward swinging poorly with his left. Billy sidestepped and shoved him away and said, "You dumb fuck, you broke your wrist on my head."

The boy turned and came back, the left fist raised.

"Quit now."

He swung and Billy deflected the swing and shoved him to the car face-first, held him there squirming and spitting blood on the windshield.

"I said quit now, for fuck's sake. She's gone."

The boy tried to pivot and Billy seized the injured hand in some extra-ordinary way and the boy pitched forward again, his lips peeled in a red grin of pain.

"I mean it," Billy said.

"Fuck you."

"Fuck me? Really?" He torqued the boy's wrist. "You gonna quit?"

The boy turned his face and shaped his lips and sent a mouthful of blood spraying over the windshield, and without another word Billy wrenched on the hand and he felt the bones give way like twigs and they each heard the snapping of the bones.

The boy relaxed and Billy let go and stepped away. The boy turned and slid slowly to his haunches, then sat hard on the snow, holding his right hand in his left.

Billy stood over him, panting. He spat into the snow and wiped his mouth. He looked up the path where the girl had gone and there was no sign of her or the horses other than the fresh hoofprints and the dark shape of hat in the snow.

He looked back to the county road and he looked at the boy again heaped against his car, blood running from his nose in a dark ooze.

Billy shook his head. "A man gets out of bed in the morning and he has no idea. Just no idea." He looked up at the high teeth of the pines, the darkening lane of sky.

The boy sat coddling his arm. Before him at Billy's waist was a silver oval with two ruby eyes and a red enamel fork of tongue. It was the bejeweled belt of the pugilist, and staring from its polished surface was his own bloodied, distorted face in miniature.

Looking good, Dudley.

Billy took out his phone and held it loosely in his palm, as if it were a stone he might sling.

"Fuck it," he said finally, slipping the phone back into his pocket. He bent to grab the boy by the jacket but the boy pushed his hands away and climbed to his feet on his own. They walked to the passenger's side and Billy opened the door and waited for the boy to get in.

"Keep your head back." He found him a mechanic's rag already red to press to his face and he shut the door and walked around and swung in behind the wheel. He got a cigarette in his lips and tapped up another and looked at the boy with the rag pressed to his face and put the pack away. He lit the cigarette and looked at the boy again. Then he leaned to grope under the seat and he found the bottle by feel and brought it up and unscrewed the cap and held it out.

"Here," he said, and the boy lifted the rag to look. It was a fifth of Jack Daniel's, half gone. He took the bottle and tipped it up and the whiskey splashed cold into his mouth washing away the copper taste of blood and running down his throat in a cold burn. He handed the bottle back, shuddering, his eyes weeping and a great hot snake uncoiling in his gut.

Billy checked the bottle for blood and tilted down a deep swallow and restashed the bottle under the seat and turned the key. Electric guitar burst forth and he snapped it off. He sat a long moment looking at his windshield, shaking his head. At last he flipped the wiper lever and they both watched as the blood spread across the glass, smearing away the world in bright arcs of gore.

45

As Grant stepped out of the truck, the red door opened and the old dog hobbled out to greet him, her wrappings gray in the dusk. He walked up to the stoop and halted. Maria stood in the partial opening, one hand on the door and one on the jamb, as if the matter of his admittance were still in question.

"I'm late," he said. "I'm sorry."

She made him stand a moment longer, the canvas tool bag in his grip like an overnight bag, and then smiled and swung open the door. "Don't be," she said. "We're not on any kind of schedule here."

He pawed at the welcome mat with his boots and stepped in, passing near her and into the scent of her, a brief miscellany of perfume and cooking and wine.

"Do you want to give me your coat?"

He glanced down at the old canvas jacket and brushed at it.

"The only other jacket I have makes me feel like I'm going to my own funeral."

"I love this jacket. But you'll get hot if you keep it on."

"Maybe I'd better see about that door first. Unless dinner is ready."

"There's time. But Grant, honestly, I'll feed you either way, you have my word."

"And I gave you mine."

She led him to the back of the house, through the kitchen—the smells of seared garlic and bubbling meat sauce and baking bread bringing his stomach alive—and into the small utility room.

"Can I get you something to drink? Glass of wine?"

Behind her the dog plopped with a grunt to the kitchen floor to watch him.

"Damn," Grant said. "I forgot the wine."

She shook her head and pressed two fingers to her breastbone: "Italian, remember? If the sheriff saw my stash, he'd arrest me. I'll pour you a glass."

"I'd better not. Not yet. I've got some sharp tools here."

He unbolted the back door and lifted on the knob and jerked the door open, rattling the old pane of glass.

"Can I help?"

"No, ma'am."

She stood watching him.

"I wouldn't mind the company, though," he said. "Unless you're needed in the kitchen."

She gave a kind of glance over her shoulder. "I think they've got it under control. I'll just grab my glass."

The door sagged from its hinges and he shut it again and studied the gaps. Then he collected hammer and screwdriver from the bag and tapped the hinge pins from their thick paint encasements and lifted the door free and set it edgewise on the floor. The cold dusk poured into the house.

"I'll try to be quick," he said.

"No, take your time."

He began backing out the old slot-head screws, and while he worked he told her why he was late: it was because he'd caught Emmet up on a ladder chipping at gutter ice with a screwdriver, and he'd spent about an hour talking the old man down, and then he'd gone up and finished the job, and then spent more time getting the old man inside and making sure he was in for the evening.

He looked up from his work, and Maria looked up—she'd been watching him, his hands—and she smiled. "He's lucky you came along," she said.

"He was doing all right."

"I mean in general."

"So do I."

"If breaking your leg is your idea of doing all right."

"It's not that he doesn't like help. He just can't stand the idea of needing it."

"He doesn't like getting old."

"He's funny that way." Grant unrolled the chisel bib atop the dryer and selected one and began shaping out the new mortises in the door edge and in the jamb, tapping gently and exactly with the Estwing hammer.

Maria sipped her wine. "I think he's gotten younger, actually, since you've been around. You and Sean. There's a light in his eye that wasn't there before."

"That's the light of pure evil."

She laughed. "The devil himself."

"I'm serious. Not an innocent word comes out of that mouth."

"What does he say?"

He dry-fit the hinge and picked up the chisel again and began teasing up fine curls of wood.

"He's got a thing or two to say about this here," he said. Not looking up.

"This here?" She would not help him. "What do you mean by this here?"

He brushed a curl to the floor and reset the chisel. "My coming over here. Over to the cafe."

"Does he now."

"Not outright. Never outright. He's too sly for that."

"I see." She watched him. "Does it bother you?"

"Does what?"

"Him being so sly."

"Nope." He replaced the hinge and tapped it with the butt of the chisel and it sat dead flush to the wood. "Sean might, though. If the old man goes down that path."

"What path?"

He rigged his cordless with a bit and predrilled for the new screws. "Oh, he was very sly today about Sean and Carmen."

"Sean and Carmen?"

"My son and your—"

"Yes, thank you. What about them?"

"It seems those two mares went out for a walk today with those two kids on their backs."

She lifted her glass and said into the bowl of it, "Does that bother you?"

"Does what?" Grant changed bits and looked at her. "Why should it bother me?"

When the screws were set he lifted the door upright and walked it to the jamb. The hinge barrels slipped together and he slid the upper pin into place and then the lower, and lastly he tapped the pins down and swung the door to with a neat and solid click. He tested it again, and as there was no binding he threw the deadbolt and put the tools away and took up the broom and began to sweep.

"Let me do that at least," she said, but he shook his head. Cleanup was part of the job, he said, and sometimes the best part, although not this time. She asked him what was the best part this time and he smiled and said he didn't know yet, but so far it was the smell of that food while he worked. Then he reconsidered and said no, it was talking to her while he worked, and she smiled, but it wasn't the way she usually smiled.

"Listen," she said after a minute. "I want to say something."

He held the broom.

She'd not eaten anything but two Greek olives and she could feel the wine in her tongue and she could hear it in her words but she went on anyway. "Listen," she said. "I know this isn't exactly happy-couple land here. You know? I don't know what it is but I know it's not that. And I know that's not why you're here. In Colorado. You and Sean. And I just want you to know that I know it. Everybody knows it."

"Everybody?"

She sipped her wine.

"What do they know?" Grant said.

"They know that you—" She met his eyes, and held them, and smiled, and shrugged. "They know that you aren't here for us."

Grant looked down on the meager pile of paint and wood chips at his feet, then turned to look out the old pane of glass in the door, but the night had come down and there was nothing to see in the glass but his own skewed face and the shape of the woman behind him.

"I don't believe she's gone," he said without turning. "Did you know that?"

Maria nodded—then said, "Yes."

"How did you know?"

She watched him. "Because you're her father."

He nodded to the images in the glass.

"Without evidence," he said, "without definitive proof, a father would never give up believing, would he."

"No."

"Long after everyone else has given up and gone home and gotten on with their lives, he would keep on believing because, without evidence, you could never kill his belief."

"No, you couldn't."

He nodded again and said nothing for a long time. She watched his back, his shoulders.

"But it's not belief," he said. "It's not belief. Whatever belief is, whatever it once was, it's been destroyed by something else. It's been kicked all to hell by something else."

She watched him. She held the glass of wine in both hands.

"Belief never stood a chance against disbelief," he said.

After a moment she said, "Disbelief?"

"Disbelief in the world," he said. "The way it is. The way it works. Its god."

She waited for him to go on.

He said: "I stay because I disbelieve. I disbelieve. I don't hope. I don't pray. I disbelieve. I disbelieve and I reject and I renounce, and there's nothing more to say about me."

He turned and his face was perfectly composed, his look detached and calm. Then he saw her and she saw the change in his eyes, in his face, as if he'd stepped out of one kind of light into another.

"I'm sorry," he said.

"Why?"

"I don't know. You're a good person. A good woman."

She stared at him, and then she looked about the utility room—at this and that, at nothing. She wiped at her cheek and sniffed, and then smiled. "All I wanted was to cook you a decent meal, for God's sake, and you lay this on me."

He held her eyes. He could think of no reply.

He took a step toward her, but just then the dog labored to its feet and clicked off across the kitchen floor, and they heard the front door slam and a moment later Carmen appeared in the kitchen, the dog at her heels, and she came to the threshold of the utility room and stood taking in the strange scene: her mother wet-eyed, holding a glass of wine, and Grant Courtland in his canvas jacket behind her, holding the broom.

46

The young man in his bed did not hear the click of the lamp, or feel the light on his eyes under their lids, but went on sleeping as before, openmouthed and dreaming of God knew what. He slept on his side, facing lampward, hair spilled across his eyes, curled upon himself with one loose fist exposed above the hem of the blanket near his chin. The air smelled of ash and sour breath and the rank humid interiors of leather boots. And he would've gone on sleeping but for a noise in the room, a true noise heard and felt, like a blow to the headboard, which jerked him blinking into the light—"What?"—raising his head and squinting at the lamp, squinting into the room.

A figure sat there in the weak light, having pulled the little chair bedside to sit upright and formally, as a doctor would, or a priest.

"What the hell you doing, Pops?" he said thickly, and the figure leaned forward, elbows to knees, hands clasped, and the face clarified and Billy beheld him groggily. Beyond him the door stood open.

The alarm clock showed 3:35.

Billy uncurled and stretched himself, yawning. He smacked his lips and said, "How long you been sitting there?"

Grant looked at him closely. The greasy, fallen hair, the hooded eyes, that mouth.

"Not long."

"That's good to hear." Billy drew himself up and rested his head against the headboard, the pillow mounded under his neck. This new position, the angle of his neck, gave him the look of a man who was helpless to make himself more comfortable.

He regarded his visitor and said, "What's on your mind, Grant?"

"I couldn't sleep."

"You couldn't sleep."

"I was lying over there, trying to sleep, but I couldn't. So I got up and came over here. I thought maybe I could talk it out of me."

Billy looked at him. He sniffed the air for alcohol and smelled none. Grant sat studying his own fingers.

"You couldn't find anybody else to talk it out with?" Billy said. "That old man across the hall don't even sleep. You could talk to him till the cows come home."

"It doesn't concern him."

"It doesn't."

"No."

"It concerns me?"

"Yes."

Billy grinned and wagged a finger and said, "I bet it concerns that boy of yours too. Am I right?"

"Yes."

"So why don't you talk to him?"

"I did talk to him, earlier. But they sedated him at the hospital and he's sleeping."

"They sedated him at the hospital?"

"Yes."

"Why'd they do that?"

"That's what they do for a broken wrist."

"He broke his wrist?"

Grant stared at him. Billy stared back from his strange position. "And you think I had something to do with it," Billy said.

"I do."

"Because that's what he told you."

"No. He told me the horse threw him."

"Yeah, they do that."

"The girl had a different story."

"What girl was that?"

Grant reached up and scratched his jaw. Billy watched his hand until it came down again.

"You know what girl," Grant said. He could hear the younger man's breathing and Billy could hear his.

"And now here you are," Billy said. "Come into a man's room while he's still in bed. Well, do what you gotta do, Grant. But before you begin I think you ought to know something that maybe nobody else has mentioned."

"What's that."

"It was a fair fight. A fair fight. And if your boy got his wrist broke it was only because he didn't know when to quit. He's no fighter, sorry to say, but he's got no fear either."

"A fair fight," said Grant. "What does a shit like you know about a fair fight?"

Billy's eyes had been glazed, then faintly lit as he warmed to the conversation. Now they turned hard and bright.

"I'm sorry junior can't handle himself better in a scrap," Billy said. "But I'm done talking to you." He reached and clicked out the light and then rolled away and slugged the pillow. "Shut that door on your way out."

Grant sat as before, like a man at vigil, his eyes adjusting to the dark. A moon had come into the west-facing window, white as the eye of a blind man. Light enough to see by. There was the tock tock of the grandfather clock at the foot of the stairs.

"How are you fixed with God, Billy?" he said, but Billy did not stir—until finally he exhaled with a sound of exhaustion and said, "Worse than a woman," and he rolled again to face Grant. Faint moonlight in his eyes. "What do you want from me? An apology?"

"Want you to answer my question."

Billy stared at him. He shook his head and propped himself again on the headboard and grabbed his cigarettes and lighter from where they lay by the lamp. He struck the flint wheel and his face lit up garishly with the flame, then darkened again.

"How am I fixed with God? Was that the question?" The eye of the cigarette flared and dimmed. The exhaled smoke rolled overhead in a blue squall.

"I'm not fixed with him one way or another, Grant. We mostly leave each other alone. Does that answer your question?"

Grant nodded, frowning.

"I used to be the same," he said. "It was a challenge for my wife, who was raised Catholic." He opened his hands and observed the two white pools that were his palms. Then he told Billy the story he'd told the boy: of the two sixteen-year-old girls, Angela and Faith, twins, and their baby sister on the dock. Told him of the splash and the dive and the mouth-to-mouth while Faith didn't come up, and she didn't come up.

Billy tapped ash into a glass ashtray. "Your wife lost her Faith," he said, and Grant said, "Yes, but it brought her closer to God. Now she understood him better. Understood that he saw to all things in the world, the beautiful and the ugly. The joyful and the heinous. There was nothing he didn't touch. No beautiful summer day on the lake without him nor dead twin sister on that same day. He was whimsical and violent and hard but this was better, much better, than a godless world that was whimsical and violent and hard. Because you could not talk to the world. You could not pray to it or love it or damn it to hell. With the world there could be no discussion, and with no discussion there could be no terms, and with no terms there could be no grace."

"Or damnation," Billy said, and Grant said, "No, that was damnation. You mind if I smoke one of these?"

Billy told him to help himself, and he did.

They were silent, smoking. The moon sat in the very corner of the glass as if lodged there. The grandfather clock tocked away.

"I didn't understand any of this until my daughter was taken from me," Grant said. "I never talked to God, not even to ask him to watch over my children. I believed that the terrible things that happened in this world every day could not happen to me, to my family. I suppose every man believes that. Until shown otherwise, he believes no evil can touch the people he protects with his love. Then, one day, another man takes his daughter from him. Simply grabs her and takes her. He has no name and no face, this man, and he vanishes back into the darkness and he takes the man's daughter there with him. What can he do, this father, in the face of such cruelty, but ask the God he never believed in to bring her back? And if he won't bring her back, or show him how to find her, then some other deal must be made. Some other terms. I never believed in God like I never really believed in the truly bad man. In his power to touch me."

The cigarette ash flared, then dimmed.

"Now I ask of this God, that if he will not give me my daughter back, at least give me my bad man. At least give me that. I spend my nights dreaming of nothing else. Of getting this man in my hands. I wake up with the taste of his blood in my mouth, only to find I've ground some tooth until my gums have bled, or I've bitten through my lip."

He paused. He drew on his cigarette. He seemed almost to smile.

"For a time," he said, "I would see a man and follow him. It could be any man, going about his business. I'd watch and I'd follow, driving sometimes to the man's very house. I couldn't help myself. Like the man I sought. Sick to my bones. I believe your brother, Joe, came up with this arrangement down here as a way to keep me away from those men up there in the mountains."

They smoked, the clouds from their lungs merging and seething in the space between them. Somewhere in the room was a small constant buzzing, as of some feverish insect.

"So," said Grant. "That's how I'm fixed with God. If he will not give me my daughter back, then he owes me one bad man. And you want to know the hell of it? The hell of it, Billy, is that I don't give a damn anymore if it's even the right bad man. I have reached the point where any bad man will do."

Billy appeared to study the tip of his cigarette. He tugged at the hair under his lip.

"And you get to decide that, do you? You get to decide if a man is bad enough to kill or not? That's thinking kind of highly of yourself, isn't it?"

"Deciding won't have a thing to do with it, Billy."

"It won't."

"No."

"What will then?"

Grant looked at his hands. The pale weave of fingers. "God," he said.

"God," said Billy, and Grant nodded.

"If God put that man on that path to take my little girl, then I expect him to put a man on my path too. I'm demanding it."

"And how will you know him, Grant? How will you recognize this bad man God has sent you?"

"That's the easy part," said Grant, and he looked up from his hands and Billy saw his eyes in their sockets like small openings to some blue flame of the skull. "I will know this man because he will be the next man who attempts to hurt anyone I love."

Billy stared at him and Grant stared back from the chair and they remained that way in silence for a long time, until finally Grant reached forward and crushed the cigarette in the glass ashtray, and placed his hands on his knees and pushed himself up. He appeared beset by some brute weariness as he bent to collect the shotgun from where it leaned against the chairback.

"That's what I got to thinking about over there," he said. "That's why I couldn't sleep."

Billy watched the gun in the dark, the moon's blue scrollwork along the barrels. Grant turned for the door and stopped. Neither of them knew how long the old man had been standing there, but when they saw him they knew he'd been standing there long enough.

"Sorry to wake you, Em," Grant said, and eased himself by and descended the stairs, and Emmet watched him go until he reached the landing and turned the corner and was gone.

He turned to look at his boy in the bed. "What the hell did you do?"

"Me? Are you blind now too? Didn't you see your buddy there with a shotgun in my bedroom in the middle of the night?"

Emmet had not put on a housecoat and under the thin pajamas he appeared to shake.

"I want you outta this house."

"What? What was that?"

"I said I want you out of this house. I'm all give out, Billy."

Billy stared at him, then fell back on his pillow in the moonlight, laughing.

"You crazy old man," he said. "You can't kick me outta my own goddam house."

"I ain't, son. I'm kicking you outta mine."

He lay there, his eyes on the ceiling. Then he moved, and Emmet saw something flash in the center of the room like the blink of some ghostly eye, or a spinning moon, an instant before some other thing shattered on the door trim to the left of his head. He stood a moment looking at the wreckage of glass and cigarette butts on the floor, and then he backed away, closing the door behind him.

47

Grant had reached the bottom step of the porch when the screen door pushed open and Emmet came backing out, an aluminum travel mug in his gloved hand. He saw Grant and stopped.

"You're up early," he said.

"So are you."

"This ain't early." He gripped the railing and came carefully down the steps. He wore his good dark overcoat, dark slacks, black shoes, and the bright red cap pulled down over his ears. Gaining solid ground he looked up and met Grant's eyes. "How's that boy?"

"Sleeping it off."

"How bad?"

"Not as bad as it looks. Two good shiners and a somewhat enlarged nose."

"Broke?"

"What?"

"The nose."

"No. Just the wrist. They put a cast on that."

"I want you to give me that hospital bill, Grant."

Grant waved this away. "It was just a scrap, Em."

Emmet cocked an ear at him. "How's that?"

"It was just a scrap."

"If my dog gets loosed and kills a man's chickens, is that man gonna come to me and say, don't you bother, Emmet, it was just a scrap?"

"Not the most flattering analogy, Em."

The old man cocked an ear at him again and Grant shook his head. He looked to the corner of the house where the tail end of the El Camino jutted. Emmet sniffed and looked at the sky.

"Why don't you let me drive you, Em?"

"They ain't took my license from me yet."

"I know it. I feel like a drive myself."

"What about the boy?"

"He's fine," Grant said. "He's sleeping."

WITHIN THE BORDER OF ponderosa pines were a few decorative birch trees, bare and white amid the stones. Grant got out to walk but there was no place in the cemetery from which he could not see the old man clearly, and he watched him trek through the snow until he reached a rose-colored stone of modest size and began to clear the snow from its crown, whisking left and then right, the way she must have once brushed snow or dander from his shoulders. When the stone was clean he pulled the cap from his head and rested upon the stone, his back to the graveyard, his fine white hair bristling.

Grant swept the snow from a bench and sat on the cold slats. The bench was aligned for a view to the north where on a clear day the mountains must be visible, rising above the hills, but this morning there was only the low thick clouds like a gray canopy over the world. In the corner of his eye he saw the old man at the stone. The white head nodding, cocking as if to listen, nodding again. Sipping his coffee. After a while the old man stood and turned and touched the stone once more and began walking toward Grant. Grant brushed more snow from the bench, and Emmet sat down beside him.

"Her folks are buried over in that corner there, where that birch is. She wanted to be closer, but them plots was bought up long ago."

"It's a nice spot she's got," Grant said.

"I bought the two plots for us and two more for the boys if they want them. If they don't, they can sell them at a good profit." He paused. "Twenty-five years ago that was, and I never once saw myself sitting here."

Despite the cold and the snow there was the damp, moldering smell of the graves, or Grant imagined there was, and he took out his cigarettes unthink-ingly, and then returned them to his pocket.

"Go ahead and smoke."

"I can wait."

"It ain't gonna kill me."

"That's not what I hear."

"That wasn't the smokes, that was the goddam chemo."

Grant brought out the cigarettes again and got one lit and blew the smoke well away, Emmet watching him closely. Emmet sniffed at the air. He sipped his coffee. Then he reached two gloved fingers casually toward Grant.

"What?" said Grant.

"Give a man a puff."

"Forget it."

"Come on now."

"No."

"One goddam puff, God damn it. Night I had."

Grant looked into his eyes and handed over the cigarette.

Emmet sipped at the filter, held the smoke briefly in his lungs, and ex-haled it slowly from pursed lips. He handed the cigarette back, grinned, and pitched forward on the bench coughing with such violence that Grant reached over and took hold of his arm.

"Em," he said. He tossed the cigarette and began to pat the old man on the back, unprepared for the slightness of him under the coat, the racking thin basket of ribs and spine. "You need water," he said, and Emmet shook his head and raised the travel mug, or attempted to—black gouts of coffee leaping from the sip hole before Grant reached to stabilize it, guiding it to the gray, contorted face. Emmet sipped, swallowed, sipped again. Grant let go of the mug and sat back again.

"Lord," Emmet gasped, wiping at his chin. "Holy mother," he said.

When the old man was quiet again, and a long moment beyond that, Grant leaned forward and said, "Want to say I'm sorry, Em. About last night. I don't know what I was thinking."

Emmet reached up and reseated the red cap, tugging it forward and down, as a man facing a gale might.

"I told him it was time for him to go," he said.

"When?"

"Last night, after you left."

"What did he say?"

"Don't matter what he said."

"I'm sorry about that, Em."

"Don't be." He looked over at the rose stone. "Alice," he said, and stopped. He shifted on the bench. "She'd tell you the same thing."

Grant rubbed at his fingers, at the two knuckles that were now the tips, nailless and printless and bone hard under the skin; yet still sometimes when he reached for a coffee cup or to scratch his jaw, he would experience again as if for the first time the bewildering moment when fingers that had been there, indisputably, suddenly were not. The loss that was more than physical.

Emmet said: "I know I never said it, and I guess I should of. But that's your home as long as you want it, Grant. You and Sean both."

"I appreciate that, Emmet. I can't even tell you."

"But you're leaving just the same. Ain't you."

Grant said nothing.

"And just where are you gonna go?" the old man nearly demanded.

"I don't know."

"Back to Wisconsin?"

"I don't know." Grant stared at his hands. "I haven't taken very good care of that boy. If he got in his head to just leave again . . ."

There was movement and they both turned to see a pair of cardinals, males both, sitting bright red in the ribs of a birch. Beyond the birch was the rose headstone, the only one not snowcapped. Grant had seen the chiseled words but not read them. They named the woman whose remains lay there, ALICE MARGARET KINNEY, with her dates, and they named the man who sat beside him on the bench, EMMET THOMAS KINNEY, for whom there were no dates, for whom the stone carver waited, and below these were the words

MAN AND WIFE and nothing more. The face of his own wife came to him then, Angela Mary Courtland, and a time of graves he could not imagine.

He turned back and Emmet was watching him.

"What?" Grant said.

The old man looked away and shook his head. "Leaving's hard," he said. "But it ain't the hardest thing. Is it."

48

The boy walked the mares to the front pasture, released them, and walked back to the barn, passing the El Camino coming and going; his blood on the windshield was long gone and there was no other sign of that day but the caved-in door where Billy had kicked it.

Some cowboy, Dudley. Some Marlboro man.

In the barn he picked up the rake and began to muck the stalls. A black farm cat gathered herself and flew up to one of the saddles and sat there, tracking the flights of swallows in the dusty heights.

Two Saturdays gone by and now a third and he knew she wouldn't come and he knew he would have to go to her, but what would he say if he did? And what did it matter anyway?

Then why don't you stop thinking about it?

About it?

Her.

He was hindered by the cast but not as hindered as he had been, and before long he removed his jacket and continued working in his T-shirt, and this was how his father found him, planted in a dry blizzard of dust and straw, bending and forking and pitching the soiled straw into the wheelbarrow.

"Sean," he said, and without stopping the boy said, "What."

Then he stopped and turned and saw his father standing in the bay door.

It was the first day of April, a bright day with the smell of spring in it. She'd been gone for two years and eight months.

The deputy met them at the interstate and they followed his silver SUV down toward Denver, and they exited where he exited and followed him up again, climbing the pass toward Estes Park and Boulder. Spring had come indisputably to this county and the tires hissed as they struck the dark bands of thaw that lay across the road. The high bends of blacktop as they took them ignited in waves of granular light, starfields of quartz and mica, and they saw in memory the black dazzle of the cinder track in the spring—the brilliance of the white lines on the oily black, her long-striding legs scissoring between the lines as she neatly snipped one girl, and another, and then another from the picture. The gleam and heat and sun-smell of her after. The other girls, their parents, stepping into their circle of happiness, circle of pride, congratulating and stepping away again.

There was no other sound in the cab but the rushing wind at their windows, and watching these new trees in this new county, the deep gorges and the far piney walls, they remembered the first time they'd climbed such a road and it could have been the same road, same mountain, a family from the plains who'd never seen such country before. And if the country was no longer strange to them, it was still strange in that it had never again astounded them, nor awed nor excited them again, but only reminded them every day and almost from hour to hour what it had taken from them and what it had made of them. The deputy's signal winked and his taillights flared and he veered from the blacktop onto a sudden unpaved road, a narrow passage where such sunlight as reached their windshields, their faces, was green and trembling and heatless. The deputy's SUV and the Chevy after it yawing and pitching in the graveled wallows until the road summitted and fed them down into a bowl of cleared land where four other cars sat waiting. Two of these were official SUVs like the one they followed and two were the meaningless parked cars of hikers.

Sheriff Kinney and his other young deputy stepped from the silver cruiser and moved toward Grant and the boy who were coming to meet the lawmen in the middle ground. Gravel and needles and deadfall crushing under their boots. The sheriff stopped and his deputies stopped and stood behind him, their young faces grave. He reached to shake Grant's hand as he always did and then put his hands on his belt and regarded the boy.

"What happened to you?"

The boy looked at the cast on his wrist, as if he'd not been aware of it. He'd worn it for three weeks now and it showed the dirt of that time and could not be cleaned. He said he'd fallen off a horse.

"The hell you say. One of ours?"

"Yes, sir."

"Why wasn't I told?"

"It wasn't the horse's fault," said the boy.

"Don't make no difference." The sheriff studied him. He adjusted his hat and looked at Grant, and he remembered why he was there.

"You sure you all want to do this?" he said, and Grant looked up from the gravel.

"What else can we do?"

"You can wait down below."

"Up here or down there, we have to look," he said. "Don't we, Joe."

"That's why I called you," said the sheriff. "Though I shouldn't of. I should of done it by the book and called you later. But it's likely to be hours yet before we even get this"—he hesitated—"recovery under way."

"I'm grateful you called, Joe."

The way he figured it, said the sheriff, the perp had driven her up here to the trailhead and parked. Then he either took her life here and carried her up the trail or else forced her to walk up there with him and then did it.

Took her life.

The boy stood remembering another shaded hollow in the woods. A cold bench and white crooked headstones. A tarnished metal plaque that promised forty days and all of it attended by the white statue with her maimed blessing and all of it so long ago.

What do you think will happen this time?

Nothing. Let's go.

The path followed the mountain's edge with only a thin median of pines separating the climbers from the gorge and the open sky. The going was steep, yet for every step there appeared a stone or a thick knee of root made bone smooth by time and weather and the treads of hikers, and the men ascended these crude steps single file, the sheriff in the lead and the deputies bringing up the rear, giving Grant and the boy the look and the feeling of two men on their way to some high alpine arraignment. Through the trees and not fifty feet off in the blue sky, two brown eagles rode the updrafts wing tip to wing tip, without effort or urgency, absolutely soundless, their hunter's eyes searching.

Above the climbers, on a level stretch of trail, two more men in uniform stood waiting, peering out through the trees into the sky. They saw the eagles bank suddenly, pinions riffling, and dive down into the gorge like Messerschmitts.

"Oh, they saw something," said one of the men. "They saw dinner," said the other, but when they heard the climbers they said no more and waited for them to come over the rise of the trail: sheriff, father, son and deputies, all winded and all ready for the level strip of trail, crowded though it was with the seven of them clustered there. The two waiting men were the Boulder County sheriff and one of his deputies. Introductions were made and the Boulder sheriff, whose name was Price, tipped back his hat and said that this was where the hiker had spotted her. She was hard to see, said Price, you had to step through the branches, right up to the edge, and look straight down.

"What made the hiker do that?" said Kinney.

"I asked him the same thing, Sheriff."

"What'd he say?"

Price glanced at Grant, the boy, and then at the ground.

"Said he was relieving himself."

Within the trees there was only one place where a man could stand like that and Kinney stepped into it and looked down. After a moment he stepped back and stood with his hands on his belt, not quite yielding the spot to Grant. He seemed to be in argument with himself. Then he moved back to the trail and let Grant pass.

Grant stepped between the branches and all of his vision and all of his heart spilled over the bluff and fell to the rocky outcrop some forty feet below, a dun-colored shelf piled with tumbled scree and sun-bleached wood and rimmed around by stunted, clinging pines. South-facing, there was no snow or even any trace of thaw on the shelf, and at first he saw nothing but a gray and dry twist of fallen tree on which someone, or the wind, had hung faded rags of cloth. Then he saw the sweep of black hair, the back of her head, and his mind corrected the image and he was tottering in space. One of his legs back-stepped of its own accord and his arm came into a strong grip and he turned to see who held him and it was his son.

He looked into Sean's eyes and the boy looked back with his matching eyes. "I don't know," Grant said. "I can't tell."

He stepped back and the boy took his place at the edge of the bluff. Leaned out and looked down.

"I'm sorry, Grant," said Kinney. He glanced at Price and his deputy. "I shouldn't have brought you up here. I thought you'd be able to see. Why don't you go on back down and—" He stopped. The other sheriff and the deputies were staring.

"Be damned," said Price, and the others turned to see the boy going over. He'd taken hold of a branch at the edge of the bluff and swung his leg out over the lip and was climbing down.

"Sean," said Kinney, "don't do that."

"Sheriff, he can't do that," said one of the deputies. "That's a crime scene."

"I said don't do that, son." Kinney came forward to take hold of the boy and Grant put out his hand.

"It's all right, Joe."

"Hell it is. He's got a broke hand and a bum leg. I wouldn't let a healthy man climb down there."

"It's all right," Grant said.

"It ain't all right, Grant. Son," said the sheriff to the top of the boy's head, "I want you back up here. That's an order."

The boy went on. Backing steadily down the face of the bluff by way of tree root and rock and fissure. He knew that under the cast the bones would hold and that it was the cast itself that opposed him, and his progress was slow; finding a foothold with his good leg, reaching down and finding a handhold with his good hand, lowering himself to the next foothold and

This is your plan, then, to make him watch you fall to your death? and with every movement sending small rockslides of talus chattering down to the ledge below. When he was perhaps twenty feet from where she lay, he looked over his shoulder and saw only the green void behind him and he turned back and said aloud, "Don't do that. Do not do that." A few feet farther down, his bad leg slipped and for a moment he scouted the place where he would land below on the ledge, but his boot, scrabbling at the rock face, found purchase and he continued on.

Five or six feet above the ledge his strength gave out, or he allowed it to give out, and he pushed off and fell clear of the wall and landed good leg first and the leg skidded out from under him in the tailings and he came down violently on his back in a cloud of dust beside her.

High above him through the haze of dust was his father's face.

"You hurt?" he called down.

"I'm all right," the boy answered. Up there, one of the men said something about evidence and the other sheriff, Price, said, "I know, Deputy."

The boy coughed and got to his knees and turned to her. Under the veil of what was once a plaid flannel shirt her back was wrapped in a colorless leather, the leather so tight it showed every rib and every vertebra. Where her waist had been was a pebbled stretched material like the webbing of a duck's foot. One arm lay under her and the other lay tangled in the roots of the clinging small pines, more root now than arm. There was no smell but the dry smell of the pines and the dusty, chalky smell of the scree.

He reached and gathered a handful of black hair and it was like the hair of any living person except that when he moved it, it shed twigs and pine needles and small moltings as if it were some derelict nest and he thought maybe it was. He lifted the hair aside and leaned to see her face. What had been her face. The drawn gray mask of it in profile. The empty slit of eyelid deep in its bowl. Cheekbone like an elbow. Fallen nose. The toothy ghoulish half smile.

"Sean?" called his father.

He looked at this face, this maybe-sister. Maybe-daughter. He looked along the wasted length of her and saw nothing he recognized. The clothes were like none he'd seen on her before. The remains of the shoes were not the remains of running shoes but of some kind of hiking boot. He looked again at her clothes. A fallen threadbare flap of backside pocket trembled in a breeze. Something glinted dully in the talus where it had piled up against her, and he grubbed there with his forefinger and brought forth a key and pulled on the key and following it out of the pebbles was a short length of chain and at the end of that, popping loose with a tug, swung a small gray clump. He stilled the swinging clump and held it close to his face and blew on it and a dingy white fur stirred in his breath.

There was something else in the debris below the pocket. He dug again and unearthed a thin plastic wallet folder. He prized a finger into the folder and it fell apart and the cards spilled out. Two faded credit cards and an ID. At one corner of the ID the lamination had curled away and the paper inside had been soaked and dried many times over, yet the picture and much of the printing had survived. Her name was Kelly Ann Baird. She had been a student at the University of Colorado. He could not read the date of her birth.

He sat back in the rubble with his bad leg out and studied the ID. Pretty girl. Pretty smile. Her image unchanged all these seasons while the source of that image inches away grew old and unrecognizable, a lonesome desiccated remainder of herself, of family and of love and pride and delight and hope. He looked out over the valley. A bird flared at eye level and screamed at him and flapped away. Perhaps it lived here on this ledge, high sepulchral roost, watching over her. Keeping her company until her people could find her and claim her and carry her back down the mountain, as if in victory.

"Sean," his father called. "*Sean.*"

He turned and looked up and waved the ID. He called up what he'd found and from where he sat on the ledge he felt the heart swing back into his father like a stone pendulum, flesh once more and filling with blood again and going on with its work.

One of the deputies had gone back down the trail for the towrope, and while he waited the boy sat beside the girl, facing where she faced. Trying to see what she'd been seeing all this time.

49

The boy went to bed and Grant lay down on the sofa and remained there in the fitful light of the TV, watching the webbing up in the vigas, the dusty swags pulsing with color. Voices from the TV reached him in strange incantation, voices undertowed into dream and his dreams playing on before his open eyes, all of it vivid and repeating until at last the hours delivered the new day, its gray light in the windows, and still in this fevered state he sat up, hunched and exhausted. On the screen a woman stood at a rostrum in a purple robe, small black ball of microphone near her mouth. She spread her arms wide and he raised the remote and the screen went black.

The air outside chilled his sweat, his clammy, clinging shirt. Porch floorboards popped under his weight and he felt the burning cold of them through his socks. He inhaled too deeply and the air came retching back up and he stood gripping the post, convulsed less by the hacking than by the effort to stop it—until the cigarette was lit and he drew the calming smoke into his lungs.

Before him, across the clearing, the house was taking shape in the dawn. No movement and no sound anywhere but the first tentative notes of the birds.

He crushed the cigarette in the ashtray on the railing and went back inside and got into a dry shirt, and then he returned to the kitchen and set the coffee to brewing and stood at the window looking at the old man's house, the light already changed. He poured coffee into a mug and left the mug sitting there. Across the way the windows were dark, upstairs and down. The rockers on the porch stilled and empty.

He looked at his watch, then drew his fingertips slowly over his jaw, as if he were deciding whether or not to shave. He stood that way for a long time. Then he pulled on his boots and got into his jacket and stepped once more into the cold morning. Down the cold popping steps and the pops returning to him in echo off the face of the old man's house.

He wasn't in the kitchen and there was no sound of the TV in the living room but Grant looked there anyway. No sound in the house at all but the tocking of the grandfather clock, and after he'd checked every place a man could be downstairs, he climbed the stairs heavily and he knocked and stood a moment with his hand on the knob, then opened the old man's door and looked in and there was no need to say his name but he said it just the same.

"Em," he said.

Silent and still in the big bed where he'd slept with his wife so many years. Silent and still and gray and so small in the big bed and all the heat gone out of the bed and out the body, and all the history and all the love gone out of it too.

Part IV

50

Billy Kinney lay against the headboard with the bunched pillow under his neck, watching the smoke in the middle space above him. It was so quiet he could hear the burning of the tobacco each time he inhaled. He lay very still, listening, and after a while he realized it was the grandfather clock at the foot of the stairs: sometime in the night it had wound down and ceased its ancient tock tock tock. He had seen the waxen and painted face, had heard the old pastor's entreaties to God, the platitudes of the condolent—but it was this, finally, the abandonment of habit, of sound, of time itself, that made it true and real.

Downstairs next to a half pot of coffee was a hundred-dollar bill and a message. *This money is from me, not the estate. I'll be back in a few days with the auction people.*

"Good morning to you too, brother," he said, his voice strange to himself.

No more sheriff now so no more neighbors bearing casseroles and pies. No more hard heels rapping the porch at dawn and the sheriff thanking them for the food and for the sympathies and seeing them off with no further awkwardness, for they'd come early and wished to leave early, before the other one came down, and wasn't it just remarkable they asked each other as they drove away how two boys from such two good souls could grow up such entirely different kinds of boys? One of the mysteries of the Lord, they allowed, and always would be, but today our prayers are with them both.

He uncapped his lighter and held it to a corner of the note and watched the flames climb, the paper twisting and blackening until the ink purpled and rose again in a phantom script, the flame going at his fingers before he dropped it into the sink. He lit a cigarette and thought of Denise Gatskill in her black funeral dress. Hair done up and showing her neck. She had come by the house but he'd sent her away. Now he had money and he ought to take her down to the city, to a bar where they served the red wine she liked.

He stood before the window. Nothing moving out in the gray midday world. Not a bird in the sky and nothing stirring over at the old ranch house either. The blue Chevy gone and those two likely gone off with the sheriff for some brunch or to the diner on their own. Monday, Monday. He began to whistle but abruptly stopped and looked quickly over his shoulder—at what? Nothing. The empty kitchen. The view into the empty living room. Dark blank face of the TV. Nothing.

He grabbed his jacket from the chairback and frisked it for phone and wallet and keys and slapped up the hundred-dollar bill, and then he went out onto the porch and past the wooden rockers and down the steps and across the yellow and crusted and spongy turf. Rich stink of earth in the air, pungency of rootbeds and tunneling worms. Grass and hay and horseshit.

He drove by the cafe and he saw the blue Chevy there and drove on. He drove by the Gatskill house and he drove by his old high school up on the yellow and snow-scabbed hill, and everything he saw was old and tired and pitiful. It was as though he'd gone away for many years and had not seen the process that changed things but only the change itself, all at once, which was the same as seeing your own life gone by. Then he reached the interstate, and with the speakers pumping through him he gunned the El Camino and headed down toward Denver.

HE LEFT THE CLOUDS and the dregs of snow and descended into the full green outbreak of spring. There were good cheap places on the east side of the city but there was a place he liked on the west side with a billiards table and where you could still smoke and where if you got too lit you didn't have to drive all the way back through town, through all that traffic and highway patrol. He also hoped to see an old boy he knew there, although this old boy wouldn't show until much later if he showed at all.

It was just one o'clock in the afternoon when he pushed through the back door into the near-empty barroom; the room itself was hardly more than a passageway, dominated by the old Brunswick with its three good lion's feet and a fourth blocky stump of blackened oak, its stained and burn-holed felt.

Behind the bar was Louis, the old man with the tremendous hands. Louis didn't care for a song during the day and if someone got one going he'd limp over and unplug the machine and after that the billiards cracked more smartly, voices sailed, a girl's laugh turned the heads of the daytime drunks.

Billy took a seat at the bar, leaving an empty stool between himself and two men who'd been talking quietly when he came in and who now stopped to watch him in the backbar mirror as he settled himself, as if he were a strange new development that might or might not be suffered.

Louis came and Billy asked for a seven-and-seven and the old man set to mixing it. In the mirror, beyond the image of himself, was the bright reflected square of the bar's only window, and within that bright square were the shapes of a man and a woman. The man leaning close to tell her things no one else could hear in the hushed and daylit bar.

Louis centered the seven-and-seven on a bar coaster and Billy palmed the hundred-dollar bill down and the old man held the bill to the light, made change, and placed the smaller bills exactly where the hundred had been. Billy pushed two singles back and folded the remaining cash into his shirt pocket and raised his drink to Louis, who nodded, and he drank.

"Can a man still smoke in here, boss?" he said, and Louis said, "He can if these boys don't mind," and the two men turned to look at Billy—the far one older than the near one, who might've been a little older than Billy.

"Smoke 'em if you got 'em," said the older man, and Billy looked to the younger, nearer man, this man staring at him for a moment from under the bill of his cap, then shrugging and facing forward again.

Billy said Much obliged and got one going. Louis placed the ashtray on the bar.

He drank. He smoked. The two men resumed their conversation, the older man monologuing low and steady, speaking about his wife, or his ex-wife, telling the younger man in the cap all the things he and the ex-wife had done in their marriage, good and bad. Billy ordered another drink and the man spoke about the things he would like to do to his ex-wife now, now that he was no longer blinded by love, and he said many graphic things he'd be sorry he said, Billy thought, if the woman ever turned up dead. If she wasn't dead already. He stirred his drink and drew the little double-barreled swizzle between his lips and sipped at the fizzing glass brim.

"It's like a man just goes along for years," the man said, "and he thinks he's living his life, he thinks he's a normal Joe living his life with a normal woman, but he ain't, he ain't, and one day he sits up in bed and he sees his life for what it really is. Sees his wife for what she really is. You know what I'm talking about, Steve?"

The younger man nodded.

"Right, Steve?"

"Right," said the younger man, Steve.

The man lifted his beer, swallowed, set it down again. "Same thing as when I was in the service, Steve, which, as I said, I ain't at liberty to talk about. Five years of high-level shit and then, one day, boom, there I am, staring at myself in a mirror, covered in blood and no idea how or why. Same motherfucking day different motherfucking story."

Billy caught his own eye in the backbar mirror. *He ain't never gonna stop, this old boy.*

Well, I don't see the chain keeping you here.

But the seven-and-seven was smooth and he had the twenties in his pocket and he sat watching Louis wash out glasses and dry them and set them in their places, big pint glasses that in the old man's hands became abruptly, unbelievably smaller. When he came over to see if Billy wanted another, Billy ordered a beer just to watch the effect. He drank half the cold pint and then he stood up and walked to the men's room, and when he returned, the talker was gone.

The other man named Steve sat staring into the mirror, one hand on what remained of his pint. Billy nodded at him in the mirror; Steve nodded back and both drank from their beers.

Louis wiped down the bar and stocked the cooler. Behind them, in the window, the man held the woman's throat in his hand, she the wrist of that hand in hers.

"Quiet in here," Billy said, and the man named Steve said, "Nice and quiet." He sipped his beer and caught Billy's eye in the mirror. "It must be a terrible burden," he said, "having to keep so quiet."

"How's that?" said Billy.

Steve nodded to his right. "Military man," he said. "Keeping it all locked in like that. Terrible burden."

"Terrible," said Billy. "He sure had some stories he couldn't tell."

Steve picked up a pair of sunglasses from the bar and frowned at the lenses. "I like a good story, don't get me wrong. But a man should never be the hero of his own stories. Nobody likes those stories." He jiggled the sunglasses, as though he were thinking about putting them on and going.

"Do you shoot?" Billy said.

The sunglasses stopped jiggling.

"Sorry?"

"I said do you shoot."

Steve sidled his eyes at him. "Do I shoot what, bud?"

"Guns. Firearms."

"What kind of a question is that?"

"A simple one. I saw your shades. Usually see those on boys at the range. Or po-lice. Or po-lice at the range."

Steve regarded him. "You ever see me at the range, bud?"

"No. I don't go there much myself." He gave the man an easy smile. "Too many po-lice."

"You think I'm a *po-lice*?"

"No, I'd wager you're not."

"Why would you wager that?"

"What's a cop doing in a place like this?"

"Looking for bad men."

"He'd be in the right place. But he wouldn't have mud on his boots. A lawman can't abide mud on his boots. Everybody knows that."

Steve did not glance down at his boots. "You have some particular interest in my boots, bud?"

Billy smiled. Steve did not smile but neither did he appear hostile under the bill of the cap. Did not appear anything. The cap, entirely featureless and of a nameless color between green and brown, matched the canvas jacket he kept zipped to his throat, a bland and homespun uniform of unguessable protocols. Seated he somehow gave the impression of a man who, on his feet, would not be very big but whom you would not take lightly in a fight. It was early for a fight but men who drank in the daytime would fight in the daytime and Billy was one of them.

He didn't want to fight. He was enjoying his drinking and he had the twenties in his pocket and he didn't want to get thrown out by old Louis with his great hands.

"None whatsoever, Steve. Why don't you let me buy you one?"

"Did you just call me Steve?"

"I did. I heard the military man say it before. What's your pleasure?"

"My name isn't Steve."

"My mistake," said Billy. "I must of misheard." He teased one of the twenties from his pocket. "Mine ain't bud, either. It's Billy." He floated the twenty to the bar and watched Louis come over. "Seven-and-seven for me, and whatever this man is drinking."

"Same?" said Louis, and after a moment the man nodded.

They sat in silence until the drinks came and were paid for and Louis had been tipped.

"I thank you for the drink and I apologize for my rudeness," the man said. "I guess I got all talked out by Mr. Covert-Ops."

"My feelings ain't hurt," Billy said. "Cheers."

"My name's Joe," the man said, offering his hand, and Billy laughed, shaking his hand.

"What's funny?" said Joe.

"I got a brother named Joe."

"That so?"

"Guess what he is."

"What?"

"Po-lice."

THEY DRANK A WHILE, and then this man Joe said: "Joe the cop"—smiling for the first time.

"Joe the sheriff. Up in the mountains."

"Which mountains are those?"

"Are there some other mountains around here?"

"There's all kinds of mountains in the mountains, Billy."

Billy looked over at him. The man looking back from under the bill. Still smiling.

"Brother Joe is sheriff in the Grand County mountains," he said, and the man picked up his beer and sipped it.

"Grand County," he said thoughtfully. "Grand County. Seems like there was something in the news with a sheriff from Grand County, while back."

"Probably some drunk on skis waving a cap gun."

"No," said the man. "No, this had to do with a girl. Teenage girl went missing up there. Or am I misremembering?"

Billy gave him a frown of admiration. "Good recall, Joe. That was over two years ago."

"You remember things like that. Things like that they stay with you."

They drank. A tall man at the end of the bar stood, looked about, saw nothing that pleased him, and then seemed to follow his own wooden legs out the back door.

"There was this one boy I remember from grade school," said Joe. He looked up from his beer, up from under the bill, and when Billy met his eyes in the mirror he looked down again and stared into his glass. As though pondering what he'd just said or what he would say next. Whether to say anything more at all.

"What boy was that?" said Billy, and Joe tilted his pint for a sip.

"That boy was Delmar Steadman. Plain, ordinary boy we all called Smell-mar for some reason. He wasn't fat or ugly or smelly or anything, but we'd decided to make him something to make fun of, I can't even tell you why. Maybe because his daddy was the Roto-Rooter man. Maybe because he had a big sister named Bonnie who gave us all boners, I don't know. Well. His backyard,

Delmar's backyard, came fence to fence with Becky Clark's backyard, and those two had grown up making eyes at each other through that cyclone fence. Sneaking kisses, pressing up against one another before they even knew why. It happens. Happens all the time. Some people find the love of their lives at that age. Tell stories about it when they're sixty, seventy years old." He glanced at Billy in the mirror, raised his glass for a sip, and set it down again.

"Trouble was, at about age ten, Becky lost interest. Just dropped old Delmar cold. We knew this the way you knew everything about everybody back then and not because of computers and cell phones either. You remember how that was, Billy?"

Billy said he did and the man went on.

"Well. Along came the summer between grade school and middle school. Magical summer. All of us shooting up like weeds, smell of chlorine and cut grass. It's about the Fourth of July—day before or day after I don't recall—and young Becky is out back suntanning on the patio. By now it's been a good two years since she's said a single word to Delmar, through that fence or at school or anywhere else. Fact is, she's hardly even *seen* Delmar in all that time. The boy never comes out in the yard anymore, not even to play with that sorry little dog of his. The back door opens, dog goes out, pisses, shits, back door opens again and dog goes in. Like living next door to Boo Radley. You know who that is?"

Billy didn't. It didn't matter.

"So Becky's out on the patio, which was nothing but a concrete slab with weeds growing in the cracks, catching some rays in that red bikini she wore that summer, oh Lord. Browning those arms, that stomach. Smell of coconut oil. She's got the sunglasses on and the headphones going and she doesn't hear him. Never even turns her head."

The man fell silent, staring into his glass. He gave the glass a turn as if to set the contents in motion and thereby his story again.

"Her own daddy found her like that, Billy. Lying there in the July sun with those headphones still going and her little forehead pushed in like a bad melon. Glass of iced tea sweating on the concrete and a red Stillson wrench lying there beside it. You know what a Stillson wrench is, Billy?"

"Pipe wrench."

"Big one. His daddy's, about yea big." He shook his head like a man in dismay. He drank.

After a minute Billy said: "Did they think he did it?"

"Think who?"

"Delmar's daddy. The Roto-Rooter man."

"They might of, at first. But then Delmar himself came out with the whole story."

"What was the whole story?"

"What do you mean?"

"Why did he do it?"

"He said it just come to him. He couldn't say why."

Billy picked up his cigarettes and got one in his lips and lit it with the Zippo and set the Zippo carefully down again. He pulled on the cigarette and side-blew the smoke away from the man.

"What happened to him?" he said. "To Delmar."

"They took him away. Becky's folks got divorced and moved away. Old man Steadman moved away and we never saw nor heard another thing about any of those people again. The world just rolled on." He lifted his beer and tilted back a drink. Made an adjustment to his cap. "I don't know," he said. "Sometimes I think he was just too young for himself, old Delmar." He raised his glass again but didn't drink. "I think if he'd of waited, if he'd of just let himself grow into himself, he'd of been all right."

Billy drew on the cigarette and blew a slow cloud into the space between himself and the image of himself.

"I never told that story before," the man said. "I wonder what made me tell it now. Talking this man's ear off."

THEY SAT. THEY DRANK. After a while the man drew the edge of his thumb over his lips corner to corner and said: "They ever find that girl?"

"What girl?"

"Up in those mountains."

"No, they never did."

The man shook his head. "How about that boy, then?"

Billy had drained his drink to the ice and was preparing to stand. "What boy is that?"

"There was a boy too, wasn't there? A little brother or something? Got hurt up there on his bike?"

Billy looked at him.

"And she left him there," the man said. "That girl. Threw a blanket on him and just left him there, as I recall."

"That's right," Billy said. "A boy on a bike."

"Where's he at now? That boy?"

"Damned if I know. They were just tourists." He raised his glass and tumbled an ice cube past his lips and broke it in his molars, the sound enormous and concussive in his skull. Then he said: "That boy wasn't worth shit for evidence."

"He wasn't?"

"Anything he saw got knocked clean out of him."

The man shook his head. "That's a pity. That's a flat-out pity." He sat staring into his glass. "It sure is a funny world, isn't it, Billy."

"That's one word for it."

"What's another one?"

"I don't know."

Billy sat another minute, and one minute more, then peeled off a five and got to his feet. "Gotta hit the road, Joe. But I'd like to buy you one more. Just for calling you Steve."

"You're off, Billy?"

"It looks like weather and I'm heading right into it."

They both turned to look at the window behind them. The man and the woman were gone and the grayness that Billy had left in the hills had rolled down onto the city as though it sought him out.

"Good talking to you, Billy. Next time I'll buy."

"That's a deal, Joe. You take her easy."

"Drive safe now."

Coldness had come down with the gray and it had a sharp coppery taste to it like blood. Three cars sat in the lot: his own El Camino, a burgundy and white Oldsmobile, and an old, high-sitting black Bronco with new mud on the tires and sprayed along the body in heavy four-wheel-drive patterns.

He stepped up to the Bronco on the passenger's side and peered into the front seats and there was nothing in there but car. Seats, dash, floorboards. As if it were newly bought or up for sale. He looked more closely at the paint job and saw that it was not the original, nor the work of someone who painted cars for a living. He moved to the rear and bent to the tinted glass of the hardtop and saw in the cargo space an orderly array of gear: five-gallon gas can, fat coil of towing rope, a good-sized tool or tackle box, and two paper grocery bags, all of it seized in a black elastic webbing.

He stood and looked at the back door of the bar. He shook his head. "Shit," he said, and walked away. Then he stopped and went back. He made a diving mask of his hands and peered inside again. One of the grocery bags was less than full and no way to tell what it held. In the other the tops of two boxes were visible, one box top rectangular and anonymously white, the other a square of light blue with the word *Tampax* in bright yellow.

He straightened and looked about him with his hands in his jacket pockets. His right hand playing the weight of the lighter around and around. He could feel the liquor swimming in his brain.

"Shit," he said again. And turned and walked to his car.

He sat with the engine off and watched the first volley of sleet break across the glass. After a while he started the car and drove across the road to the 7-Eleven, backed into a space, and killed the engine again. He took his phone from his pocket and checked the time. Two thirty in the afternoon.

He drew on his cigarette and held the smoke, staring at the phone. Then he exhaled and dialed. The call was forwarded and a deputy answered and Billy asked to speak to the sheriff.

"He's fairly jammed up right now, Billy. I'll have him call you back."

"I need to talk to him now, Denny. It's critical."

"Critical?"

"It's important, Denny."

"Donny. I'll tell him to call you, Billy."

Billy blew smoke from his nostrils and grinned. "I'd be very grateful, Donny."

The sheriff called back an hour later. By then, Billy was climbing the interstate through a heavy sleet going to snow.

"Thanks for returning my call, Sheriff."

"What is it, Billy?"

"I got a question for you."

The sheriff, in his office, was going over some of his father's—their father's—old papers. Some so old the ink had begun to fade. "Ask it," he said.

"Those Courtland kids, up on that mountain, when the girl went missing."

The line was silent as the sheriff got his bearings. "What about them?"

"There's something you never told anybody. Isn't there."

"Not following you, Billy."

"There's always something you don't tell. That only the cops know about. That's how it's done, right? Procedurally speaking."

"Billy, are you drunk?"

"I ain't had a drop."

"Sounds like you're driving too."

"Listen, God damn it. I just want to know what you didn't tell nobody, that's all. It's a simple question."

The sheriff was silent. Billy watched the fat wet flakes coming down. The dark grooves of tiretrack in the gray slurry of the road. The Bronco's taillights simmering far ahead, hot and beady.

"If I didn't tell nobody," said his brother finally, "I didn't tell nobody for a reason, so why would I tell you now?"

"Because I'm asking. Because who gives a damn now?"

The sheriff said nothing. Then: "You better get off the road, Billy. We got a storm up here and it's headed down there."

The line hissed and crackled. He was climbing higher now and losing his signal. He thought he'd lost it, was about to hang up when the sheriff said, "Go home, Billy. I mean it. Those folks ain't none of your business now."

"Now?" he laughed. "Hell, Sheriff, they never were."

51

The Bronco held a good pace on the interstate, a legal but bold pace for the conditions, which had gone from sleet to a heavy snowfall in a matter of miles as they drove upward and westward, leaving the new foothill greens behind and traveling back into the high old winter of the mountains. The El Camino was not a mountain car nor a snow car but in the winter Billy kept two hundred pounds of sand in tubular bags heaped over the rear wheels, and on this day in early April the snow was not too deep, and he had the tracks of the cars before him, the tracks of the Bronco, to keep his treads close to the pavement, and he climbed the mountain interstate with ease.

The light was flat and gray and there were two good hours of it left and he drove without headlights, keeping well back from the Bronco. He'd passed the exit for home eight miles back and now he was approaching the exit for the pass that would take him up to the divide and down again into the resort town where the Courtland girl had gone missing, in the county where his brother was sheriff, and he slowed, anticipating the exit—but the Bronco's taillights went on, and the tracks went on, and he shook his head and smiled. Old Steve was a smart one: You did not go hunting in your own backyard. Or shop or drink. You got your goods from some other man's backyard far away, and up here you did not have to go very far to be far away.

"But how far, Steve?" He checked his fuel gauge and saw that the tank was half full. And half empty.

"Where we going, Steve?"

Fourteen miles beyond the exit, just short of the great tunnel that delivered travelers all at once to the far side of the Rockies—to entirely new weather systems, to the long, slow descent to the western deserts and the coast and the ocean—the Bronco's signal light began to blink, its brake lights flared and it took the exit for US Highway 6 and the Loveland Pass. It crossed under the interstate and picked up speed again on the winding two-laner and Billy let himself fall farther behind, as there would now be no place for the Bronco to go but up to the top of the pass and down again on the other side.

He took a switchback turn at its posted speed, the car slewing mildly, and when the road straightened again he checked his phone for a signal and found that he had one—a very scant one—and he entered a short text message and sent it.

The road wound high into the mountains, into heavier snowfall and finally into a gusting chaos of snow like the white rioting heart of the storm itself, before cresting and beginning its steep descent into the valley on the other side. Down and down and the snowfall growing lighter again at the lower altitude and the mountain switchbacks cutting once, twice, and a third time across the Snake River before settling into an easier alliance with the river at the floor of the valley, both road and river turning according to the same geography, the same logic.

He kept the radio off, wanting to hear nothing but the engine and the regular sweep of the wipers. The liquor had left him all at once, leaving him edgy and wishing for a cup of coffee. He asked himself if he knew what he was doing, and answered that he knew exactly what he was doing, he was taking a drive, that was all.

There were no exits or even turnoffs for many miles. Then the posted speed limit fell, and another sign announced their arrival at a resort village, and the speed limit fell again and his heart lifted at other signs of organized humanity: the high shedroofs of the lodges, the Christmassy lights in the restaurants and shops, the cheering reds and greens of traffic lights. But there was little traffic so late in the season and when the Bronco caught the village's outermost red light Billy knew he would have to pull up behind it or else draw more attention to himself. He was fifty, perhaps forty, feet away—the shape of the driver's head visible through the rear window—when red turned to green, and signaling, the Bronco turned left.

"Go on through and double back," he told himself; but he was afraid of losing him in the grid of streets, and at the last moment he signaled and turned through the yellow and followed.

The Bronco immediately turned left again, heading east along the rim of a large and nearly empty parking lot. Then it turned right onto a county road, which took them all at once out of the village and into the long mountainous valley to the east, and as there was no other traffic coming or going Billy let the gap between the cars grow once more. With his free hand he collected his phone and punched up and sent another text.

The road turned south and the speed limit fell and Billy rounded a bend to see that the Bronco had come to a stop at a T in the road. The intersection had come up suddenly and there was no hiding, and if the man checked his mirrors there'd be no missing the El Camino behind him. Likewise when the man went one way or the other there'd be no missing that the El Camino had done the same, and so he hoped the Bronco would turn right, where a sign indicated the town of Montezuma lay, instead of left, where there seemed little incentive or encouragement for any single vehicle to go, let alone two.

The Bronco sat idling at the T as if awaiting a break in traffic, but there was no traffic. The El Camino idling behind it. The snow drifting down.

"Go left, you son of a bitch, I dare you."

The Bronco signaled left and turned, and Billy took his place at the T, signaled, and followed.

HE CAME TO ANOTHER intersection a few miles on but the Bronco had not taken it, and he followed the tracks deeper into the range. The Bronco ignored two more turns and the road began to climb in increasingly steep cutbacks, as if here were yet another pass that would take them inevitably to another summit and another vortex of snow. But the snowfall remained light and the El Camino continued to find traction. His luck was holding, and he climbed another few miles toward the white ghostly peaks before his luck ran out.

It ran out all at once, without warning, when the Bronco's taillights disappeared, as though the car had gone off the road. Yet when he arrived at the place where the taillights had vanished he found no tracks careening from the road—found no road at all but only the sudden crunch and ping of loose gravel under him, and the road, such as it was, diving into the evergreens ahead.

He pumped the brakes and brought the El Camino to a halt and sat looking into the trees. The mountains that lay above and beyond the trees were obscured by the trees themselves and by the fog of snowfall. He rolled down his window and looked out into the white emptiness of the gorge, the air thin and cold and pungent with the smell of snow and pine. He picked up his phone and sent a final text, then sat looking at the road ahead. Or what had been the road and which, but for the tracks, might have been just a minor clearing at the end of the road where the makers of roads, going back to men in wagons, had abruptly and inexplicably stopped.

He tugged at the hairs below his lip. He thought of the set of tire chains back at the barn hung on their barn spike with the horse tack. He sat a few moments longer, sensing the rising dusk in the bowl of the gorge, in the shades of the pinewood. Then he said, "All right, son, let's see it," and he lifted his foot from the brake and drove on.

52

The road tunneled in wide swings through the woods and was not too steep, the snow not too deep, and he made good progress with the Bronco's tracks before him. The road looped back upon itself, and on the far side of every loop he expected to see no more road and the Bronco parked before some ordinary mountain homestead, the man, Steve, stepping out of the car to the ordinary jubilation of dog and wife and children, and nothing for Billy to do but laugh and drive away. But around every turn there was more road, more trees, another turn, and no Bronco, and no house and no wife.

The road narrowed as it climbed. Trees and scrub trees crowding in, low-hanging boughs lapping at the windows. If a man were to stop he could not turn around but would have to back all the way down and good luck with that, pardner. He drove on and the road grew steeper, a fact he could not see or feel but knew by the increasing slippage of his tires. He shifted on the fly into his lowest gear and pressed on more slowly, all his senses wired to the messages of the climb, and still the tires spun, the tail swinging drunkenly toward tree trunks, righting, yawing again the opposite way, and he understood with a rising fury that she would not make it and that he'd known she wouldn't. He made one more bend, tires spraying a wet slag over the undercarriage, and with his fingers light on the wheel he worked her with all his skill but the rubber spun and the motor raced and there was nothing to do but stop and hope the car held. It didn't. Brake, no brake, it would go back the way it came. He hooked an elbow over the seat and attempted to take the curve one-handed but he overshot it and the bed of the El Camino slammed into the sudden, ungiving trunk of a pine and went no farther.

He killed the engine. He lit a cigarette and sat watching the snow mutely finding the windshield. Falling heavier now. The Bronco's tracks were filling.

He pulled the keys from the ignition and pocketed them and buttoned the leather jacket and collected the rawhide gloves from the glovebox, and then he reached under his seat and hunted down the bottle and took a swig. He reached again under the seat, groping deeper, "Come here you mother-fucker," the blow to the tree having sent it to the very back of the cab, and at last he felt it and tugged it free. He peeled away the black watch cap and put it on his head and checked to see that the gun, a nine-millimeter he'd bought off a man in Nevada, was loaded, the safety on, then he dropped the gun into his right pocket. He picked up his phone from the seat and put that in his pocket too but then took it out again and left it on the passenger's seat, centering it on the cover of a magazine. Finally he pulled on his gloves and got out.

He took a few steps up the road and turned to look back. His car rested nearly abeam to the road so that any vehicle coming up or going down could not pass. He stood thinking about that, then dropped his cigarette into the Bronco's track and continued on.

The treadless cowboy boots he'd won at billiards sent him to his hands and knees, and sent him there again before he adopted a wider, splay-footed stance, digging the inside edges of the soles into the snow. By the time he reached the next bend, no more than thirty yards from the car, his legs were burning and his lungs felt pierced through by the thin air. He stopped, hands to knees, unable to curse for his wheezing and his wheezing the only sound made by any living thing on the mountain.

Before him the road looked less a road than some wide chute carved out by falling rocks or by water or both, and still the Bronco's tracks went on, and finally so did he, staggering on until he reached the next bend where he rested again. When he came to the bend after that and there was still no sign of the Bronco other than its fading tracks, he fell once more into his wheezing stance of rest and fought with all his heart the desire to drop to his knees, to his back, in the snow.

The day was now all but gone, the sun fallen behind some distant peak. He judged that within a few minutes there'd be no light at all but the light of the snow itself where it lay on the trail.

He glanced back down the mountain at the tracks of the Bronco and his own thin herringbone footprints between. He removed a glove with his teeth and found his cigarettes and the Zippo.

"You got to the end of this to decide," he said, and when he finished the cigarette he dropped it in the snow and went on, and he'd not gone very far before the tracks of the Bronco turned abruptly from the trail, plunging down into a deeper, scrappier woods.

He stood at the top of this gully looking down, his heart thudding in his neck. He studied the trees for possible handholds and felt for the nine-millimeter in his pocket, making sure it was secure, and then he reached out for the first tree and stopped. There was a bootprint in the snow. Nearly as fresh as his own but not his own, the floor of this print waffled with good tread. It led to its left-footed counterpart, and he saw that the tracks had come up out of the gully and continued up the trail. He looked ahead and saw nothing in the snowfall but the white, snaking trail and the dark pattern of prints along its back.

He looked down the gully once more where the Bronco was stashed, and he looked back up the mountain.

"All right, asshole," he said, addressing himself. "It's a fair fight now."

He knew by the clarity of the tread that the man's lead on him was not great, and he tried to stare not at the snow but into the darker woods ahead so that his eyes would be rightly adjusted to see the man before the man saw him. But he never saw the man. He'd climbed another fifty steep yards of mountain when he saw to his right, or thought he saw, a wink of light deep in the woods, so faint that had he come by this spot only a few minutes sooner, a few shades earlier in the gradients of dusk, he would not have seen it at all.

The man he tracked had seen the light or not seen it or didn't care. His tracks had gone on, stamping their regular seal on the trail until both trail and tracks curved around a low rampart of boulders and passed out of sight.

Billy stared into the woods where he thought he'd seen the light. He began to believe he'd not seen it at all, that it had been some trick of the high altitude, of the mixed fuels of exhaustion and adrenaline. Then he saw it again, far back through the trees, dully orange and faintly guttering like a candle orphaned in the woods, and on nothing more than the lurching of his heart at the sight of it, he abandoned the trail and began to make his way through the pines and the snow toward this light.

53

Sheriff Kinney considered the papers before him sorted in their various stacks. He picked one up and read a few lines. It was a letter from his father's sister, his aunt, from a time when people wrote letters. It seemed all about the weather and he set it down again. He swiveled in the chair and looked out the window at the shallow field of snowfall and the white world beyond.

"Out in this in that goddam car of yours," he said.

"You ask me something, Sheriff?" his deputy said from the outer office.

"What? No. Talking to myself."

The deputy appeared in the doorway holding the coffeepot. "You want any more of this or should I toss it?"

"Go ahead and toss it and go on home before this gets worse."

The deputy looked out the window. "What do I care about a little snow, Sheriff?"

"Well, why don't you go on out and make a snowman then?"

The deputy stood with the coffeepot.

Kinney looked up at him. "I'm sorry, Donny." He gestured vaguely at the papers before him.

"That's all right, Sheriff. Your dad sure kept track of things, didn't he."

"He sure did."

"You look like a bookkeeper there, or a lawyer."

"I feel like both." He randomly lifted a paper and it was the deed to a cemetery plot for himself. "A man never knows how many pieces of paper he collects in his life because there's never any cause to look at them all together until he's dead. And then it's somebody else and not him who gets the job of looking at them, and it is a hopeless task, Deputy. Hopeless and thankless. Every man knows this and yet every man still saves up all his goddam papers. Now why is that?"

"I guess a man can't help himself, Sheriff. I guess it's his nature."

He stared at the deputy. "I reckon," he said. "Now go on home, Donny."

"Want me to wash that mug?"

"Thanks, Donny."

He leaned back in the swivel chair and set his bootheels on the edge of the desk and he looked at the picture of his daughter there on the desk. Josephine on that good roan pony, Laddy, the reins so easy in her hands. Sixteen on that day and she'd taken the blue ribbon by five entire seconds.

A junior now at the university in Boulder studying journalism. A good way to see the world, she said. As if the world were something her father and mother couldn't imagine. She had not known the girl they found up there on the mountain trail, Kelly Ann Baird. But people at the school remembered when she'd gone missing. A pretty white college girl just vanishing. It was always news.

He wanted to call Josephine every day but he didn't. She wouldn't have it. The closer he wanted to keep her, the farther away she wanted to go. That's what being a father was.

He stared at the papers and thought of the ranch and his life there as a boy, the only child for many years until Billy came along. Now he'd done the math and there was no way to keep the ranch without selling his house up here and moving back down there and nobody wanted to move back down there, least of all his wife. He'd sell the ranch, and Billy would get some money and move on, maybe for good. Grant and his son would move on too, you couldn't worry about that. Grant was a smart man who'd once run his own construction company, a good man, now a man who'd suffered the most unthinkable thing. You could help but you couldn't help him, not really.

His phone sounded the tone that told him he had a text message. He picked it up and it was Billy again. That made three. He read the message and set the phone down again and stared at it, and while he was staring at it the phone sounded its note once again, and he picked it up and read the message. But whereas the others had been the names of highways and passes and county roads, here was a single word that by itself made no sense to him: *blanket*. He scrolled to see if he'd missed something. He waited for the rest of the message, but it never came. He looked again out the window at the snow. He looked at his daughter on the horse.

When his boots hit the floor his deputy called out to see if he was all right.

Kinney gathered the two-way from the desk, his sheriff's hat and jacket from the coat tree, and stepped into the outer office. Donny stood in his jacket and gloves near the front door.

"What's going on, Sheriff?"

"I see you got your snow boots on."

"I saw it was snowing."

"Did you already tell Linda you were coming home?"

"Just sent her a text."

"All right. You can call her from the road."

"Where we going, Sheriff?"

"Loveland Pass."

"Loveland Pass?" The deputy glanced through the panes of glass at the tumbling storm.

"I thought you didn't care about no snow, Deputy."

"I don't, Sheriff. But that's Summit County."

"Is that a fact?"

The deputy tugged at his gloves. He adjusted his hat.

Kinney looked at him. "I just gotta check something out, Donny, and I need your help."

"Hell, Sheriff. You don't have to ask for it."

54

It was altogether nightfall under the pines, and while this helped him to track the orange light it also rigged his path with deadfall he didn't see until he'd snagged his boot and pitched headlong into branches that raked at his face like the hands of ghouls. One twisted ankle pulsed in its boot and he struggled to hold his direction. It was necessary to detour around the boughs of the pines and each time he did so he lost the light, then stopped, then moved again laterally through the trees until he reached a place where the light and his eye aligned once more and he could move forward again. Then, abruptly, he smelled woodsmoke, and he said in the silence of the trees, *Jesus, Jesus.*

He made progress but the light seemed to grow no brighter or nearer, as though it were borne through the woods ahead as a lure is dragged through water. He pursued it, moving through the woods tree by tree, until he came around the broad skirt of a blue spruce and stopped.

Before him in the smallest of clearings sat an unlikely structure, so squat and spare, so colorless and rough-hewn and artless, that if not for the weak pulse of light in the seams of the door he never would have seen it. And but for the light never would have believed it to be anything but some crude and temporary shelter that rightly should have rotted back into the mountain a century before.

There were no windows that he could see, and even the pale vine of woodsmoke rising from the roof pipe, hardly distinguishable from the snowfall into which it climbed, seemed a sign of abandonment and disuse.

He stood almost within the spruce, pulling the air into his lungs as quietly as he could. He looked for signs of the man he'd been tracking and saw none. No footprints before the door of the shack and no visible trail or footpath in any direction. There was the hunkered little structure and there were the trees all around it and there was the vast, snowbound mountain. He watched the seam in the door to see if anyone would pass between it and the source of light within but no one did. He looked all around him through the trees, alert to any sound. He reached into his pocket and brought out the nine-millimeter and, muffling the sounds with his gloved hands, chambered a round and thumbed off the safety. He removed his right-hand glove and stowed it in the opposite pocket with the whiskey bottle, restowed the gun carefully, and stepped away from the spruce.

Crusted snow lay under the new powder and his boot steps announced him to the woods but there was no help for that and he moved ahead unhurriedly, favoring the bad ankle, until he reached the cabin. He raised his fist to knock on the door and it was then he saw the lock, a large outdoor Master, the fat boltshackle passed through an equally fat staple of a heavy-gauge hasp, which was itself fastened to door and jamb not with screws but lags, or perhaps through bolts. In the moment he took to consider such hardware he understood from its gleam and the smell of oil that it had been used recently and would be used again soon. Then he struck the door a few knocks with his bare knuckle and called out Hello as casually and quietly as he could.

He lowered his hand and found the gun grip inside his pocket. Held his breath, listening. The ticking of the snow on his shoulders, the faint pop of firewood on the other side of the door. He glanced around the clearing and it seemed even smaller now that he was at its center, the woods that shaped it more immense and dark. He let go of the gun and raised his hand again but then held it still. There was a sound from the other side of the door, as of a chain, as of chain links unspooling over a wooden floor, like a hound hauling itself to its feet, some old mountain breed chained up against doing damage or breaking free in its master's absence. And then the hound spoke. It spoke in the voice of a girl and it said, thinly, "Hello? Is someone there?"

Billy swallowed.

"Who's in there?" he said.

The chain dragged again and came to rest.

"Who's out there?" said the girl. Nearer to the door but still some distance from it.

"What's your name?" he said, and waited, his heart pumping. He asked again, and she said: "A man is keeping me here. Please help me."

He took hold of the gun again. "Is the man in there?"

"No. He's gone. Please help me."

"I'm trying, darlin. Just tell me your name. Please."

She was silent. The chain was still.

Then she said her name. So quietly that Billy wondered if it had been his mind that said it.

55

After dinner the boy got into his jacket and went down the porch steps and out onto the April snowfall. He headed for the barn, stepping again and again into his own blue shadow, until abruptly he stopped and looked up and saw the full moon burning overhead. For all its wintry sharpness the night smelled of the thaw the snow had covered, of loam and grass and pitch. As he neared the barn he smelled the hay bale he'd busted open earlier, and he smelled the horses and the saddles, odors as pungent as they'd be on a hot day in the summer. The mares stretched their necks and snorted as he unpocketed an apple and held it out to be smacked up by one mare and then he did the same for the other. They snuffed up the apple scent from his palm and, finding only scent, permitted him to stroke the warm ridge of bone from forehead to muzzle. On the rail before the tack wall sat the two saddles, and he put his hand on the seat of one, feeling along the smooth cool curve of it.

He'd seen her just once, since: dark-haired and pretty in her black dress at the old man's funeral . . . looking up to find her looking at him. But that was not the time to talk to her, that was not the time, and what did it matter anyway?

When he got back to the house, his father had broomed off the porch steps and was sitting on the top step, smoking a cigarette. The boy sat beside him and took one of his cigarettes and leaned toward the offered flame.

"You ever look at that old man's throat?" his father said.

"Yeah, I looked at it."

"But it made no impression."

"It made an impression." He drew on his cigarette. "I'll quit when you quit."

Grant looked at him and looked away. "All right."

One of the mares whinnied and stamped in her stall.

"They're going to miss you," Grant said.

"Who?" said the boy. Flicking his ash.

"Those horses. Who did you think I meant?"

The boy shrugged. "Thought you meant the horses."

"Then why'd you ask who?"

The boy said nothing. They smoked.

"Maybe we should make an offer," Grant said. "Take them with us. The horses, I mean."

"Take them where?"

Grant lifted his cigarette and drew on it. Across the blue clearing sat the old man's house, dark and silent. There was no wind or movement or sound anywhere. The El Camino had been gone all day.

"You think he's coming back?" said the boy.

Grant straightened his arm to tip his ash. "It doesn't much matter now, does it?"

"It never did," said the boy. "Not to me."

Grant looked at him in his wrist cast, looking up at the moon. The moon in the very middle of the sky, in the black bowl of stars shaped by the snowy ridgelines all around, the ridgelines themselves bright and stark and close in the moonlight.

"It's going to snow again," Grant said.

The boy scanned the sky. "There's not a cloud in a hundred miles."

"That's a halo moon."

"So?"

"So that means more snow."

"Says who?"

"Says everybody."

The boy glanced at him. "You were watching the news," he said, and Grant nodded.

"It's snowing in the mountains and headed this way." He pointed his cigarette at the moon. "But anybody can see that."

The boy shook his head.

To the north above the ridgeline a falling star burned and died, leaving a faint scratch on the black lens of sky.

Did you make a wish, Daddy?

Yes I did. Did you?

Yes.

Shoulder to shoulder in summer's grass, a concert of summer's insects in their ears. The dizzying, burning heavens.

How many stars are there, Daddy?

Too many to count, Caitydid.

Will they all fall?

No, just a few.

Where do they go when they fall?

I don't know. Where do you think?

"Did you see that?" he said to his son.

"What?"

"Falling star."

"It wasn't a falling star."

"Sure it was."

"Stars don't fall. It was space debris. A piece of rock."

Grant looked at him.

"What?" said the boy.

Grant looked to the north again. As if where one star fell there would be another.

The boy drew on his cigarette and surveyed the sky all around. "See that little group of stars there, just above the ridgeline?" He was pointing to the southwest.

Grant shook his head.

"Right under Cancer?"

Grant looked at him.

"That little cluster," the boy said, "right there, above that high point of trees?"

"All right," said Grant. "I see it."

"That's Hydra, the water snake. Its head, anyway. Longest constellation in the sky. It was charted by the Greeks over two thousand years ago, and guess what?"

"What?"

"Not one star has ever fallen out of it."

Grant nodded. "What else?" he said.

The boy told him that Hercules had fought the water snake as one of his twelve labors, that the snake had many heads and each time Hercules chopped off one head, two grew back. Grant asked how Hercules solved this problem and the boy told him that each time he chopped off a head, his nephew came along with a hot sword to burn the stump.

They were quiet, each looking up, as if watching such things unfold. The boy turned to the north and pointed again. "See those five stars up there? Looks like an upside-down house?"

"Sure," said Grant.

"That's Cepheus, the king."

"What'd he do?"

"He had a wife who bragged about her beauty so much Neptune sent a sea monster to destroy his kingdom."

"Did it?"

"What?"

"Destroy his kingdom."

"No. As a sacrifice to the sea monster the king chained his only daughter to a rock by the sea." The boy tipped his ash.

Grant sat studying the distant lights. Distant cold debris field of falling objects and her hand so warm, so small in his, her grip so strong.

I think they turn into little children, she said.

Like you?

No. Little children who don't live in houses. And who know magic. And who no one can see but God.

Are they angels?

No, Daddy, I told you. They're just little children.

56

Billy pressed his bare hand to the grain of the door. "Caitlin?" he said.

"Yes?"

"Caitlin, my name is Billy."

"Are you with the police?"

"My brother is the sheriff, Caitlin. Sheriff Kinney."

"Is he with you?" These words spoken with such desperation, such hope.

"I'm gonna get you out of there, Caitlin."

He took the big lock in his fist and felt its heft. He doubted the nine-millimeter's capacity to damage it; heard in his mind the shot replaying all over the mountain.

"Does he hide a key out here?"

"I don't think so."

"Is there another way in?"

She told him about the window but that it was boarded and locked from the inside, and he limped around the shack and found the small window at head height and the glowing little sparrow-hole in the batten and he thought to look in but did not. Instead he continued around the shack and on the last unseen side he came upon a scrap of blue tarpaulin, and underneath the tarp he found an ax embedded in the face of a log. The blade popped loose with a tug and was in his hands, the handle smooth from use, the head weighty. Then he saw the sled—old-fashioned wood sled propped against the wall, long enough for three, maybe four sitting children. A heavy towrope and runners of bright red. He could make no sense of it.

He carried the ax back to the door and looked slowly about the woods. "Caitlin?" he said.

"Yes?"

"I found an ax. I'm going to try it on the lock."

She didn't answer. Then she said, "Billy?"

"Yes?"

"There was another man. Last spring. A hiker."

"Yeah?" he said.

"He shot him, Billy. He killed him."

Billy held the ax. He grinned at the door, at the lock. "Thanks, darlin. Now please step back."

He struck the padlock dead on the boltshackle with a ringing blow and the blade threw sparks and delivered a hard shock through his hands and up to his shoulders. He squared off with the door and struck again with another burst of sparks, another jolt of pain in his hands. He swung twice more and took the lock in his fist. Invisible burrs pricked his skin but the lock and the hasp were solid. He thumbed the ax blade, but he hadn't checked before and couldn't say how much of the nicked dullness was his own doing.

He glanced around and once again squared off, and this time he began to chop at the door itself near where the hasp was bolted. But either the blade was badly dulled or else the wood was aged and hard and thick beyond any wood he'd ever experienced, for the ax merely dented and gouged but did not sink or give any sign of splitting the wood.

He held the ax, getting his breath.

The girl made no sound. He asked if she was all right and she answered that she was.

He raised the ax and resumed his work, trying each time to strike the same spot just to the right of the hasp where a pulpy kind of cleft was forming. He learned the best stance and swing and angle, and after a dozen blows to this deepening seam there was a cry of rupture and the ax head sank into the door and stuck. Immediately after, from the trees behind him, something rustled and he turned and reached for the nine-millimeter. but all he saw was the shape of a large night bird winging through the boughs. He watched the place in the trees from which he thought the bird had launched but nothing more stirred save the snowfall. No sound but the deep, thick valving in his ears, which was his own blood.

If you're there, what are you waiting for?

He turned back to the ax handle, and as he did so something bit deeply into his back and he pitched against the door and heard bounced back from it the small flat report of the gun. The bullet had entered him high in the ribs and to the right of his spine, punching a hole in his right lung coming and going, the lung already collapsing, but all he knew was that he'd been shot and could not get his breath.

Fallen against the door, his forehead to the wood, he heard on the other side of it the chain dragging on the floor. She said his name but he didn't answer. He became aware of the approaching footsteps and began fumbling in his pocket for the gun but before he could get it in his grip he felt the pressure at the base of his skull, the dull cold hardness of metal.

"I know what you're looking for and I'd leave it if I were you."

Billy withdrew his hand and placed it flat to the door. He waited for the sound that would be the last. It didn't come. Nothing did. Then the pistol barrel lifted from his skull and he received a blow that sent a white-hot rod coring through his brain. Wave upon wave of pain he'd never imagined and he slumped to the ground, piled against the door. He reached for his head and rolled against the door until he blindly faced the man. Nausea swept through him and he rolled again, his guts convulsing. The heaving brought fresh waves of pain, and fresh nausea followed that and he lay for some time retching up the last of it, and then he lay wheezing through his punctured chest, his body rocked by spasms.

In the midst of this the man took and pocketed the nine-millimeter and he found the whiskey bottle and took that too. Now he grabbed Billy by the shoulder and rolled him back against the door to look at him squarely. He dropped into a squat and sat regarding him, the gun hanging loose between his thighs.

"I figured it was you."

"Did you," Billy wheezed.

"You asked a lot of questions, bud."

"So did you, Steve."

"I told you my name's not Steve. Look what you did to my door. I waited one too many to pop you."

"What were you—" He sucked in a cold length of air. The hole in his back rattled like the strange new gill that it was. "Waiting for."

"I wanted to see if this door would hold up."

"It held pretty good."

"Better than you. You don't look so good, Billy."

"Don't feel so good. What'd you shoot me with?"

"Nothing but this little pop gun."

"Tell you what, Steve."

"What."

"You take off now you might get away."

"Get away from what?"

Billy spat again. "Sheriff."

"Sheriff," said the man. "Sheriff that's your brother? Sheriff Joe?" He studied Billy's face. He looked at the door, as if everything beyond it were visible to him.

He said: "If I thought Sheriff Joe was on his way up here, what chance of living would you give this girl?"

"Same chance," Billy said.

"Thought that through, did you?"

"Wasn't hard."

The man smiled. "No, I bet not."

Billy knew that the moment the man had seen him on the mountain, the girl's fate was decided: sheriff or no sheriff, he would not remain up here and he would not let her live. Billy's only hope was that the man would panic and run. It was not even a hope.

Thin light rippled along the man's teeth. "You know how I know you're full of shit, Billy? The fact of this ax stuck in my door. Why would a man do a thing like that if Sheriff Joe was on his way? Why wouldn't he just sit tight and wait?"

"'Cause he's dumb and reckless."

They were silent. No sound on the other side of the door but the soft popping of firewood. The snow had stopped, and the clouds above the clearing were infused with light, as if beyond them lay a bright city. Billy coughed and spat and the effort raised red blots to his vision. The ground beneath him moved like a bed of rolling logs.

The man glanced up at the ax again. "Before you go, Billy, why don't you tell me one thing."

Billy said nothing.

"Why don't you tell me why you came up here? What's this girl to you?"

"Nothing. I know her people."

"I'm her people, Billy."

"Her daddy might not agree."

"The same daddy who let her go off by herself up in those mountains?"

"Wasn't by herself."

The man huffed. "Might as well of been."

Billy coughed. He felt the wet cling of his shirtback where the blood had soaked it.

The man watched him. Then he looked down and with his forefinger began writing in the snow. He seemed to be working out some calculus but the figures he made resembled none Billy had ever seen. Working on these equations, the man said: "I suppose you think I had my eye on this girl. This particular girl. That I built up a plan around her." He glanced at Billy as a professor glances up from his notes, saw that Billy was listening and went on. "People don't want to give dumb luck any credit for the turns in their lives, good or bad. People want to believe in some plan, or design, when all around them is the evidence that the whole world is nothing *but* dumb luck. Going back to the first cells in the ocean. Going back to the stars."

He glanced up from his ciphers again. "You think I saw this girl and followed her up into those mountains? Hell. I was up there looking for a girl all right, I don't deny that. But it was another girl altogether. It was this other girl who liked to ride her bike up there with her one-legged boyfriend—had some kind of a gadget leg for riding, this poor bastard. I had my eye on *that* girl. That was my plan. But then along comes nothing but chance, Billy, nothing but dumb luck to put this other girl in my path."

Billy leaned and spat. "I guess it was dumb luck made you hit that boy with your car."

"Are you listening? If I'd gone up into those mountains just a few minutes earlier or just a few minutes later, I never would of seen either one of those two. They'd be back in Wisconsin watching the corn grow. Why is that so difficult to understand? You of all people, with that bullet in you, ought to understand."

Billy attempted to grin. "I got shot by dumb luck?"

The man studied him. "Let me ask you something. That bar down there, where we talked earlier. How often do you go there?"

"What?"

"How often do you go to that bar we were at today."

"I don't know."

"Once a week?"

Billy shook his head.

"Once a month?"

"Few times a year," Billy said, just to stop him.

"All right, a few times a year," the man said. "Now ask me how often I go there."

Billy stared at him.

"Go ahead," said the man.

Billy spat. "How often you go there?"

"Never, Billy. Never. I can't even tell you the name of the place. I never once stepped foot in there until today. Today, for no good reason at all, I decide to pull over and I go into that bar and I sit on that stool and who sits down beside me?"

Billy said nothing.

"And now look at you. Lying there with that bullet in you. When you woke up today did you think, hell, I reckon I'll go down to town and meet the man who knows where that girl is my brother the sheriff never could find and while I'm at it get myself shot?"

He looked at Billy as if expecting an answer. When he got none he shook his head. He said, "You're the same as that girl in there, Billy. You are both nothing but demonstrations of how the world really works."

"You crazy bitch," Billy said. "I chose to come up here. She didn't have no choice. You just took her. What you call dumb luck," he wheezed, "the world calls fucked-up perversion."

The man's eyes narrowed. "She did have a choice, Billy. She could of stayed with her brother. She got in my car of her own free will. You can ask her. Go ahead. She's listening to every word of this. Aren't you," he called out.

Billy looked away. His head felt so heavy.

The man made a long study of him.

"Perversion, you say? Thinking the world gives one damn what you do or don't do, whether you live or don't live—that's the greatest perversion there is, Billy."

Billy coughed up more blood. He thought he might be about to pass out or die. Likely both. Like this. Just like this. Nothing but a rapist son of a bitch to see him off. "Are you done?" he said.

"Why?"

"'Cause if you're gonna keep talking . . . I'll have some of that whiskey."

The man produced the fifth of whiskey and unscrewed the cap and offered the bottle. Billy lifted it to his lips and tilted the hot whiskey down his throat. The man took the bottle back and screwed down the cap and chucked the bottle into the snow.

Billy licked the blood from his bottom lip, from the tuft of hair below it.

"Tell you one difference, Steve," he said. "Between you and me."

"What's that."

"I ain't the one keeps pussy on a chain."

The man stared at him. Faintly amused. "No?"

"No."

"Maybe you don't like girls."

"I like girls."

"I know you do, Billy. I bet there's one somewhere right now wondering where you're at. Why you're not with her. Why you haven't called. Wondering what other girl you might be with." He looked at the door and shook his head. "That is a long chain, Billy. Going both ways."

Billy lay wheezing and the man watched him with a look of false concentration. Like a chess player who has seen the endgame far in advance.

Billy gathered his breath and said, "Let me ask you something."

The man sat waiting.

"Your old man," Billy said.

"What about him?"

"What was he."

"What was he?"

"Yeah."

"You mean besides a drunk and a son of a bitch?"

"Yeah."

"Nothing. He worked on crews. He wasn't anything."

"He wasn't," said Billy, "the Roto-Rooter man."

The man watched him, puzzling—and then slowly smiled. "Damn," he said. "Is that what you think?"

Billy watched him.

"It never occurred to me you'd think such a thing. But I can see how you might." He gave a quiet laugh. "Be damned." He looked down at the designs in the snow, his calculations, as if finding something new in them.

"I suppose I could of been," he said. "I suppose I could of been. And I won't say that what old Delmar did with that Stillson wrench never left an impression on me. I won't say that. But I just didn't have it in me, Billy. Not at that age."

A black wave rose up before Billy's vision and rolled on.

The man looked off toward the woods. "Charlotte Sweet," he said. "That was my first."

He glanced at Billy with an odd little smile.

"Can you believe that? I saw her one day on the tennis courts in the park. Her and none other. Chasing those balls around with her friends. Ninety pounds and sweet sixteen, Charlotte Sweet. Can you imagine?" He watched Billy's face. "You can imagine. You have imagined. All men have. Kings and emperors had them like candy—are still having them—while your average Joe—*Billy!*" he barked and Billy's eyes slid open.

"Don't talk to me about chains, Billy. Men are bound by chains their whole lives. That's the difference between you and me. That's why you are lying there now with that bullet in you, don't you see?"

Billy turned and spat and did not look at him again.

"I'll say one thing for you, Billy, you've got sand. I'll grant you that. But it's like I told you down at the bar: a man should never be the hero of his own story. So here's what we're going to do. Are you listening? We are going to go up to this place I want to show you, this little crack I damn near fell into once. Three, maybe four foot wide and no saying how deep. Only one way to know, really. Sometimes in a real blow it will get drifted over with snow—that's how it almost got me, day I found it—but it doesn't ever fill up with snow or anything else and I think you're gonna like it down there, Billy. You'll have some company with you. Another hero down there you can swap hero stories with. A couple of young ladies. And you can have this one too, soon enough."

He stood then and raised the hem of his jacket to button the gun into its holster, and Billy saw the leather sheath at the opposite hip and it was the last thing he saw before the rolling logs parted and the water swam up to carry him down into darkness.

57

When he came back to the world, or to whatever world this was, he was on his back, staring up into the skirts of the pines. The skirts sweeping by. Or he sweeping by them—each ridge and divot of the earth transmitted to him through the hard slats on which he lay and through the heels of his dragging boots.

At his head his lone bearer towed him along, easily as any horse or mule, his breaths visible in the light that came from the bright clouds beyond the tree tips, and Billy watching these breaths as he rocked and jostled on the slats, having no idea how far he'd traveled or how far he had yet to go. When his mouth filled with blood he lolled his head to one side and let the blood run out.

The man pulled his load another thirty yards and at last stopped, dropping the rope. He took a few moments getting his wind, then got his hands under Billy's arms and dragged the dead weight of him from the sled. He drew him nearly upright and began to haul him backward up a series of small rises in the earth, black stones like ancient steps and each step striking a sharp note of pain in Billy's twisted ankle. The man bore him up the stones and when they reached the top he turned him and making a belt of his arms stood him on his bootheels before the pit he'd described and shook him like a doll.

"Wake up, Billy," he said. "I know you ain't dead."

Billy's head swung from one shoulder to the other. Arms slack at his sides. "Wait," he said. Hot drool of blood on his lip. Blood running down the chute of his lower spine.

"There you are. Good. I want to show you something." One arm peeled away and the other tightened, and when the free arm came up again Billy saw the nine-millimeter, the dark empty socket of the grip where the clip had been removed. "Now," said the man, hefting the gun, "listen"—and he lobbed it into the pit. It fell silently at first into that blackness as though into a great, soft throat. Then the gun struck rock, chimed into rock again, and thereafter rang wall to wall in a long echoing descent, until at last the gun either struck bottom or else dropped soundlessly again through space. There was a faint chasing of rock chips, then silence.

The man's breath pulsed hot on Billy's neck. Both arms around him again in that weird embrace, grotesquely half tender, brute and awkward. As he must have held her in the little shack, in the light of the stove. Night upon night and she didn't fight, she didn't resist but instead opened her arms to him, her legs, did as he wanted, as he liked, good girl, every which way and again and again and even kissed him because each time was another hour, another day, and she was alive now because of it.

"Are you ready for this?" the man said quietly into his ear.

He shook his head. His hands hung at either side of the man's hips, his fingertips landing and relanding there, light as moths. Then he felt it.

"Well, courage, Billy. You won't hardly feel a thing, shape you're in," and he puppet-walked him to the mouth of the pit, from which there rose a rich cavernous reek of earth and decay, as if here indeed was the vent to some very deep, very grim storehouse.

"Wait," Billy said as the man positioned him.

"What for?"

"I ain't ready." And he raised his left fist in a punching motion behind his head and felt it slug into solid meat. The man's arms fell away and Billy pitched forward over the pit. But the pit was not wide and there was strength enough in his legs and he pushed off and was briefly airborne before he slammed chest and gut to the stone ledge on the far side with his legs swimming over the pit. He began to slip—but then his fingers found holds in the rock and he dragged himself clear, rolled to his side, and rolled again onto his back. His heart hammering. Red bombs of light in the trees. He propped himself up on his elbows and looked back at the man.

The man stood as before on the opposite side of the pit. He'd raised his gloved left hand to the left side of his neck, exploring with his fingers the haft and hilt of the bowie knife embedded there, as if it were some newly discovered lesion or chancre under his collar. No part of the blade was visible. Without lowering his left hand from his neck, he fumbled with his right at the holster. The button snap popped and Billy watched as he pulled out the pistol, aimed it, cocked it, and dropped the hammer on the empty chamber.

The man's lips parted in a terrible grin. Blood like ink in the seams of his teeth. He attempted to step away from the hole but his knees failed him and he dropped hard onto them. He worked his jaw as if to speak but no sound came out that Billy could hear. They watched each other across the pit. Then the man, his hand now firmly on the knife grip, keeled to his left and fell to the stones like a man already dead and lay there unmoving.

Billy let his own throbbing head fall to the stone. He breathed with his one good lung. Overhead a bright tide of clouds ebbed thinly over the pines, black starry rents in its surface like night ships steaming counter to the current. He rolled his head and looked at the man on the far side of the pit and then he shut his eyes, just for a minute—*Just give me one minute here, son, and then we'll get the man's keys and go on back to her.*

He closed his eyes and dreamed of the pit, of beings from below, the deeply entombed climbing one over the other like crabs toward the moonlight, issuing from the pit's mouth to consider the two men lying there, poking and sniffing and deciding at last, *This one, him,* and with their claw-hands dragging him back down with them, and he awoke jerking, choking, pressed to the flat rock as a man to the side of a cliff, his heart pounding. He sat up and spat out the blood. He thought he hadn't been out long but it had been long enough for the moon to burn off the clouds and center itself directly over him, a round and burning sun of the night. He rolled his head to look at the man and the man was gone. Nothing but an empty shelf of rock where he'd fallen. As if the dream had been no dream and only wrong in one of its particulars.

"Get up, damn you," he said. "I know you. Ain't dead."

He got up on his knees, from there to his feet, a long tottering moment, the pines in sickly carousel all around him—and then *Slowly, slowly, son, down the old stone steps.*

58

They sat in the heated cab studying the woods before them, their headlights boring a vague passageway under the boughs.

"You think those are Billy's tracks, Sheriff?"

"I don't know. They might be."

They looked again at the GPS screen, which seemed to place them in a dark void at the edge of the world. The device told them the time was 9:32 p.m. Their speed was zero.

"How far you reckon he could get in that car, Sheriff?"

"I don't know. I guess we'll find out."

"You want me to get Summit County on the radio, tell them we're up here?"

"No, let's see what's up ahead here a ways first."

The deputy shifted into the low range of four-wheel drive and they drove into the woods and followed the primitive road as it wound through the trees and grew more steeply pitched, more wildly switchbacked, the foreshortened way brilliant in their headlights until at last they rounded a bend and saw the El Camino. There was time and slope enough for the cruiser to stop short of the car, and the deputy skillfully worked the gas to keep them from backsliding more than a few feet, until at last they achieved a kind of stasis on the slope.

The El Camino sat aslant the road, anchored to a tree by its tailgate.

They sat watching it for a moment.

"He sure drove that car, didn't he, Sheriff."

"He sure did."

"You want me to throw the lights?"

"No, there ain't nobody in it."

"How can you tell?"

"Well, I see that snow built up on a cold hood, and I see a car that ain't even tried to get itself unstuck, and lastly I see them footprints going away from the car and on up the road."

The deputy drew himself to the wheel, as if he'd lacked the proper vantage to see such things. He sat back again and shook his head. "I don't know, Sheriff. I got a funny feeling."

"All right," said Kinney after a moment. "Cover me with the shotgun if it'll make you feel less funny."

The deputy put the cruiser in park and eased his foot from the brake, and the cruiser held. They got out and the deputy took his position in the wing of the door while the sheriff approached the El Camino. Kinney put his light into the cab and called back that nobody was home and the deputy raised his shotgun to port. Kinney tried the door and then walked around and tried the driver's door. It opened and the dome light came on and he stooped to look in. He picked up Billy's phone and checked for the messages he himself had left but none had arrived. The two phones were now less than a foot apart and not a word could pass between them.

"That his phone?" said the deputy.

"Yep."

"Why do you reckon he left it?"

"Why do you?" Kinney was reading the sent messages.

The deputy grew pensive. "For one, it wouldn't do him any good up here. For two, I reckon he wanted us to find it."

Kinney pocketed the phone. "That's how it looks to me."

He shut the door and returned to the cruiser and handed the deputy a magazine and asked him to get on the horn and call it in, and he'd begun to walk back to the El Camino when he stopped and turned back. The deputy was staring at the magazine.

"You want me to call in this magazine, Sheriff?"

"Look again, Deputy."

He looked.

"There on the fanny," said Kinney.

"Oh," said the deputy. "Got it."

A few minutes later the deputy told him the number had come back a New Mexico plate registered to one Reginald Smites who, like the plate itself, was long expired.

Kinney was skimming his torchbeam along the surface of the snow to reveal what was left of the other set of tire tracks continuing up the road.

"Looks like he got out and followed on foot, Sheriff."

"That's how it looks to me."

"Think we can move this car?"

"He didn't leave the keys."

"We could tow it out of the way."

"We could try but I don't want to spend the time. Go grab a torch, Donny, and lock up and let's go."

"You want me to bring the shotguns?"

"I guess one ought to be plenty."

The moment the deputy extinguished the headlights the woods grew deep in every direction. Tree articulating from tree and the steep expanse of mountain unveiled in the blue flood of moonlight. They saw where Billy had twice fallen and they saw his adjustment and they followed these strange impressions up the road with the flashlights off and no sound anywhere but their own footfalls and the faint hiss of wind in the boughs. When the sheriff's two-way squawked he grabbed it and thumbed it into silence and the deputy did the same to his.

59

The wood split and there was the sudden edge of blade, the dull gleam of silver in the black face of the door. She did not believe it. A thing from the outside world had broken into hers. She stared at it, heart-stopped, waiting to see what it would do next. The sight of it awakened in her thin legs the memory of a day long ago on snowshoes—afloat on the deep snow, thighs full of blood, lungs stretched and burning and each step another step downslope, away from the shack, away from the cot, from the bathroom, from the chain. She watched the blade in the door and it didn't move, and then she heard the pop of the gun, and she dropped to her knees, and the voice she heard next was the Monkey's.

She backed away, dragging the chain with her to her place on the cot and to the sour old sleeping bag, which for a moment she had let herself believe would never again touch her skin. She drew up her legs and cowled the bag about her and watched the dim edge of blade in the door, dully lit by the glow from the stove where her next-to-last log withered on its bed of coals.

After a while he and Billy were quiet. Then he told her through the door that he would be right back, and there were a few more sounds, and she heard the sled runners cutting through the snow and away into the trees, and there was no more sound from out there and she didn't move. She watched the edge of the blade in the door, staring so intently that it burned into her retinas—and it became in this uncanny way more than the edge of the ax but the edge of the outer world itself, as the thin blade of the crescent moon suggests the whole round moon, and she remembered a book she'd once loved about a circular being who was missing a piece of itself, like a slice of pie, and went rolling around the world singing, *Oh, I'm lookin' for my missin' piece,*

I'm lookin' for my missin' piece. The smell of the book's paper and the smell of sawdust on her father's shirt in whose arms she rested like a small circular being herself. The deep man-tremor of his voice down in his chest passing into her back and into her chest, and his heartbeat too, like a separate voice speaking in a register so low that only her own heart could hear it, and she knew by this memory, by her willingness to allow it to bloom inside her, that she would not see him again. Or her mother or her brother.

So she sat thinking of each of them, all she could remember of them, while another part of her listened for the return of his footfall, the dragging of the riderless sled, the sound of the key fitting into the padlock. He'd told Billy he did not believe the sheriff was coming but he would not take the chance. It was time. And he would do what he should've done long ago and then he would come down from the mountain and never return to this place and he would never be found and she would never be found, nor her sisters before her nor the two men who had tried to help her. Her family would never know and she knew now that that was the worst thing of all, to never know, and she hoped that if there was no God or no heaven that at least she might be allowed to make herself known to them one last time, to tell them everything she'd not told them when she'd had the chance, and she began to tell them now, hastily, in a fevered whisper, for once more she heard the footsteps beyond the door, distant, then steadily louder, slogging heavily in the crusted snow. She did not hear the sled runners and she did not hear the jangle of keys as he reached the door, but instead the door shuddered and she saw the ax blade pulled from its place in the breached wood, and then there was no sound other than her whispers as she closed her eyes and spoke to her parents and to Dudley. These would be the faces she saw, not his, the faces of Dad, Mom, and Sean. She tried to see what he must look like now, her little brother. He would be the age she'd been back then. Taller, leaner, more like their father. No longer a boy but a young man. Lastly she imagined herself, not as she was now but as she had been. She put her own remembered face into this portrait and in this way they were reunited, complete once more, a fully round thing.

In the next moment the wall behind her shook and her eyes leapt open and the edge of the ax was in the door again, more of it than before, rocking

in the splintered wood. It withdrew again and she heard the wheezing effort
of his backswing and the ax came crashing once more through the wood, the
entire axhead now, wrenching in the ragged seam like the head of a panicked
animal. Freeing itself, crashing through again. She didn't understand. She
didn't understand. Had he lost his keys?

The axhead fell again and pieces of wood flew across the room, and the
axhead was jerked from the door and did not return. There was hole enough
now she could see the white of the snow in the trees beyond, luminous in the
moonlight. Then the hole was blacked out and she knew he'd blocked it with
his head. She held her breath. White fingers sprouted in the black hole and
gripped the wood. The door shook. The fingers withdrew.

There followed another blow of the ax and this time the axhead did not
stop but continued on its downward arc as the plank of the door split all
the way to the floor and the entire door shook in its frame. For a moment
all was still. Then the door banged violently once, and a second time, and at
last swept open in an explosion of light and snow and shards of wood spinning through the air, followed by the man himself, crashing into the room
like someone stepping through a rotted floor. He fell to his hands and knees
and remained that way, gasping, the ax pinned to the floor under his right
hand. He'd fallen in with the moonlight, and the longer he remained in this
all-fours position the more he appeared to be captive to the box of light in
which he crouched. When he looked up at last his face was ghastly in that
light. Ghastly in any light. What may have been the very last of his blood
ran in a black syrup from his mouth. Something rattled deep inside him, as
though every breath passed through a wet cloth.

She shrugged off the sleeping bag and Billy watched as she separated from
the heap of bedding like bones from hide, so skinny, so pale in her thin rags.
Dark hair snarled about her face, her filthy bare feet. The dragging chain and
the padlock rocking at her ankle like some grotesque idea of jewelry. They each
looked into the other's eyes and saw there the pitiful thing they had become.

She put a hand on his shoulder. The first touch of another human not
him in so long. Kept her hand there, fighting the desire to wrench the ax
away—*Mine, give it to me.*

"Billy," she said. "Where is he?"

He spat blood and wheezed, then pushed himself to his knees and sat back on his heels. He knuckled the blood from his lips and looked about him. "My God," he said.

"Billy," she began again, but then his balance gave out and he toppled backward, landing heavily against the doorjamb. His legs unfolded before him one at a time, and now the only part of him she could easily reach was his boots. She put her hand on the ax and slid it closer to her.

He was blinking at her sleepily. The smell of him, like the moonlight and the cold, had invaded the room. He was the smell of cigarettes and car exhaust, of pine trees and snow and mud. Of unwashed hair and vomit and alcohol. He smelled of sweat and flesh and of cowhide and of something metallic and primal that she thought must be his blood. He smelled of the world.

"Billy," she said again. "Where is he?"

"S'who?" he said.

"The man. The man who shot you."

His raised his hand in a vague gesture. "Stabbed."

"You stabbed him?"

He nodded.

"Is he dead? Billy, is he dead?"

He sighed. He closed his eyes. "I don't know." His lips were blue; his teeth had begun to chatter.

She looked beyond him, into the moonlight, at the trees and the mountain. She could not see high enough to see the moon but she knew it was up there, bright and whole.

The room was growing cold but she didn't feel it. She was burning up. Her heart was punching at her wasted ribs.

"Billy," she said. She grabbed his boot and shook it. "Billy."

He opened his eyes. Glassy, drowsing eyes struggling to focus.

"Billy, you said the sheriff was coming. Is that true? Is he coming?" He winced, and she realized it was his ankle and eased her grip on it.

He wagged his head. "Don't know," he said. "My phone."

"Yes?" she said, "yes? You have a phone? Where? Where's your phone, Billy?" She reached out toward him.

"Not here," he said. "Down. In the car."

She stared at him, disbelieving. "Why would you leave it there?"

"You go," he said. "My car." He shuddered. His gloved hand lifted from the floor and stabbed at his jacket pocket and at last found its way in. She heard the sound of keys and he brought out his fist and held it out to her. She could just reach it. Her hand touched his bloody glove and she had the keys.

"My tracks," he said. "Down the mountain. Understand?"

She nodded. She clutched the keys. They were not the set of keys she wanted and he seemed to know it. Such sadness in his eyes.

"I'm sorry," he said, shuddering. "Can't chop. Anymore."

"It's okay. You rest. I'll get you some water." She'd begun to stand but he raised a hand to stop her. He wanted to speak again.

"Do you know," he said, "what timezit?"

She turned and looked instinctively for the coin of light on the floor but it wasn't there.

"Ten," she said. "Maybe ten thirty."

He nodded.

"Your people," he said.

She looked at him. She held absolutely still.

"Your people," he said again. "Down there still," he said. "Still looking."

She bowed her head. She placed her hand on his boot again. Her thin small shoulders shaking. After a moment she wiped her face and looked up again and said she would get him some water.

She dragged the chain into the bathroom and collected the quarter-full bucket, the last of her water, and returned to the outer room, and stopped short, and set the bucket down, for she could see from there that he was dead.

Outside, the wind blew in the pines. A flurry of snow seethed over the floor and settled alongside his leg. She looked behind her at the dark stove, the last small chunk of firewood next to it. Then she looked beyond him, out into what she could see of the world in the corridor of door and moonlight.

"Come on if you're coming," she said, and stood holding the ax.

60

She'd never used one before but the shape of the handle and the weight of the head told her how it must be done and she took her stance over the chain, raised the ax as high as the ceiling would allow and with all her strength brought it down. Sparks leapt and the axhead twisted and the handle convulsed from her hands like something alive. The effort left her panting and dizzy and furious with her body. She bent and gathered the chain in her hands and found no sign of the blow and only a scrape of raw steel in one tarnished link, the link itself unharmed, and she understood at once a combination of truths: the chain was too strong, the ax too dull, her body too weak. In the air was an acrid, ferric smell, like the smoke of sparklers that burns in the nose on the Fourth of July.

She took up the ax again and this time aligned herself over the bolt plate in the floor, over the half hoop that was conjoined with the final link of the chain, that perversely enduring union that had defied her every effort to break it. She raised the ax and brought it down and the axhead did not twist but merely rang out a flat note and bounced back into the air, having struck the face of the plate an inch from the hasp.

Dizzily she raised the ax again and brought it down again and the blade glanced off the hasp but she held on. She knelt to feel the hasp and the link but they remained bound to each other as ever. She turned the ax and drew her thumb along the nicked and blunted edge. Despair rose in her and she fought it down. She looked at the door, the thick wreckage of it, and she looked at the floor around the bolt plate. Having swung the ax she now understood what it had taken to break through the door, and what it would take to do the same to the floor, and she knew she could never do it.

Cold air spun about the room. Snow continued to drift in and collect at Billy's leg, a climbing dune. She knelt there watching it, shivering.

What are you doing? said the girl—the strong one, the one she thought had abandoned her.

"I'm thinking."

I hope you're thinking how you'd better stoke this fire and get in that sleeping bag.

"Fuck that sleeping bag."

The girl said nothing.

Caitlin held the ax, listening. Then she said: "Do you think he's coming?"

Who?

"Either one."

The girl was a long time answering and Caitlin knew what she would say. *I think what I've always thought. There's no one coming. There's only us.*

Crystals swam in the air and landed cool on her face. Billy's keys where she'd left them on the floor glinted blue in the light. Follow his tracks, that's all. Get to the car. That's all. She remembered snowshoes, the deep powder and her pounding heart, the Monkey in pursuit and *no fall, no fall* . . . He had bagged it all up, snowshoes and boots and jacket and gloves, took it away without a word. Bad girl.

She held the ax. Her heart clocking away the seconds, the minutes. Now that she'd let the faces of her family into her mind she could not get them out. Faces of the life before. And they were down there still, he said, still looking. Still looking and what will they find?

She listened for the girl—listened for anything. But there was nothing. Wind. The snow whispering along the floorboards.

She got to her feet and opened the stove gate and with the last length of firewood prodded the length that preceded it, now nothing more than a smoldering black bone of itself which at first touch fell into glowing red cubes. Flames arose and she placed the new wood carefully atop them and closed the gate incompletely so that the air would draw and the wood would burn more quickly and intensely. She set the bucket of water next to the stove and the ax next to that, and then she went to the cot and picked up a flannel boy's shirt, once red now gone almost to black, and she put this on and buttoned it to her throat. Lastly she got down on her hands and knees and reached far under the cot until she felt what she was looking for and dragged them out. They were dusty and gray and shrunken, like creatures who'd crawled under there long ago and died together side by side. She took one in each hand and clopped them sole to sole and the sound and the feel of this nearly made her sob. She clopped them and the red dust of the trail and the gray dust of the years fell from them like snow.

There were no cans of food or snack bars or child's boxes of juice or anything at all on the larder shelves and she dipped her hand into the bucket and drank three cold handfuls of water.

She looked at the man named Billy on the floor.

"I'm sorry," she said, and she took him by the ankles.

61

The way became more trail than road and before long they reached the place where the tire tracks dove down into the brush and one set of boot-prints became two and they raised their Maglites and probed the gully with the beams, but the light struck the thick latticework of brush and went no farther. They switched off the torches and stood in silence, in moonlight.

"Want me to go on down there, Sheriff?"

"I guess not, Donny. We've got two men afoot now and we'd best see where they've gone to. Though by the looks of these tracks I'd say they've already got there."

The deputy sniffled and looked back down the way they'd come, and up to where they were going. "What do you suppose made him do a thing like this anyway, Sheriff?"

"I quit even asking that question a long time ago, Donny."

They went on.

The two sets of tracks progressed in tandem up the narrowing trail, one set landing wide of the other as if out of some compulsion, or superstition. As if one man were loathe to place his foot where the other's had been.

"There ain't no mistaking which is which, is there, Sheriff."

"Let's go quiet, Deputy."

They came around a bend and, seeing only more trail, more tracks, stopped to get their wind. Kinney wanted a cigarette but put that out of his mind.

They'd turned to go on when a sound reached them, traveling in echo from up the mountain. A dull flat chock, as of an ax blow to solid wood. They stilled themselves and listened. Less than a minute later the sound came again and after that there was no more sound like it nor any sound at all. The deputy looked at the sheriff and the sheriff nodded, and they went on.

The trail grew more difficult and Kinney yielded the lead to his deputy so that he himself might concentrate on the surrounding woods, listening for any single thing which was not of the woods. They'd not climbed another fifty yards before he reached and put a hand on the deputy's shoulder and they halted.

The deputy looked where the sheriff pointed and he saw the small flare of color deep in the monochrome woods, simmering and orange and geometrical—a doorway. And seeing it he immediately smelled woodsmoke, as if one could not exist without the other.

"Damn, Sheriff," he whispered. "Damn."

Kinney lowered to a squat and removed his hat, and the deputy did the same, the shotgun bridged across his knees. They watched to see if anyone would pass before the door or window or come to shut it against the cold, but no one did.

The deputy whispered, "Sheriff, look up ahead here," and he pointed to where the two sets of tracks abruptly diverged. The men rose and went stooped-backed up the trail and dropped once more to their haunches to study the tracks.

The deputy drew a gloved forefinger under his nose. "What should we do, Sheriff?"

Overhead, the white points of the pines sawed through the stars and sent a fine brilliant dust sifting down.

"I don't like it," said Kinney, "but I guess we'll have to split up." He leaned and spat dryly. "You go on ahead with those tracks and I'll take these here. Set that radio to beep mode. If you see anything, beep me twice and wait for me to come, and I'll do the same."

They restored their hats to their heads, squared them, and stood. "Don't use your torch if you can help it, and stay sharp, Donny."

"Okay, Sheriff."

He watched his deputy out of sight, then turned and stepped into the woods as his brother had done when he spotted the same remote light two, perhaps three hours earlier.

THE MOON FOLLOWED HIM, sidling through the treetops and attaching to him a disturbed version of his own shape, a liquid shadow that moved with perfect stealth while he himself blundered along behind. He kept an eye on Billy's tracks and an eye on the light ahead, and he made himself stop every twenty paces and count to ten, just listening. He heard a twig fracture thinly in the distance, in the direction his deputy had gone, and nothing more. He considered whether he'd made the right decision splitting up. Made the right decision not calling Summit County to meet them up here.

Meet us for what, for Jesus' sake?

He had stopped to listen at a place where Billy had tripped over a tree that lay hidden under the snow. "Up here in goddam cowboy boots," he said, and continued on.

He followed the tracks where they dodged through the pines, and when he glanced ahead once more to the lighted rectangle, now unmistakably a doorway, something passed darkly and soundlessly before it, like a tree felled in the middle ground but with no sound of its landing. He stood still and the tree came swinging back to darken the doorway again, and he saw then that it was no tree but some figure careening through the woods.

He stepped behind the branches of a young pine and watched the figure come on, antic and wayward, wildly lame in one leg. Bereft of all ballast or compass yet moving doggedly on some course, and it was the same course, he saw, that he himself was on and that was stamped in the snow by his brother's boots.

He peeled off his gloves and stashed them in his pocket and unholstered his sidearm and found his stance behind the small pine, digging his boots into the snow. He raised the Maglite and rested it on a branch at eye level where the sight line was clean, training both gun and unlit flashlight on the place twenty feet ahead where he knew the figure would come into view.

Through the intervening boughs he made out the hobbling shape and he saw the blue-black gleam of leather in the moonlight, and although he believed he recognized the jacket he saw nothing else in those palsied movements or in the blanched face under the watch cap resembling his brother. He thumbed off the safety of the gun and released the air slowly from his lungs.

The sound of erratic footfalls arrived in advance of the figure, and Kinney watched the white breaths erupting before the white face, and in time he heard the breaths too, hearing not only the exertions behind them but also the ragged bursts of speech within them—a breathy convulsive incantation as fierce as it was unintelligible.

At last the figure came lurching into his line of fire and he threw his light on it and a gloved left hand swung up reflexively and there was no weapon in it, nor in the right, which remained down and fisted and close to the right thigh.

"Not another step," said Kinney, and the figure stopped. The splayed, outstretched hand wavered in the torch beam, its shadow covering the face like a huge smothering glove. He saw that it was not his brother but some impostor in his brother's clothes and a poor one at that: swamped in the leather jacket, blue jeans lapsed into accordion folds from the ankles up. Or rather from one ankle up, for on the opposite leg the pant leg was bunched above a cowboy boot, where a strap had been fed through the pullstraps of the boot, the impostor holding the resulting loop in his gloved fist like the bridlereins to his own right foot.

"I want to see both your hands in the air right now," Kinney said, and after a moment the unsteady figure let go the strap and fell at once to both knees and then to all fours with a high, awful whimper. Black hair spilled from the shoulders and hung trembling in the sheriff's torchlight.

"Look up," said Kinney. Such shoulders as there were under the jacket shook visibly. Droplets fell amid the lank hair, dazzled in the light, and were consumed in the snow.

"Come on now," said the sheriff more gently. "Look at me." He lowered his beam and when the light was off of it, the fallen head lifted and showed him the face under the cap and for a moment he believed he was seeing the face of his own daughter—haunted and drained and ravaged by illness.

"My Lord God," he said. He came from behind the tree holstering the gun and knelt beside her and looked into her wild wet eyes. "Sweetheart," he said, "what's your name?"

62

They had been silent a long time, smoking in the moonlight, when Grant said: "I thought about trying to stay on here. I talked to Sheriff Joe about it. I thought I might cover the mortgage for a while. But it would mean selling the house back home. It would mean going back there and putting everything in storage. Or selling it."

The boy thought of the house in Wisconsin, his bedroom above the garage, all his childhood things, bed and books and fighter planes hung on fishing line. The ribbons on Caitlin's wall like a bird wing, her trophies and posters and the stuffed ape he'd given her one Christmas and that sat on her bed still. Everything untouched in the cold dark and not a sound anywhere. He lowered his head and blew into his cupped hands and said into them, "What about Mom?"

"What about her?"

"Is she planning on staying with Aunt Grace forever?"

"I don't know."

"Are you getting divorced?"

"I don't know."

"You don't know."

"No. We haven't talked about anything but one thing in a long time."

The boy thought of the waitress, Maria, and of Carmen.

Grant reached for the ashtray on the porch rail and stubbed out his cigarette.

The boy said, "You think she still believes in God?"

Grant nodded. "Yes."

"What about you?"

"What about me?"

The boy looked at him and looked away.

"I don't know," Grant said.

"Do you think it would've changed things?"

"Would what have changed things?"

"Believing. Before."

Grant stared at him, at his profile in the moonlight.

"Is that what you think?"

"Sometimes."

They were quiet. Across the clearing from out of the shadow of the house slipped the shape of a cat, sinuous and black on the snow, stalking something. She was nearly to the blue spruce when she stopped, one forefoot stilled in midstep, and her eyes ignited in her face like tiny headlamps, green-gold and molten. For a moment the world was still. Then the boy scraped his boot on the step and those lights blacked out and the cat turned and slunk back into shadow. They watched to see if she would reappear but she didn't.

"That house back there is the only thing left," said the boy.

Grant got another cigarette in his lips and offered the pack to his son but he shook his head. Grant lit his cigarette and exhaled a blue, ghostly cloud.

"I don't know what else to do," he said. "Do you?" He looked at the boy. Blond whiskers silvering in the moonlight. He still saw the young boy he'd been not long ago, but he knew that he alone saw it, that it was the image a father carries, burned into the eyes by way of the heart.

The boy shook his head and said that he had wished for something terrible. Terrible.

"When?" Grant said. "Just now?" He was thinking of the falling star.

"No. When we went to see that girl."

Grant looked at him. "What did you wish for?"

"I wished it was her. I wished it was Caitlin."

Grant looked away.

"I wanted it to be her so we could take her home."

Grant shook his head. "I shouldn't have let you go down there."

"You couldn't have stopped me."

Grant sat shaking his head. "I've had this conversation a thousand times," he said. He stared into the sky. "I never should have let you go up into those mountains, I say."

The boy was quiet. The moon sat in the eye of its ring.

"You couldn't have stopped me, she says. Maybe not, I say." He stared into the heavens, his eyes burning with its lights. "But I should have tried."

63

Kinney told the girl who he was and that he'd followed his brother, Billy, up there. She was still on her hands and knees, and he scanned the snow for blood.

"How bad are you hurt, Caitlin?"

She gave a sob and faltered and he caught her by the upper arm. More bone than arm under the leather. He knew by this how light she would be.

"All right, sweetheart," he said. "You're gonna be all right now. We're getting you down off this mountain." He found his radio and pushed the button twice and waited. He pushed twice again and as he waited he heard someone coming through the woods, moving smartly but cautiously. He doused the torch and drew the gun again and leveled it over the hunched girl, who grew silent and rigid.

"Who all's up here, Caitlin?" he said under his breath. "Is he up here, the man who took you?"

"I don't know. I think so."

"What about Billy? Where's Billy, Caitlin?"

Before she could answer, a man appeared in silhouette and Kinney saw the shape of the man's hat and he lowered the gun and blinked the torch twice to guide him. He told her it was all right, it was just his deputy, and she began to breathe again.

The deputy came through the trees at a lope and he stopped beside them and set the shotgun across his knees and leaned upon the shotgun gasping like a man at the end of a hard race. He was as pale as the girl and when he met the sheriff's eyes the sheriff saw he was badly shaken.

The deputy looked at the girl on her hands and knees in the snow. He looked at the one big cowboy boot she wore and the loop of belt making its dark smile in the snow. He looked at the running shoe on her other foot. He seemed not to have the breath or words to speak.

"What did you find, Donny?"

The deputy lowered himself to his knees beside the girl, as if to pray, or beg. The girl watched him with her wet eyes.

"Did you find him?" she whispered.

"Find who?"

"The man," she said.

"All I found was Billy," he said.

Her eyes searched his. Then her head dropped again heavily, black hair spilling to the snow.

Kinney looked from the girl to his deputy. "Tell me, Deputy."

"Sheriff, I think we need to get this girl to a hospital."

"I know it. Tell me what you saw up there."

"Sheriff, I don't know if I can."

"By God, Donny."

The deputy shook his head dismally. He reached to touch the girl's shoulder but stopped himself. "Miss?" he said. "Can we take a look?"

She did not answer or move. Then, in silence, she pivoted onto one hip and shifted around to sit in the snow with her arms stiff behind her and her legs stretched out, and thus arranged she raised the single boot into the air before the deputy, as if proffering it. As if in some weird invitation of undress.

The deputy handed the shotgun to the sheriff.

"What are you doing, Deputy?"

The deputy took the boot in his hands and began, gently, to pull. It came off more easily than Kinney would've predicted and when it slipped free he did not understand what he was seeing. At the end of her white thin leg there was no foot. There was the heel—and nothing else. A stunning illusion. As if the rest of the foot were still inside the boot. The deputy tilted the boot and the blood ran from it like oil and Kinney looked again and saw the black sooty wound and he smelled the seared meat smell of it.

"My God," he said.

The deputy tilted the boot farther and something heavy slipped along the shaft from bootheel to mouth and landed in a dark clot on the snow.

"What is that?"

"I think it's his socks, Sheriff. Billy's socks."

Kinney looked at him.

"He got shot, Joe. He didn't make it. I'm sorry."

Kinney frowned. He adjusted his hat. Then he handed the shotgun back to the deputy and slipped an arm under the girl's knees and the other around her back and rose to his feet lifting her easily.

"Don't," she said. "I can walk."

"I know you can, sweetheart, but this will be faster."

"Let me help, Sheriff."

"No, she don't weigh nothin. Grab that belt there and get it on her leg." The deputy did so. "Higher," said the sheriff. "Just below the knee. Pull it tight. Tuck in the end. Are you in pain, sweetheart?" he said, and even as she shook her head he said, "Jesus, what a question." To the deputy he said: "Now watch our backs with that shotgun, Donny. Anything else moves in these woods you go ahead and shoot the sonofabitch."

The girl hooked one arm around his neck and with her face to his chest he turned and they headed down the mountain, moving slower than they might have, not for the weight of her but for the care he took not to jostle her or allow her to come into contact with any branch or bough or to himself slip on the steep trail. She was not bleeding badly and he didn't believe she'd lost much blood, and if she'd not gone into shock by now he didn't believe she would and his sole desire in the world was to deliver her gently and safely to the cruiser.

The girl for her part rode in his arms like a child to whom sleep has come no matter what, no matter where, though it wasn't sleep she surrendered to but something more absolute, more exquisite, which was abandonment.

Abandonment of thought and of fear and of responsibility and of strength. She surrendered to abandonment and in her surrender she felt the downhill pull of gravity and she believed that the man who carried her was in fact a man-shaped sled or toboggan and she its only passenger. Sailing down the mountain slope with the song of speed in her ears, beat of his heart against her ribs, whole unto herself but also belonging to the snow and the wind and the moon and the mountain. Altogether more effortless and fleet than she'd ever been in any footrace and putting nothing but distance and more distance between herself and the life up there, which was no life but only the momentary interruption of life, and every second on this man-sled delivering her farther and farther from shack, chain, sleeping bag, Monkey. Down and down the great slope, the sweetest ride, joy of speed, down and down and unstoppably down.

64

They came around a final bend and found the El Camino broadside to the road as before and the cruiser beyond it downslope. Both the sheriff and his deputy were breathing harshly. The full moon hung above them on its high sweep, and on the deputy's wrist a small round face lit from within told them it was just midnight. The deputy unlocked the cruiser and opened the rear door and went to the other side to help the sheriff arrange the girl along the bench seat, her body so meager in the folds of clothes. He saw something protruding from one of the jacket pockets and after a moment understood that it was a shoe. The other running shoe.

"How's that, Caitlin?" said Kinney. "Can you ride like that?"

She nodded, gazing around the interior as if it were the cockpit of a spaceship. Kinney told the deputy to start up the cruiser and get the heat going, then he had him radio Summit County for ambulances and officers. When that was done the deputy came around again and stood behind the sheriff who was still tending to the girl.

"You want the emergency kit, Sheriff?"

Kinney looked more closely at the wound in the dome light. The blackened curled lip of skin with its bright scarlet fissures. "No, I'd rather spend the time driving toward the EMTs. And anyway I don't believe we can do much better than what's been done." He reached for the belt below her knee and noticed for the first time the silver oval of buckle, the snakehead with its ruby eyes, and for a moment it froze him, as the face of a true viper would. Billy had put it on that morning, or whenever he'd gotten up. Mindlessly fastening the buckle and getting on with his day. Then Kinney thought of the girl's father, Grant, and the boy Sean, down on the ranch. Going about their day, their night, with no idea, just no idea. He uncinched the belt and watched for the blood to seep from the wound and cinched it again.

What in the hell, he thought. Just what in God's own hell.

"Sheriff," she said as he was withdrawing from the cruiser. She'd removed Billy's glove. She held out her bare fist. He reached in and cupped his hand and the keys dropped into his palm.

"He gave them to me," she said.

"Okay. You lie still now. We're gonna get you to the hospital before you can say boo." He moved to shut the door and again she said, "Sheriff."

"Yes?"

"I'm sorry. What I did to him."

He didn't understand. "Hush, now," he said. "Don't talk."

"Sheriff?"

"Yes?"

"Do you have a phone?"

"There ain't no signal up here, sweetheart."

"Can I just hold it?"

He found the phone and she closed her bare hand around it and rested her fist on her chest.

He shut the door and handed Billy's keys to the deputy. "I need a favor, Donny."

"Ask it, Sheriff."

"I need you to stay up here with this car. Just stay here with the shotgun and don't do nothing else but keep an eye out. If there's another man up here I don't want him getting by you, is that clear? You put him down before he gets by."

"I will, Sheriff."

"It won't be long before Summit County gets here."

"Don't worry, Sheriff."

Kinney clapped a hand on the deputy's shoulder and stepped to the driver's door, and then stood there, ready to open the door. The deputy hadn't moved.

"What is it, Deputy?"

The deputy sawed his finger under his nose.

"Donny," said Kinney.

"She was chained up like a dog in that shack, Sheriff. Looks to me like she did that to herself. With an ax."

"How do you know?"

"Well, Sheriff." The deputy looked down. "Hell. There was two feet up there. Human feet. Just lying there. Like shoes. One of hers and one of his. Billy was already dead when it happened, you could tell."

He looked up again. "Now why would she do a thing like that, Sheriff?"

Kinney studied the dark shape of the girl in the back of his cruiser. Pale oval of face in the shadows. He heard again the sounds they'd heard from the trail: one wooden blow. Then the other. Lord God if only she'd waited fifteen, twenty minutes, he thought. But there was a man up there with a gun and she might not have had twenty minutes or even ten.

He turned back to the deputy. "Why do you reckon she did it, Donny?"

The deputy bumped the barrel of the shotgun against his leg. "I'd say she did it for practice, Sheriff."

Kinney nodded. "That's how it looks to me."

He opened the cruiser door and got in and switched on the headlamps, spilling light once more over the road and the deserted El Camino. He turned to speak to the girl but she was out, the phone still clutched to her chest. He powered down the passenger's window and told the deputy to look sharp. Told him to be nothing but smart and he would see him later at the hospital, and then the deputy stood to watch the sheriff back the cruiser deftly down the road.

65

The boy fell asleep quickly and all at once and in his sleep he re-turned to the glen on the mountain where the stone Virgin watched over the crooked stones. There was the coldness of the stone bench and no sound but the chattering aspens, a sound like wind chimes made of bird bones, and in the dream he leaned to search for the tarnished plaque but behind the scrub growth there was only more growth, and he rooted and pulled in despair until something moved at the tree line and he looked up and there she was: black toss of ponytail, bare legs blotched pink and red, the scant shorts and the running shoes all brilliant white in the shaded hollow. She said *There you are* and pulled up before him winded, hands on hips, her head cocked to one side. She asked him where he'd been and he said he'd been right here, and she asked why and he said because he was waiting for her and she asked why and he said because he didn't know the way down and she shook her head and said, *Dudley, the way down is down. It's always down. Didn't you know that?* Then she knelt to retie one shoe and as she was doing this something else moved in the woods, some plodding and reckless thing, and she looked up and smiled, and then, like a sprinter in the blocks, she rose and flew, leaping once more into the woods. He tried to follow but when he stepped into the trees there was no sign of her, nor any sign of trail. He stared into the pines and he heard his name, and when he opened his eyes a hand was on his shoulder and a face was hovering in the dark, eyes shining, and he said *Don't, don't* . . . but the words were only in his heart and his father shook him again, almost violently, and said, "Sean, wake up. Wake up. You have to get dressed."

"Why?" he asked, still in the woods.

"Because they found her."

He stared at his father in the darkness, his father staring at him.

"How do they know?" said the boy, and his father said, "Because she told them."

Part V

66

Something was buzzing—a terrific and malevolent insect, a great scarab. It sat wide and hard-shelled on her chest, it sat on her mouth, and she couldn't breathe; she swung an arm and struck a soft small creature near her head and the animal released a childish, laundered smell and the smell told her where she was, who she was, and when she knew this she knew what the buzzing was and she blindly reached for it, toppling the capped water bottle onto its side, the bottle sending the vial of pills rolling off the table and bouncing on the carpet with the faraway sound of a fallen baby rattle.

She swung out her legs and sat with the phone in her hand, reading the bright small screen. The room faced east and the windows were a deep shade of blue. No idea how long she'd slept. The alarm clock sat blank and pointless, unplugged long ago by her husband. The phone buzzed twice more before she answered.

"Angie," Grace nearly cried. "Where are you?"

"At the house," she said thickly. She picked up the water bottle and unscrewed the cap.

"The house?" It took her sister a moment. "What are you doing there?"

"Running the streams."

"Running the what?"

"The . . . water. Running the water. For the traps."

"Angie, are you all right?"

"Yes. I'm fine. Why?"

The heat had stopped blowing, the furnace paused. No one, nothing, moved in the house. It felt empty as a museum after even the guards have gone home; the paintings unlit in the vast gloom, gazed at by no one but the white-eyed statues. She looked about her at the posters, the furniture, her daughter's things; they were losing their power to devastate her. They were becoming like her memories.

"Well," Grace said, "I've been calling. Did you lose your phone, or what?"

Angela could see her sister's face: the anger and disbelief. The fear. The face of an adult woman whom she loved without question and into whose tiny lungs she had once blown life, a fact that was known but could not be felt.

"It was in my bag," Angela said. "I didn't hear it. I'm sorry, Grace."

"Well—" said Grace. She took a breath. "How did it go this morning?"

"How did what go."

"Teaching, Angie. Did you teach?"

"Not really."

"What does that mean?"

"They sat and read their book. They pretended to. Real teacher-of-the-year stuff."

There was a long silence. Angela glanced at the screen. "Are you there?"

"I'm here." Grace's tone became casual. "Have you been at the house all day?"

"No. I walked around. I rode the bus."

"You rode the bus?"

"Yes."

"Where did you go?"

"Nowhere. The library."

Grace's son hollered at her from somewhere in the house; she didn't answer. "Angie," she said. "I'm coming over."

"Don't, Grace. Seriously, I'm fine." She was putting her things back into the tote bag. Shouldering it. She restored the teddy bear and the ape to their places. Smoothed the duvet.

"Well—are you coming home? I mean, are you coming back for dinner?"

There was the sharp rap of the little brass knocker on the front door downstairs.

"Go ahead and eat without me," Angela said. "I'll warm something up later."

"But Angie—"

The door swept open and a man called "Hello?"

"I have to go, Grace, someone's here."

"Who's there? Who was that?"

"It's no one."

Hard-sole footsteps on the oak floor at the bottom of the stairs. "Angela?"

"I mean it's only Robert from across the street. He must have seen the light on downstairs." She stepped out of her daughter's room and closed the door.

"Angela—"

"I have to go, Grace. I'll call you back."

HE HAD SEEN THE light and no car in the drive and had come over to make sure it was her. Or one of them. A good neighbor. Watching her come down the stairs—"Are you all right?"

"Yes, of course. Just checking on things."

"Is everything all right?"

"It seems to be."

"Good. Good." He stood there nodding, looking about in the light from the kitchen. His shirttails out, cuffs turned back. Blue jeans and black loafers. Smiling at her uncertainly. "You look nice," he said. "Did you teach?"

"Yes. Thank you."

Nodding. Checking his watch. "Have you eaten?"

She locked up and they crossed the darkened street, their footsteps lost in the scuffling sounds of two boys playing basketball in the spilled light of a garage. April cool but a feeling of the coming summer too, the hardest months. He followed her in and shut the door and offered to take her jacket but she kept it despite the warmth of the room. The air was densely spiced with the roast he'd been cooking for much of the day. He did something with computers and could work from home.

He turned down the music, an opera, and stepped into the large open kitchen and picked up the bottle. "Italian," he said. "Insanely good." He poured her a glass and she came to the bright plum color of it and sat in one of the high bar chairs and watched him lifting lids, stirring the steam, giving names to the smells. One thing he'd learned was food. Another was wine, though he wasn't a bore about it. His hair was gray but had not thinned and there was the cowlick at the front, a springy disobeying forelock he wore long, like something from his youth he couldn't give up, like something which served him still.

He stirred and spiced and tasted, talking all the while. It might've been a summer night with the children chasing fireflies over the back lawn, the dog, a little terrier, yapping in dismay.

Both boys in college now and the terrier, like Pepé, buried under a tree.

"Don't you like it?"

"Hmm?"

He indicated her glass.

"Oh. No, it's lovely." She raised it for a sip.

He had good manners and would not ask after her family nor talk about his boys. He talked about his house and the improvements he would like to make this summer and the Chinese elms he was thinking about planting.

"Do you know a good realtor?" Angela said.

He stopped stirring to look at her. "A realtor?"

"Yes."

He stood there. The thick, wet blurpings of the sauce. He turned back and began stirring again, but absently.

"I've done some work for a couple of them," he said. "People speak very highly of Leslie Brown. I'll give you her info."

"Thank you."

He checked the roast and lowered the flames under the pots and they took their glasses to the living room. She had always admired Caroline's taste, and she let herself sink into the deep sofa, fabric the color and fineness of a wheat field in a painting. There had been a time, a very long time, when she could not admire, could not even notice; pleasure lay at the bottom of the sea. She toed the sneakers from her feet and put her head back. Robert joined her on the sofa, crossing an ankle over his knee. On the mantel were the same pictures in their silver frames: Peter and James growing up and grown. He and Caroline much younger. The dog alive. Everybody happy.

The male tenor began to sing, the notes rich and pure.

Robert sipped his wine and held the glass to the light.

"I saw him today," he said.

"Saw who?" She rolled her head on the sofa back. She was tired. It took her a minute.

"Oh," she said, and sat up a little. "Where?"

"At the gym. My gym. He has joined, apparently."

"Oh." She didn't know what to say.

"I was just coming out of the steam room and he was just coming in. Five minutes earlier and there we would have been. Like Romans."

"I'm so sorry, Robert." She touched his forearm.

"Ah, shit—that's life, right? You run into the man your wife prefers to sleep with. One day we'll go for a beer, he and I. Watch a bit of the game. He'll turn out to be a pretty good egg. Life goes on. Isn't that the idea?"

"No," she said. "That's not the idea."

He looked at her and his face changed. He uncrossed his leg and turned to her. "I'm sorry, Angela. I'm an idiot. I—"

She shook her head, "No, I didn't mean that. I was only saying . . . I was only saying I'm sorry, that you had to go through that today."

"It's nothing. Christ. It's so trivial."

"It's not nothing," she said.

He glanced at the mantel and then looked down. He seemed to be studying the sofa, the square of cushion plumped and risen between them like bread.

Outside, in the window, trees reared in a wave of sweeping light, appeared to pirouette, lapsed again into darkness. A man said gently: "Come on, we haven't got all night." There was the jingle of shaken tags.

She reached to touch the fallen forelock. Training it back, hopelessly. He looked up. His entire story in those eyes. Story of the world.

"Can we just be quiet for a while?" she said. "Can we just sit here and listen to the music?"

67

They took the blue Chevy, Grant at the wheel, and they smoked and said nothing, staring out at the darkness and the traffic and the signs and the tire tracks in the snow and the setting moon, and she was safe, the sheriff said, she was in no danger. Every mile taking them that much farther from the mountains where'd she gone missing and where all the men and all the searching and all the hours in the world never would have found her, she was fine and resting and they shouldn't hurry. The lights and the land rushing by at that unreal hour and wondering had she seen this, and this, that day so long ago in the strange car, in broad daylight. They wanted to speak just to know it was real, but they did not trust the sound of their own voices not to rip it all apart, road and mountain and moon and truck, throwing them back to their beds and to the dawn and a heartbreak all the greater for how much they'd believed. And what would they say anyway that they didn't already know without saying? She was safe, she was resting. There was nothing else to know and nothing to do but to get to her, and when they saw her, when they truly believed in this night, then they would make the phone call, and this too was understood without either of them saying it.

The sheriff didn't want them driving at that time of night in the mountains; he wanted to send his other deputy down to get them, but the deputy would have been an hour just getting to the ranch and it was that hour that ended the discussion.

Grant followed the sheriff's directions at least and did not take the Loveland Pass but drove ten miles beyond it and came back from the west on the state highway, and at last they saw the lights of the little resort town and they saw the blue hospital sign and they located the emergency entrance and Grant parked in the first space he saw without reading any more signs and they crushed their cigarettes in the tray and stepped out of the truck.

The sheriff awaited them outside, leaning against the wall near the glass doors, and the sight of him swung Grant back in time to a different hospital, different child, but same sheriff waiting. He and the boy crossed the parking lot and as they stepped up to him the sheriff unleaned himself from the wall and removed his hat that his face not be in shadow, and the gesture stopped them both cold.

"She's fine," Kinney said, raising his hand. "She's just fine."

"Where is she?" said Grant.

"You can't see her, not just yet."

"The hell I can't." He took a step and the sheriff caught him by the arm.

"She's in with the surgeon, Grant."

"The surgeon. You said she was fine."

"She is fine. She's not in any danger. It's just that, well . . ." He tapped his hatbrim against his leg.

"Joe. Just tell us."

He told them, there in the humming yellow light, speaking evenly and accurately, and when he was finished Grant and the boy stood still. Kinney tried to imagine what it would be like to be this man before him, this father, hearing such things. His own daughter unconscious within the building. He could not.

At last Grant nodded. He looked at his son and his son nodded too.

"We'll go in now, Joe."

"All right. But one more thing."

They waited.

"She didn't want to be carried, Grant. After all that, she wanted to come down on her own." He looked from one to the other, father to son. They stood looking at him, as if expecting him to go on. "That's all," he said.

"Did she?" said Grant.

"Did she what?"

"Come down on her own."

The sheriff looked at him. "Hell no," he said. "I by God carried her down."

Grant put his hand on the sheriff's arm. "I'm sorry about Billy, Joe. I don't even know what to say."

Kinney raised his hat and set it on his head. "Me neither."

Then the boy, who had said nothing, said, "What about the man?" and Kinney looked at him. He was not even recognizable as the boy he'd first seen in a hospital bed himself not very long ago, knee like a purple cannonball.

"I can't say about him," said Kinney. "There's a good twenty lawmen up there now, dogs too, and unless that sonofabitch can fly they'll track him down."

Grant hardly heard. He'd already turned toward the glass doors.

THEY HAD WAITED ALL this time and now they waited some more, standing and sitting and standing again, the night-shift nurse tolerant of their pacing and their repeated demands for information, for updates, the sheriff bringing them coffee and stepping out to smoke and talk with other lawmen, the TV in the corner muted and the clock ticking loudly from its place on the wall, ticking off most of an hour before a woman in blue scrubs emerged and came up to them. She was small in her scrubs, her face dark and without makeup and open and kind. She introduced herself as Dr. Robinson and Grant held her hand and said, "How is my daughter?"

She smiled at him and at the boy. "She's going to be just fine, Mr. Court-land. She's a strong young woman. But she's been through a great deal." Her face grew somber and Grant told her that they'd talked to the sheriff and they knew about her foot, and the doctor nodded and told them more about it: the cleanness of the wound and the undamaged tibia and fibula and how Caitlin had likely saved her own life by cauterizing the blood vessels as she had. A surgeon could hardly have done a better job of it, said the doctor, and she looked at them as if this, above all else, was the brightest fact.

"Can it be reattached?" Grant asked, voicing an idea that, until that moment, had not occurred to him.

"The foot?" She turned to the sheriff, who stood apart, and the sheriff shook his head.

"Even if we had it," she said, "too much time has passed and the soft tissue is too damaged and, well . . . Dr. Wieland will tell you more precisely when you see him."

"Dr. Wieland," said Grant.

Dr. Wieland down in Denver, she explained, was one of the finest podiatric surgeons in the country. He worked on soldiers and he would finish what Caitlin had begun and he would see to a perfect stump.

Grant looked at her. *A perfect stump.*

She glanced at the clock on the wall and said they would take Caitlin down by ambulance in about an hour.

"Ambulance," said Grant. "What about a helicopter?"

"She's in no grave danger, Mr. Courtland. And Dr. Wieland won't be able to see her until the morning anyway."

Grant nodded. He and the boy stood waiting.

The doctor looked at them. She looked at the sheriff and she glanced around the waiting room.

"Is Caitlin's mother here, Mr. Courtland?"

"No, she's in Wisconsin. I wanted to see her first. Caitlin. I wanted to be sure before I called."

"I see," said the doctor. "All right. Well. I need to talk to you a moment before you see your daughter." She looked gently at the boy and said to Grant, "Perhaps just the two of us would be best?"

"You can tell us both."

"All right."

She didn't have to glance at the sheriff; he'd already left the room. She mated her hands before her and looking into Grant's eyes she told him that an examination in these cases was automatic and mandatory, and that their examination of Caitlin had shown that she'd been pregnant.

Grant stared at her.

The boy hung his head.

"Where is it?" Grant said.

"It?"

"The child."

"The pregnancy never came to term, Mr. Courtland. She miscarried."

"Miscarried."

"Yes."

"How long ago?"

"She's not sure. She thinks last spring."

The boy looked up.

"She told you that?" Grant said.

"Yes."

"When?"

"Before we put her under to work on her leg." She held Grant's eyes. "She didn't want you to know, Mr. Courtland. Not out of shame, which is a normal reaction, but because she couldn't bear the idea of you having to think about it—of having it in your head." She smiled faintly. "Finally, just before we put her under, she agreed to let me tell your wife."

The doctor regarded them both. "As I would have told Mrs. Courtland, I believe it's best for Caitlin that you all know all the facts, here. But she doesn't need to know that you know, not right now. Do you agree?"

Grant nodded. The boy nodded.

"Is that everything?" Grant said.

The doctor told him that the HIV rapid test had come back negative and that they'd have the confirmation results in two days and that Caitlin would need to be tested again in a few months.

"She's weak, she's malnourished," said the doctor, "but her heart is strong. And so is her head. She wasn't happy that we wouldn't keep her awake until you got here." The doctor smiled, she looked at the clock—then turning back to them with a crease in her brow, she said, "Oh, I meant to ask: who is Dudley?"

In the end there was nothing but a wide birch door and a nickel latch handle, and the doctor closed her brown hand on the handle and it gave a soft click and the door swung in without a sound and she held it open for them to pass, and Grant stepped in first and the boy came behind and they stood in the first bright wave of the room and everything they saw and heard and smelled amid the lights and the machines and the tubes and the propped meager figure in the bed was utterly alien to the girl they expected to see. Yet when they stepped closer and saw the dark hair on the pillow and saw her sleeping face, so gaunt now, aged as theirs were aged and more so for having aged all at once, yet when they saw this face, the years and the machines and the room fell away and they would've known her had it been twenty years, had it been a hundred, and the love held back so long became undammed inside them and because they could not fall into her arms with this love they turned and fell without a word into each other's.

THE EMBRACE, BRIEF AS it was, cost them the moment when the girl, fighting her way into the most painful light, opened her eyes and saw the two men standing there. She did not believe it. She felt the blood so thick and heavy in her veins, the dull drifting of her brain and the tremendous weight of sleep like stones lashed to every part of her and she knew she was drugged and she did not believe what she saw, but the tears came just the same, hot and fast, and she said the word she had waited so long to say.

Daddy, she said.

68

He could not speak but only stood there, hunched over her, careful of the tubes and wires and the incredible thinness of her under the bedding. His jaw was pressed to her wet neck, and she trembled with the quaking of his body. There was no sound in the room but the chirping of the machines and the soft patting of her hand on his back and her reedy voice saying It's okay now, Daddy, it's okay, it's okay, Daddy.

She opened her eyes again, the pupils so large and black even in that light, and Sean, standing back from the bed, tried to hold her gaze, but he could not and he looked instead to the floor.

"Dudley," she said, just audibly, and he looked up and she was smiling at him over their father's shoulder. She said something more he didn't hear and he stepped forward and she swallowed and said in her drugged whisper, "I knew you were alive."

SHE SLEPT AGAIN AND they stood looking down on her. Grant reached to draw a strand of hair from her face, passed his knuckles softly over her cheek, her chin. Then he turned to his son: "I'll call your mother now. Are you all right?"

When he was gone, Sean stepped closer to the bed. He took up her limp hand. He looked at her feet: the tented shape of the left foot under the bedding and the footless right in its enormous white wrappings, like a swaddled child. When he looked at her face again her eyes were open. Wet and glazed and looking at him.

"So tall," she said.

She looked beyond him to the closed door, and before she could ask he told her that she wasn't here, that she was still back home, in Wisconsin. "We wanted to see you before we called her," he said.

"Is she all right?"

"Yes."

She studied him. "Do I look as old as you?"

"You look just the same."

"Bullshit."

She saw the cast and puzzled at it. "What happened to your hand?"

"It got in a fight."

"With who?"

"The wrong man."

She stared at him. Then she looked beyond him again toward the door, and he turned to look but there was no one there.

"Are they still . . . ?" she said.

He nodded.

The machines beeped and hummed. He looked around at their mysterious faces. When he came back to her, some fresh wave of pain was in her eyes and she said, "Sean, I'm so sorry."

He shook his head.

"I never should have left you," she said. "I'm so sorry."

"Don't," he said.

"I was supposed to take care of you—"

"No," he said.

"And I left you there."

Her lids faltered and the grip drained from her hand. "But you stayed," she said. "You stayed, all this time."

Next she knew, the world was in motion—walls and ceiling panels and lights all sliding by in a lurid hallucinatory blur. Then she saw her father beside the bed and the sight of him walking and the feel of his hand around hers told her it was not the world in motion but herself.

The small woman doctor walked ahead of him. Her brother walked on the other side of the bed and a man she didn't recognize was pushing the bed. A bag of clear fluid swung from a chromium hook.

She squeezed her father's hand and he looked down and his haggard face reset itself.

"Hey there, sleepyhead."

"Where we going, Daddy?"

"Down to Denver, sweetheart, to see another doctor."

"Will Mom be there?"

"Not right away but soon."

He smiled and she said in sudden desperation, "I wanted to call you but they took my phone away and wouldn't give it back!"

"It's all right, sweetheart. We're here now."

"But I wanted to call you and they took my phone away. Why'd they take my phone away, Daddy?"

The woman doctor with the pretty face smiled and said, "It was the sheriff's phone, honey, remember?"

They passed through the parting glass doors and into the harsh outdoor lights of the stone canopy. Beyond the canopy the mountains and the ski runs and the sky were all blue-gray in the coming dawn and she felt the cold air and saw the sky and began at once to weep.

"Billy," she said.

"Shh," said Grant.

"Daddy," she said.

"Yes, Caitydid."

She closed her eyes and Grant touched her face.

"I'm so sorry," she said.

"Hush," he said.

"He found me, Daddy."

"I know, baby."

"He stabbed the Monkey."

Grant and Sean looked at each other.

"He stabbed the Monkey," she wept, "and I chopped off his foot."

The EMTs took command of the gurney, buckling the legs and rolling it into the ambulance all in one motion. Grant shook the doctor's hand a final time and thanked her and she told him again that Caitlin was going to be just fine, that she had never met a stronger young woman nor a braver one.

She stepped away and the sheriff came forward.

"I just got off the radio with my deputy," he said. "They found him."

"Alive?"

"No, sir, he's as dead as they come. The dogs found him sitting under a tree with a bowie knife stuck in his neck. His own, from the looks of it."

"Billy," Grant said.

"That's how it looks." Kinney adjusted his belt. "Dogs also found a hole up there."

"A hole."

"A kind of pit. In the rocks. Deep. Looks like he was trying to put Billy down there when he got that knife stuck in his neck. Then he crawled away and died and Billy went back to the cabin. How it looks."

"So he's dead," Grant said.

"Dead and gone to hell."

The EMT had his hand on the ambulance door. The sheriff didn't move.

"What else?" Grant said.

"Bodies. Down in that pit. At least two. We won't know how many till morning."

Grant nodded.

"I can take you up there, if you want," said Kinney. "After you get Caitlin settled down in Denver. If you want to see that shack. That man. I figure it's your right."

Grant looked into the ambulance. He shook his head. "I've already seen it, Joe."

He climbed in and sat beside his daughter and found her hand, and the EMT shut the door and the ambulance pulled away with the colored lights flashing but no siren, and when they passed through the parking lot Sean put the blue Chevy in gear and fell in behind them and he stayed behind them all the way down to the city.

69

She dreamed that night of a house in the woods. They were not the woods of the mountains that went on and on like the sea, but a small woods, and through the trees she could see the sun on the lake, a rich, wobbling yolk of deep yellow, and the windows of the house, which was no house she recognized, were struck with the same rich light, as if the house had been designed, oriented, to blaze in just this way at just this hour of every day, like the cathedrals of Europe. A woman sat on the porch steps waiting, a woman no older than herself, and at her approach the woman stood and smiled and drew the hair from her forehead in a certain way, and love flooded into Angela's heart as her young mother took her into her arms and held her and kissed her and said, *Angela, my love.*

Mom, what are you doing here, where's Daddy?

Daddy isn't here, sweetheart, but Faith is.

Faith's here? Where?

Inside, inside. They're all inside, and Angela's heart grew faint. *All?*

And the door swung open and within was a vast room like a ballroom, and everywhere she looked there were girls, young women, all in marvelous clothes, the loveliest dresses—slender modern girls dressed for someone's wedding, or graduation, their smiles, their eyes catching the light, their faces open and luminous—so many faces! She looked and looked and at last she saw her own face among them, her own smile, and Faith came running into her arms, and they kissed the tears from one another's cheeks . . . and happy as she was in this dream of reunion Angela was uneasy, her stomach like a fist— there were too many girls, and taking Faith's hand she moved more deeply into the room, and there were many girls she knew by name and many she did not and her heart was pounding and her legs were unsteady. They were nearing the back of the vast room, nearing windows full of the dying light of sundown, when at last she whispered, *Is she—? Faith, is she—?*

And Faith smiled and said, *Don't stop, Angie, keep looking.*

Hair of every shade, thick, shining hair of youth and she saw a ponytail like walnut silk, and she could not breathe—but it wasn't her. And here was another girl, and another, all of them so young, so full of love, and none of them Caitlin, and she awoke then in sobs, swimming in the scents of hair, of warm smooth faces and of kisses, saturated in them, and her palms were full of the most incredible— *"Smell, smell!"* she demanded, but the arms that held her were not a sister's, not a daughter's. "It's all right," he was saying. "It's all right, Angie, it was just a dream." But he didn't understand, he didn't understand how she had loved them, all of them, his arms so thick and muscled and hard in the spinning, fragrant dark.

THIRTY, PERHAPS FORTY MINUTES later, as she was falling asleep again, her phone began to rattle on the tabletop, and Angela freed herself from him and groped and found it and lifted the blue light to her face thinking, Grace, oh God, you forgot to call Grace . . . but it wasn't Grace.

70

When they reached the clinic Dr. Wieland was in surgery and Caitlin was set upon by a swarm of purple-clad nurses and orderlies who moved and spoke and touched like a single entity whose only purpose was to reassure and calm the hearts of all who came before them. Grant and Sean were diverted to a small waiting room where three oversized leather chairs sat around a well-made walnut coffee table. A sweating pitcher of water, a hot pot of coffee on the table. Living plants in festive Mexican flowerpots. They were alone in the room and they knew without being told that no one else would come into the room unless it was one of the nurses or orderlies in purple scrubs or the doctor himself.

They had been in the room fifteen minutes, according to the wall clock, when there was a knock at the door and a young man stepped in to tell them that the doctor would be in surgery with another patient for a little while longer and to ask if there was anything they needed. They both wanted to say an ashtray but didn't. Fifteen minutes later the same young man returned to say that the doctor had finished with his surgery and was now with Caitlin and he would come talk to them soon.

Grant looked at the wall clock and he looked at his watch and he went to the window and looked out on the city in the early light. He remembered standing at another window on another morning, his naked wife behind him. Naked for the last time. His for the last time.

"She'll be landing in half an hour," he said. "And it'll take about that long to get to the airport."

Sean poured more coffee. "What did she say?"

"What did she say?"

"When you called."

Grant thought but couldn't remember. He'd made the call in a dream, unable to believe what he was doing, what he was saying. What did you say to a mother who believed her child was dead? How did you break that news? *She's alive? We found her? We have her?* Or were those the sheriff's words to him?

He met his son's eyes and shook his head. "I don't remember."

They were quiet. The wall clock ticked. At last, with a sharp stab of pain in his knee, Sean pushed up from the chair and opened the door.

"Sean."

He turned back.

"I'll tell her . . . the rest," Grant said. "I'll do that."

Ten minutes later, with a brisk rap for warning, the door opened and a tall man in purple scrubs and a white doctor's coat walked in and introduced himself as Dr. Wieland. Grant looked for blood on the white coat and saw not one spot. The doctor was silver-haired and slightly stooped in the way of tall old men although he was not so old and his hand as the two men shook was alive and strong and did not let go of Grant's but instead kept hold of it, turning it over to see what his fingers had felt.

"Not bad, not bad," he said, reading the old suture scars with his thumb. "Are you a carpenter, Mr. Courtland?" The thick and laconic drawl was somehow at odds with the purple scrubs and the keen eyes and the strong antiseptic smell of him. In his other hand he held something, which at a glance appeared to be a human foot, absently carried away from the operating room.

"A poor one," said Grant.

"Not as poor as some. I've seen men who didn't know better than to stop at two fingers but came in with all four in a sandwich bag. Table saw?"

"Yes."

The doctor nodded. He released Grant's hand. "Was there no chance of replanting?"

"Replanting?"

"Reattachment."

"I forgot them. I'd been drinking."

"Ah," said the doctor. "Please, sit," he said, and they lowered into the deep laps of the chairs with the coffee table between them. The doctor paying no mind to the thing in his hands.

"I saw a young man once who'd cut off his hand with a circular saw. One of those powerful ones—what are they called?"

"Worm drive."

"Yes. A worm drive. The saw kicked back as such saws are inclined to do, I'm told, and severed his free hand cleanly at the wrist. In his panic, or whatever it was that ruled his thinking, he did not apply a tourniquet but instead plunged his wrist into the fireplace, much as Caitlin has done." The doctor shook his head. "Remarkable, the human will," he said. "This young man then drove himself and the severed hand to the hospital, where I told him I could replant the hand but that because of the burning I would have to shorten the forearm a bit, and do you know what the young man said? He said, I ain't gonna be no short-armed freak, doc. Throw that hand out and let's get on with it."

The doctor sat smiling pleasantly.

"How is my daughter, Dr. Wieland?"

The doctor's face grew serious, though his eyes shone brightly. "She is wonderful, Mr. Courtland, she is wonderful. The entire staff is in love with her."

"What about her foot?" said Grant.

"I understand we do not have the foot."

"Her leg, I mean," said Grant.

"It's a pity we don't have the foot. I'd have liked to see the incision, even if there was no hope of replanting." He now regarded the foot in his hand. They both did. It was a plastic anatomical model, the bones and sinews all exposed in their grisly articulations.

"Because of the burning?" said Grant.

"That's right."

He searched the doctor's face. "And if she'd used a tourniquet instead?"

The doctor stared at him, smiling faintly. "As I understand it, Mr. Courtland, Caitlin expected to be going down the mountain on her own two feet—as it were. Is that not correct?"

"That's correct."

"That's why she cut off her foot in the first place, is it not? Because as far as she knew that was her only hope?"

"Yes."

"Well. I have operated on the toughest young men and women you will ever know, and if any one of them had told me they'd performed such a feat as walking down a mountain with one foot severed and managing a tourniquet all the while, I'd have said it was nothing but the morphine talking."

Grant had no response.

"No, Mr. Courtland. Your daughter did what she believed she had to do to get down the mountain. A tourniquet? No, sir. She never would have made it."

He peered at Grant and began shaking his head again. "Remarkable," he said.

"Will you have to shorten her leg?" Grant said.

The doctor was staring at the plastic foot. "No, I don't believe so. But I have to ask, Mr. Courtland—has your daughter any interest in medicine? As a practice and science, I mean?"

"Not that I know of."

"No special interest in podiatry? In surgical technique?"

"Not that I know of. Why?"

"Remarkable," said the doctor, then was silent.

Grant watched him. "What's remarkable, doctor?"

"All of it," he said. "But most especially the disarticulation itself."

"The disarticulation?"

"The cut, the cut. With an ax, no less. If I didn't know better, Mr. Courtland, I'd say Caitlin consulted with Dr. Syme himself before she picked up that ax." Then, using the plastic foot for reference, he explained the particulars of the Syme's procedure. He spoke of the disarticulation of the ankle joint and the resection of the malleoli and of the removal of the calcaneus by subperiosteal dissection, and as he spoke, his slow-moving drawl was gradually overtaken by a narrative of escalating passion, as though the very language of surgery caused in him a kind of unmanageable excitement. As though he'd taken Grant with his missing fingers as a fellow enthusiast of the amputation arts.

"Caitlin's disarticulation is beautiful," the doctor said. He smiled, his eyes catching the light. Then, sobering, he admitted that there was, however, a good deal of soft-tissue trauma that would require some complicated grafting, which would slow down her healing.

"But she is strong, by God," he said, "and I'll tell you something else, Mr. Courtland: in about six months, when she gets one of these Flex-Symes carbon running feet under her, she'll wish she'd lost both feet."

Grant stared at him. "Did she tell you that?"

"Tell me what?"

"That she's a runner."

The doctor looked at him, puzzled.

"I'm told your daughter brought only two things down with her from the mountain, other than the clothes on her back," the doctor said. "Is that not correct?"

Grant didn't understand.

"May I?" said the doctor, and he leaned over the coffee table and picked up the white plastic bag that sat near Grant's feet and had been sitting there all that time. Grant looked at it and wondered who had given it to him and when. The doctor loosened the plastic drawstring and reached in and peeled the bag away from a pair of running shoes. They had once been pink and white, and one of them, the left, was shaped and cleaned by its recent usage in the snow while the other was dingy and stiff, and the moment he saw them Grant took them from the doctor and held them in his hands and wept.

71

Sean was inside the terminal on time, but his mother's plane was delayed and he passed the time wandering with his limp and his cast in the massive weave of travelers, until finally he took refuge in a small shop. He pretended to browse the magazines, then bought a toothbrush and a small tube of toothpaste and went to the men's room where he stood brushing his teeth and washing his face and running his dripping fingers through his hair. The face he saw in the mirror looked old and foreign to him. Men came and went. After a few minutes he threw away the toothbrush and the small tube and went back to the terminal corridors to wait for her.

He didn't see her at first among the passengers emerging from the security exit. He saw a woman he mistook for her, looked past her, and looked back and it was her. She saw him at once and walked over to him with her red eyes brimming. She was older and somehow smaller and her blonde hair was styled in an unfamiliar way and within it were new streaks of white. She stood looking him over and shaking her head and saying nothing. She raised her hand to his face and swept her thumb over his dry cheekbone as though to wipe away a tear.

"Is your father with you?"

"No, he's with Caitlin," he said, and at this sentence her face fell and she reached for him and held him while passengers dodged all around them. He could not remember the last time they'd embraced, but it seemed he'd been a boy then, reaching up to her from far below.

When she released him her face was wet but composed. He took the small bag from her shoulder and hung it on his. She asked was it a long drive to the clinic and he said no, not long, and they turned and began to walk. Soon they were on the highway in the Chevy, driving back into the city, back into the west, as they'd done long ago, toward those same formations looming so incredibly in the sky.

At the clinic, at the first sight of her aged and joy-wrecked mother, Caitlin knew her better than she'd ever known her before, seeing in her eyes nothing of what she herself had gone through but only the full and terrible love of a mother for the child who came from her and was part of her and was all of her and the loss of whom could not be borne.

72

The funeral was held on a damp and chill Thursday morning. It was only ten days since the old man had been buried here, but now the last of winter had been washed away by the rains, and the grass was coming in pale green and tender over his grave.

There had been no formal service—Sheriff Kinney had seen enough of the press and other gawkers and wanted only to get his brother laid to rest and for all of this business to be behind them, although he knew it never would be, and those who attended the burial had received a call from him the day before, when the time and day had at last been set. Among the mourners were the Gatskill girl, wearing the same black dress she'd worn ten days ago; the old veterinarian, Dale Struthers, and his wife, Evelyn; Maria Valente and her daughter, Carmen; the sheriff's two deputies and their wives, and Kinney's own wife and his daughter, Josephine, who'd driven down from Boulder again and who was unable to keep her eyes from the Courtland girl, so thin and quiet in her wheelchair, so pale in her dark dress and dark hair, her eyes gazing into the distance while the pastor spoke graveside once more, committing on behalf of those gathered this soul to God's keeping. The breeze took up his words and carried them along over the graves and into the far border of trees where the crows sat in the boughs watching.

The casket descended mechanically into the earth and a few flowers were cast down onto its black enamel hood and Denise Gatskill dropped some small unseen thing that rang lightly along the curve of the lid and fell down into the dark. Then she was led away in the care of another young woman and a young man who, like her, had nothing more to say to anyone there.

One by one the remaining mourners turned from the grave and shook the sheriff's hand again or embraced him, and then moved on to the Courtlands and the girl in the wheelchair, the men nodding to the girl and patting her stiffly on the shoulder, the women bending to press their faces wetly to hers. They shook hands with Grant and Sean and Angela, and as there were no words for what they felt they said none and moved on, some to pay respect to other graves, the rest returning to their cars.

Kinney lacked the heart to open up the ranch house again and instead the mourners were invited to the Whistlestop Cafe, where Tom Hicks was preparing a brunch buffet, and for this reason Maria Valente and her daughter were brief with their respects, Maria saying as she held Angela's hand that she hoped she would see her again at the cafe and then turning from Grant Courtland and his family and walking away hand in hand with her daughter. At their car the girl stopped and looked back, and Sean, holding his tie down against the wind, went to her. Maria slipped into the car, and Sean and Carmen stood talking for just a moment. Then she raised up on her toes to kiss his cheek, and he turned and came back, head down, refusing to meet his sister's eyes or to acknowledge in any way her sly smile.

Kinney walked the old pastor to his car for the chance to press a fold of bills into his hand, but the pastor would not take the money, as he had not taken it when he'd buried the sheriff's mother, and then the sheriff's father, who had been members of his parish. On his way back Kinney stopped behind an iron bench and lit a cigarette, and after a moment Grant walked over to join him. Kinney shook another cigarette up from the pack and Grant looked as though he would take it but then didn't.

"Told myself I'd quit," he said.

"You can quit some other day."

He took the cigarette and leaned toward the sheriff's cupped hands, and they stood smoking, watching the small huddle of their families in their dark clothes, all standing but one.

"How's she coming along?" said the sheriff.

"Healing fast, the doctor says."

"I ain't surprised."

"I appreciate you putting this off like you did, Joe. We all do."

Kinney waved this away.

Grant read the inscription again on Emmet and Alice's shared stone, and he read the new stone already in place: WILLIAM MICHAEL KINNEY, BELOVED SON AND BROTHER.

"I don't know how else to put it," he said, "but I wish your dad had lived to see this."

Kenny nodded. "I do too."

"My last words to him weren't very kind ones," Grant said. "To Billy. I would like to have them back."

Kinney blew a stream of smoke. "Mine weren't either, Grant. He didn't go out of his way to bring out the best in people."

"Well," said Grant. "I'm not likely to remember that part."

They smoked. They watched their families, each one of whom glanced in turn to see that the men were still there behind the bench, still smoking. As the wives talked and the men looked on, Caitlin slipped her hand into the sheriff's daughter's hand and without looking at her simply held it.

"I guess she didn't get to them other funerals, then," Kinney said. "Them two girls and that other man, the hiker."

"No. But the families came to see her at the clinic. The girls' families." Grant looked away and drew on the cigarette. "I'll tell you, Joe, it reminded me of when she'd win a race, and the parents of the other girls would come over to shake her hand, hug her."

Kinney flicked the ash from his cigarette. He peered into the gray sky.

"They ever find any family of that man?" Grant said after a moment.

"Not much. Both his folks are dead. They found his old granny in a nursing home in Sterling but she didn't hardly know her own name so they just let her be."

Grant stared into the distance. Then he said: "I'd have killed him if I had a chance, Joe. You know that?"

"I know it."

"I pictured it a thousand times. Walking up to him with your dad's shotgun, putting it in his face. I wouldn't have cared what happened to me."

The sheriff looked down at his boots.

"I had the TV on this morning at the motel," Grant said. "And they were talking about a little girl nine years old got taken by some man down in, I don't remember the name. It wasn't too far from here."

"Pueblo."

"Pueblo. Yes. Little thing got away when the man's van broke down and he took her into a 7-Eleven and she started screaming."

"Brave little girl."

"Yes," Grant said. "But say that van didn't break down, Joe?"

"Well," said Kinney. "I guess some would say God was looking out for her."

"Is that what you'd say?"

Kinney looked out over the stones. "Some days I would," he said.

Grant nodded. He said, "Sometimes I wonder if I didn't make a mistake, not seeing him for myself, that man. His body. Seeing it with my own eyes. I wake up sometimes and I know he's not dead. That he fooled everybody and he's out there still."

Kinney looked at him until he looked over. "That was some other man took that little girl, Grant. I can by God guarantee it."

"I know it, Joe. I know it. But it's no comfort."

At the cars Kinney leaned down so Caitlin could put her arms around him once more, and Grant lifted her from the wheelchair as he had once lifted his son, and he and Angela got her settled in the backseat of the new car with the pillows behind her and more pillows under her leg along the seat. A few days before, down in Denver, he'd traded in the blue Chevy for the wagon. He'd wanted to throw in the green Chevy too, but Sean said the car would be too crowded and that he'd follow along in the old truck.

Angela reached to embrace Kinney and he stood stooped and patting her back while his wife and daughter waited. He shook Grant's hand and he shook Sean's casted hand, and Sean wanted to tell him something but the sheriff raised his free hand as if to deputize him and said that everything that ought to be said about Billy had already been said. None said *good-bye* and neither did they say they'd see each other at the cafe, and the two families got into their cars and Kinney sat behind the wheel watching until the new wagon with its three riders and the old Chevy with its one had both passed under the arms of the ponderosas and turned onto the county road, and he waited a little longer still before putting his own car forward, knowing he would never see any of them again.

73

Three days later and a week sooner than he'd predicted, Dr. Wieland pronounced Caitlin fit for travel and she was discharged to the care of her family and to the postsurgery specialist who awaited her in Wisconsin. That afternoon, she and Sean left their parents in the motel as they'd left them one July morning long ago and they drove out of the city in the new car and up into the mountains, Sean at the wheel and Caitlin arranged in the backseat with her pillows. Up and up the winding pass as before to the Great Divide where the waters decided which way to go, east or west, and without stopping they looked at the families who'd pulled over and they saw children on the slope above the parking lot making snow angels in the high old snow, in the warm April sun, and they drove down again, down once more into the small resort town and everything was as she remembered it and they passed the motel where her parents and the boy had lived while they searched and while the sheriff and his people searched and the rangers and the FBI searched and the whole world searched and none of them ever more than ten miles from where she was as the crow flies and none of them ever anywhere near her for that.

The road was called Ermine, she remembered that, and they found it and followed the black swings of it up into the pines again, and at each intersection Sean stopped while Caitlin studied his old map in its four faded pieces, and he went whichever way she told him to go and they were not up there long before she had him pull over and park.

It did not look like the place to him but he killed the engine and got out and collected her crutches from the back and stood by as she wrestled herself up out of the car, and when she was up on her one foot he handed her the crutches. She took a few steps on the blacktop and stopped and lifted her face to the sun and breathed slowly.

"You get used to them," he said.

"I know. I remember."

"You remember?"

"I had them when I was seven."

"I don't remember that."

"I do."

"What happened?"

"Dad ran over my foot."

"Dad ran over your foot."

"I came running out of the house and he backed over my foot. My own stupid fault."

"Was he drunk?"

She shrugged. "All I remember was he was leaving and he hadn't said good-bye."

They stood in the sun. There was the smell of the desiccated needles and of the sap weeping from the pines. Then they left the blacktop and made their way through the pines, Caitlin choosing her steps carefully and Sean following, ready to reach out but knowing he would not have to, that already she'd integrated the crutches into the thoughtless mechanics of movement, as she'd integrated the absence of one human foot and would integrate the mechanical one when it came.

They entered the glen and sat on the stone bench in the freckled light. The white and maimed Virgin stood as before amid the white trunks of the aspens and the chalky headstones. There was the weird sense of being back in time, at the beginning, a sense of knowing what was coming. Everything in the glen had an arranged, artificial look to it, like staging—even the light, even themselves. She was winded and as she caught her breath he leaned to look for the plaque, expecting it to be covered in growth as in his dream, but it wasn't.

She saw him reading the plaque and turned to read it herself.

Right Reverend Tobias J. Fife,
Bishop of Denver, Mercifully Grants,
In the Lord, Forty Days of Grace
For Visiting the Shrine of the Woods
And Praying before It,
           1938.

The little aspen leaves stirred and they felt the breeze, brief and cool.

"Go ahead if you want to," she said.

"Go ahead and what?"

"Eat your Snickers." She smiled and he tried to smile back.

He dug the cigarettes from his pocket and got one into his lips and lit it and blew the smoke away from her. They were quiet. He looked once at her bandaged stump where it lay atop the opposite ankle, the way anyone would sit. After a minute he said, "The old man we were staying with, the sheriff's father?"

"Emmet."

"Emmet. He told me this story one time about his great-grandfather busting up his son's foot, Emmet's grandfather's foot, with a hatchet, the blunt end, when he was just a boy. To keep him from going off to war and getting himself killed like his brothers. He'd been the last boy left."

"Did it work?"

"I don't know. Emmet found out later that his grandfather made the whole thing up. I still don't know what to believe. Sometimes I wonder if I dreamed it."

She sat looking at the face of the Virgin.

"When you were little," she said, "I'd hear you through the wall at night, talking. I'd come into your room and sit by your bed and you'd go on talking, as if you knew I was there. As if your eyes were open. I'd ask you things and you would answer. You'd say the most hilarious things."

"Like what."

"I don't remember. I just remember wanting to laugh so badly I thought I'd pee myself." She looked at him, her eyes bright.

"I don't remember that," he said.

"You never did, the next morning. But you knew, when you were sleeping, that it was me. You'd say my name."

They were silent. Sean smoked. He looked at her bandages again and she saw him looking and elevated the stump a little.

"It doesn't hurt," she said. "Not much. It just kind of pulses. And itches."

"The stitches," he said, remembering his own.

"No. My foot. The bottom of it. And my toes. I swear I'm wiggling my toes and I look down and there's nothing there. And still I swear I'm wiggling them. Like they're invisible. Like there's some kind of hole in my vision."

He thought about that. Then he said, "Why didn't you bring it?"

"Bring what?"

"You know what."

She looked down at the stump. "I don't know. I could have. I thought I would. But when I saw it sitting on that floor, in that place, I didn't want it anymore. It wasn't a part of me anymore. I don't know how else to explain it."

He drew deeply on his cigarette and blew the smoke.

"I saw him," he said.

"Saw who."

"That man."

She turned away.

"When he hit me with the car, I saw him," he said. "I saw his eyes. I tried to tell you but I was so—Jesus, Caitlin I was just so . . ." She put her hand over his fingers and squeezed. And when she did this he was a boy again, and she was eighteen, up there in that mountain hollow while their parents waited below at the motel, and everything that had happened did not have to happen but could be altered by some simple act, by some slightest change in the unfolding of the day, and there would be no man in yellow sunglasses and there would be no crushed knee, no months and years of pain and no raped girl in an alley and no Emmet and no Billy and no girl on a horse nor girl on a ledge and no shack and no chain and no ax either, and they would come back down the mountain together and Caitlin would go on to college and she would run and the world would not miss it, the world would not care if these two young people slipped away and lived that other life instead.

She squeezed his fingers and there was no sound in the glen but their own breaths. At last she released his fingers and picked up her crutches and began to haul herself up, only to abruptly sit down again.

"I'm so weak I can't fucking stand it," she said.

"Just sit," he said. "Just rest."

"No. I want to go now. But I need a favor, Dudley."

He turned and she looked at him.

He hooked one arm under her knees and the other around her ribs and he lifted her from the bench and she was so light this girl, this stolen sister, this king's daughter sacrificed for what offense and to appease what god or gods he didn't know, and he swung her around so her back was to the statue and the headstones, and when they were under way she said with her arm around his neck, "You think they'll still give me that track scholarship?" and he said, "Maybe." And then he said, "Maybe half," and she laughed, and she weighed nothing as he carried her back down the trail, careful of her head, careful of her invisible foot, back to the car.

74

They sat drinking coffee in the motel coffee shop, staring out the window at the passing cars and the reflections of the passing cars in the glass of the building across the street, and each time the cafe door opened they turned to look and each time it wasn't their children the air darkened and the blood emptied from their chests, and there was time enough to see themselves on that other morning long ago when they'd stood naked in the motel room as the world instantly became something else, themselves with it, time enough to see all that had passed since then too, their two lives playing out between them like silent film, one imposed upon the other as if those two histories were a common one after all and could never be viewed except together—until at last and when they thought they could not bear it another second the cafe door opened and there he was. Blond like his mother, holding the door for his dark-haired sister on her crutches, and the blood poured back into their hearts and they stood and Grant left twenty dollars on the table for two cups of coffee and the four of them went together out to the parking lot and a few minutes later they slipped into the traffic going east, into the dusk. Grant at the wheel and Angela beside him and Caitlin in the backseat with her leg stretched out. Behind them, for now, was Sean and the old green Chevy, and behind the Chevy was the lit and diminishing city and beyond the city were the high summits, undiminished by distance, and beyond these the sun was falling into the west but they did not see it—nor the mountains nor the city but only the darkening sky ahead and the climbing moon and the road, and it was a road as straight and flat and bare as any they'd ever seen and it raced away before them over the plains, hiding nothing.

Acknowledgments . . .

. . . is a poor word for what I owe so many, beginning with my father, Joe Johnston, and stepmother, Amanda Potterfield, without whose dream of Colorado this book never would have been written, period. Also: nieces Brenna and Chloe, who grew up waiting for me to finish; and their father, my brother Tyler, who believed and safeguarded all along the way. And my mother, Judy Johnston, whose constancy and bone-deep goodness have meant more than I can say.

For years of friendship, shelter, and wisdom I thank Mark Carroll, Carmela Rappazzo, Jim Hodgson, Nancy Russell, Nicolette and Henry. I thank Chris Kelley, steadfast reader and countryman; I thank Mark Wisniewski, P.D. Mallamo, and deep snow consultant Ted Mattison. I am forever indebted to my teachers and friends David Hamilton, George Cuomo, and Roberts French. I thank Thomas Mallon, Faye Moskowitz, and the George Washington University for a life-changing year in DC. I am deeply grateful to the MacDowell Colony, the MacArthur Foundation, David Sedaris, Don Foster, Erin Quigley, and Marianne Merola. For all the beautiful hard work she put into my manuscript I thank Genevieve Gagne-Hawes, and I thank my agent, Amy Berkower, for being the finest advocate a book and its author could hope for. I thank my editor, Chuck Adams, for taking such good care of this story, and I thank *everyone* at Algonquin for an exceptional book-making experience start to finish.

Lastly and ongoingly: sister Tricia, brothers Tad and Harris, Uncle Rick and Aunty Kathy, for all the love, complexity, and humor of family, amen.